Footballers Don't Cry

BRIAN GLANVILLE

Selected Writings

First published in this form in 1999 by
Virgin Publishing Limited
Thames Wharf Studios
Rainville Road
London
W6 9HT

ISBN 0 7535 0312 3

A catalogue record for this book is available from the British Library.

Typeset by SetSystems Ltd, Saffron Walden, Essex
Printed and bound in Great Britain by Mackays of Chatham PLC

Contents

Ruud Gullit

Prospect, December 1996

Ruud Gullit has enjoyed a King's Road honeymoon since he arrived last season – a *deus ex machina* – at Chelsea football club, to play, and subsequently to manage. With his famous dreadlocks, his sporting talents, his polyglot charm, Gullit has enraptured London. Last month he acted with typical poise and dignity during the public mourning for Matthew Harding, the Chelsea director; so many other football stars would have been at best trite, at worst an embarrassment.

Of his prowess as a player, there has never been any doubt; he is one of the great footballers of his age, a glorious amalgam of technique and power. The Gullit of today, now 34, clearly cannot have the pace he once did, not least after a series of operations on his right knee which cost him a whole season with AC Milan in 1989–90, and which could so easily have ended his career. That he should come back to the field at all was remarkable. That he should do so to such effect was even more so.

Under full galleon sail, there have been few more exciting players; and very few more versatile. After a season with DWS Amsterdam and then three with Haarlem, it was with the Feyenoord club of Rotterdam that Gullit made his name; there he blossomed as a sweeper, playing behind the defence, but always ready to make forays upfield. But by the time he was transferred to PSV Eindhoven in 1985, he was best known as a midfield player, a stupendous sight when, dreadlocks flying, he launched his huge frame upfield. For such a big man – indeed, for any man – his touch was delicate, and he used his height to dominant purpose when the ball was in the air.

Arriving so unexpectedly in London after eight years in Milan and Genoa, Gullit delighted football reporters by the way he would slip into the press room – quite unbidden – to hold court after Chelsea's games at Stamford Bridge. Speaking very serviceable English, which he learnt at school (his Italian is perfect), Gullit would chat away in a most engaging manner, often laughing, always amenable – a welcome change from the grudging suspicion of so many English players and managers. All this makes you wonder why, after he had left Sampdoria of Genoa in 1995, a Genoese journalist should describe him, caustically, as 'an opportunist', comparing him unfavourably with the Englishman David Platt.

But Gullit's brilliant career has inevitably had its darker moments. A hero for so long in Italy, his last season was an unhappy one as he oscillated between AC Milan and Sampdoria, increasingly unwelcome at both clubs. And for all his prowess, Gullit has never received the true accolade of a great player: success in a World Cup.

In 1988, when Holland so emphatically won the European championship in West Germany, Gullit bestrode the field, supported by AC Milan's other two Dutch stars, Frank Rijkaard and Marco van Basten. Two years later, when it came to the World Cup in Italy, Gullit, who had still not fully recovered from his knee operations, was never at full throttle; and the Dutch, quarrelling among themselves as their footballers (like the Germans) often do, stuttered out of the tournament.

Four years later, Holland were among the favourites for the 1994 World Cup in the US, with Gullit their trump card. It was never played, for Gullit walked out of the training camp before the tournament began, to the bitter dismay of his team-mates. In the event, Holland were knocked out by Brazil, a game which they lost only narrowly, and which they might have won had Gullit been playing.

On that occasion at least, it was not a case of *cherchez la femme*. Gullit might be – indeed he was – accused of acting like a prima donna. But his motives and objections, such as they were, involved football, rather than his personal life. The same cannot be said of his flitting between Milan and Genoa. After leaving his first wife, Yvonne, with whom he had two daughters, he married a young Italian journalist called Christina. She, it is said, was bored by the provinciality of Genoa after Gullit had moved there to play for Sampdoria. She longed for the lights of Milan and urged him to return. This, in mid-season, he did, but he no longer fitted in with the way AC Milan were playing, so back he went to Genoa. The plan was that he would next play in Monaco, where Christina wished to live, and that he would leave Monaco before the end of the ensuing season to play, for a fortune, in Japan. In the event, his second marriage broke up, he formed a new liaison, and went not to Monaco but to London.

Gullit was born in Amsterdam but, like many outstanding Dutch footballers of his time, his father came from the former Dutch colony of Surinam. The contribution made by Surinamese players to Dutch football has been immense. Twenty years ago, the famous Ajax Amsterdam team and the fine Dutch international team (almost one and the same) were entirely white. Johan Cruyff, the centre-forward and inspiration of both teams, was born of Dutch parents and brought up in Amsterdam. Dutch journalists of the period lamented that, after Cruyff and company, there would be a steep decline: young talent was simply not emerging. But it did and it was largely Surinamese, with none more refulgent than Gullit.

Is Gullit a greater player than Cruyff? He is certainly more versatile, although possibly less technically remarkable. In Italy, he emerged as a centre-forward in his latter seasons, as effective in his own way as Cruyff – larger, more muscular, and probably better in the air. In his earlier days, he used to say that the best goal he had ever scored was for the unfashionable Haarlem club in the 1981–82 season, before he grew dreadlocks. 'Playing against Utrecht, I went past four defenders then the goalkeeper, and scored. It was an unforgettable goal for me' – a memory which must have been obscured by so many other goals since then.

It was while he was playing for his next club, Feyenoord, that he locked horns with the club's manager, Thijs Libregts – a clash which would bear bitter fruit when Libregts was made manager of the Dutch international team a few years later. Gullit, a public critic of apartheid and devotee of Bob Marley, found it hard to forgive a racist remark.

Libregts has done his best to explain his gaffe away, but to scant effect: 'That's an old story from when I was with Gullit in 1984,' he said. 'Remember, in football, you have black people, tall people, short people and some with glasses. It's normal to have nicknames. You say, "OK. Blackie, kick the ball, then." And then we had some discussion and I said, "Blackie must run more because he's a little bit lazy." And they wrote down, "The coach said all black people are lazy." And then all that started.'

It was inevitable that, like any talented, strong-willed player, Gullit should have had his brushes with authority. Libregts was no longer in charge by the time of the 1994 World Cup but Dick Advocaat, the new manager, was little more accommodating. Advocaat wanted Gullit to play out on the right flank. Gullit wanted to play a more focal role in the centre. Matters came to a head when Holland played England at Wembley in the preliminary World Cup tournament in 1992.

Initially deployed on the right flank, Gullit kept moving into the middle, so Advocaat substituted him. For Gullit, this was a humiliation, exacerbated by the fact that Mark Overmars, who proceeded to play on the right wing, was instrumental in gaining Holland a draw. Gullit refused to play for the national team, then changed his mind only to walk out of the pre-World Cup training camp.

Why did he do it? His own explanation never quite carried conviction. When a French journalist suggested, the year after the finals, that Holland might have won had he played, Gullit laughed and said in English, 'There's a proverb which more or less says this: if my aunt had a dick, she would be my uncle.' He added, 'I knew Holland couldn't be world champions with the tactics and players they had announced. I tried to make my reasons known. There was no appropriate response, so things went ahead without me. My departure took place at a surprising moment, I admit, but that's how it is. That's how I am.'

He expanded on this in an Italian interview. 'Almost everything I know, I have learnt in Italy,' he said. (He joined the

Milan team in 1987, a £5.5m transfer from PSV, replacing England's Ray Wilkins.) 'I've had long experience in the strongest championship in the world. When I knew I was going back to play for my international team, I also heard people saying: you can come, but you must keep quiet. We shall play as we want. My experience was being discounted; everything I had won counted for nothing. But you cannot always say yes. For me, the World Cup was very important, it was my last great chance. The heat, the humidity and the times of the games were going to condition the championship. You had to play with your brains. Anyone who went for all-out attack would have used up his energy in no time. Holland was incredibly overrated by the press and the fans. I was sceptical. Advocaat told me I was right, but then the two wingers who should have been playing in midfield went back to being wingers after ten minutes and we were all in trouble and out of breath . . . I said these things, but the others laughed in my face. I felt a sense of frustration. And then I left. I didn't want to expend my energy for nothing. I didn't want to put my prestige on the line and then get slaps from the press.'

His Dutch team-mates have not been sympathetic. Wim Jonk, the Dutch midfielder, who came to play for Internazionale in Milan, was especially cutting. 'It's never nice when a player leaves the national team,' he said, 'and all the less so when he walks out the way Gullit did. He just said, "Ciao, goodbye, everybody," promising he would explain his reasons only after the World Cup. If Ruud had behaved like the great star we all knew he was, he wouldn't have gone like that. He would have stayed there with us, he would have argued to impose his views. But he didn't; he didn't even deign to explain anything to us after the World Cup. Now he's speaking, but it's too late, and it isn't right to say that Holland deserved to be knocked out, because they played badly. In fact we played well: we beat Ireland and were knocked out by Brazil at the end of an intense, dramatic clash, in which we played on equal terms with the South Americans . . . All things considered, though, Gullit did well to desert Holland. We forgot about him at once. We were more at ease without Ruud.'

One doubts that, but the bitterness over what Jonk and

others clearly regarded as a betrayal is all too apparent. It is unlikely that this would have bothered Gullit too much. He is a man who manifestly follows his own star, as the journalists in Genoa noticed. But it would be unfair to regard Gullit only as a calculating individualist. Like any decent middle-class Dutchman, he has a highly developed social conscience and emphasises his public duties as a star footballer. 'I try to speak prudently, looking for the right words, and to tell people things face to face. Football has given me a place in society which obliges me not to avoid any subject, however difficult. I cannot play the ostrich; too many supporters, too many children, hang on my words.'

But he is also, by his own admission, something of a latter-day troubadour. He once cheerfully told a French interviewer – in immaculate French – 'I have no house, even in Holland. I live like a nomad, like a citizen of the world. I am a gypsy!' When Gullit did decide to sign for Chelsea, one wondered how long he would stay, which was perhaps another way of wondering how long his current liaison would last. In the event, he did stay, and when, in 1996, with Glenn Hoddle's elevation to the England job, he was appointed player-manager at the club, he went to work with a will, drawing on his huge store of experience. In pre-season training he put great emphasis on stamina, employing a former international sprinter to put the players through their paces. On the field, he tried to persuade them to run less and think more, so that, when the moment arrived, a forward, such as Scotland's little John Spencer, would have the breath and energy to accelerate.

To Chelsea's dismay, he was out of the game for several months at the start of this season after a calf operation. He was determined not to play again before he was completely ready. Simply to recover from an injury is not enough; there has to be a further period of recuperation. 'One spends one's time listening to, assessing one's body,' Gullit says. 'The human body isn't made to play football. So you have to force it, gently, above all when age begins to weigh on you. I spend time talking with my body. The body never lies. I know that one day it will say, "Stop! I can no longer bear what you're asking me!" I cannot say whether that day is coming. The better I know my body, the more able I am to decide if it's demanding a massage or some training, some work, some effort, or a rest. Thanks to such attention, I am still capable of playing.'

At Chelsea, he seems to have struck up a good relationship with the club's demanding chairman, Ken Bates. But in Italy he was badly bitten, and a falling-out is quite possible, especially if Chelsea's early success this season fades. He was justifiably aggrieved when AC Milan so readily let him go to Sampdoria. Silvio Berlusconi, Milan's president, was quoted as saying in private that he thought Gullit was 'finished' – a spur for Gullit to prove that he was nothing of the sort. In happier times Gullit was full of praise for Berlusconi. He said in 1993 that the good spirit in the Milan dressing room 'reflects the personality of Berlusconi. Since he bought the club, he has fashioned it in his own way.' But by 1995 he was saying, 'Let's say that my leaving Milan can be explained by the fact that I did not rediscover the atmosphere there that I had left. The way Milan played had changed, too. My first departure from Milan took place in circumstances that I didn't like.'

The fans at Chelsea, who not so long ago were notorious for a significant racist element, have taken Gullit to their hearts. His appointment as player-manager was immensely popular at a club which has won little for decades. Beginning as *libero*, or sweeper, subsequently moving up into midfield, setting doubts about his stamina to rest, Gullit has delighted the fans with his inventiveness, and shooting. On the training field, he was virtually working as a coach even before he was made manager. And the training field, if not the playing field, is where he wants to be; office work has no appeal for him.

Gullit's international prestige enabled him to sign for this season such foreign players as the Italians Gianluca Vialli and Roberto Di Matteo, and the less well-known but immediately successful French centre-back, Frank Leboeuf. Vialli, the prolific striker discarded by Juventus, after helping them to win the European Cup final in Rome last season, could have gone where he liked, but Gullit charmed him to Chelsea.

If the 'gypsy' does stop wandering and stay at Stamford Bridge, he will surely bring some success. Perhaps his problem will be, as he says, that he so much enjoys playing football.

When the time comes, as eventually it must, that his body tells him enough is enough, will he be satisfied with what must ultimately be a secondary managerial role? Chelsea and their fans must hope he will.

Matthews Returns

Sunday Times, 22 October 1961

'NO, BUT YOU must have butterflies,' said Stanley Matthews. 'Everybody has.'

He was talking about next Saturday when, forty-six years old, after fourteen and a half years with Blackpool, he wears once more the red and white Stoke City shirt in which he became famous. Indeed, it was thirty years ago that he left school in nearby Hanley to become an office boy with Stoke City, subsequently winning innumerable international honours, becoming the greatest outside-right the game has ever known, giving, in the 1953 Cup final, perhaps the greatest of individual performances.

Now, back in the narrow, changeless streets of his native city, he's marvellously relaxed and cheerful; pink-faced, slender, the hair going dignified grey, a silver bar behind the knot of his white silk tie, a sporty trilby on his head.

In the tiny Stoke dressing room, where the benches are an unlikely pink and a television set sits on a cupboard, the photographers are busy. 'Hold up the shirt, Stan! Could we see the number seven on the back?'

'Well, Stan,' says Tony Waddington, the young manager, a sturdy, sandy-haired man with a Manchester accent, 'a bit different in here from the old green and yellow. Sere and yellow, if you like.'

'We used to have an old stove there, you know,' says Matthews. 'Coke. I walked in, and the fumes hit me.' He gestures cheerfully towards Jackie Mudie, the Scottish international, his partner in Blackpool's 1951 Cup final team. 'I recommended him here – I'd been carrying him on my back for years. Then I come back, and here he is!' They'd been playing together in Canada, this summer.

'Jackie was writing to me every week,' says Waddington. ' "There's a young lad playing over here in Canada at outside-right; if you can get him, he won't half do us some good." Of course, we had that about shortening the pitch a bit and bringing the touchlines in, but he said, "No, make it wider." '

'Harry Weetman wouldn't be able to drive from end to end,' says Matthews, 'it's that long.'

A photographer says to Waddington, 'A man jumping for joy. Something like that, you see.'

'It's a good idea, but . . .' says Waddington, doubtfully. 'I'd prefer not to make an exhibition of it. I'll tell you what . . .' and he suggests a compromise.

'I've got a *much* better idea than that, though,' says the photographer. 'Stan stooping there, and you *vaulting* over him.'

Out on the field, the cameras point and click. Nobody does any vaulting. 'If he scores three goals on the first Saturday,' says Waddington, 'I'll do a handstand for you.'

'He knows he's safe,' says Matthews.

Why has he come back? 'Well, when Tony asked if Blackpool were prepared to let me go and they *were* prepared, I thought, well, if I can help Stoke, this is the time to move. I wouldn't have considered any other club. I feel a little frightened, in a little way, you know – it's a very big occasion. It'll be all right, I feel sure.'

'You see,' says Waddington, 'Stan's nature is something of a romantic.'

'It'll be all right,' says Matthews, as though he isn't sure. 'It'll be all right.' Then, with a sudden change of mood, he extends his small, neat hands and allows them to shake. 'I've been in bigger matches before!'

Though he'll play for Stoke, he won't move from Blackpool.

'No, you see I have my routine of training, which is very important. It will be more beneficial to me there, because I go out on the beach every morning. I go for half an hour's walk, a lot of breathing exercises, I have a lot of brine baths. I don't need so much training, you see, half an hour's training for me is the equivalent for someone else of an hour and a half. When you're thirty, the stretching exercise is very important. It's more important when you're forty than thirty, and more important when you're fifty than forty. And deep-breathing exercises done properly, that *really* is important. If I'm not on the beach, I do them somewhere. I must do them by hook or by crook, or I get worried. Everything I do I get a kick out of. Enthusiasm is the goal to success.'

'He must be nearly always fit,' says Waddington, 'because he never does anything to make himself *un*fit.'

'You see,' says Matthews, 'I may have a different outlook on life from a lot of people. I never think what's gone by in the past. I always think what's going to happen tomorrow. Even if I only have a walk, I'll get the biggest thrill.'

'We've got some wonderful snapshots of Stan at the ground,' says Waddington. 'Old ones.'

'What're you looking back for?' Matthews asks. 'Don't look back!'

Looking for an Idiom

Encounter, July 1965

BRITISH SPORTS JOURNALISM is still looking for an idiom; still waiting for its Red Smith, its Damon Runyon, its AJ Liebling, let alone its Ring Lardner; still waiting for the columnist who can be read by intellectuals without shame and by working men without labour. Meanwhile, it is afflicted by dichotomy: a split between mandarin indulgence and stylised stridency, this in itself a valid reflection of the class structure.

Each of these particular groups of journalists has its own special cross to bear. The more sensitive popular writer knows that almost every piece he writes is a self-betrayal, a selling-out to the cruel machine which has produced him, a wilful limitation of his powers. He is thus particularly sensitive to any form of outside criticism.

The quality writer, on the other hand, is an isolated, if not an alienated figure, writing for an informed minority when, given the wide reference of his subject, he should be speaking to the generality. Besides, he is often poorly paid, while the successful popular columnist is affluent, a creature of jet travel, bottomless expense accounts, and first-class hotels.

What is wholly lacking is an idiom which will throw a bridge across the two cultures, avoiding, on the one hand, bathos, which is the nemesis of 'good' sports writing, and on the other stylised vulgarity, the nemesis of the popular school. The American sports writer, though now in a barren period, a period of pygmies, has never had this problem, precisely because, in a more fluid society, the idiom lay close at hand. Thus it was possible for Ring Lardner, a serious artist as well as a journalist, to take that idiom and do something quite new with it, in creative terms. Lardner was for years a travelling reporter with the Chicago White Sox, who nicknamed him 'Old Hawk Eye'. He was perhaps the first writer to exploit the possibilities of working-class speech and idiom in fiction, particularly in his *Letters from a Busher* called *You Know Me, Al*, and in stories such as 'Alibi Ike', 'My Roomy', and 'Hurry Kane'. When the White Sox threw the 1919 World Series and became, by popular baptism, the 'Black Sox', Lardner grew disillusioned with the game, and tended to cultivate a homespun, Mid-West newspaper personality which made him one of the ten most famous men in America, but hardly impinged on his central talent. (One of his sons, John Lardner, was probably as good a sports writer, writing a gifted and urbane column for *Newsweek*, though he had none of his father's antic creativity.)

AJ Liebling, again a fine journalist rather than a creative writer, had the same bland personality as the younger Lardner. He wrote splendidly on boxing (and even, while covering the 1952 Olympics for *New Yorker*, produced a memorably amusing piece on soccer). Red Smith (of the New York *Herald Tribune*) is possibly not quite in the same category as these three, but again the idiom has been found and used. Though whimsical at times, he is naturally and unforcedly funny, knowledgeable yet at the same time light and diverting. One has the impression of a man, a definite man, writing naturally, rather than of a hoarse voice, shouting into the wind in somebody's else's dialect.*

The different attidues to popular sport, with their considerable consequences, were perfectly illustrated by a photograph pub-

---

* In Europe, the best sporting journalists – Gianni Brera, Jacques Ferran, Robert Vergne – write as whole men, whose subject happens to be sport. This, again, contrasts them with many of their British equivalents, whom one could scarcely imagine writing on anything *but* sport. A football report in *L'Équipe*, the finest of all sports daily newspapers, or in its sister weekly, *France Football*, might well begin (and has): '*Pends-toi, brave Fontaine! Nous avons battu à Monaco, et tu n'y étais pas!*' The multiplicity of Brera's allusions, in the Italian press, are such that the mere subject matter threatens to founder helplessly beneath them.

lished, many years ago, in an American magazine. It showed President Roosevelt clowning, baseball in hand, at a match which opened the season. What British Prime Minister has been seen, in similar circumstances, at a soccer match, though soccer is as indubitably our national sport as baseball is America's? At most, he might pad on to the turf of Wembley before a Cup final, to exchange patronising handshakes with the contending teams.

The Establishment game has always been cricket and it has led, inevitably, to Establishment writing; writing which can often be excellent, but which is far outside the province of the ordinary sports fan.

This rigid polarity, this lack of a solvent idiom, is shown by the way our popular sports writers tend to model themselves on the Americans. Inevitably, there is no rationale, no inner direction, so that the result has been a hybrid disaster, as tasteless and inorganic as a mid-Atlantic television series. Thus, the popular British sports writer is never being himself. He is a mimic, a febrile ventriloquist's dummy, using somebody else's eye and ear and experience, and trying pitifully to pass them off as his own.

The results are twofold: first, an appalling waste of talent; secondly, the reluctance of really gifted working-class boys to go into popular sports writing, when they are the very people who might fructify it.

Whatever the sports pages of the popular newspapers may suggest, their sports journalists are not all crass, insensitive men who go through life with their eyes shut and their ears closed. Many of them, indeed – one thinks of Alan Hoby, columnist of the *Sunday Express*, Sam Leitch of the *Sunday Mirror*, Frank McGhee of the *Daily Mirror*, Reg Drury of the *News of the World* – are shrewd, perceptive men with a splendid gift for anecdote and observation; qualities quite unwanted by the Moloch of mass circulation.

The popular press, indeed, has been strangely unaffected by changes in the structure of British society, the gradual levelling-up, the vastly increased chances for a clever working-class boy to get a good education. If anything, it has become much more resolutely low-brow than it was before the war, stylistically much more rigid.

The bright working-class boy, therefore, is no keener than he was then to become a popular sports journalist, for the cultural pattern of the society is all against it. Having acquired, against the odds, a good education and a literary style, he is naturally loath to mortgage them. There could scarcely be a more cogent example than Neville Cardus, the very father figure of mandarin cricket writers, who was brought up in the backstreets of Manchester at a time when poor, clever boys did not get to university. The struggle was proportionately harder, the determination not to squander his literary gifts proportionately greater.

Of a younger generation, there is John Arlott, once a Hampshire policeman, later a celebrated radio commentator on cricket, whose style is as literate, precise, and rounded as Cardus's own. It is worth quoting a passage from each of them.

Here is Cardus writing an obituary for Hubert Preston, a cricket journalist who died in 1960, at the age of 91:

> I didn't dare go into the Lord's press box during my first season as a cricket writer for the *Manchester Guardian*. I was shy, provincially raw. I wrote my reports sitting on the Green Bank. I wrote them on press telegraph forms, and at close of play handed them in at the telegraph office under the clock at the Nursery End.
>
> One afternoon, Hubert Preston saw me as I sat on the Green Bank, scribbling my message. 'Why don't you come into the press box?' he said in his own brisk, rapidly articulated way. He took me by the arm and led me up the steep iron steps. The tea interval wasn't over yet. Preston introduced me to Sidney Pardon, who then introduced me to other members of the press box, some of them life members. Each made a courteous bow to me; it was like a *levée*. Pardon pointed to a seat in the back row. In time, he assured me, I would graduate to a seat among the elect . . .
> Hubert's deafness was the reason why, now and again, the aristocratic Pardon was obliged to raise his voice. Pardon

once apologised to me for an occasional voice crescendo. 'You know,' he said, 'Hubert is quite sensationally deaf.'

This is the 'quality' school at its most engaging; evocative and concise, controlled yet informal, free from inflation and the straining for effect which are inevitable when the writer forgets that what he is writing about is, after all, only a sport.

By the same token, no one has captured better the romance of professional football for the young fan than John Arlott:

> Bacon was a tall man from Derby County, with a shaving-brush tuft of hair growing out from a shallow forehead above a mighty jaw. His chest was like a drum, his thighs hugely tapering, and he had two shooting feet which he threw at footballs as if with intent to burst them. It was on April 3rd in the Year of Our Lord one-thousand-nine-hundred-and-thirty-one – a Good Friday, as I recall, with Reading's relegation virtually certain – that A Bacon, at centre-forward, realised all his dreams. The match was against Stoke City at Elm Park, and Bacon proceeded to score six goals against them; six goals of immense excitement. He had a habit of hitting a ball well forward on his instep: not a toe-ender by any means, but from about the line of stitching joining the toecap to the instep – a point of impact only possible to a man of immensely strong legs and ankles. That day, everything he touched flew at the Stoke goal like a shell. But for some great saves he must have scored twenty, and his last goal was scored from an angle of about one degree to the goal line on the right of the goal, and the ball, flying vertically into the goal, as I shall never forget, thrust the roof of the net high above the crossbar.

There may be a sentimental moment or two here but, once more, the observation is fresh and precise; the writer has used not only his memory but his eyes. The popular sports journalist, on the contrary, is so thoroughly the prisoner of his style, takes his ambience so utterly for granted, that his language tends always to be inexact and merely emotive.

This, for instance, is Peter Wilson, the procreator of the modern English sports column, on the world heavyweight title fight between Rocky Marciano and Don Cockell, in San Francisco:

What is courage? I give you the answer, fellow Englishmen, in two words – Don Cockell . . . this was the kind of extra courage which makes you proud to belong to the same race as the boy who grew up in the backstreets of Battersea . . . And that is why the high and the mighty, the men with riches and the men with power, the women with beauty and vast possessions are rising in a kind of primaeval mass . . . sympathy and acclamation for a man from thousands of miles away, whose tongue they can hardly understand.

The contrast between Wilson, on the one hand, and journalists such as Arlott and Cardus, on the other, is a curiously ironic one. For it is Arlott and Cardus, writers of working-class origin, who have developed a mandarin style in the quality press, Wilson, the Old Harrovian, who has been one of the architects of the popular style.

What is strange about this style – or stylisation – is that it has evolved so little since Peter Wilson began his *Sunday Pictorial* column in 1938. This, for better or worse, was certainly a breakthrough. Till then, the acknowledged innovator of popular British sports journalism had been Trevor Wignall of the *Daily Express*. In his time, he was regarded as highly daring and dangerously outspoken, though, in retrospect, his columns seem dull, prosaic and tame.

In 1937, for example, when Fred Perry returned to England as a professional tennis player, Wignall wrote, 'He does not want to cause embarrassment either to himself or to those with whom he was formerly associated, and so he will not be here to use a couple of tickets for the Wimbledon stand, even if they were sent to him. Yet he has a better right to them, even when the professional aspect is introduced, than some who have been financially assisted to make an appearance on the Centre Court.

The simon-pure amateurism of tennis is no better or more worthy of respect than it is in ice hockey.'

Or again – with almost engaging innocence – 'It is one of my sorrows that I always know ten times more than I can ever print. If I were to publish, for example, the details of a talk I had last Friday with a man prominent in fighting, a sensation would be created that would last for weeks.'

Wilson, from the first, was less ingenuous. His column began with the authentic, now familiar, hollow boom, the Lear-like promise of apocalypse:

> . . . I will do such things
> What they are, yet I know not, but they shall be
> The terrors of the earth.

One-sentence paragraphs, endless reiteration of the first person singular: Sport With the Lid Off. Peter Wilson Exposes.

Yet nothing seems to *get* exposed; we are in the presence of a great gun, filled with blank ammunition:

> Let's kick off with Soccer.
>   I believe the stars of the boot-and-shoe game [*why shoe?*] are the worst paid of all our public entertainers.

A valid point, forcefully made, yet it is not sustained nor, in the weeks and months ahead, is it resurrected. Instead, the valid social issue is quickly obscured by vague accusations of rough play, assertions that there are players who put a knee in their opponent's thigh or kick him in the ankle; a fact woefully apparent to any of his readers who stood, Saturday by Saturday, on the terraces.

Aggression seems to stop short at the merely offensive statement:

> The possibility of Great Britain eventually winning the tie brings to my mind that O Schmidt of Rumania is quite the worst player who has ever appeared in Davis Cup matches in this country.

Tennis, in fact, is a sport which Wilson played with success, and on which he is indisputably expert, while he is perhaps the most knowledgeable of all his contemporaries on boxing. This expertise – however disguised by stylisation and the struggle for effect – tends to set him apart from most of the columnists who followed him, few of whom had a deep technical knowledge of their sports.

Over the past quarter of a century, Wilson has remained steadily at the top of his profession, moving briefly to the *Daily Express* in the fifties, then back to the *Mirror* group, and the *Daily Mirror*. At the *Daily Express*, there were visible efforts to produce more memorable writing, for a more sophisticated audience, but the results were not happy. The world cruiser-weight title fight between Sugar Ray Robinson and Joey Maxim gave rise to one pleasing image – 'there was always artistry in what Robinson did in his hemp and canvas studio' – but it also produced this:

Maxim was no longer the plodding clod. He was the descendant of those Italian men who ploughed the baked iron furrows with wooden ploughs while their women work beside them like oxen. He was as strong and brown and terrifying as the executioner who comes at dawn.

He also wrote of 'Len Harvey, so finely chiselled that he looked sculpted out of whitest marble – never was there such a marmorean boxer. Would there had been some Praxiteles of pugilism to immortalise the symmetry of young Harvey.'

Wilson, of course, was in no sense an original; he derived from the harder-hitting, more egocentric reaches of the American school of sports journalism. With Desmond Hackett and JL Manning, however, he has been the most significant, and symptomatic, figure in post-war British sporting writing, though the phenomenon of Hackett, who succeeded him on the *Express*, shows how far the cult of personality has travelled.

Until the advent of Hackett, it would be quite inaccurate and misleading to talk about an *Express* style of sports writing, for it simply did not exist. Writers such as the verbose Wignall, the whimsical, literate John Macadam (who could, at his occasional best, bridge the gap in idiom), the precocious Frank Butler, and Wilson himself, were utterly dissimilar in kind. But Hackett was far more purely an *Express* man, an *Express* creation. The time had clearly come when the popular press was sufficiently sure of itself to manufacture its own sports columnists, in its own house image.

Hackett was in no sense a prodigy. He had, when he was given his opportunities – there was what appeared to be a trial period, a hiatus, and an eventual confirmation – already been with the paper for twenty years. Though his style of writing was something new to the actual sports column of the *Express*, the public *persona* was derivative. Hackett himself would doubtless gladly acknowledge how much he owed to the flamboyant, inventive Henry Rose, with whom he worked for many years in Manchester, and for whom he wrote an obituary sharply distinguished by its sincerity.

Rose, by origin a Cardiff Jew, had made use of a finely developed sense of showmanship to become the idol of Northern sports journalism. When he came into the press box at Liverpool, the fans on the famous Spion Kop terrace behind the goal would ritually boo him, and Rose, immaculate, with cigar, overcoat and brown trilby hat, would raise the hat to them. Famous for his generosity to other journalists, immensely skilful in deploying his network of 'contacts', he was a mine of exclusive news stories. He belongs, as Dr Leavis remarked in another context, 'to the history of publicity', rather than to any history of sports *writing*; the matter was always secondary to the manner. But in Desmond Hackett's brown bowler hat, his cultivation of the jaunty image, it is not unfair to discern an echo of Henry Rose. The difference between them is that Henry Rose failed when he was uprooted from the North and tried in London; Hackett, after a difficult beginning, survived.

It is generally accepted in Fleet Street that he made sure of his job with his report of the Hungary *versus* Brazil World Cup quarter-final in Berne, in 1954. It was a match of alarming violence, in which fists, boots, and – afterwards – even bottles were used. Hackett's report, which appeared on the front page, began like this:

The World Cup quarter-final was a riot. My jacket is ripped, my shirt torn, and I am minus a tie. And I have been thrown over a fence. So I do mean a riot . . . I tried to cross the field and ended up thrown over a fence by two policemen. Considering the riot going on around me I was grateful to be out of it.

But I was able to help Mrs Ellis, the wife of the Halifax referee, and her two young sons through a side entrance into her husband's dressing room.

Bob Ferrier's version of the incident, in the *Daily Mirror*, was a little different. 'Mr Ellis' wife, Kathleen, pale and frightened, was "rescued" from the packed stands where the fans were fighting by Scottish referee Charles Faultless.'

FIFA, the International Football Association, appeared to be sceptical; they held an inquiry into the incident which established nothing concrete. The *Daily Express* were enormously pleased; they are said to have presented Hackett with a bonus – and a new suit.

Since then, Hackett's column has been an unswervingly loyal reflection of the post-war ethos of the *Express*. The event is always secondary to the personality – or the predicated personality – of the columnist, whether it be the Hungarian revolution ('I am besieged by Russian tanks') or a boxing match.

In 1958, Hackett went to the Swedish World Cup, and wrote this about an injured Russian footballer:

Netto had his Kremlin-treasured left leg in an elastic support. He cut out the tougher leg tests and worked with one of the half-dozen trainers in this Russian soccer circus. Being a helpful kind of chap, I kicked a few stray balls in Netto's direction, and they were all carefully steered back to the trainer with a RIGHT foot.

The *Express* man works under relentless pressure. He must always be one jump ahead, one step farther 'inside' than his competitors. He is, one feels, in some sense the embodiment of Wenlock Jakes, in Evelyn Waugh's *Scoop*, a man who can arrive in a Balkan town to cover a revolution and, when he finds there is none, produce one with the sheer, purple force of his prose. His competitors see him rather in the guise of Waugh's Sir Jocelyn Hitchcock, lurking secretly in his hotel room, spinning stories they can never hope to match.

Once more, the idiom is as far away as ever; the *Express*, in any case, has an idiom of its own.

JL Manning, the columnist and former sports editor of the *Daily Mail*, has certainly bridged the gap between the classes in terms of his appeal, but he has done so through opinionation, rather than through language. One reads Manning because, at his best, he is genuinely controversial and well informed, because he expresses views which, however antipathetic they may seem at times, appear to be seriously held. The technique, the colour, and the occasional passion of sport are beyond his range. He is neither a natural reporter nor a vivid phrase-maker. He is essentially a political writer (it is no coincidence that he has stood for Parliament as a Conservative candidate). 'More often than not,' he has said, 'I write about the reconstruction of sport' (a subject which similarly engrossed his father, the late LV Manning, the authoritative and much-quoted columnist of the *Daily Sketch*).

He can deploy facts with telling skill, has a sense of the development of sport over the years, and has ridden some good hobby horses: tighter control of professional boxing, for example, and a limitation of the subsidy to horse racing, when less patrician sports cry out for money. He is most effective when the tension between self-absorption and involvement with his material is evenly maintained. When he is not seriously involved, the humour grows ponderous, the style coagulated, and there may be solecisms; a rough tour made by a Rugby team was once described as a *tour de force*. But if he is not a naturally humorous writer, his slightly archaic, heavy touch can sometimes work well:

Does it not worry you, Manning, that the way things are going in sport, the next amateur to relinquish his status or retire will hire the Albert Hall . . . to sponsor it, and make so much money that it will be possible to afford amateurism after all?

It is arguable, I think, that certain writers have appeared who might have been capable of finding the idiom, building the bridge, were the popular press not so cautious and hidebound. Indeed, one of the most interesting appointments of the new *Sun* was that of Clement Freud, a gifted and sophisticated natural writer, as their first sports columnist.

The late HD Davies, who wrote for years on cricket and football for the *Guardian*, as Old International, was one who might have succeeded. Certainly his idiosyncratic football reports on the popular BBC programme *Sports Report* were widely appreciated. The style might have been polished and mature; the voice, beguilingly, was as Lancashire as hotpot. After Davies had been killed in Manchester United's 1958 air crash at Munich – the team, and several reporters, were on their way home from a match in Yugoslavia – Neville Cardus wrote this of him:

Old International was the first writer on soccer to rise above the immediate and quickly perishable levels of his theme and give us something to preserve in terms of character, vivid imagery, and language racy of Lancashire county ... Only a few weeks ago [he] told us of this sceptical man in the Maine Road crowd, and how he shouted, 'Look at 'im tryin' to dribble. Why doesn't he learn? 'E's nothing else to do.'

Davies, again, was a quality writer who emerged from the working classes, for his father was a cotton warehouseman who, as a boy, walked to Manchester from the Midlands with sixpence in his pocket, in search of work. He had a fine eye for character, eccentricity and appearance, and a love of anecdote. Of Bill Foulke, the 22-stone goalkeeper who played for Sheffield United and England before the First World War, he wrote:

The sight of Foulke's stomach in goal was said to have been the one thing which would persuade Bloomer [a legendary goal scorer] to abandon his golden rule when shooting – namely, never to let the ball rise above knee high. The story goes that in one match Bloomer twice knocked Foulke insensible with violent shots in the stomach, and sought to do it a third time. But this time Foulke incontinently fled and let the ball through.

But an idiom grows – it cannot be manufactured – and for a very long time to come the gap between such writers as Arlott, Cardus, Alan Ross (on cricket), Geoffrey Green of *The Times* (on football),* and the popular press will remain a vast one. Before popular sports journalism can rid itself of its shoddy inexactitudes, its weary stylisation, another gap must disappear, that between the quality and the popular newspaper, and this, in turn, is largely dependent on social change.

* To this company I would add Hugh McIlvanney of the *Observer*.

The Great Dictators

The Oldie, August 1993

RECENTLY THE CHAIRMAN of Arsenal football club, Peter Hill Wood, announced that George Graham was the greatest manager Arsenal had ever had, and that a statue of him would be erected on the premises. This suggested that he was a still finer manager than the late Herbert Chapman, whose bust has long stood in the marble entrance hall of Highbury's East stand.

On the face of it, Hill Wood's statement seemed a kind of sacrilege, though football fans have memories too short to declare the equivalent of a fatwah. Chapman died when I was two years old, but as one who has made a study of Arsenal's history – like Graham himself – I find the comparison both odious and ill-founded.

Whether Chapman's paternalist methods would work today who knows, but it's significant that they or their equivalent worked for Brian Clough for all but the last of the eighteen years he spent in charge of Nottingham Forest. Graham, a manager often at odds with the press, not seldom at odds with some of his own players, winner of two League Championships and both last season's major cups, is neither a Clough nor a Chapman.

One of Chapman's greatest friends was the Italian Vittorio Pozzo, who first took charge of the international side in the 1912 Olympics. Later, after the Great War, he ran it for twenty years, during which time it twice won the World Cup.

Then there was Stanley Rous. It was in 1934, the year in which Chapman died (he caught pneumonia after watching a game in bad weather), that Rous became secretary of the Football Association. He held the job for the next 28 years before transferring to the presidency of the international body FIFA; Denis Follows then became his successor at the FA.

The night this appointment was announced, I was waiting in the anteroom of a BBC radio studio to interview Mr Follows. As we waited, Follows remarked of Rous: 'The secretary of the Football Association is the servant of the Association. And we all knew what happened. The servant became the master.'

And a good thing too, you might say, given the bumbling ineffectuality, the self-seeking pomposity and the nitwitted incompetence of those FA councillors who sat above him. Rous had his faults, as any dominant authoritarian has, but he was honest, he had a true vision of the international game, and he cut a clean path through obscurantism and folly. In fact, Rous, Chapman and Pozzo might all be described as benevolent dictators.

Vittorio Pozzo

Stocky, bushy white-headed, a tremendous egoist but a fascinating raconteur, Pozzo became very well known to me in his latter years. I met him first at Wembley when I was a nineteen-year-old journalist, on the occasion of a match between England and Argentina. Next day, a magical one for me, we travelled all over London together while he told me tales of his career. When the following year I went to live in Florence, I travelled overnight up to Turin, eight hours in third class on wooden seats. I hardly slept, but he kept me enthralled all the next day.

An unusual coincidence linked Pozzo and Rous. Both had problems with fascist salutes during matches, and both incidents took place in 1938.

First was the occasion with Rous in Berlin. Relations between Britain and Nazi Germany were taut. At the Olympics, held in the same stadium two years earlier, the British team had boldly offended the Nazis by refusing to raise their arms in the Nazi salute. Sir Nevile Henderson, Britain's appeasing ambassador, asked if the England team would 'Heil Hitler'. Rous mediated. The reluctant players saluted: then went on to thrash Germany 6–3. Soon afterwards Pozzo's *azzurri*, the Italian team defending the World Cup they had won at home in 1934, played Norway in their first-round match in Marseille. When the players gave the fascist salute, which was obligatory then, a burst of whistling and jeering came from Italian dissidents on the terraces. Pozzo obliged the team to hold the salute until the noise abated. He wasn't a fascist himself. A sturdy Piedmontese, a mountain man, he told me once he couldn't join the Resistance because his figure was too well known.

What he did do, beyond doubt, was channel the chauvinism of the times to his advantage. A French journalist once called him 'the poor captain of a company of millionaires'.

He was a wily psychologist. If two players had clashed in a match he made them share the same room. 'We are trying to build a team,' he'd tell them. Next morning, he'd poke his head round the door. 'Well, cannibals, have you eaten each other yet?' Embarrassed grunts would greet him. Then each man would take him aside in turn to say, 'He's not such a bad fellow. The public set me against him.'

Pozzo, ironically, learnt his successful tactics in England. As a student, pre-World War I, he fell in love with this country. When his parents cut off his allowance, he taught languages all over the Midlands. He'd wait shyly outside stadiums to talk to the great players of the day – Charlie Roberts, Manchester United's centre-half, or Steve Bloomer, Derby's legendary goal-scorer. Both inspired the pivotal, attacking centre-halves of Italy's World Cup wins.

Herbert Chapman

Chapman was a Yorkshireman who'd played inside-forward for Spurs, and was suspended, initially for life, by the FA over illegal payments made to players by Leeds City. Chapman took the blame, saying he'd burnt the club's books, but was soon triumphantly back as manager of Huddersfield Town. Both they and Arsenal would win three championships in a row.

Arsenal, then a mediocre club, appointed him in 1925. Together with the famous player Charlie Buchan (bought from Sunderland on a unique '£100 per goal' transfer) he devised the Third Back Game. With its stopper centre-half, this counteracted the avalanche of goals which followed the just changed offside law.

Chapman was both inspirational and innovative, taking a keen interest in more than just tactics – he was a Svengali to his players. 'He told you how to dress,' his left-back and captain, Eddie Hapgood, once said to me. 'He told you how to do your hair.' But Chapman's partner at full-back for Arsenal and England, George Male, said to me in the early 60s that there might be players now who'd answer, 'Well, I'm not staying here for that.'

Male was one of Chapman's great successes. Arriving as an amateur left-half from Clapton, he was persuaded by Chapman to become a full-back. 'By the time I left his office, not only did I know I was going to be a right-back; I knew I was going to be the best right-back in the world.'

Stanley Rous

Rous, a fearsome figure behind his desk at Lancaster Gate, large white cuffs covering the sleeves of his suit, began obscurely as a schoolmaster in Norfolk. He kept goal a bit, taught sports at Watford, became an international and Cup-final referee, then got the job at the FA.

Even he couldn't push England into the World Cup before the war, but he steadily conquered our football's xenophobia. The FA, who'd withdrawn from FIFA in the 20s, returned after World War II.

That Rous was a snob and a social climber could scarcely be gainsaid. He hadn't much contact with the troops on the ground. 'Stanley Rous was up here yesterday,' said Gerry Hitchens, England's blond centre-forward in World Cup camp, Chile 1962. 'He said: "Morning, Bobby!"' Bobby was of course Bobby Charlton, then as blond as Hitchens.

A military figure, middle-aged, with short hair and brief moustache, would train with England's players then, and take part in their practice games. Who was he? A rich friend of Rous's, who'd been hospitable to him in Australia. The word was that when he sat down at their table England's players would move away.

Rous was famously at odds with the FA president, Graham

Doggart, who'd once played centre-forward for the Corinthians and England. Once when I was in his office Rous said to me: 'I've just had Doggart round. He had this little piece of paper in his hand. He said: "There were two spelling mistakes in the latest issue of the FA News. Secondly, I've had two letters from the FA which were insufficiently stamped. If I hadn't known the postman I'd have had to pay the postage due."

'I said to him: "Good *God*! I've just come back from the US with a £100,000 contract, and you're talking about *stamps*?"

'He said: "I do have some other points but perhaps I'd better not make them now." I said: "Perhaps you'd better *not*!" '

But Rous did get things done. He never let FIFA slide into the shoddy ways which have afflicted it since 1974 (when he was deposed as president by the ineffable Brazilian water-polo player José Havelange) – not least of which was the dubious and mysterious awarding of the 1986 World Cup to Mexico, despite the height and heat and the fact that it had staged it once before, in 1970.

Vanished giants. Pygmies have followed. Chapman, who immediately got rid of Tommy Black, a Scots left-back who gave away a penalty when Walsall sensationally beat Arsenal in the FA Cup of 1933, would never have paid Tony Adams his full whack when he was jailed for drunken driving, as the new Arsenal did. Rous would never have cravenly involved the FA with the so-called Premier League as his successor Graham Kelly has. Pozzo would surely still have been a poor but dominant captain of Italy's present company of multimillionaires.

Footballers Don't Cry

Love Is Not Love, 1985

T HE PHONE WENT at one in the morning, and I knew who it was. Oh no, I thought, not him. But it had to be him. We'd only got the baby off an hour ago.

'Peter,' he said, 'I've lost me job.' There were tears in his voice. It was pitiful, honestly. Him. The Iron Man. But I couldn't sound surprised. It had been coming for weeks.

'Called me in tonight and sacked me,' he said. 'The bastards.'

This was what shocked me: his tone. The feeling sorry for himself, after all he dinned into me over the years, right from the very beginning. 'Don't squeal. Pick yourself up and get on with it. Footballers don't cry. Football's a game for men, not lasses. If they kick you, you kick 'em back.' All that, and so much more. Never give up. Never feel sorry for yourself. And now here he was, how they'd done this to him, how they'd done that to him, full of self-pity, wanting comfort, till it was almost like I was him now and he was me.

'Peter,' he said, 'Peter, I hope you'll never know what it's like to have this happen to you. To be stabbed in the back by a lot of ungrateful, fat-arsed businessmen that know fuck all about this game. That's what hurts. To take it from them. Me, who's given my life to the game.'

I was still half asleep. I said, 'Yes, Dad. I know, Dad.'

Marion came out of the bedroom, yawning and rubbing her eyes. 'Who is it?' And I said, 'It's Dad. He's just got the push.'

'Not again,' she said. 'It's the middle of the night. You're going to wake John.'

'Dad,' I said. 'I'll phone you in the morning.' I felt bad: I knew he wanted to go on, pouring it all out, and I felt worse, because I knew I didn't want to listen. 'God bless you, Dad,' I said. 'I'll phone first thing tomorrow.' Then I put down the phone and took it off the hook, else I knew he'd be back. It was a terrible thing, that. Little moments, little movements, yet you're changing a whole life.

I didn't sleep. I lay awake, thinking. What he'd done for me, how much I'd always admired him. Just a little lad, going to watch him play, at Bolton and at Rotherham; then later on, when he dropped out of the League, at Wigan and Boston and Kettering. Get in, Dad! Go on, Dad! A centre-half, great big fellow, coming in bang with his thick legs, ploughing through the mud with his sliding tackles, taking the man, the ball, the lot; jumping above the centre-forward, thump with his head, always first to the ball, a hard man, very tough, very brave, very strong, a bit dirty – though I never thought that, then.

All those little back gardens. Left foot, right foot, left foot. 'Come on, Peter, come on!' I was frightened of him, me. Him so big and me so little. Like Mother, never really growing.

'You'll be a winger,' he said, when what I wanted was to be a centre-half, like him. Big and strong. Coming in like a tank.

Later, there were all the piddling little jobs he had, coach of this, manager of that, of nothing. Clubs in the Midland League, clubs in the Northern Premier, always in debt, playing in front of a few hundred people; him having to do everything, mark out the pitch, mow the grass, treat the injuries.

'Peter,' he'd say, 'you're my answer, son. When you make it, I'll make it. The war did me, Peter, as a player. Took the best years of my career away. Stopped me realising my potential. If I'd played for England like I should, there'd have been no stopping me afterwards. Manager of Arsenal, Manager of Everton. Look at Matt Busby. Captain of Scotland, end of the war – Manager of Manchester United. A great team ready waiting for him. Me, I had to start with rubbish. I've done miracles with rubbish. Worked wonders with rubbish. I knew about recycling before it had ever been invented. But you get no medals for that.'

And he hadn't. He'd last three months here, six months there, then something would snap. He'd quarrel with the chairman, blow his top to the press, even thump one of the players, and out he'd go, off we'd go. Another little house, poor Mother packing and unpacking all over again. No wonder she was worn out. No wonder she died.

'But you, Peter,' he'd say, 'you will justify me. By your career. By your skill. By your determination. And then, Peter, they may begin to listen. They will begin to see that I practise what I preach – through my own son, who nobody can say I did not develop.' He'd put his hand on my shoulder, this very emotional look in his eye. 'You'll never disappoint me, Peter. I know that.'

I wouldn't. I knew it, too. I'd rather cut my leg off.

I'd never been so chuffed as when he got that job with City. More than when I came to Rovers, and to London. Even more than when I first played for England. And, to be honest, I think I know why. There was relief in it. Not just because he'd be happy now, he'd stop complaining now, but because, in a funny sort of way, things were like they should be again. Me an England player, but him a top manager. With only one thing spoiling it – for him, not me. Knowing people were whispering and hinting. Would he have ever managed City if he hadn't been my father, if I wasn't playing for England?

Ignorance, that was.

'And why did I play for England?' I asked, whenever I got wind of it. 'Because of him. Dad and his coaching.' But you could see by their faces that you'd not convinced them.

I couldn't even convince Marion. 'He didn't make you,' she said. 'I'm sick of hearing that, from him and you. He was lucky to have you.'

'No, no,' I said. 'You don't know football, Marion.'

'I know him,' she said, 'and I know you.'

The next morning, when we woke, the first thing she said was, 'He's not coming to stay, is he?'

'I don't know,' I said. 'I've not thought.'

She'd never forgiven him, though I've always told her it was nothing personal, nothing against her, even if he was wrong; just his feelings for me, and my football.

'You mean him and your football,' she'd said.

He'd always told me, 'Don't get married early.' I tried to explain it to Marion. 'It's not you,' I said.

'No,' she'd said, 'and it's not you either – it's him, everything for him. He wants you to be a little puppet, dancing to his strings.'

It was a bad time for me, that, pulled one way and then the other. My form suffered. I loved her; and I loved him; and I loved football. That was the time I missed a penalty in the semi-final against Leeds at Villa Park, and we went out of the Cup. I didn't see her for a week and I wouldn't talk to him. Then one day I walked into the hairdresser's where she worked and said, 'Come on, I've got the licence,' because it had to be like that. I either had to marry her or give her up, and if I gave her up it would shatter me.

'My mother,' she said. 'My father . . .'

I told her, 'Never mind them, and never mind my father. I've got two witnesses. We'll have the church wedding later.' And we did. I'd had to do it like that. For the first time in my life, I'd started hating him.

'My own son,' he's said since, 'and I wasn't invited to his wedding.'

When we stepped out of that gloomy little registry office, I went straight into the Post Office along the road and I sent him a telegram: 'MARION AND I MARRIED TODAY BIGGEST MATCH OF ALL LOVE PETER.' We didn't hear from him for ten days, and then he sent a silver teapot that must have cost him a bomb.

'Marion,' he said, when he came over from Hartlepool, where he was coach then, 'I want you to know I've got nothing against you. I never have had. I've always thought you're a wonderful girl, but Peter and me, we've always lived for football, and I'll admit I've been anxious for his career.'

'No more than what I am, Mr Coleman,' she said.

But things changed; it was inevitable. The moment we walked into that registry office, they'd changed. It was the first big thing in my life I'd ever done without him, the first I'd ever done against him. But when he got the City job, that changed things, too; it helped to change them back again. It wasn't me getting two hundred quid a week while he got forty any more, and much too proud to accept anything. Time and again I'd say, 'Look, Dad, it's yours. You did it. I'd be nothing without you.'

'I'll not take a penny,' he'd say. 'The satisfaction I've had from you, you can't buy it.' He's a wonderful man, if you only but know him.

So after breakfast, while Marion was feeding the baby, I telephoned him. He was still in the same state.

'They're being very vindictive about it,' he said. 'There's still nearly eighteen months of my contract to run. Ten grand they owe me, and they've as good as told me I can sue them for it. And this club house – they're turning me out of that, as well.'

'Dad,' I said. What else could I say? 'Come down and stay with us.'

'You're sure?' he said. 'How about Marion? What about the baby?'

'There's tons of room, Dad,' I said. 'Marion won't mind. Just until you get settled. Till you get another job.'

'For a week then,' he said. 'But only that, mind. Just till I get fixed up.'

She was choked when I told her. 'Without even asking me,' she said.

'Just for a week,' I told her, 'while he looks around. He's shattered, Marion.'

'He'll shatter us,' she said.

He was in a state when he got to us. All tense and taut, that twitch at the left side of his mouth.

'It'll be down to your knees, soon,' he said, looking at my hair. His was the short back and sides he'd always had. 'Hello, Marion,' he said. He kissed her on the cheek, and she took it like it was a vaccination. Then he kissed John, the baby, and his face relaxed; he liked the baby. He started playing with his fingers, but he burst out crying.

'He's tired,' Marion said, and took him away.

The old man glanced around the place. It was a lovely house; it had cost thirty thousand. Nice, big rooms, big picture windows, looking out on a golf course at the back, colour telly.

'By gum,' he said, like he always did, 'things have changed a bit since I were playing.'

I hoped he wasn't going to come out with the usual rigmarole, about my hair, my hundred-pound suits, my embroidered shirts, because I knew it by heart: 'What's that? The Sportsman Club? In my day it was eight pound a week and a pint at the boozer.'

Now he looked out the front and said, 'That your new car?' It was an XJ Jag. He shook his head; I was used to that as well. 'I don't know,' he said. I hoped he wouldn't go on about buses and bicycles.

He sat down on the leather sofa, he slapped himself on the knees, he gave the laugh he always gives when he's miserable, and he said, 'Well! Now let's wait for the offers to come pouring in!'

'It's early days, Dad,' I said.

'Oh, yes,' he said, 'I don't expect them to come rushing. Not falling over themselves. After all, where did I leave City? Only three places off the bloody bottom. Where will they finish now I've gone? Right at the bottom.'

'Don't feel bitter, Dad,' I told him.

'Bitter?' he said. 'I'm not bitter. I'm resigned to it, me. Directors, bloody amateurs, obstructing a professional.'

'That's the system, Dad,' I said. 'You'll not change it.'

'It's a bloody diabolical system,' he said, and I was afraid he'd be off on another of his favourite moans – directors and how ignorant they were – but instead he went quiet, not even looking at me, sitting there like he was embarrassed, till at last he said, 'You don't think there'd be something for me at Rovers?'

It left me speechless. It was the first time in my life he'd ever asked me for anything. 'Well, Dad,' I said, 'there might be. Not as manager, just now, nor as coach. They go together, do those two. Everywhere Geoff Creamer goes, Bobby Birchall goes with him.'

'I know,' he said, 'I didn't mean that,' which made it worse, because what else was there? Scouting? Looking after the Reserves? Those weren't for Dad; they never had been.

'Maybe I could help with the coaching and the scouting,' he said. 'Something like that. Weighing up teams they're going to play.' He looked at me. The look was new as well, almost pleading. What had happened to him?

'I'll try tomorrow,' I said. 'I'll see the boss.' Then I made an excuse and left the room. It was too much for me.

I did talk to the boss, Geoff Creamer, next day. He was uneasy; I could tell he didn't want to upset me. At the same time, obviously, he knew about Dad, his reputation.

'There's not much for him here, Peter,' he said, 'not for him.'

'Just a bit of scouting and coaching,' I said, 'to be going on with. It's shattered him, this. I think maybe he needs to get his confidence back.'

'I'll talk to the chairman,' he said. A couple of days later he called me in and told me, 'We've got something for your father, on the lines he asked for. I'm afraid we can't pay him a lot, but if he regards it as a port in a storm . . .'

So he started with them, coaching and scouting like he'd wanted, going to look at teams and players for the boss, taking individual players for special skills, out at Epsom, where we trained, nice and near my home. Of course, I was glad he'd got the job, very glad – for him – but it made things strange. Him being at the club; him living at the house. We'd gone back, and yet, if you see, we hadn't gone back. Dad couldn't change; you couldn't expect him to. He'd still tell me what to do, how to play, when to go to bed, even when to go on the job – 'Never the night before a match. It's like losing two pints of blood' – like I was still a kid. Marion could hardly keep quiet if she was there when he did it: she'd wriggle; she'd make faces. I was afraid any moment she'd say something, and afterwards she would. 'I don't know how you put up with it. Treating you like a baby, and he wouldn't have a job if it wasn't for you.'

'I know,' I said. 'That's why I put up with it. He knows it, too. He's on forty-five a week – our reserves earn more than that. But without him what would I be earning?'

But it wasn't easy to get her to see it like that, especially with the baby keeping her up and taking all her time. She said, 'I've heard of mothers-in-law . . .'

Once a day he'd say, 'I must move out. I mustn't burden you. I'll find a room in a hotel.'

'If I hear that once more,' Marion told me, 'I'll go straight out and find one for him.'

I took her hand; she looked very tired. 'I know,' I said. 'I know.'

But I couldn't hurt him, even if it sometimes drove me up the wall: the diagrams, the salt and pepper pots on the table, the 'action replays', going over and over some move I'd made or hadn't made, like after a game we lost at home to Newcastle.

'The one-two,' he said. 'It was on. It was screaming at you. Even with that big camel of a centre-forward of yours. Going through alone. That was daft. But then you always were a greedy little bugger.'

Another time I missed a penalty at Birmingham. That was good for a week, that. My run-up. The way I'd struck the ball. Hitting it high instead of keeping it low. The position of my body. The goalkeeper's position. 'Low and angled, low and angled. How many times do I have to tell you that?'

A million.

Mind, it was only a year ago or so I'd stopped the phone calls, or most of them, the postmortems we'd have after every big game, even in Europe, especially with England – I remember phoning him once from Caracas, when I really felt I'd played bad. It began to fall off after I got married. Marion would say, 'Phoning your father again?' or 'I suppose you'll be on the phone for an hour tonight.' Perhaps I'd outgrown it; I didn't need it so much now. But she could never realise how it had helped me all those years.

Now and again I'd look at his face when he thought I wasn't and I'd see the bitterness, the disappointment. That was the end, with City – I knew it and he knew it – the end as far as managing a big club was concerned. He'd upset too many people. No wonder he was afraid to leave us; no wonder he was for ever lecturing me: I was all he'd got left.

And then it started at the club. I'd been afraid it would. First he didn't reckon the coach, Bobby Birchall, which was par for the course; he never reckoned any coach, especially one that was coaching me. He'd be out on the field there at Epsom when Bobby was working with us, shaking his head, clicking his tongue, making faces, till it was obvious that Bobby noticed and naturally he didn't like it. There was no future in it either. It was like I'd told him: where Geoff Creamer went, Bobby Birchall went. Geoff Creamer sat in the stadium and handled the directors and the press; Bobby Birchall was out at Epsom looking after the tactics and the training. If you knocked Bobby, you were getting at Geoff.

One day Geoff had me into the office. He said, 'Peter, you'll have to talk to your father.' I'd been expecting this. 'We're glad to have him here,' he said, 'till he gets something else. But he must realise Bobby Birchall is coach, and I'm manager.'

'I know,' I said, 'but it's difficult for Dad. He's used to helping me.'

'Just a quiet word,' the boss said. 'I shouldn't like anything to go wrong,' and he gave me what we used to call his Man Management smile, the smile on the face of the tiger.

Of course, I didn't talk to Dad. How could I? He'd no time for Bobby, and even less for the boss. 'They'll burn you out, this club,' he'd say, 'using you like they do. This four, four, two. They want you on both bloody wings, and fetching and carrying in midfield. I'm going to have a word with Geoff Creamer if it goes on. You'll not last three seasons. I'll tell him, "You're killing the goose that lays the golden eggs."'

'Please don't, Dad,' I said. 'I can tell him myself.'

'Ay,' he said, 'but you haven't, have you? It's just as well I'm here.'

The trouble was there was truth in what he said, like there nearly always was. They had been working me hard, for a couple of seasons now, and I was beginning to feel it, but it wasn't any good telling them – it would just make it worse. I'd wince, sometimes, when the boss and the old man were together.

'Work rate?' the old man would say. 'What's all this bloody work rate? Footballers aren't factory hands. Footballers aren't navvies.'

The boss would cock his little head and stick out his little fat arse in the way he had and smile his smile and say, 'Football's changed a lot, you know, Ted.'

'Maybe,' said Dad, 'but it hasn't changed for the bloody better.'

The big blow-up came when we played Milan in the first leg of the European Cupwinners' Cup quarter-final, at our place. Everything went wrong in the first half. They were playing this packed defence with a sweeper, body-checking a lot, shirt-pulling, and when they broke away and scored we got desperate, just banging long balls into the middle, which their defence were eating.

At half-time, Bobby and the boss came into the dressing room with the old man, who'd been sitting on the bench with Bobby – they'd sent him out there to watch Milan. As soon as I saw him I could tell we were in for trouble; I knew that look on his face. He was bursting to bollock everybody in sight and, to make matters worse, the boss and Bobby just stood there like a couple of dummies with nothing to offer at all. I was longing for them to say something, anything, just to fill the silence, before the old man leapt in, which he did.

He started: 'Well, if you two haven't got anything to say, I have. I've never seen such a pathetic exhibition. You're playing right into their hands. No skill, no method, no intelligence.' On and on he went, and whether the other two were too surprised to try and stop him or too chicken, I don't know. The fact is they didn't. He bollocked us for using long balls into the middle; he bollocked us, especially me, for not going to the line and pulling the ball back – 'You try getting there,' I said, 'with the shirt-pulling and the obstruction' – and he was still at full blast when the buzzer went for the second half. Bobby and the boss hadn't opened their mouths. We left the three of them behind us in the dressing room, and I wondered what they'd say to one another.

The thing was that his pep talk worked; I think that's what they couldn't forgive him. We did get our tails up; we did start playing better; we did start going round the back of them; we equalised, and very nearly won.

After the match the boss didn't show in the dressing room at all, just Bobby, looking a bit sheepish, and the old man, who, of course, was just full of it. He never could read situations outside football. 'That was better, lads, that was better. If you'd played like it the whole of the game, you'd have bloody annihilated them!'

All I kept wondering was where the boss was, and what he was saying to the chairman.

There was a reception afterwards, the usual drag: speeches, a cold buffet, and a couple of beers at most, because you knew the boss was looking. He didn't speak to the old man, nor did any of the directors. There was what you might call an atmosphere.

The word went round that a few of the lads were going on to the Sportsman's Club. I asked Dad if he'd like to come, and nearly got my head bit off. 'A club? After a game like this? If you'd been trying, you'd all be too tired to do anything but go to bed, which is what you should do, after a match' – another of his favourite moans. So it was a confrontation, the last thing I wanted; the two of us standing there, glaring at each other.

I couldn't back down, not in front of the lads. 'Well, I'm going, Dad,' I said. 'I'll see you later.'

He went on staring for a while, and then he said, 'You little tyke,' and walked away. I felt bad leaving him.

We were there till nearly three in the morning, but when I got home the light was still on in the front room. He was sitting there with his head in his hands. I'd never seen him look that shattered, eyes all red. He looked a hundred years old.

'They've sacked me, Peter,' he said, and he began to cry.

'I'm sorry, Dad,' I said.

He said, 'Sorry? Is that all you can say? You're not going to stay there, are you? You'll ask for a transfer?'

I shook my head.

Get up, I thought; get up; footballers don't cry. The words sprang into my throat and choked me. I knew he'd never get up now.

Are Boxers People?

Cavalier, August 1964

OXING IS A world – or an underworld – apart. It has its own legend, its own heroes, above all its own vernacular. Logically and ethically, there's not a thing to be said in favour of its continued existence. It exploits the young, the poor, and the underprivileged, caters to sadism and violence, has long been the preserve of the gangster. Sweep it away, however, and you sweep away with it, from an increasingly conformist world, the character, the colour, the malapropisms, the vitality.

Brought into contact with it a few years ago, with sudden surprise, I should now miss it dreadfully if it disappeared. The actual fights aren't even the half of it: boring where they are not brutal – but the background is priceless and unique.

Above all, the boxer himself is usually a sympathetic figure full of idiosyncratic ways, chronic overconfidence, decent simplicity.

One knew, of course, many of the myths. Of Tony Galento, who, when asked what he thought of Shakespeare, replied, 'I'll moider da bum.' Of Rocky Graziano, who came back from a title fight and said, 'They trut me good.' But one was used to the milder eccentricities of the soccer world, where characters were characters, but didn't make such a profession of it.

Then, endowed with a sports column, I made a visit to the Thomas à Becket gym, down the Old Kent Road. It's here, above a pub, that most of the leading British fighters train, and I was greeted by Ted Kid Lewis, the greatest Jewish boxer ever to come out of the East End, a former world champion; now a kind old man with gold-flecked white hair and a squashed nose, who looked as if he'd never harmed a fly. Everyone was for the best in this best of all possible worlds.

Lewis presented me to Ted Broadribb, who used to manage Tommy Farr. 'Ted used to be my idol as a boy,' he said.

Lewis then introduced me to Joe Lucy, the former British lightweight champion, behind the bar. 'A gentleman. Never insults anybody. Never abuses anybody. I'm full of praises for him.' Going upstairs, Lewis said of a young boxer, 'Does his training properly. Looks after himself. I wish he was my son. I've got a wonderful son. Best son in the world, he is. That was a happy day, when I married. The happiest day in my life.'

Inside the gym, a long light room full of mirrors, plastic buckets, and fight posters, a trainer in a black blouse and a black beret, wearing a little silver badge inscribed 'Victor', came forward and said, 'I think you must regard Ted Lewis as the non-parell [sic] of all non-parells. And it's important to note that, as one of the best known of our sporting mortals, he retains all his faculties, which is synonymous of the fact that he has always taken good care of himself. And a more humane human being you could go to the four corners of the world to meet.'

The next gym I visited was England's Gymnasium, in a Cardiff backstreet where rain water swirled rotten vegetables along the gutters. Joe Erskine, the Welsh heavyweight, a swarthy, amiable man, was preparing for a return British title fight with the champion, Henry Cooper. Their last fight had been controversial; Benny Jacobs, Erskine's manager, a man with dark, knowing, heavy-lidded eyes and drooping silver hair, had jumped into the ring to protest. The ring, he maintained, was too small and, worse still, Cooper had hit Erskine after the bell had gone. Pinned to a board in the corner of the big dingy gym was their Christmas card: one boxer was knocking another boxer over the ropes of a tiny ring, while Father Christmas, as timekeeper, rang the bell. The greeting ran: HOPING YOU DON'T STOP ONE AFTER THE BELL.

'I used to like him,' said Erskine, sombrely, 'but after what he done anything goes. I may do a few little naughty things, myself.'

I bore the news to Cooper, at the Thomas à Becket. He's a placid agreeable Cockney with eyes that cut as easily as paper and a twin brother, George, who also fights and says, 'You expect *to get* cuts; I mean, me and Henry do.'

'Joe's a silly boy,' said Henry. 'I mean, boxing; that's his long suit. Him and me's the best of friends, like I knew him in the army, but I hate his manager.'

The two duly fought again. Erskine was plagued by sinovitis; Cooper won with ease. No one did anything naughty. Cooper trained at an old pub down in the country at Wrayesbury, living in a riverside bungalow where you could watch the blobs of detergent floating by like great white ducks. His father was there, a little man wearing an expression of perpetual amazement that one so small could have produced two so vast. From time to time, he would reiterate the theme of Henry's docility outside the ring. Once, a journalist had betrayed the secret that he was getting married. 'Henry said to him the next day, "*You're* a right one. I know I give you a story, but don't go making it fan*tastic*." The man said, "I'm sorry." He thought he was going to get a coating, but Henry said, "It's over now." '

I met Dick Richardson, too, the hulking heavyweight champion of Europe, who made a fortune with the crudest of ring techniques till his shrewd little Cockney manager, Wally Lesley, persuaded him to retire. 'If I was a racehorse trainer, and Richardson was a racehorse,' Lesley told me, 'I'd have got warned off years ago. In Dortmund, I took seven nerve tablets from about four o'clock till the time he got in the ring. I only take 'em on big fight nights, just to bolster me up. He may fight well, he may come in and stink the place out, but don't ask *me* which Richardson you're going to see, because *I* don't know.'

As we sat in the living room of Lesley's little semidetached house in Staines, just beyond London, somebody used the word 'bastard'.

'Don't swear,' cried Richardson, huge and rugged, a terror with his head in the ring. 'It's his wife, see; she's a Catholic. No. I mean, Wally and me, when we're outside the house, we'll say anything, but not in here. It's his wife. It's her religion.'

But none of these had quite the deadpan pungency of Terry Downes, once the world middleweight champion, with his flattened nose, remarkably youthful face, and thick, sometimes impenetrable, Cockney ('Me 'ooter; I could fight *you* and get cut'). I heard him speak at a luncheon given before he met Paul Pender at Wembley for the title. Pender spoke first, deploring the fact that a newspaper had described everything as far too friendly. 'When you go on to a football field, you don't *growl* at one another,' said Pender.

Downes got up, in his turn. 'Well, I've done a bit of growling in me time,' he said. 'But I reckon you're a fool if you go around growling at a bloke don't want to growl at *you*, making a right idiot of yourself.'

I once asked him how he felt when he knocked someone out. 'I feel surprised,' he said.

In 1962, Ray Robinson arrived, complete with entourage, to fight him. 'Blimey,' Downes said to me, 'I feel old myself at twenty-six in the mornings. I wake up and I think, I got to run six miles this morning. "This old fight game's getting hard," I say to myself. *There's* a man forty-one been doing it twenty years. How does *he* feel, some mornings? He's only human.'

'Let me say this,' I was told by George Gainford, Robinson's manager, a big bald man in a brown suit, who looked like a revivalist preacher. 'You know, a famous statesman said once that he did not become Prime Minister to disband the British Empire. Let me elaborate on that. We did not come here to lose a fight, *al*though the best-laid plans of mice and men oft go astray.'

Robinson did lose, and the title went round and round – from Fullmer to Tiger to Giardello, the first American fighter I ever met. Giardello came to London with Tony Ferrante, his manager, and Joe Polino, his cut man (later to work in Sonny Liston's corner). Downes fought Giardello and beat him.

Ferrante said, 'I'm a funny man, which Micky Duff knows that today, my woid is my bond.' Polino said, 'One time Joey Giardello was on crutches, and a guy hit him. He was helpless, so he hit the guy with the crutch.' Giardello said, 'No, no, no. Somebody else hit him with the crutch. He didn't pick me out at the station. When he found out who I was, he sued me for $25,000.'

At a luncheon one day, I sat opposite the three of them,

transfixed, as Polino explained, 'One time *I* was a fighter. I hit a guy with a left cross. Then I hit him with a right cross. Then he sent me to *Red* Cross. So I quit. When I talk about Joey and I say "we" I don't mean I'm going to take the punches. Joey's going to take the punches.'

'Sweet,' Giardello said.

Years later, Giardello – with no Ferrante, no Polino – beat Dick Tiger for the title. I telephoned Downes and asked him what he thought. 'Didn't shock me too much,' he said. 'He's a musclebound fighter, Dick Tiger. He just waits for you to stop and then he belts you. If you don't stop, he can't belt you. He beat Fullmer, who didn't need much beating. You get out to Nigeria with ten thousand of them shouting; what would have happened to Fullmer if he'd won? He'd have been soup for the next day's dinner. I wouldn't have fancied it there much, them sitting there with all their spears and bows and arrows.'

But my meetings with Floyd Patterson – one in London, one in New York – are what I remember most vividly of all. He was champion at the time; shortly before the first meeting with him I spoke to his manager, Cus D'Amato. 'When you have an organisation,' said D'Amato, darkly, 'you don't *have* to hurt anyone. All you have to do is starve a man to death.'

Patterson was hard to get hold of. Strange, unidentified voices would answer the hotel phone, one of them curiously high-pitched. His mother? one wondered. It seemed unlikely. At last, a harsh New York voice said, 'Hallo. This is Mr No*vem*ber.'

'This is Brian Glanville,' I explained. 'I wanted to get hold of Floyd Patterson before he went away.'

'*He* isn't going anywhere.'

I got hold of him and was impressed. He seemed, I told him, to represent the new, evolving heavyweight. Had he had a good education? Oh, no, said Patterson. He'd left school at fifteen.

Then perhaps he read a lot?

'I don't like to read books,' said Patterson, 'because my manager, he reads books, and my sparring partner, *he* reads his books, and to me it seemed to be a sort of disease or something. They used to read until they fell asleep and then wake up and read again. Well, if reading makes you that way, I'm not interested.'

Patterson, Downes and Cooper were certainly people. Farther out towards the fringe lay the heavy menace of Liston, the endless cacophony of Clay. I drove down to Philadelphia to interview Liston. He sat in the office of his lawyer, with arms like great black hams resting on the arms of his chair; a massive man, massively chewing gum.

'This man has been exposed to calumny!' cried the lawyer. 'He's paid the government every cent he owes! He loves kids! You said you wanted to talk to him about Father Stevenson. As soon as you talk about Father Stevenson, it comes out: he learnt boxing in the penitentiary! No! I will not permit it! You know, a lot of people think I'm a son of a bitch, but this is just the way I talk.'

By the time he had finished talking, each word had to be laboriously pried out of Liston. 'Yah,' he said, or, 'No,' then went on chewing gum. At last, in desperation, I mentioned that Patterson had just published his memoirs in which he recalled how distressed he was by the sight of Ingemar Johansson lying on the canvas, one leg twitching. Did Liston feel the same?

Liston chewed gum and at last spoke. 'After the Westphal fight,' he said, 'a newspaperman asked me, "How did he look, lying there?" I said, "He looked very good."'

Wasn't he afraid that, with a punch like his, he might one day kill a man?

'How did you come here?' Liston asked.

'By aeroplane.'

'Yeah. What was that plane that crashed the other day, with a hundred and eleven passengers? How many survived? Three? After that plane, another plane took off.'

His lawyer, since replaced, saw me to the office door. 'I apologise for my attitude,' he said. 'But not for my action.'

The following year, Cassius Clay came to London to beat Henry Cooper on a cut eye. By now I was less easily surprised. 'I'm going to whup him like I was his daddy,' Clay announced, face perfectly blank, like a spoilt child reciting lines in the school play. 'I'm going to whup him like he stole something.' Then, despite himself, he suddenly gave way and giggled. Now that he is heavyweight champion of the world, the psychopathology of everyday Clay remains a mystery, most of all to those of us who followed him to Miami Beach.

There, he was inseparably accompanied by his hypnotist in ordindary, Bundini, a large man wearing a baseball cap, who said he'd been ten years with Sugar Ray Robinson, Clay's hero. He was going to make a champion of Clay: 'I've brought *that* on him, now.' Someone who'd been 25 years with Robinson said Bundini had, indeed, been with Ray ten years – as waiter and cook.

One would see them storm into the dingy Fifth Street gym together.

'I'm the champ!'

'You the poor man's *dream*!'

'I was *born* the champ!'

'You born the champ in your *crib*!'

Once, as Clay pirouetted under the shower, a photographer called to him, 'Hey, Cassius! Yesterday I tried to make you look like an Adonis . . .'

'*No!*' said Clay, with menacing finality.

'Just with your leg up, Cassius.'

'*No,*' said Clay. 'I'm a *fighter*, not a *sex* maniac.'

A fighter? An exhibitionist? A perennial child? Perhaps we shall never know. Soon after he had won the title, Doug Jones, the heavyweight who so nearly beat him, gave a simpler explanation. I met him, the last of these fighters, in Harry Wiley's gym in Harlem, where black boxers endlessly skip and punch and lift and sweat as though preparing frantically for Armageddon.

'Money,' said Jones, 'is funny. Money make some people funny. Yes, it *does*; yes it *does*.'

Are boxers people? Yes, I would say; only more so. I should hate to see them disappear.

The Brothers

Triangles, 1973

NOBODY COULD HAVE wanted more for him than I did. No one could have cared more. No one could have looked after him better. That's what hurt me, when it turned out like it did; that, more than anything. Everything I done, I done for the best. For him. For my brother. But the worst thing I done, definitely the worst, was that day on the plane, chatting her up for him.

It's funny, isn't it? You do something with the best intentions, just out of kindness, and what you're doing is you're crucifying yourself. You might just as well say, here you are, here's the hammer, here's the nails, get on with it.

How many times have I thought about it, that moment on the plane? 'Fancy her, Joe? I'll fix it for you,' then stopping her as she come back down the aisle, a big bird, solid, blonde, turning them slow, grey eyes on me: 'Got a smile for my brother?'

I needn't have opened my mouth; I needn't have said a word. Come to that, she could have said, 'No,' and walked on, instead of, 'Why?' and stopping, looking from me to Joe, obviously liking him, starting to smile. I said, 'That's it! That's the smile!'

Or we could have travelled on another plane; or she could. Or turned down the telly thing in Newcastle. Anything. Any one of a thousand bloody things, anything but what happened; what I made happen. 'Why?' she said. 'Can't he ask himself?'

Bang-bang. Love at first fucking sight. Two weeks – engaged. Six months – married. Then all the trouble. Because he was the same with birds as he was with boxing, Joe. He'd got it all, but he wasn't interested. Good-looking. Nice, black curly hair. Fantastic physique. Everything to pull them, and yet he didn't want to know. I'd think about it at times, how unfair things were. All these things that he'd been given, and he wasn't interested; all the things I'd had to do for myself.

I fought, I fought quite well – I always reckoned I was dead unlucky, not being with the right manager, never getting the right fights – but I never had Joe's punch, I never had his body, I never heard that 'O-o-oh,' just coming into a ring and taking off my dressing gown.

The same way, *I* wanted birds, but birds wanted *him*. I had to work for them; I had to learn all the moves. I did all right, I pulled them OK, always have and always will, but with Joe, again, it came natural; and he didn't care. Maybe, though, you do better in the long run when you have to work at something, make it happen for you, but there it is. The two biggest things in a man, fighting and fucking; I always liked both of them, but Joe, he could take 'em or leave 'em.

The trouble I had getting him down the gym; the coaxing.

'I don't fancy it, Ted.'

'What do you want to do?' I'd ask. 'Get fat? It's a disgrace, a body like you've got.'

'That's not for me,' he said, 'boxing ain't.'

'You don't *know*,' I'd say. 'How do you *know*?'

He owes it to me, the fact he ever started it at all, the fact he's got all that he has. Where would he be, now? Still in some filthy garage, on his back under a car all day, twenty quid a week, if he was lucky.

'You don't have to box,' I said. 'Try the weights at first. Do a bit of skipping. Medicine ball. Get some fat off. Then, if you change your mind . . .'

'I won't change me mind,' he said.

He was eighteen, then, never put a glove on. It took a lot of work, I can tell you. Yet he used to come to all my fights; never missed; he was proud of me, like I was proud of him. Shoreditch he'd come to, Albert Hall, Lime Grove, even up to Nottingham and Leicester, but instead of spurring him on, it seemed to turn him off. People'd look at him, trainers and that, other fighters, and they'd ask, 'Taking it up, then, is he? Fighting amateur?'

and I'd have to say, 'No.' It'd choke me. 'No,' I'd say, 'he ain't interested.'

In a way, I suppose, we didn't seem like brothers, and yet we *were* brothers, good brothers, different but close, different in looks, different in age – twelve years – very, very different in character, yet with this bond that none of the others in the family had, me the eldest, him the youngest, perhaps *because* of that.

One of the things that made me laugh, so ridiculous it was, she said to me once, Janet, 'It's Joe that gets hurt,' as if I didn't take every punch myself. When he was up there in the ring, they hurt me more than they did him. I mean that. Because you don't feel them in the ring; not if you're fit, not if you've trained. When you're keyed up, with the old adrenalin going, they bounce off of you, and the good ones, the ones that put you away, those are the ones you feel least, at the time.

I wanted him to box, because there was so much I knew I could give him, so much I could do for him, so much I'd learnt, fighting myself, that now I couldn't use for myself; that if I'd known then, I'd have been more than just a British contender. I'd have done the lot: I'd have fought for the world title, even though I may never have beaten Clay; I don't think anyone would, not then. That's what I mean when I say I was part of Joey, that I felt for him, that in a way there was really no division; when he was in the ring, I was in the ring. Managers always talk about 'we'. 'We'll do this to them, we'll do that to them,' and of course the old chestnut: 'We was robbed.' Personally it used to sicken me, but with me and Joey there was really something in it, it was true. Like I said, nobody could have looked after him better than I did.

I planned it all, too, right from the first amateur days. The club he joined, the fights he had, when to let him go in the amateur championships. I had to handle it all very, very carefully, like breaking in a stallion, because if I'd done the wrong thing, pushed him too hard, got the wrong fights, he'd have bolted, he'd have packed it up. So it had to be slow, it took a long time; it was like I was juggling two balls at once: one, bringing him along, keeping him interested; the other, handling his career. Believe me, it wasn't easy, not to keep the two of them going.

His first knockout; I won't forget that. A club match, over Canning Town; he was still fighting welter. *Bop!* A lovely punch it was, one I'd been showing him, a right cross, after feinting to the body with the left. The boy he was fighting went down wallop, it must have been five minutes before they got him round, and Joey had this sort of smile on his face. I knew the feeling, there's nothing like your first knockout; it's like having your first bird.

'There you are,' I said, 'what did I keep telling you? How does it feel, eh?' and he shook his head, like he still couldn't believe it.

That was the moment it took, when he started moving under his own steam, without me having to keep shoving and pushing. Not that I still didn't have to go on at him a bit, because there was still two things that worried me about him: one, lack of ambition; two, lack of a killer instinct. Everything else, he had; all the strength, plenty of bottle. He wasn't scared of no one, even in his very first fights. One club match, he was up against a fellow who'd fought the last European Championships, a very hard puncher; no real style, but a hell of a belt, specially the left. But Joey just went in there after him as though it was the other way around, he was the experienced one, the other fellow was the novice, and this bloke was so surprised he never got going. Joey took it on points.

In a three-round fight, which of course is all you have in the amateurs, it can go like that; a good start's half the battle. At the same time, another difference between Joey and me, I knew I had to make him harder, and that wasn't easy. He didn't like hurting people. 'Joey,' I'd tell him, again and again, 'it's you or him. That's the way you've got to think of it. If you've got him going, put him away, because, if you don't, he may come back, and put *you* away.'

He'd say, 'Yes, Ted, OK, Ted,' but I had to make him *feel* it. You know the old saying, a hungry fighter's a good fighter, and Joe hadn't never gone hungry. Something had happened in them twelve years between his generation and mine. Things had got easier, softer. People weren't struggling no more. A hungry fighter knows if he don't fight, he don't eat and if he don't win, he probably won't fight no more, and once he's known what it's like to go hungry, it's always there, driving him on, no matter how much bread he makes. He's been poor, and he knows he can be poor again.

So there was this difference between us. When I was in the ring and saw someone going, saw that glaze in his eyes, that old wobble in his legs, I didn't feel no pity; it was bang, bang, and out they went. Afterwards I'd maybe go over to them, when they was up on their feet again, put a hand on their shoulder, ask them were they OK; but that was afterwards. Whereas with Joe, there was actually times I'd see him step back. I'd bellow at him, 'Get in, you daft berk, get in and finish him!' which sometimes used to get me into trouble, because they don't like that kind of thing, not in the amateurs.

It's very, very hard to instil that in a fighter, if it isn't there already, and to me, it was all Joe lacked, because he'd got the power, he'd got the punch, left *and* right. When they landed properly, that was it; it was only a question of improving his timing and his footwork, so that he could set them up.

I started him in quite early, sparring with professionals. Illegal, of course, but everybody does it and, if you want to make a career in the pros, it's the only way. Naturally I kept him away from places like the Board of Control gym in Hampstead, the Thomas à Becket down the Old Kent Road, the places we'd be seen, but there was plenty of others.

Day after day, night after night, I'd din it into him: what he could do, what he could be, how at thirty he could be set for the rest of his life. Another thing was, I wanted him to be seen, I wanted word to get around. I wanted him to get the best offer from the best promoter. There were plenty of managers wanted to take him off me, people I'd known when I'd been fighting. Some of them tried to get at Joe behind my back, but they was all wasting their time. I'd open my eyes wide, and I'd say, 'Pro? Who says he's going to turn pro?' because when he did, there was only one person that was going to manage him, and that was me.

One advantage he had, once he'd more or less matured: he was a natural middleweight. He come out of the welter class in less than a year, and he never had no trouble making middle-weight, whereas with me, which was part of the trouble, I was always too heavy for a cruiser, and not really big enough for a real heavy. Normally speaking, Joe would weigh about twelve stone, but half a stone of that would come off very quick, once we got down to training. He was always strong around eleven six, eleven seven.

One of the greatest things for me was being back again; back to all the old sounds and smells. Gymnasium smells: sweat and dust and leather and liniment. The old sounds: those jangling bells for the rounds, the ropes going tap, tap, tap against the floor, the punchball shaking on the wall, the *ugh-ugh* as the fighters jabbed and crossed; even all the old ugly faces, them scars and broken noses, and them cigars, as big as brown bananas.

It was all part of it. I could never step into a gym without this feeling coming up inside me. There was nothing to beat it except the real thing, the arenas themselves, the light and the dark, the tension in the air. Amateur; that was nothing. Small promotions; they were really nothing. I wanted to be back at Wembley – I'd fought there twice – or maybe Earl's Court, and one day, please God, in Madison Square Garden. I'd never made that, I'd never been to the States, but Joey would, I'd see to that.

What I did know about him was this. He was an exciting fighter. He was box office. He'd draw people. At a time when boxing was on its arse, when there wasn't a dozen fighters in the world that would fill a big hall for you, Joey had got it. Joey was the kind they'd come and see. He had the looks and he had the aggression and he had the punch. He'd keep on throwing punches and he'd keep on coming forward. He wasn't one of those fighters that'd win a fight and send you to sleep that we'd got so many of in Britain, duckers and divers, that won their fights without ever landing a proper punch. All right, he'd never be a Sugar Ray Robinson, he'd never have those moves, but how often does a Sugar Ray Robinson come along? Once in thirty years. With what he'd naturally got, and what I could teach him, I knew he could be the best in the world.

The first time his club coach wanted to put him in for the

national amateurs, I said no. He'd only been boxing nine months and it was too early. Not that I didn't expect him to do well; with a bit of luck he could even have gone as far as the quarter-finals, but that wasn't enough. I was trying to build this image around him; he was a winner. When I thought he was so good he'd have to win, and if he didn't win it could only be because of something like a cut eye, or one of them diabolical decisions you can get in the amateurs, then I'd put him in, but only then.

He worked a bit with his trainer at the club but mostly he worked with me. He learnt the professional way, right from the beginning: how to look after himself in the clinches, what to do when a bloke started using his nut, things that didn't matter so much in the amateurs, but that you had to be prepared for in the pros.

As soon as I could, I'd decided to give up my job and devote myself to Joe entirely. For me, it couldn't be soon enough. Since I'd packed up fighting, I'd done various things. Minder in nightclubs, which I still was, a bit of second-hand-car trading, some scrap-metal dealing, and one or two things I'd rather not talk about, the sort of things you can drift into when it ain't going for you, when you're disappointed, plus something like your marriage breaking up.

It was interesting round the gyms, round the promotions, to have them talking to me again – Hallo, Ted? How are you, Ted? – where before they'd been turning their backs on me, like they was afraid I'd try to touch them. They made me sick. I despised them.

He lost a couple of early fights, Joe, both of them on points, one of them ridiculous, when I made him a good half a point ahead, but otherwise he was winning. They suited him, three-rounders, with his aggressive style: there wasn't time to burn himself out. Later on he'd have to learn to pace himself, just like I did, but for the moment I let him go his own way. In any case, you can't change a fighter's basic style: you can only work on what he's got, and try to improve it. Joey to me was what I'd been, a fighter not a boxer, and if you tried to take that away from him you finished him. Of course I didn't want him to be a goalkeeper, one of them fighters that stops everything, both for his own sake and his career, because his looks were part of him, part of the image. I'd have him bobbing and weaving for hours, slipping left leads, covering up for left hooks, blocking shots to the body, but like I said, he wasn't a Robinson. If anything he was more of a Marciano: he might take a punch, but he'd land two or three.

As for our parents, the old man liked the idea, but my mother didn't, which I'd expected. Being the youngest, she'd always been inclined to spoil him. It may have been part of his trouble.

'Joey don't *want* to box,' she said. 'Leave him alone. He's happy as he is. We've had one boxer in the family.'

'What do you want him to be, Mum?' I'd ask. 'A garage mechanic all his life?'

'Well, what's wrong with that?' she said. 'You father's still working on the building sites. Where's it got *you*, this boxing? What's it done for *you*?'

'It's not what it's done for me, Mum,' I'd tell her, 'it's what it can do for Joe, because of what I've learnt. Because I've already been through it.'

'You've been through it,' she said. 'Why should Joe go through it? He could come out the same as what you did.'

It was no using talking; the only way was to show her, and we did, we did.

What put him right on the map was the European Championships; after them, everybody wanted him. We could pick and choose, just like I'd wanted. The funny thing was, he was lucky to get the chance. Well, lucky in a way, unlucky if he hadn't, because to my mind he was out on his own and there was no other middleweight to touch him, whatever happened at Wembley in the national amateurs, and what happened was he got stopped on a cut eye in the semi-finals, nutted if ever I saw it, though an amateur nut. Maybe not even intentional, which didn't make no difference. The referee stopped the fight, middle of the second round, and that was that, just when Joe was beginning to run away with it. Then the bloke that wins the title turns pro; the runner-up, the one that beat Joe, gets in a car accident; and Joe goes into the team for the Championships.

In Warsaw, they were, and he was brilliant, even if it's me that says it. Joe loved going abroad, even to those miserable

Iron Curtain countries full of shabby people, lousy food and nothing in the shops. His eyes lit up, everything he saw he seemed to like, he'd always load himself with souvenirs and local gear, fur hats if it was somewhere like Poland, ten-gallon hats later on when we were down in Houston, naturally a sombrero when we went to Mexico, and it would carry over into his fighting, the enjoyment.

In Warsaw, the first two fights, he knocked them out, which is the only safe way in tournaments like that and the Olympics. The next round they slung in the towel, and in the final he was up against a Russian, to me a professional, one that had been around at least the last five years, silver medal in the Olympics, a heavy-set bloke with hair like a brush. He could tie you up in the clinches, use his thumbs a bit, be a bit naughty where he hit you. I was worried for Joe, I admit it, especially with this twot of a team coach going on about straight lefts and counter-punching.

Not that any of it mattered in the end, because what did Joey do but go and knock him out in the first round? A beautiful punch, too, a right cross, just as the fellow had missed him with a left, something I'd been working on with him. I was up on me feet, shouting and yelling, while they counted over the Russian, though you could see that he'd never get up, because when Joey landed he landed, and I knew that punch had done everything we ever wanted.

He was a hero when we got home, photographers at the airport, picture in every paper, television interviews, reporters after him, the phone going in my flat all day. 'Look, Ted, we've always been mates, Ted, put in a word for me, I'll see you're looked after, Ted.' Even Harry Fish, my old manager, he comes down the East End to see me, and I laughed at him – I'd been waiting years for this.

'You?' I said. 'After what you done for me; or rather, what you never did. Don't make me laugh,' I said.

Promoters, too: Solomons, Levene. Invitations, lunches. Come here, come there. That yiddisher restaurant in Soho with the names on the back of the chairs; Bob Levinson took me there, another promoter, with Sammy Kane, the little, old white-haired yes-man who went with him everywhere, who'd been a bit of a bantamweight about ninety years ago, and now just hung about like an old dog, waiting to be put to sleep, pathetic.

In that restaurant everyone seemed to be big; everyone seemed to be fat. Even I felt quite small. You got the impression they wouldn't let you in if you were under fifteen stone or ate less than four courses, and there were so many of them putting on cigars it was like ringside at a title fight. I don't mind yiddisher people, which nearly all the big promoters were and a lot of the managers. If they were smart I could be smarter and, in a way, at least you knew where you were with them: you were always on your toes, looking for snags, looking for angles, and they respected you for it, whereas with some of the others you might drop your guard, and then they'd really move in on you.

'Ted,' he said, this Levinson, 'it's a long time, it's been a *very* long time,' though I didn't remember his ever having spoke to me before. 'Didn't I say it was a very long time, Sammy?'

'You did, Bob,' Sammy said, 'you did.'

The point about Levinson was he needed me a lot more than I needed him, because he wasn't the power he'd been while I was fighting, not by any means; in fact I knew he was desperate for a new drawing card.

'Just a chat,' he said, 'that's all I wanted, a chat about old times, and maybe a word or two about *new* times.'

'Very nice, Mr Levinson,' I said.

When we got on to Joe, which was about the steak course, he said, 'All I'm interested in, Ted, is to help both of you. All I want is to see you get the best possible advice, when Joe turns pro.'

'If he turns pro,' I said, with a very straight face.

'When, if . . .' he said. 'And *if* you become his manager, which I know you may do, then I want to tell you I think that's a wonderful idea, as well. It's unusual, but it's a wonderful idea. Because blood is thicker than water, eh, Sammy?'

'Quite right, Bob,' Sammy said, 'it certainly is. A brother's a brother.'

'And if you want advice, Ted, you can always come to me,' Levinson said, 'whether he's fighting for me, or whether he's not. In fact especially if he's not, because if he *is* fighting for me, believe me, you won't *need* any advice.'

'Of course he won't,' said Sammy. 'Bob'll look after you; looks after everybody, Bob.'

But it was Harold Maxwell we went to, another yiddisher, though a lot younger than Levinson, a lot more up to date, finger in a lot of different pies, who really did look after fighters – when he wanted to – set them up in this, set them up in that. Levinson was down, now, Maxwell was up, and they hated each other.

'To me, Ted,' Maxwell said, when we were sitting in the Astor one night, 'Joey is now, Joey is the new image. Young people will go for him. The girls will go for him. He's with it and he's exciting and that is how I want to promote him.'

He was bald, Harold, a biggish man, carrying maybe a stone and a half too much, wore very expensive suits, diamond cufflinks and a gold signet ring, always smoked the best cigars, chauffeur-driven Bentleys, and he didn't care what he spent. There was always more where that came from, which suited me.

It was a wonderful deal I got: sixty grand guaranteed in the first two years. When I told Joe, it knocked him sideways. 'You're joking,' he said.

'No, I'm not,' I said. 'And this is only the beginning.'

As for our mother, she didn't know what to say; I wanted to laugh, looking at her face, because it was all there, happiness, surprise, a bit of resentment. 'Maybe you'll start believing in me, now, Mum,' I told her.

The very first fight we had was at Wembley on the same bill as Henry Cooper, and you'd never believe the publicity we got before the fight. The new Golden Boy. Britain's Brightest Hope. Tom Cummings of the *Star* was one that came down to see us – we were still training then at Bethnal Green, which was near enough where he came from himself – stumpy little fellow, very well in with Harold Maxwell. I'd known him ever since I turned pro.

'Going to be any good, is he, Ted?' he asks, giving me that kind of a look he's got, half a smile, half-cynical.

'My life, Tom,' I said, 'he's going to make it. Stand on me.'

'Stand on you?' he says. 'They all bloody stood on you. What're you going to do now? Stand on *him*?'

'Tom,' I said, *'you've* seen him. *You* know.'

'Good amateur,' he says, 'good banger. He can hand it out. What happens when he has to take it?'

'You'll see,' I said, 'you'll see.'

He said, 'You're already talking like a manager.'

Picking that first opponent was a very, very tricky thing: one mistake, and that could be it. If Joey lost, even if he won and looked bad, the public could say, another bum, just blown up by the papers. He had to win, he had to win well, and he had to beat somebody worth beating. Ronnie Milne, the match-maker, put a lot of names up to me, and I didn't like any of them, most of them because they looked too easy, fighters who'd been around when I was and hadn't got no better, or otherwise fighters I knew nothing about, from Italy and the States and all.

In the end we agreed to a Yank, one called Billy Navarino from Jersey, that had been fighting a long time, been knocked out by Emile Griffith in a world title fight, third round, and once boxed a draw over here with Terry Downes. Like Ronnie said, winking at me, 'He's been around, Ted, he's been around quite a while.' Because a bloke that's been fighting this long, especially if he's a bit of a banger who'll give a few, take a few, he's a little like an alcoholic. An alcoholic's got so much booze in his blood that he's gone after just a drink or two, and a fighter that's had a lot of punishment will go where another one might just shake the punch off. 'I think Joe may have a chance,' Ronnie said, and he winked at me again. He'd have made a good villain, Ronnie.

'Too right he'll have a chance,' said Tom Cummings, who was there at the time; he always seemed to be there, whenever it was anything to do with Harold Maxwell. 'He'll have a chance of doing time for manslaughter, if the other fellow doesn't die of old age on him, before that.' But he didn't write that, not in the *Star*: he wrote what an interesting fight it would be, youth against experience, a good first test for boxing's new Golden Boy, and in his opinion, youth would be served; which it was.

In fact in the fourth round there at Wembley – he had his very first fight there, in the Empire Pool, where I'd only fought those two times bottom of the card, right at the very, very end, after a couple of title fights, when all you see is empty seats, people packing up and going home, the whole place dying. It was wonderful for Joe. The only thing that worried me was, how would it affect him this first time, the build-up, the atmosphere, the pressure; was he liable to freeze?

The worst thing, to me, was that walk to the ring. It can seem a terrible long way, even though it's not as bad at Wembley as Earl's Court, which has the stairs, as well. Still, with the spotlights, the trumpets, all the old carry-on Harold loved – for this one of Joey's, he had beefeaters – it was going to be long enough, believe me.

Mind you, he'd been all right before on big occasions, the Amateur Championships – which of course were at Wembley – the Europeans; in fact if there was anything I held against him, it was that he hadn't taken them seriously *enough*.

I went to watch the other fellow spar once or twice, Navarino, over The Load of Hay, and to me he didn't have nothing but a good right hand; the rest was all from memory. He got caught a lot by his sparring partners. Even allowing for the fact that most experienced fighters don't push themselves sparring, it still looked to me like he was made for Joey.

We even had a big press lunch, in a posh West End restaurant. Henry Cooper was there, as top of the bill, and the bloke he was fighting, Navarino and his manager, and of course Joey and myself. Everybody had to get up and say something. Harold Maxwell said he was very, very proud of being the first promoter to present to the British public one of the most exciting young fighters to emerge for many, many years, a fighter who he was sure was going on to the highest honours as a professional, just as he had as an amateur. Then Joey had to stand up, which embarrassed him, though we'd been rehearsing it. He stood there pink in the face, smiling, crumpling up his serviette, and said thank you very much, he hoped it was going to be a good fight and he wouldn't let people down, and he was grateful to Mr Maxwell for the opportunity.

Then we had one of the usual stuffed shirts from the Board

of Control, with all that old may-the-best-man-win crap; about six and a half words out of Navarino, of which I understood maybe three; and finally Tom Cummings, who used to come on at times like this as a kind of clown, taking the micky out of Harold Maxwell, but, if you know what I mean, never going too far. 'I've seen a lot of Harold's prospects,' he said. 'I've had a good long look at them, because most of them were lying down. But I'm going to stick my neck out about this one, because I think he's a bit special, he's a little bit different. In fact, at the end of this fight, he may even be standing up. And with respect to Mr Navarino here, you never know, he may even not have lost.'

That night, the whole family was at the ringside, our father, our brother and sisters, even our mother, who normally wouldn't come near a boxing promotion; I never remember her coming to one of mine. Naturally as his trainer and manager I was in Joey's corner, and I'd got Wally Beckett with us, who was a fabulous cut man. I'd had white jerseys made with 'Joe Rogers' on the back in fancy lettering, scarlet – it looked great, very, very smart – and Joey's dressing gown had cost ninety quid, dark-blue silk, all gleaming in the lights, with his name on the back in yellow, in the same writing.

In the dressing room, the little pokey dressing room we had, I kept talking at him, partly to din into his head what I wanted him to do, partly to keep his mind occupied, like when some-one's climbed to the top of a building you try to stop them looking down. I could see he was a little nervous: he licked his lips once or twice, his attention wandered a bit. He said, 'Yes, Ted, OK, Ted,' but I could feel the tension; in fact I was feeling it, myself.

Then Harold come in there in his dinner-jacket, the third time he'd been in. He was here, there and everywhere at all his promotions, wandering round the ring, shaking hands with people, organising this, organising that. Tom Cummings once said about him, 'Harold is the only promoter who personally counts every bloody spectator.'

'Come on,' Harold said, 'come on,' like an old hen, all nervous, as though, if we weren't there in the ring on time, they'd start without us. Then he said, 'Good luck, Joey, see we're all proud of you,' give him a smile, and we were away, into that dark arena, even the ring dark for the moment, just the spotlights playing on us, the trumpets blowing, the old beefeaters shuffling along beside us with their pikes, Joey banging his gloves together as he walked, his face set, no expression, people shouting, 'Good luck, Joe; have him over, Joey!' and suddenly the lights in the ring coming up again, brighter than day, this blinding island, picked out high up in the middle of the dark, the loneliest bloody place in the world.

It seemed forever before that first bell went, all the announcements – Joey was a pound and a half the heavier – the referee's instructions – it was Duggie Jones, who usually I liked – then finally, 'Seconds out!' I squeezed Joey's shoulder, ducked under the ropes; we were away. I *mean* we.

People told me afterwards I was bobbing and weaving down there in the corner, throwing every punch that Joey threw, blocking when he blocked. 'Be first, Joe!' I was shouting at him, 'Be first!' which was better advice than what it seemed, because I wanted him to show this Navarino right away who was boss; I wanted him to dictate the fight. I wasn't worried about him lasting the six rounds, which was what it was this first time, even though he'd never gone more than three. He'd trained well, and as far as I was concerned he'd be ready for eight, once he'd learnt to pace himself.

The crowd was with him all the way, right from the first bell – it was wonderful – cheering every time he threw a punch, really excited when he landed, booing when the other fellow held in the clinches, which he was doing a hell of a lot. Hitting on the break was another little dodge he had, and he caught Joe once like that with a nasty right, on the side of the head, which the referee spoke to him about; but Joe just shook it off and kept on coming after him. They loved that, the crowd. When he caught Navarino at the very end of the first round with a lovely right uppercut, a tremendous roar went up. Harold was standing near me with a big smile on his face, a big cigar in his hand, looking like he'd swallowed the canary. 'Ted,' he said, 'we *are* going to be proud of him, I'm telling you.'

By the end of the third, I could tell the Yank was going. He'd obviously banked everything on a quick finish, and it hadn't happened; it was Joey who'd run the fight, and anything he'd took he'd just shrugged off. There was a very slight cut above his left eye, but nothing bad, nothing the other fellow could open. In fact, after Wally had worked on it, you couldn't hardly see it. 'Get in close,' I told Joe, 'get inside and work at the body. Then, when you've got him going, you can move upstairs.'

The round wasn't halfway through when he did just what I'd said. He got Navarino in a corner and landed a tremendous right, above the liver, really hurting him, and the fellow went into a clinch. I was doing my nut yelling at Joe, yelling at the referee, telling him to pull Navarino off, telling Joe to stay in there. He caught him again, there was another clinch, and finally Joey went in bang, bang, a left hook and another terrific right, both to the head, and you knew the fellow was out before he'd even hit the canvas. Lovely.

I went mad. I was in that ring almost before they'd finished counting, lifting Joe, hugging him, and you should have heard the crowd. What an answer it was to all those people that had said he'd never be worth all this money.

Because they existed all right, right from the first, the knockers and the disbelievers, some of them people that didn't like Harold Maxwell, other people who'd like to have managed Joe themselves, or reporters who went in for being snide. Plus, of course, the jealousy that you'd expect: why should a young kid who'd done nothing yet be entitled to all that money? To which my answer was, why shouldn't he be?

'All right,' I'd tell people, 'Joey's a beginner. I know it; *he* knows it. But people are prepared to pay to see him fight. It's something he's got – that all the experience in the world won't give you.'

It was a very, very different sort of life for Joe and me, now. Asked here, invited there; dinners, promotions in the posh hotels, forever on the telly. In the end we took a place together. I moved out of my flat in Clapton and Joey left home, which to me was the making of him, something that had to happen, however much Mum was against it; in fact even *because* of that. We got a flat just near the park in Battersea, which was perfect for Joey's roadwork, and nice and near a gym, another big reason. Harold Maxwell found it for us. In fact I believe one of his companies owned the block.

Joey's second fight, he did even better. Earl's Court, this time, and he was a semi-final, which choked some people, I can tell you; against a flash Italian called Marchini that had fought for the European title. He went in one; Joey got him with a terrific left hand in the first thirty seconds, and after that it was just a question of when he'd put him away.

At this time, I had him fighting nearly once a month. Of course I wouldn't let him go on like that, but on this I did agree with Harold: I wanted people to get to know him. I wanted him to build up his following; then, when he'd done that, we could pick and choose.

'Joe,' I said to him, and I meant it, 'if you think it's too much, if you find it's a strain, I want you to tell me. Right away. No messing. Because it's your career, Joe. It's your life. All I want is to do the very best for you.'

'I know that, Ted,' he said, 'I know that.' A lovely boy, Joey. None of it had changed him. He spent a bit more on his clothes, now – though, mind you, he'd always dressed well – he ran around in a Lotus, but still completely unspoilt. Still the same as he'd always been. 'I'm enjoying it,' he said, 'as long as I keep winning.'

'You *will* keep winning,' I told him, 'but just remember. If it's too much, tell me.'

Because there'd come a point, I knew it, when Harold was going to want one thing and me another: he'd want his money's worth, whereas my job, my only job, was to look after Joey. Which I did, in every way, especially medically. Regular check-ups by the finest doctors. Encephalograms. No expense spared. Nothing left to chance. If he got a bad cut, we didn't just stitch it and leave it: I took him to a plastic surgeon, the best. It was common sense, and it was an investment. Like I've said, his looks were important, they were part of it all.

The first time Joey didn't look good – though he didn't look so bad, either, nothing like as bad as some of the reporters made out – was against Danny Robins, in his sixth fight, at the British Sporting Club.

Robins was a southpaw, which is always difficult, and he was a counter-puncher, which was another problem. He'd been around a long time and he was quite a clever boxer, I'll give him that, but the way he boxed, he could send you to sleep. I wasn't that keen on Joey fighting him, not at this stage, but Harold and Ronnie Milne were on about his being over the hill, that whatever happened he couldn't hurt Joey, which was true, and in the end I allowed myself to be talked into it; a mistake, I admit, because we was really on a hiding to nothing. If we won, then so what – who was Robins, anyway – and if we didn't, or won poorly, then there was a lot of people waiting, ready to put the boot in.

It was at the Carlton Hotel, the fight, everyone in dinner-jackets. They'd eat, they'd drink, and then they'd watch the boxing. The ring was set up in the middle of this ballroom. Personally, I'd never liked fighting in front of this kind of audience, getting myself knocked about while they stuffed themselves with food and knocked back the booze. To me, it was completely out of date, those days had gone, like going in with lions in the Colosseum. The thing that made it all the more ridiculous was that, with the money we were getting, we were probably much better off than what a lot of *them* were; in fact I said to Joe, 'I wonder how many of them had to hire their dinner-jackets,' because ours were our own: we'd had them made.

This was the worst crowd we could have had on a night like this, ignorant, intolerant, biased. They were on at Joey from the first round: 'Come on, Rogers! Get it moving! Let's have some action!' You'd get a better-behaved crowd down Shoreditch Town Hall or the Lime Grove Baths. There wasn't no one more anxious to get moving than Joey, but the other fellow wouldn't let him: he was poncing about out of range, and when he wasn't out of range he kept on holding.

Joey was getting very upset, and I didn't blame him. He said in the corner, 'He won't fight me, Ted, he won't come near me. I don't know what they want. I'm doing the best I can.'

'You keep after him, Joe,' I said. 'Just keep after him, and you'll catch him. There's eight rounds to do it in.' Because I reckoned that the other fellow would go tired; he couldn't go on running for ever, and once he stopped Joey would nail him.

Maybe he would have done if it had been a longer fight, fifteen rounds or even ten, but as it was this Robins had enough steam to keep going, or at least to stay out of Joey's way. The disgusting thing was the way the audience came on to his side. They started jeering Joey; they cheered whenever Danny landed a punch, which believe me wasn't often; then at the end, when the referee give a draw, which to me was just ridiculous, you should have heard the booing and the whistling, the way they banged their glasses on the table, half of them pissed.

Some of the reporters wrote terrible things about the fight, how Joey had been exposed, how he'd been made to look like a novice, his style had been crude, and a lot of cobblers like that. Naturally he was very upset; this was the first time anything like this had ever happened to him. He sat there next morning with the papers all round him and he said, 'I know I was bad, Ted, but I wasn't that bad. They don't make no allowances.'

'They know fuck-all,' I said, 'don't take no notice of them. How many of them ever put a glove on? A fight like that is something you learn from. I'll get him for you again in six months, and he won't last two rounds.'

But Harold was worried and he sent for me; not even to his office, but to his house in Bishop's Avenue, colossal it was, with three big cars outside, a Rolls, a Jag, a Bentley, an enormous front lawn, and a butler to open the front door. Ronnie Milne was there, as well. It was the first time I'd been in Harold's house, and it was what you'd expect, every possible comfort, fantastic, really: thick carpets, colour televisions, sofas you sank into half a mile, pictures on the walls, anything you fancied to drink, though Harold didn't drink much. To tell you the truth, I felt a bit uneasy: it was like foreign territory, where he and Ronnie were at home; I was a stranger.

One of his kids came in, a little girl, maybe about eleven, quite good-looking, and he put his arm round her, you could see he was nuts about her. She was going out somewhere, and he put his hand in his pocket and gave her a quid. He said, 'Will that be enough?' and she said, 'I hope so,' never thanked him, and went out of the room, didn't say a word to me, like *she* knew I didn't belong, too.

'I'm not happy, Ted,' Harold said to me. 'I know the press we got was a scandal. I know it was difficult for the boy, but we can't afford to let anything like that happen again,' like I'd wanted this Robins, and he hadn't.

'It won't,' I said, 'I can promise you that.'

'Look, Ted,' said Ronnie Milne, 'we don't expect miracles. The kid's young. He's got a lot to learn. That we know.'

'So if you don't expect miracles,' I said, 'what's worrying you?'

'*We* don't,' said Harold, blowing out cigar smoke, 'but the public does.' Then everything went very quiet, because I realised what they were on about.

'Listen, Ted,' Harold said to me, finally, 'Joey's not an ordinary fighter, and I haven't given him an ordinary contract. I knew what I was doing when I offered you that money. It wasn't just good for you and Joey, it was good for me, it was good for all of us. But because Joey's had more, people want more.'

'They'll get more,' I said.

'They want more now,' said Ronnie. 'They want more right away.'

I felt sick. All my life, the whole of my career, I'd never thrown a fight or been involved in any kind of fix. I couldn't speak; I couldn't even look at them. For a minute, I thought I was just going to get up, tell Harold where to stick his bloody contract, and walk out of that house. But it wasn't just me: it was Joe as well. I had to look after him, even though I knew he'd feel the same as me, so what I said in the end was, 'Joey would never wear it.'

'He don't have to know,' said Ronnie. Then there was another of them silences. There was so much going on in my head, so many things battling with one another, I thought I'd go spare.

I told them, 'Do what you fucking want to do, then.'

'That's not very nice, Ted,' Harold said. 'Remember we're not suggesting this just for us. We're all going to gain. In any case, you've been in boxing long enough. Do you really think every big fight's on the level? What about Carnera? What about Maxim?'

'I know every fight *I've* ever had anything to do with has been on the level,' I said.

'Two or three,' said Ronnie, 'that's all we'll need. Just till the kid finds his feet.'

'Two or *three*,' I said.

'Maximum,' said Ronnie. 'I promise that'll be the maximum.'

'It chokes me,' I said. 'And anyway, what if Joe finds out?'

Harold gave me this big cat's grin of his and said, 'He won't find out. He'll never find out. That I can promise you.'

'Who are you?' I asked him. 'God, or something? These things get around in no time, always.'

'Not with us, they don't,' said Ronnie.

So in the end I'd got no alternative, I had to accept it; but it was for him that I done it, him and only him.

The first fight was at Earl's Court, and the bloke was a Puerto Rican; in my opinion, Joe could have taken him anyway. He was experienced, yes, but he'd never done very much, and besides, he was another of these that had taken a lot of punishment in their career.

It crucified me, I can tell you, having to go through all the usual motions with Joe, in training, knowing what I knew, and another thing was, they'd insisted I make Wally Beckett joint trainer, which to me was just ridiculous. Cuts he knew about, but otherwise I reckoned he was twenty years behind, with far too much concentration on roadwork, and the worst thing of all, he wanted to change Joey's style; which was obviously what they were after.

'Look,' I said, 'leave him alone, will you? He's done all right so far. Let him fight the way that's natural to him.'

'You let him fight the way that's natural to him,' he says, 'and he'll be punchy inside a year.' I very nearly filled him in for that, but it was difficult with Harold and Ronnie backing him, protecting their bloody investment; or so they thought.

Joey didn't like it at all. 'It don't *feel* right,' he said to me. 'All this dancing about. All this ducking and diving. I like to go forward.'

Ronnie said to me, 'It's bound to take time, and we're *giving* you the time. Now do you get it?'

'Yeah,' I said, 'I get it, but I don't fucking like it.'

'You'll like it, Ted,' said Harold. 'I promise you you'll like it.'

It was at Earl's Court that one, and it went three rounds. All I'll say for that Puerto Rican is that he wasn't a bad actor. Joey caught him – or he let him catch him – with a right to the head, and he slid down off the ropes, made like he was really trying to get up again, eventually did get on his feet, lifted his guard as if he was in a daze, and the referee stepped in between them and said, 'Enough.'

'He was easy, Ted,' Joey said to me back in the dressing room. 'He's a strong-looking bloke, I expected a lot more trouble.'

'I've told you before,' I said, 'if you catch them right, they all go, anybody,' and to the reporters I said, 'Now maybe you'll stop writing we're a flash in the pan.'

'I never wrote that, Ted,' Tom Cummings said. He looked at me deadpan. I looked back at him, and I wondered how much he knew.

A month later it was a Spaniard, Fernandez, former European title-holder, thirty-two years old, so they said, though, looking at him, he could have been forty. Joey was still having trouble with his change of style, and the Spaniard caught him a few times to the body, early on. Then Joey started forcing the fight, genuinely in my opinion. He landed high with a left hook, and the fellow went down like they'd done him with a humane killer.

'Gets easier and easier, doesn't it, Ted?' Tom Cummings said, and this time there was definitely a look in his eye.

Then there was an American, Phil Thompson, and an Italian – one stopped in the fifth round and the other a knockout in the eighth – and we was on our own, again, thank God. By this time, too, I'd got them to see it wasn't no use trying to turn Joey into a ballet dancer. I got back in charge, and I was going to stay in charge.

The funny thing was, I think those fights had given Joe confidence; that, and switching back to his old style. He was really beginning to fight well, again.

'I'm going to put him on at Wembley in the autumn, Ted,' said Harold. 'I'm going to have him top of the bill, and I'm going to put him in with one of the best Americans. That's how much I believe in him.'

'One who stands up,' I asked, 'or one who lies down?'

'From now on, Ted,' he said, 'if they lie down, it'll only be because Joe knocks them down. That I promise you.'

The American was Danny Byrne, and they weren't doing us no favours. He'd only fought for the world title twice, and he'd taken Emile Griffith all the way, only a couple of years ago. He was fourth in the world ratings, and a lot of people said I shouldn't have took the fight, that Joey wasn't ready – the same people that had been saying the other fights were too easy. You can never win.

I said to Joey, 'Look, Joe, if you think it's too hard, if you think you're not ready, I want you to say so.'

'If *you* think I should, I'll take it, Ted,' he said, and it was a marvellous feeling, that people could believe in each other like this. So you can imagine what it did to me when he got such a hammering. On my life, every punch he took, I felt I was taking it myself. He showed wonderful courage that night, Joey. Nothing stopped him going forward, nothing stopped him looking for a knockout, long after it was obvious he could never win on points. He got a nasty cut over the right eye in the fifth, which Byrne kept working on. Jack Dover, who was in our corner now instead of Wally, and I did everything we could with it, but it still kept opening up again, and finally the referee stopped it at the end of the eighth – it was a twelve-rounder – after inspecting the eye.

Personally I was glad for Joey, because he'd taken enough, and I'll give the crowd this, they did cheer him, when the MC said, 'And applause for a gallant loser.' For once those words really meant something.

Of course there was all the usual knocking, how Joe had been exposed again, how he'd been brought on much too fast. One of the most big-headed boxing writers wrote, 'Byrne took Rogers back to school, and I only hope he learnt a few lessons there, one of them being that it's unwise to try to run before you can walk.'

As far as I was concerned, Joe *had* learnt, just as he'd learnt against Robins. He said to me, 'I wish they hadn't stopped it, Ted, I'm sure I would have got him, he was beginning to slow down. Another round or two and I'd have nailed him.' What a wonderful spirit.

Harold and Ronnie Milne weren't so happy. Harold said, 'We can't afford another one like that. Next time I'll find him something easier,' which he did.

First I took Joe to Majorca for three weeks, lying around in the sun, pulling a few birds, then, when we got back, we went into strict training.

Ronnie found him a Canadian called Larry Page, a bloke everybody knew had got a glass jaw, and Joey put him away in five. After that, a big step forward: I took him to the States for the first time, to fight in Houston, against an American called Willy Jones, ranked ninth in the world. Harold wasn't too keen because for him there was only peanuts in it, but I persuaded him, I told him, 'Joe needs the experience. Sooner or later he's got to fight over there.'

'The later the better,' Harold said. 'Wait until he gets a shot at the world title; and even then, I could probably get it for him over here.'

In the end, he gave in, but he said, 'Just see he doesn't lose, that's all; because if he loses, I lose, you lose, we all lose. And I stand to lose more than both of you.'

'He won't lose,' I said, and he didn't. He fought a wonderful fight; I've never seen such guts. And what a fantastic place, that Astrodome, everything under cover beneath this enormous roof, room for 60,000 people, marvellous seating arrangements, private boxes with their own apartments. We'd never seen nothing like it, Joe and I.

For three rounds I was really worried about the fight, the way this fellow was getting through on Joey, especially with the jab. He put him down once in the second, though it was more of a slip, and he was up to everything, especially the low punches. Twice the referee warned him, and in England he would definitely have been disqualified. But this was one of the reasons I'd brought Joe out here. I wanted him to learn the facts of life, and it was better now than later, when he might even have a title to lose.

By the fourth, I reckoned the American was going. I'd noticed he was inclined to drop his guard when he threw a left hook, and I told Joey to sidestep and come in over it with a left of his own. He did it beautiful, and the fellow went down wallop; I was dancing around that ring, I was so pleased.

When we got back to London, I told the reporters, 'In a year, Joe will be the British champion, and in two he'll be challenging for the world title.'

Even Harold and Ronnie had to admit he'd done well, that we'd polished up the old image, though Tom Cummings looked at his face, at all the marks, and said, 'If that's what he looks like when he wins, I don't want to see him when he loses.'

It wasn't much, though: a few little cuts and swellings round both eyes, another cut on the cheek. The old cosmetic surgeon soon had him fixed up.

The British title-holder then was Ernie Crouch, to me another fighter who'd bore you to death if he couldn't beat you any other way. If he ever won a fight by a knockout, it was because the other bloke fell asleep. Everything was left hand, jab, jab, jab, piling up the points; otherwise it was all bloody bobbing and weaving. 'Two or three more fights,' I told Joe, 'and you'll be ready,' and he said, like he always used to, then, 'If you say so, Ted.'

I'd got the whole thing clear in my mind, like I'd said: British title, world title, and when we'd won that, which we would, defend it maybe half a dozen times, no more, then finish. Out. We'd have made enough to set ourselves up for life; we already had five launderettes and two lots of flats in Camden Town.

That's what I'd tell Mum whenever she started carrying on about Joe; she didn't come to his fights, no more. 'Mum,' I'd say, 'look, it ain't for long. Maybe only two or three more years, and that's it; we'll be able to look after all of you.'

'Look at his face,' she'd say, 'look at the marks.'

'Look at *my* face,' I'd tell her, 'remember *my* marks? What's left of them now?'

'He's so handsome, Joe,' she said. 'And what about his poor brain?'

'It hurt *my* brain so much that I got him a contract for sixty thousand pounds,' I said. 'He's examined regular, Mum. If they told me anything was wrong, do you think I'd let him go on?'

He had his three fights. Two he won, one he drew, and they

all went the distance; two against British fighters, the other, that he drew, against a German, at the Albert Hall again, and they booed the decision. To me he'd walked away with it. I wouldn't have given the German more than three rounds, but by now we were getting used to this sort of thing; they expected a knockout every time.

After that one, Harold said, 'Maybe it's a bit early to put him in with Ernie Crouch,' which I told him was ridiculous. People in the game were saying things like, 'Ernie will jab his head off,' but I didn't say nothing, just laid a little money on Joe, here and there. We'd answer them on the night.

It was at Wembley, of course, the second time Joe had been top of the bill, and it was a sell-out, which to me was the perfect answer to all of them, because it certainly wasn't nothing to do with Ernie Crouch. Like they say, he couldn't draw the hat off your head.

The way we'd planned it, Joey was going to go in over the jab with his right. He'd have to go after him, because Crouch would never come to *him*, and he'd have to cut off the corners, otherwise he'd be chasing shadows for fifteen rounds.

Day after day, we'd work on it in the gym. The sparring partners I found were as close to Crouch in style as possible, and by the time we stopped the sparring I was really optimistic.

In fact, the first couple of rounds, things really looked great. Joe went after Crouch right from the bell, missed him with a few shots, then caught him with a really good right to the side of the jaw, just like I'd shown him. The rest of the round, Joe did all he could to catch him again, and Crouch did everything he could to keep out of trouble, but his corner brought him round, and as the fight went on Joe couldn't quite seem to catch him again. Stick and run, stick and run, that was all the other fellow did. To me, he turned it into a farce: he should have been thrown out of the ring for lack of effort.

Instead of which, they gave him the decision. When he walked over to Crouch's corner, the ref, and raised his hand, I couldn't believe it; neither could Joe. I'll never forget the look he gave me, like a puppy, almost, and how terrible I felt because there wasn't nothing I could do.

When Harold came into our dressing room smiling his usual

poncey smile, I'd like to have slung him out – it was nothing to fucking do with him – but Joey right away said, 'I'm sorry, Harold,' really meaning it, almost in tears, and that choked me all the more.

'Never mind,' said Harold, 'never mind, these things happen; you were definitely a little bit unlucky,' then he was off – which was Harold's way of saying, 'Fuck you!'

The press was diabolical again; the *Mirror* wrote: 'It was like a willing carthorse in clumsy and hopeless pursuit of a thoroughbred.' When Joe read that he said, 'What a terrible thing to say.'

I took him abroad again, this time to Portugal; he soon cheered up in the sunshine; then, when we came back, Ronnie Milne got us another American, Freddie Kramer, rated eighteenth in the world, and we fought him at the Sporting Club, again.

This time, thank God, it wasn't a fighter that got on his bicycle; it was one that wanted a proper fight, like Joe did, and that was how it turned out; even *that* audience had to applaud them. He had Joey down twice, in the fourth and the sixth, but he came back fantastic, had Kramer in real trouble in the ninth and the tenth, put him down in the eleventh, and in the end they just had to give him the verdict. Even Harold was really chuffed. 'One or two more like that,' he said, 'and never mind the British title; I'll put him in with the champion of the world.'

The rest of that year we didn't fight, for tax reasons, and it must have been a couple of months later that he met Janet, on this plane. I didn't take it too serious at first. There was a lot of birds in and out of our place, mostly mine, admittedly, and I thought of her as just another of them. She was a Newcastle girl, but flying: she was down in London quite a lot.

When they got engaged, I was honestly staggered. '*Engaged?*' I said to Joe. 'You're *serious*?'

'I'm in love with her, Ted,' he said, and that was that, because I knew Joe. Very shy – with birds, anyway – very agreeable, but when he made his mind up, that was it.

'Well,' I said, 'I hope you know what you're doing.'

Now and again we'd all go out together, me with some bird, Joey with her, but there was something not right, a kind of wall, them one side, me the other, and I'd got this feeling, one that worried me, that he was slipping away, Joey, like on a mountain, the rope's running through your hands, and there's nothing you can do to stop it.

When he told me they were getting married, I admit I did hit the roof. 'What about your career, Joe?' I said to him. 'What's going to happen to it? Can't you wait a year or two?'

'I don't want to,' he said. 'There's plenty of married boxers, aren't there? Clay and that. Cooper. Most of the world champions.'

It wasn't that she'd ever said anything, Janet – she didn't say a lot, anyway, at least when I was with them – it was something that I felt. She disapproved of me. She didn't like me. She was against Joey fighting, and she blamed me for it; a little like my mother.

When they were out together, her and Joe, they behaved the way kids do when they're in love, smiling at each other, kissing occasionally, talking very quietly, everything private between them. I'd got nothing against it at all; not so long as it didn't interfere with his fighting, with his future. In fact when I saw there was no shifting him, they were definitely going to get married, I told her, Janet, 'You know that if everything goes OK for the next couple of years, Joey would be all right for the rest of his life. I mean, you both would.'

'All right?' she said. 'What does that mean?'

'Financially,' I said. 'He'll have enough put away, enough business interests, to retire.'

'And how many fights would that mean?' she asked. 'In two years?'

'I don't know,' I said. 'Maybe not very many. If we get the big one, the world title fight, then it could be very, very few.'

'It can't be few enough for me,' she said, and then she hadn't even *seen* him fight. In fact the first time she went to see any of his fights was in May, at Wembley.

She took a lot of persuading. This one was against the world number three, Joe Bacon, the best man we'd fought yet, but I was confident we could do it. As far as I was concerned, I didn't care one way or the other if she came, though if anything I'd rather she stayed away, because obviously she'd made her mind up already, and there's very few wives or fiancées like to see their blokes being clobbered, even if they're doing a bit of clobbering themselves.

Unfortunately, it turned out to be a fight in which Joey took a lot of punishment. In a way, this was something I'd had to resign myself to, because it was his way of fighting, the only way he knew, take one to give one, or maybe two, but if things worked out like I wanted, then it wouldn't be for very long.

When Bacon cut him in the third round, though, it wasn't with a punch at all, it was definitely a head; a nasty one, just above the right eye. We did what we could with it in the corner, but in the next round it opened up again, and I admit it looked bad. Not that it stopped Joey: he kept going in like a good'un, just like we'd told him to, because I could tell that if he didn't finish it soon, the referee would.

When I looked down from his corner at the end of the third, she wasn't there. I only half took it in at the time, and when it registered, to be honest, my first thought was that it was just as well.

By the fifth, I knew it would have to be a knockout or nothing, because one more round was as long as the eye would hold out, even if it wasn't hit again. 'Now or never, Joe,' I said, and he was tremendous, he did everything you could have asked for, chased this Bacon all over the ring; the fellow didn't know what day it was. Joe caught him on the ropes with a left to the side of the head, he followed up with a lovely right to the body, and I really thought we might have a chance. Bacon had hardly touched him in that round; the referee had a look at his eye in the corner, but let it go on; then, in the sixth, Joey got a little reckless, he left himself open, and the fellow got in with a right. Nothing fantastic, but enough to do the damage. Blood came spurting out of it, making it look a lot worse than it was; so the referee stepped in, and he stopped it.

Joey went crazy, crying and protesting; the crowd were shouting and booing and, when he left the ring, they gave him a tremendous cheer. Harold came in our dressing room and said, 'Congratulations, Joe, that was a really wonderful fight,' then, when the reporters were in, he said, 'In my opinion, Joey is entitled to a return, and I shall do everything in my power to get it for him.'

Well, naturally that suited Joey and it suited me; the only one it didn't suit was her, Janet. I'd been expecting trouble, because naturally his face didn't look too good; she wasn't to know it would clear up in no time, he was such a good healer, and any complications, we'd go straight to the plastic surgeon. I could tell she was getting at him from the way he'd behave at times, suddenly going quiet on me, or taking time to answer things, not like himself at all. As for her, I didn't see her much, now. When I'd suggest we all went somewhere together, the times she was in London, he'd say they'd got something arranged, and when I did see her she'd hardly speak to me.

The next thing was, when I got home one night from Harold's office, all excited, with the news he'd fixed up the return with Bacon for that October, Joey said, 'Not then. I can't fight then. We're getting married.'

That stopped me dead. 'When did you decide that?' I said.

'Saturday,' he said, 'when Janet was down.'

'And you never told me?' I said.

'Well,' he said. 'I've told you.'

'And you can't change the date?' I asked him. 'A week here, a week there, what's the difference?'

'Ask Harold to change the date,' he said. He could be very stubborn, Joe, when he wanted.

All I said was, knowing this, 'Harold wouldn't be pleased.'

He wasn't either. 'After all I've done for him,' he said. 'The trouble I've taken. The sacrifice I've made. They've held me to ransom for Bacon's purse. At Wembley I can't get any other time for six months. Let me talk to him, Ted, I want to talk to him.'

'It won't do no good, Harold,' I told him, and it didn't. All he got was, 'I'm sorry, Harold, I know that, Harold, I can't do nothing about it now, Harold.'

The next thing was that Harold tried to get to Janet. He started sending round presents for her, chocolates, flowers, perfume. He said to Joey, 'Come to the Playboy Club with me. Both of you. As my guests.'

'I don't think so, thanks,' Joe said. 'Janet's not too keen on them places.'

'Then what does she like?' he asked. 'Does she like shows? We can go to Danny La Rue's, or maybe to the Talk of the Town, if she prefers that. And I promise you another thing: when you go on your honeymoon, you can have my villa at Juan les Pins. As long as you like.'

But in the end he had to give in, Harold, and settle for the Albert Hall in December, which of course didn't have half the capacity. 'Talk to her, Ted,' he said to me. 'See if you can't get her to be sensible.' But it wasn't easy even getting to be on my own with her, let alone talk to her.

I did get hold of her at last, in a flat she stayed at near the air terminal in Gloucester Road, when she was in town, one she shared with two or three other hostesses. I drove over there one Saturday morning, not telling Joe, and she opened the door herself. When she saw it was me her face went dead, but she let me in. 'I want to talk to you,' I said. Two of the other girls was in there, but they disappeared, leaving us together in the room.

'What about?' she said.

'Joe,' I said.

'You mean about this fight,' she said.

'That and other things,' I said.

She wouldn't sit down.

'Look,' I said, 'I've told you: it's not for very long.'

'Not long!' she said. 'It may have been too long, already.'

And I got a little pissed off. 'Do you know more than the neurologist, then?' I said. 'Do you know more than the brain surgeon? Because that's who we go to. That's who examines him.'

'All I know is what I see with my own eyes,' she said.

'Well, they see a little more,' I told her, 'and *they* don't see nothing wrong.'

'If they did,' she said, 'would it make any difference to you?'

'That's a terrible thing to say,' I said, 'a disgraceful thing to say.'

'Is it?' she said. We stood there looking at each other. There was a million miles between us, and I knew there always would be.

'So what are you after?' I said. 'Do you want to make him pack it in? Now, when he's just about to come into the real money? When everything's falling into place?'

'You're good at twisting things,' she said.

'I want the best for him,' I told her.

'Or what's left of him,' she said.

I controlled myself; I fought with myself; it wasn't easy. 'One day,' I told her, 'you'll understand what I've tried to do for Joe.' Then I walked out and left her; I didn't trust myself to say no more.

I told Joey, 'Look, if you think I'm no good for you, if you think I'm taking you for a ride, OK, let's turn it in. We've never had no contract.'

He got embarrassed. He looked away from me; he said, 'I don't think that. I've never thought that.'

'*She* does,' I said, 'Janet does.'

'She gets upset when I get knocked around,' he said, 'that's all. It's natural.'

'Explain to her,' I said. 'That's part of it: within reason. Like a racing driver has to take risks. Like an air stewardess can always crash, God forbid, if it comes to that.'

'I know all that,' he said, 'but it's hard to convince her.'

'Listen, Joe,' I said, 'if you give up now, what have you got? The launderettes, the hotels. OK, that's a good beginning. A few thousand quid put away. How long will *that* last? If you keep going, in another eighteen months, a couple of years at most, you could be laughing. No more worries.'

'What'll I be like in two years, Ted?' he asked. He still couldn't bring himself to look me in the face.

'That's *her* speaking, Joe,' I said, 'not you.'

He was looking out of the window, the one that faced Battersea Park. 'Maybe she's right,' he said.

In October we had the wedding, up in the Northeast, in a little village church. Her old man was a miner and a bit of a fight fan. We got along very well. He was obviously thrilled to have Joey as a son-in-law.

'When he fights Joe Bacon again,' I told him, 'you'll be there at ringside, really ringside, not what Harold Maxwell puts on the tickets when they're a hundred yards away from the ring, and you're all right if you've brought your binoculars.'

Janet and I got on OK up there. I must admit she looked good in her wedding dress, and I told her so. As I watched the two of them going down the aisle, I could understand why Joe had fancied her. She was pretty all right and she'd got character, even if at times I could personally have done with a bit less of it. She and I didn't say a lot to each other up there, but we were very polite. For the moment, she seemed to have accepted things, but I wasn't too happy about Joey moving out from me and moving in with her – they'd bought a house near Epping Forest – because now she'd have him all day, every day, except when he was in training.

They went off on honeymoon, but not to Harold's place: to Malta, not the South of France, and I knew that must be her, not Joe. He'd sent them a fantastic present, Harold, an antique silver tea-service that must have set him back a bomb, plus a huge basket of flowers, gladioli, everything, with a ribbon on them: 'God Bless and Keep Punching, Harold Maxwell.' She hadn't met Harold, yet; that was going to be interesting.

It was funny to be on my own in the flat, no Joey. In the end, I moved a bird in, a real little raver, a dancer at the Stork Club, but she could cook, thank God, as well. It was just for company; I certainly wasn't going to get married, again.

When it came time to prepare for the Bacon fight, there didn't seem to be no problems; Joey got down to it like he always did. This time I put us in a pub near the river, down at Maidenhead. It was fine, there; very green, fairly quiet, and not too far from London. He'd ring her up every night, and they'd talk for about an hour.

He was very conscientious, never skipped nothing, got through the roadwork, heavy bag, abdominal exercises, took his sparring very seriously, went through all the moves I showed him, that I'd worked out from the first fight. I wanted him to crowd Bacon more and, at the same time, see he didn't get nutted, again.

Like I say, he trained hard; and yet it wasn't the same. All of a sudden, it was like he was doing a job, something he had to get over; whereas, before, it was his life. No problems, he'd never give you an argument, but somehow there wasn't the same commitment. Outside the gym, he didn't want to talk about it like we'd always used to, though when it came to the fight, he certainly gave it all he'd got.

Unfortunately, it wasn't quite enough. For a couple of rounds, he really had this Bacon going – he landed some lovely body punches, he put him down for six with a great right hand – and in my opinion he'd have had him in that second round, if it wasn't for the bell. He got Bacon into a corner, he caught him with a left hook to the jaw that set him up perfectly, the fellow had just gone into a clinch, he was practically using Joe to hold himself up, the referee was just about to pull him off; then the bell went.

God knows what they gave him in that corner, I don't think it was anything legitimate; in fact I protested afterward. All I know is that, from being nearly out on his feet, he was recovered enough in the third to keep out of trouble and, after that, the fight turned.

In the sixth, he caught Joey with a very lucky punch, a left that was more of a swing than a hook, as he came back off the ropes, and Joey went down. It was the way he fell that did him, more than anything, I'm convinced; the way he hit his head. As soon as he landed, I knew there wouldn't be no getting up, and I had this feeling in my guts, like you sometimes get going down in a lift. It was the first time anyone had ever knocked him out.

He lay there, flat on his back, his eyes closed, his arms stretched out, the referee counting over him, every word a knife in my stomach, the longest ten seconds that I'd ever known in my life. Yet at the same time, I knew I'd been expecting it; it was like I'd seen it before. In a funny way, a way I can't explain, it had somehow all been building up to this, this moment, Joey there on the floor, even if it wasn't going to be the end of things.

After the 'ten', I was through those ropes like the clappers. He was starting to stir, but it was still two minutes before he come round. Harold was there, too, bending over him, with his great, white, pudgy face, looking like somebody had run into the back of his Rolls. Afterwards, he came into our dressing room. Joey was still lying on the rubbing table. He'd come round, but he still wasn't too clever. He'd been crying a bit.

'One thing they can't say, Joe,' said Harold, 'they can never say you haven't got courage.'

Joey looked up at him and said, 'Thanks, Harold,' then Harold said, 'And I'll tell you what. I'm going to get you that shot at the world title.'

I don't think Joey believed it. I know I didn't, not at the time. After all, the highest Joe had ever been in the world ratings was twentieth and, after this, he wouldn't even be there.

The champion was a Cuban, Pedro Borja, deadly in his time, but to my mind, just going over the top.

Ten days later, Harold rang us and told us he could get Joe the fight, Wembley again, in April, and he was promising Borja forty thousand quid. Us, he'd pay fifteen thousand. 'I must be mad,' he said, 'they'll say I don't know what I'm doing. I could lose a fortune, but I'm willing to risk it. I tell you, even if I sell it to closed-circuit television, I'm still liable to lose money.'

When I told Joey, I hoped he'd be as excited as I was; in the old days, I know he would have been. We had lunch together in Soho. I didn't let on at first. When I sprung it on him, he said, 'You're joking.' Then he said, 'I'll have to talk to Janet.'

'Janet!' I said. 'Who's your manager?'

'It upset her a lot,' he said, 'me getting knocked out.'

'Look, Joe,' I said, 'it's a gamble, this. I admit it. Borja's a great fighter; or he's *been* a great fighter. But now he's beginning to get caught more often. Now he isn't lasting so well.'

I could see he was excited by it. If it was left up to him, there'd be no hesitation. He said, 'I know that. I'll speak to her.'

How it come out was, if he lost, it was going to be his last fight. 'I had to promise her that,' he said, and what could I do but accept? After all, he might win and, even if he did lose, he could always change his mind; or *her* mind.

When the news was announced, there was some disgraceful things said. One paper wrote that it was liable to go down as the Mismatch of the Century, and another said it should be reported to the League Against Cruel Sports. You would have thought that, when a British fighter had a chance of a world title, everyone would be only too pleased to get behind him, but there'd always been this where Joey was concerned, right from the very beginning.

As for Janet, she wouldn't hardly talk to me, and I cursed the fucking day I'd spoke to her. She'd got nothing to complain of, anyhow; especially after seeing what she'd come from, up there in the North. She'd got a nice house, now, her own car, holidays abroad, all the clothes she wanted. I said to her once, it just slipped out of me, 'You don't have such a terrible life, Janet.'

'No,' she said. 'I live off Joey, too.'

So we went into training, back to Maidenhead, again, but now it was even worse than before. Joe's approach was wrong: his whole attitude was let's get it over, and I could have fucking throttled her because she was the one who'd done it, no one else. His great chance, and he was training like a zombie.

I told him a couple of times, 'If you don't want to go on with it, Joey, tell me, that's all, just tell me; I'll tell Harold, call it off,' but he said, 'I'm going on. I told you I'd fight him, didn't I?'

This Borja arrived, and I went to watch him sparring, but you couldn't tell nothing. Good-looking bloke, little moustache, seemed to get caught a fair bit, but now and then he'd open up tremendously, bang-bang-bang.

I planned the whole fight very carefully, every round, because, the longer it went on, the more chance Joe would have. After all, he was ten years younger, maybe more, because you can usually put a few years on whatever fighters from these countries say they are, especially when they've been around a while.

One afternoon, when I'd been up in town, watching Borja, I got back to the gym at Maidenhead; Joe was there, skipping. As soon as he saw me, he dropped the rope and said, 'Is it bent?'

I was so shaken, I couldn't answer him at first. 'What do you mean?' I said, eventually, and then he did his nut – there was no one else in there but us – grabbing my tie, yelling and shouting at me, 'You bent the Thompson fight, didn't you? You bent the Fernandez fight! Why not this one?'

'What do you mean?' I said, pulling away from him. 'Who's been talking to you?'

'The press!' he said. 'That's who's been fucking talking to me! The *Sunday News* bloke. They know everything.'

'It's bollocks,' I said, though inside I'd gone cold. 'I'll have them for libel.'

'They've got proof,' he said. 'They say they've got statements and tape recordings.'

What could I do but bluff? I told him, 'On my life, Joe, there's nothing in it.' I did my best to pacify him, then I rang up Harold. 'Right,' he said, 'I'm ready for the bastards. I'll ring 'em now and tell them if they print one word, I'll have them for a hundred thousand pounds. It's their word against mine. There's nothing they can prove.'

Three days it took to talk him round, Joey. At first he wanted to pack it in right away, he wanted to go home, and I knew, if that happened, that was it, because he'd talk to her. I pleaded with him, I practically went on my knees to him, I got Harold and Ronnie down to swear to him those fights were all on the level, while at the same time Harold did his best to put the frighteners on the *News*. The one thing I could say, I could honestly tell him, was that this fight with Borja was dead straight.

'Stand on me, Joe,' I said. 'And anyway, how can you bend a world title fight?'

For those three days, it wasn't good. If it had still been just us two together, I knew I could have swung it all right, but the thought was in my mind all the time, what's she saying to him? Has she been stirring it up?

As if things weren't difficult enough, she went and gave a terrible interview to some bird on one of the daily papers: 'Why I Hope This Is Joey's Last Fight', full of stuff like, 'Whenever he fights, I sit at home praying that he won't be hurt. I never go, I don't even listen to it on the radio. I think Joey's being used. I think every boxer's being used.'

I showed it to Joey. I said, 'Do *you* think you're being used?'

He didn't answer right away, then he said, 'Not used. Not really. Not by you, Ted.'

I couldn't stop myself: I rang her up and asked her, 'How

can you give an interview like that when he's just about to fight for a world title.'

'Joe knows how I feel,' she said. 'It's nothing new to him.'

'I've promised if he loses it's the last time,' I said. 'What more can I do? You think I want him to get hurt any more than you do?'

'Yes,' she said.

But by the time it come to the night, Joey was a lot better. The nearer the fight came, the more it got to him; you could see it in his face, in his eyes, the way he was training, even when the sparring stopped. After all, this was it, this was what we'd been building up to all these years, a world title fight, and whatever anybody said, he was in with a chance, like anyone must be when two professionals step in the ring.

I don't think we'd ever prepared so well for a fight. He was just inside the limit a couple of days beforehand, and at the weigh-in he was eleven six and a quarter, three-quarters of a pound lighter than the other man. We'd gone again and again through all the punches Borja threw, particularly the left hook, which he was famous for, and we'd worked out the tactics perfect: box him for four or five rounds, keep him moving about, then, as soon as he started to tire, take the fight to him.

Those opening rounds, it worked just like I'd hoped. While Borja was strong there was no point taking any risks, and Joe boxed better than I'd ever seen him, really skilful, footwork terrific, swaying away from the jabs, blocking the hooks, ducking under combinations, scoring with a few nice jabs himself, and landing one good right cross in the second.

In the third, it didn't go quite so well. He was still a lovely mover, this Borja, and when Joe missed him on the ropes with a left he landed a combination left-right to the head. For the moment I was very worried – was Joe dazed, had it cut that eye? – but luckily it hadn't, and he's a very strong boy, he shook it off. The fourth and fifth he was starting to take the fight to Borja more; the fellow already seemed to be slowing. It was very even, maybe with Joey just slightly ahead.

Then, in the sixth, it happened, and no one was more astonished than what I was. He went in and he hit Joey low, a left-hander, terrible, right in the knackers; it hurt him even with the foul cup on. The referee took this Borja aside and gave him a warning; the crowd were going crazy. Joey got up, still very shaken, but thank God he managed to hang on for the rest of the round.

We did what we could in the corner, but he was still in quite a bit of pain. 'Get on your bicycle,' I told him, 'keep out of the bastard's way.' It was all he could do.

Halfway through the next round, fuck me if the bloke doesn't do it again, this time a right hand, bang straight in the cobblers, and the referee didn't have no alternative. Disqualified.

As soon as he'd done it, sent the fellow to his corner, lifted Joe's hand while he was still on the deck, there was murder. People cheering, people yelling, people booing, people protesting; betting boys, mostly. A few fights going on; coppers breaking them up. Down at the ringside, I saw one big villain, Tommy Mallow, up on his feet, carrying on, effing and blinding, shouting that it was bent, he'd bloody kill Harold Maxwell, and as for Harold, he was nowhere to be seen, not up in the ring, nowhere, which was strange in itself, because normally at his own promotions he was right in the middle of everything, especially when Joe had won.

As for me, I didn't know what to think. I was delighted; I was puzzled; I was worried about Joey, who was still pretty well unconscious. I knelt down there beside him; 'You're the champ, Joey,' I told him, 'you're the champion of the world, son.' His face was all twisted up with pain, not able to take it in.

We lifted him up between us, me and Jack Dover, while the MC was making the announcement from the ring: Joey was champion of the world. Borja came up and tried to apologise to him; television people wanted to interview him; but in the end, we got him through the crowd with an escort of coppers, most people congratulating us, just a few of them against us, and we were there, in the dressing room.

We put him on the rubbing table; we worked on him. He didn't say nothing, just gasped a bit. Finally he sat up. 'Joe,' I said, again, 'you're world champion.'

It was then he got up off the table. I'd never seen an

expression like that on his face before, all twisted up, nearly in tears.

'You bent it!' he shouted at me. 'You fucking bent it!' and he hit me. His own brother. Hit me.

The Tokyo Olympics

Sunday Times, 25 October 1964

THE PAPER LANTERNS wither in the streets; the Olympic Flame is spent; it is all over. Over, after a week that has seen the apotheosis of Snell and Abebe, the rehabilitation of Brightwell and John Thomas, the triumph of Ann Packer, the twilight of CK Yang. The National Stadium, metamorphosed overnight from a football pitch into a hurdle-strewn gymkhana field, metamorphosed again into a floodlit secular temple for the closing ceremony.

Yet again the terraces were packed, though one still feels that the dimensions of Olympic fever were such that they'd have been packed for a sewing bee.

The Japanese, however, may well be euphoric, with their immaculate organisation, their exhilarating stadia and their sixteen gold medals, even if three of these were won for judo and one for women's volleyball, leading one to surmise that, if ever the Olympics are held here again, flower arrangement will be on the agenda.

'Weeping athletes and spectators,' predicted *Yomiuri,* a local newspaper, 'will sing the sad strains of "Auld Lang Syne".' In fact, the many and various solemnities of the closing ceremony were redeemed by the mass entry of the athletes themselves, who, refusing to take it as anything but a joyful celebration, poured into the stadium after the last flag-bearer had entered like a throng of happy children.

They waved their hands, their hats and even their umbrellas; they shouted, they danced, they sang, they clapped. It was in vain for a prim young woman to admonish them through the loudspeakers to march in eights; their exuberance was not to be contained even by the most self-conscious of quasi-religious occasions. For them, the electronic gongs had boomed in vain, the anthems had been sung without effect.

Among them, round and round the track, ran a beaming and delighted African, spindly-legged, dressed only in white running shorts and vest, waving both arms to the crowd. The band, forsaking the Olympic Fanfare which has haunted Tokyo all fortnight, played jaunty marches, and even when the floodlights went out for Mr Brundage to intone his sonorous appeal to the youth of the world to reunite in Mexico City, it was too late. The occasion had been well and truly saved and the moral was plain: if the sonorous old would only leave the exuberant young to their own devices, the athletics world, at least, might be a better place.

The floodlights went out; the bandsmen played behind a phosphorescent lake of silver; sailors in white hauled down the Olympic Flag; a choir of girls sang the Olympic Hymn and then 'Auld Lang Syne' in what appeared to be Japanese, but it was too dark to see if anyone was crying. Besides, there were the fireworks to come and what could be more appropriate to conclude a party for happy children?

In the Olympic Village there was an air of *Nunc Dimittis* about it all. The bicycles have flat tyres and doubtful brakes and they're inclined to rattle.

Berruti's coach, sitting right opposite him, says, 'I'm convinced that if he'd trained 100 per cent, a thing which he has never done, he'd have won in this his second Olympics.' Berruti remains inscrutable behind his dark glasses.

A German girl runner, asked about the marathon, replies, 'It is too long. I think a race should have a spiritual aspect,' and looks surprised when an English man cries, 'How German, how German!'

Percy Cerutty, Herb Elliott's coach, still roams abroad, Svengali without Trilby now – or, if you prefer it, the Ancient Mariner in search of the Wedding Guest. He shoots out theories with unending prodigality but there's no gainsaying his views about those hulking grotesques, the female shot-putters and discus-throwers.

'They're not worth a cracker to look at,' he says. 'The women's shot put final is absurd. What a travesty of womanhood! Huge, overweight, monstrosities of human malformation. They interest me like the fat woman in the circus does, or an elephant, but you can never really love 'em, like you can a racehorse or a giraffe.

'Freakishness is attractive: everybody pays to see a two-headed cow. But we must give up lionising and paying tribute to these freaks who, by reason of being freaks, can win at athletics.'

In our weightlifters' quarters, Louis Martin looked a fallen and crestfallen hero, the very incarnation of bitter self-disgust, his powerful hands rammed into the pockets of his smart, blue, tapering trousers.

'Terrible! How can I say it's great and cover up the sore? It's bound to burst some time. It's ten pounds less than I did two years consecutively and that's a very poor performance. I was struggling from the word go.'

'Even going out with him this morning,' said Al Murray, his coach, 'I didn't know what to say; it would all be idle chatter.'

'Suppose I just cover this up,' said Martin, 'have a gay time. As soon as you go home – poom, up it all comes again!'

Then would he go on to Mexico City, I asked. 'Am I going on? What a terrible question to ask. I think I can still win. On the right night. It's a mistimed peak, that's all.'

The Years of the Golden Fix
Champions of Europe, 1991

TWO VIGNETTES; EACH involving Juventus. First the Stadio Comunale in Turin, on a spring afternoon in 1973. Derby County have just lost 3–1 to Juventus in the first leg of the European Cup semi-final. Two of their players, centre-half Roy McFarland and inside-forward Archie Gemmill, both key men, have been booked, which means they will miss the second leg. Out of the dressing room emerges Brian Clough, the Yorkshire-born manager of Derby County. Facing him is a throng of eager Italian journalists, waiting for his comments. I am among them. Clough speaks. 'No cheating bastards will I talk to. I will not talk to any cheating bastards.' Then he, together with the former Juventus hero and Wales centre-forward John Charles, disappears behind the dressing-room door.

'*Cos'ha detto, Glanville, cos'ha detto?*' cry the Italian reporters. What did he say? Diplomatically. I feign incomprehension. The dressing-room door opens again, and there is Clough. 'Tell 'em what I said, Brian!' I do. Alarm and consternation. Headlines the following day. *BASTARDI TRUFFATORI!* Cheating bastards! No real chapter and verse, though, on the why and wherefore, the scuffle in the dressing-room corridor when Peter Taylor, Clough's lieutenant, had tried to pull Helmut Haller, Juve's West German inside-forward, away from Schulenburg, the German referee.

Forward a year, to Turin again. This time the Presidential office of Juve's Giampiero Boniperti. Blond and blue-eyed, the eternal *jeune premier*, captain of Juventus and Italy in the years when I lived there, 'Boni' sits beneath two photographs. Each was taken when a FIFA XI played England at Wembley in October 1953 to celebrate the Football Association's ninetieth anniversary. One shows 'Boni' in the FIFA team's line-up, shaking hands before the game; the other shows him scoring one of his two goals in the 4–4 draw.

I was there because John Lovesey, the sports editor of the *Sunday Times*, had sent me. We had Juventus, in the vernacular, bang to rights. They had clearly sent the notorious Hungarian fixer, Dezso Solti, to Lisbon the previous year to try to suborn the Portuguese referee of the second leg against Derby County, Francisco Marques Lobo. But Lobo was an honest man who had reported the attempt; an honourable act which had had a shabby sequel. By this time, the *Sunday Times* were ready to publish and be damned, but John Lovesey insisted I give 'Boni' his chance to vindicate, or at least explain, himself.

Boniperti heard me out in silence as I told him all we knew, which was almost everything. When I had finished, he replied, '*Brian, se ci sono questi pazzi in giro!*' Brian, if there are these madmen going about! Then he said, 'And what's happening in English football, now?' The conversation was closed.

Thus it was that the *Sunday Times*, a few weeks later, came out with a front-page story on the Lobo–Solti Affair: on the failed attempt to bribe, the disgracefully inadequate inquiry by the European governing body UEFA, the astounding letter to Juventus which thanked and exculpated them. In time we would dig up, in Holland, a letter which the 'madman', Solti, had actually signed in 1971 on behalf of Juventus. But UEFA did nothing then, and have done nothing since.

So far as I was concerned, the saga had begun with a telephone call. I heard from Budapest – which would become the fulcrum of our inquiry, a city where rogues and honest men were enmeshed in a strange network of intrigue and finagling – of the previous year's cover-up in Zurich.

There, I discovered, UEFA had held an inquiry into the Lobo Case, of which no news had percolated into England. This despite the fact that Denis Follows, then Secretary of the Football Association, was also at that time head of the UEFA

Disciplinary Committee. As an Englishman, he had stood down from the committee which passed judgement on Lobo–Solti but amazingly he had subsequently done nothing to inform the English news media of what had occurred. Indeed, when in subsequent years I had cause to turn to him for information, he had to search in his attic to discover the relevant papers. There were those in Budapest who believed he must himself be involved in the affair, but I am sure they were wrong. Continentals have so often mistaken English ingenuousness for deviousness.

I pursued the investigation as far as I could, but it was not enough. That there had been dirty work at the crossroads was beyond dispute. That Solti, notorious for years as a fixer for Internazionale of Milan in their European Cup heyday, had offered Lobo a bribe, I was convinced. Just as I was sure that Lobo had sturdily refused it. That Solti had been 'run' by the general manager of Juventus, the notorious Italo Allodi who for years had used him while Secretary of Inter, I was equally sure. Just as I was sure that Lobo had refereed the goalless second leg – which I also saw – impeccably. Derby had been awarded a penalty and missed it, while their centre-forward Roger Davies had been sent off for knocking Morini into the net with a punch.

To light the touchpaper, it was essential that someone speak to Lobo, get a statement, show what had happened. I couldn't do it: I had no Portuguese. And so I turned to Keith Botsford, a polyglot American journalist with an Italian mother and a father who'd played tennis for Belgium. His Portuguese was excellent. He also, like myself, spoke Italian, Spanish and French. German, too, and some Russian. He had worked for years in Mexico, and had acted as a secret agent in Budapest itself, just after the war, when the Russians interrogated him. He was also a passionate football fan, for many years a follower of Chelsea.

John Lovesey agreed to take him on, and sent him to Lisbon. There, he went to see Lobo, a telephone engineer when he was not refereeing, and with some difficulty and much diplomacy persuaded him to talk. Back to London he came with the whole story: of Solti's visit to Lisbon, of the car keys he dangled before

Lobo's face in Room 142 of the Ritz Hotel, of the $5,000 he offered besides – if Lobo would see to it that Juventus won their second-leg game in Derby.

Lobo played Botsford a tape recording of a subsequent telephone call he received from Solti. Now it was my turn, to go to Milan and try to trace it. I began by visiting a private detective, one of the plump Ponzi brothers. Tom, the most notorious of them, was a known neo-Fascist, by turns buccaneer and unlikely hero. His brother was somewhat less enterprising. He could not, he said, do anything to help me trace the call from Solti to Lobo. He suggested that I could best try to do it myself. How? Simply by walking into the headquarters of the telephone service and inquiring.

It seemed a very long shot, but it worked. I did as he suggested, went to the telephone headquarters, and asked a woman working there if she could find details of the call. She said she would try, and before very long produced them. Solti had indeed called Lobo in Lisbon that day. As I continued to ask questions, a senior woman appeared, and looked at me suspiciously, saying that such information was not usually provided. But it was too late: I had it, and went home with it.

It should be said that, though the revelations of the Lobo– Solti Affair came as a shock, they were not wholly a surprise. There had been dirty work at the crossroads before by Italian clubs, one well knew, even if nothing, so to speak, had stood up in court. Or ever got close to one. As long ago as 1964, as we have seen, there had been the Tesanic Case.

Reaching the semi-finals of the European Cup, Internazionale had to win the second leg at home to Borussia Dortmund to reach the final. During the match, Luisito Suarez, the Spanish international inside-forward, brutally kicked the Dortmund right-half, who was obliged to leave the field. There were no substitutes then. Dortmund struggled on with ten men and lost: Inter went on to win the final. Tesanic, the Yugoslav referee of that game, would later be found on holiday, allegedly at Inter's expense.

The following year, it was Liverpool's turn. They had gained a famous victory over Inter in the first leg of the European Cup semi-final, winning 3–1 at Anfield. In later years, Bill Shankly would tell one that afterwards he had met a large Italian journalist who shook his head and told him, sadly, 'You will never be allowed to win.' Nor was he.

The return leg in Milan was lost 3–0, with a couple of really strange goals. For one of them, Peiró, another Spanish international playing for Inter, ran back from behind Tommy Lawrence, the Liverpool keeper, who was preparing to clear the ball, kicked it out of his hands, and put it in the net. Corso scored an equally contentious goal. A free kick was given to Inter, on the edge of the box. With his famous left foot, Corso struck it straight home. Though the referee, the Spanish Ortiz de Mendibil, had clearly indicated that the kick was indirect, he allowed the goal.

Then, in 1973 itself, there was the vexed case of Leeds United's defeat by Milan in the final of the European Cup Winners' Cup in Salonika, where Michas, the Greek referee, gave a series of appallingly indulgent decisions in favour of Milan, who won 1–0. Michas would subsequently be suspended, but that was as far as it went.

Not that the Italian clubs had been the only suspected offenders. When Panathinaikos of Athens most unexpectedly reached the final of the European Cup in 1971, they were outrageously favoured by the French referee of their return home leg against Everton in the quarter-finals. During the first leg, Joe Royle, later to become an outstanding manager with Oldham, then the Everton centre-forward, remembers the Greek defenders hissing in his ear, 'Athens, Athens!' And in Athens, Everton got nothing from the referee.

Years later, Keith Botsford and I, after infinite attempts, would at last manage to obtain the full story of a Hungarian referee who did *not* comply with the blandishments of Inter and the pressures of his own Federation: but that is another story, and I shall tell it later.

Boniperti having stonewalled, the *Sunday Times* blew the whistle – an appropriate metaphor – on the Lobo–Solti Affair on 21 April 1974, under the headline THE $5,000 FIX THAT DIDN'T WORK. No one appreciated better than Botsford and myself, Italophiles and *appassionati* of Italian football, the deep irony implicit in that headline and indeed in the story itself. For our exposure was wholly due to the fact that the 'fix' had failed, had gone off at half-cock. So, indeed, it had in 1966, when Inter failed for once to bribe their man; but of that, at the time, we knew nothing.

Juventus, we would discover, had almost certainly tried before, with more success, in less exalted circumstances, when the referee was the familiar Ortiz de Mendibil. But we began by relating how Lobo was first approached, on 27 March 1973.

He was listening to a record in his home in a working-class suburb of Lisbon, when the telephone rang. 'An Italian gentleman' wanted to speak to him from the Ritz Hotel, in the city. The 'gentleman' told Lobo that he was a 'follower of football' who was in Lisbon to see an international match, the following day. He brought personal messages for Lobo from mutual acquaintances in Italy: he would like Lobo to come over to the Ritz to meet him.

Lobo was a simple, decent fellow, but he wasn't born yesterday. He had made it a practice never to meet people connected with football without the presence of a third party. He was, he said, just about to eat his dinner. Could he call back later? Or could the messages not be conveyed now, on the telephone.

No, said the mysterious caller; they were of a personal nature. He really did need to see Lobo at the Ritz. Lobo said he would call back after dinner. He put down the receiver, picked it up again, and called Sousa Loureiro, president of the Portuguese Referees' Association. Sousa Loureiro told him he could keep the appointment at the Ritz but must confine himself to polite discussion, and make no comments of his own.

So off to the Ritz, on its high hill above the Avenida Liberdade, Lobo went, for an appointment which would prove fateful, whose reverberations would sound down the years. One might compare it with the turning over of some great stone, from beneath which crawled all manner of vile, slimy, secretive creatures.

The man Lobo met in Room 142, with its pretentious decor, was a Central European in his late fifties who, said Lobo, 'reeked of money'. With him was a much younger woman, blonde and attractive. Lobo wrongly took her to be Solti's wife;

she was in fact his mistress. In time to come they would fall out, with sharp recriminations.

Solti began authentically enough by giving Lobo a message from a man who was indeed an Italian friend. He then congratulated him on his 'appointment as a World Cup referee'. This was news, though delightful news, to Lobo. How did Solti know this, he asked. From Dr Artemio Franchi, said Solti. Franchi at that time was President not only of the Italian Football Federation, but also of UEFA.

He had also heard from Franchi, Solti pursued, that Lobo had been chosen to control the second leg of the European Cup semi-final at Derby. Franchi, he said, had told him this as well. This astonished Lobo even more, but he reckoned that anyone who had such close contacts with Franchi must be an important figure indeed. 'Franchi,' pursued Solti, 'told me you were one of the best.' The unspoken message, Lobo realised, was that Solti was a close friend of Franchi and others who could promote his career as an international referee.

If Lobo were to referee that game at Derby to the best of his ability, Solti went on, it was important he attend the first leg, in Turin. Everyone in Europe recognised that the English played a tough kind of football. To illustrate his point, he produced a cutting from *Il Giorno*, the Milanese daily. If Lobo came to Turin, he could see for himself just how 'hard' English football was. Solti invited Lobo as his guest. While he was there, said Solti, he would see that he met people who could help him as a referee.

Solti announced that he'd already made travel arrangements for Lobo. He would fly from Lisbon to Madrid, thence to Milan. 'You will stay in my house there, and I want you to meet the President of Juventus and other club officials.'

Solti then made one of those gestures common in his career, at once flamboyant and insidious. He reached into his pocket, produced a car key, and dangled it in front of Lobo. 'The implication was,' said Lobo to Botsford, 'that when I left Italy, I would not have to fly back, but would have a car of my own to drive back in.'

Obeying his instructions, Lobo said nothing. Solti assumed this meant he agreed. 'Look, Lobo,' he now said. 'My friends

and I are very interested in the return match. It's really nothing
for me. I have to pay the players, anyway. There's no problem.
I already have to carry nineteen on my list, and it isn't difficult
to put down twenty. Anyway, I have a free hand to do what I
want for the club. If I put down twenty instead of nineteen,
nobody is going to say anything. The price is about $5,000,
and I can do this without any trouble.'

No doubt he could, since in his fixing days with Inter, Solti,
in 1966, had unsuccessfully offered the Hungarian referee
Gyorgy Vadas immensely more. Lobo, who had no more intention of accepting so repugnant an offer than Vadas, replied that
he really could not go to Italy as he had conflicting obligations.
Solti was at first insistent, then yielded, plainly believing that it
was merely the trip to Italy which Lobo had refused. 'Well,' he
said, 'it's all agreed, but I shall call you again at a later date to
make the arrangements.'

Still following his instructions, Lobo replied, 'If you want to
call me, that is all right with me.'

When he left, Lobo at once delivered a report to his Referees'
Association president. They decided to set a trap for Solti.
When his call to Lobo was eventually made, a representative of
the association would be there, listening on another telephone.

Now came the contentious first leg between Juventus and
Derby in Turin, culminating in those hot, strong words from
Brian Clough. The curious thing about that game, which I
watched, was that, though strange and suspicious things may
have happened, Juventus won it fairly and squarely on the field;
if one accepts the amount of licence given by Herr Schulenburg,
the referee, to the aggressive little Juve right-half Furino. José
Altafini, once upon a time nicknamed Mazzola when he played
for Brazil as a nineteen-year-old in the 1958 World Cup, had a
superb game for Juventus, scoring two fine goals, and the 3–1
score was not unjust.

This was more than could be said for some other happenings.
Peter Taylor, Clough's lieutenant, observed that when Schulenburg blew the half-time whistle, the West German international
Helmut Haller, sitting on the Juventus bench, rose and went to
him, 'talking earnestly in German' as the two walked on down
the tunnel and into the dressing room.

Taylor followed them and, he says, 'tried to intercept them' to show he knew what might be afoot, but his way was blocked, apparently on Haller's instructions, 'by a group of tough-looking Italians' and a scuffle ensued. Taylor had already been warned before the game, he said, by the old Juventus favourite John Charles that 'Haller was in with the referee again'. There is, it should be said, no evidence that anything underhand was going on. 'Nothing can ever be proved,' said Taylor, 'but I believe it was corrupt and dirty. It brought us on a ton in learning about Europe and put us on our mettle for the future.' As it was, Gemmill and McFarland were booked and thus ruled out of the return, McFarland for no reason which was immediately evident.

On 4 April, Solti did indeed ring Lobo and he, as an employee of the Portuguese telephone company, was able to have the call recorded. Botsford obtained and translated the transcript. Lobo spoke Portuguese; Solti an odd mixture of indifferent Italian and Spanish. The conversation went as follows:

SOLTI   So. How are you? Solti here.

LOBO   I couldn't go to Turin. It wasn't my fault. I had my professional obligations to attend to, but I want you to know I do take your offer seriously.

SOLTI   Well, how do the possibilities look?

LOBO   I couldn't go to Turin to see the match. I have received the notification to do the return match between Derby and Juventus, but I cannot go to Turin. How is Franchi?

SOLTI   Very, very well, for a man of over fifty.

LOBO   My compliments to Franchi.

SOLTI   Fine. I shall do that.

LOBO   I am pleased to hear that. Are you satisfied?

SOLTI   Yes. Listen. Do you know who the linesmen are?

LOBO   Fernando Leite and Caesar Correia.

SOLTI   Is he an international referee or not?

LOBO   He is on the UEFA list.

SOLTI   I am not so sure.

LOBO   He is a UEFA referee, and he has a UEFA badge. Solti, are you going to England?

SOLTI	Before that, I will be back in Lisbon.
LOBO	You're coming to Lisbon?
SOLTI	I should know next week.
LOBO	Then it is after that you will talk to me?
SOLTI	Do you understand? Can you come through Paris?
LOBO	Ah, I see. I go through Paris.
SOLTI	Yes.
LOBO	I see. We will make arrangements in Paris.
SOLTI	Yes.
LOBO	I will go earlier, and talk to you.
SOLTI	We will talk next week in Lisbon. All right?
LOBO	In Lisbon is fine. I will talk to you next week in Lisbon. Now . . .
SOLTI	That is this week. Right?
LOBO	You have my telephone number?
SOLTI	I have it.
LOBO	When you get here, call me.
SOLTI	We will talk on the phone.
LOBO	Yes. The arrangement we talked about at the Ritz Hotel was $5,000 wasn't it?
SOLTI	Yes.
LOBO	Well, I haven't got anything more.
SOLTI	I think we will discuss it personally.

After listening to the tape, Lobo told Keith Botsford, ruefully, 'I am not a rich man. $5,000 and a car is four years' work for me! I could have taken the money, and no one would have known. I'd be a richer man than today. But I didn't. I did my duty. And I didn't get to be on the World Cup list, which was the one thing I wanted. Why?'

Long before the end of our investigation, that became a pitifully rhetorical question. Gyorgy Vadas could have told Lobo why, had they ever met. Told him how, after his sturdy bravery, his defiance of all the temptation Inter put in his way and his impeccable refereeing of the Inter–Real Madrid semi-final in 1966, his reward was to be banished forever from international refereeing. You did not defy the European football 'mafia' with impunity.

Lobo sent the tape of the telephone call from Solti, with his own report, to his Referees' Association. From there it went on to the Portuguese Football Federation, and thence to UEFA in Berne. On 24 April, the day before the return leg of the semi-final at Derby, a letter arrived from the UEFA Secretary, the Swiss Hans Bangerter. It affirmed its faith in Lobo's skill and impartiality, and confirmed he'd still be refereeing at Derby. It made no mention of any possible investigation. For Lobo's protection, his Referees' Assocation sent an official observer, who gave him the highest possible marks.

He well deserved them. Again, I saw the match myself, and Lobo's refereeing was excellent. The game was a goalless draw, though Alan Hinton contrived to miss the penalty awarded to Derby by Lobo. There was also the ugly incident in the second half when, having been fouled by the blond Juventus centre-half Morini, Roger Davies knocked him flying into the goal-mouth and was promptly and properly sent off.

On 20 June 1973, UEFA's disciplinary sub-committee met to consider the case at the Atlantis Hotel in Zurich. Its Italian president, Barbè, stood down, as did Denis Follows. When, the following year, I telephoned Barbè to ask him about the case, it was to receive the panic-stricken response, '*Io non ne so niente, io non ne so niente!*' I know nothing about it! Somewhat strange for the man who was president of the committee, even if he himself had not actually been present on the day.

And what a day! A fiasco, in this author's opinion. In the event, it was the Czech, Petra, who presided over the sub-committee. The other members were Wouters of Belgium, a lawyer who received a large retainer as an advisor to UEFA; Poroila of Finland; and the Maltese, Banisci. Lobo spoke of the meeting as follows: 'There were nine persons present ... I repeated the substance of my report, and was listened to politely and asked no questions. Then, when I had finished, Franchi invited me to step with him into a neighbouring room. We went in alone, without any other member of the committee, and there I was shown a group of gentlemen and asked if I recognised any of them as the person who had offered me the bribe. No words were exchanged when I was in the room, nor could I put any questions. I quickly said that it was none of those present, and with that I was given permission to withdraw.'

The men in the room, it transpired, were directors of Juventus, though they did not include Giampiero Boniperti, the president; still less Solti.

Mystery was piled upon mystery. Artemio Franchi subsequently insisted that he was not present at the meeting of the sub-committee. This, he told us, was because the separation of executive and disciplinary functions was a matter of policy, even if, in his own words, 'I [can] think that in some specific situations, which involve not only disciplinary problems but perhaps matters of major international importance, this policy is too rigid, is wrong, and should be altered.' Yet were we to suppose that Franchi wasn't there at all, that Lobo didn't meet him in the Atlantis Hotel, that he mistook somebody else for Franchi? Not to mention his female companion, whom Lobo said he recognised.

Then there was the farcical 'identity parade' – a parade without the suspect! And Solti was in the Atlantis Hotel, because Lobo caught sight of him. Curiouser and curiouser. The disciplinary sub-committee did, however, decide that Solti be declared *persona non grata* in European football; a decision which would not, in the event, be implemented for another eighteen months.

Nine days later, meeting this time in Glasgow, the sub-committee decided that there was insufficient evidence to take such a step without fear of legal repercussions. Instead, it would circularise its clubs and members, warning them about Solti in more general terms. This, too, was not done. Franchi's explanation to us was that, again, Solti might sue them. In December 1974, when Solti was at last made *persona non grata* in Budapest, such gossamer objections were simply brushed aside, or ignored. That the sub-committee, with a highly paid lawyer such as Wouters on it, should have thought for a moment that Solti could sue with any hope of success leaves one baffled.

More baffling still was the fact that, on 5 July 1973, Hans Bangerter, the Secretary of UEFA, sent Juventus a letter, thanking them for their co-operation and telling them that they had been exonerated. It transpired that Franchi, the President of

UEFA, knew nothing of that letter, with which such great play would subsequently be made by Juventus and the Italian sports press.

A rank odour hung over the deliberations and actions of the sub-committee and indeed of UEFA itself. The only person initially to suffer was Lobo himself, and again, in puzzling circumstances. It emerged that the decision not to send out a circular, warning clubs about Solti, was taken on the advice of a Berne lawyer called Hodler, recommended by Bangerter. Yet it also transpired that, when he gave this advice, Hodler had not even been given the chance to listen to the damning tape of Solti's telephone conversation with Lobo.

The reasons given for Lobo's exclusion from international refereeing were less ingenious than squalid. Never did he get another game, though at the time of the revelations in 1973 he was on the World Cup supplementary list. Behind this banishment was the Austrian Friedrich Seipelt, chairman of the UEFA Referees' Committee. He had personally decided, he told us, that since the Lobo–Solti Affair remained *sub judice*, it was best that Lobo be removed from circulation. No one in UEFA authorised such a move.

Artemio Franchi utterly rejected Solti's statement to Lobo that Franchi himself had informed Solti of Lobo's selection to referee the Derby–Juventus second leg, a month in advance. In that case, we wondered, who did tell Solti? Franchi did admit that Solti was well known to him by sight, from his presence at UEFA draws for the three European Cup competitions. We had to presume that, if Solti did not gain this information from Franchi, it was either leaked to him through UEFA, or through a club. No prizes for surmising which.

It is time, though, to present in greater detail the *dramatis personae* of this horrid affair. Who, in the first place, was Deszo Solti?

He was a notorious figure in European football long before the Lobo affair, but he had been associated chiefly with Internazionale of Milan. A man by then in his late sixties, a Hungarian Jew, he had survived the war, taken Argentine citizenship, lived in Vienna and eventually settled in Milan, in an expensive apartment. But Budapest still saw a great deal of him. There, he would sit in a café endlessly greeting and being greeted.

Before he moved to Vienna, Solti already had strong connections with Hungarian clubs. In Austria he promoted 'cabarets', living in a sleazy demi-monde and maintaining his café connections with people in the football world. He fell out with at least one partner, who claimed he had been cheated. By 1949 he was in Rome, using his acquaintance with Bela Guttmann, another Hungarian Jew, who had played before the war at centre-half for MTK Budapest and the Viennese Jewish club Hakoah. In later years, he would become a major manager, twice winning the European Cup itself, with Benfica of Lisbon, as we have seen.

In 1955, after Guttmann, to his chagrin, had lost his job with Milan, he and Solti were involved in a hit-and-run motor accident in which two children were killed. The investigating magistrates, however, did not press charges.

'I was full of ambition,' wrote Solti, in a memoir published in Budapest in the mid-1970s. 'I knew I wouldn't be able to play football well enough, but I decided to become an administrator.' The turning point came the year following the motor accident. 'In 1956,' wrote Solti, 'a very rich man became president of Inter. Signor Moratti was an oil millionaire and a typical Italian, very temperamental ... Moratti took me into his confidence. He seemed to discuss football several hours a day.' Solti was hired; but not for long.

The first deal he did on behalf of Inter was to acquire, or so he thought, a Hungarian team manager, Kalmar. But Kalmar instead signed with Panathinaikos of Athens. An infuriated Moratti gave Solti the boot. 'As soon as that happened,' Solti wrote, 'Moratti chucked me out. My whole world collapsed. It was nearly the end of my career.'

Nearly, but not quite. Significantly, Solti now began 'helping Real Madrid with their European Cup games'; how, one can only surmise.

In the meanwhile, Solti became a kind of travel agent deluxe in Milan, assisting visiting foreign teams; an ideal opportunity to build up his network of connections in football.

In 1961, according at least to Solti's version of events, the flamboyant Helenio Herrera, an Argentine brought up in Casablanca and by then manager of Barcelona, 'asked me to help him get a job with one of the Italian clubs'. Solti said that he at once approached Moratti at Inter, and thus got back into his good graces. At Barcelona, Herrera, using methods at once authoritarian and incantatory, had built a powerful team, capable of challenging Real Madrid, and all but capable of winning the European Cup. Herrera joined Inter as their new manager, and Moratti, according to Solti, told him, 'I would like to employ you as "manager" of my club.'

The word 'manager' must be interpreted somewhat loosely. 'Fixer' would come a little nearer to Solti's subsequent functions. Public relations played a part in it. We may take with a grain of salt Solti's claim that he was sent to report on Inter's opponents in European tournaments. Though Keith Botsford and I would, poring through agency photographs in Vienna, turn up photographs of Solti, Italo Allodi, Herrera and Moratti exulting with the European Cup at Prater Stadium after the 1964 European Cup final, Solti had no credentials as a football analyst.

Wheeling and dealing was more in his line. Thus he writes that in 1963 he went twice to Liverpool to obtain dates favourable to Inter for their two legs against Everton. On his first trip, he says, he failed. Moratti sacked him again, according to Solti. But then he was allowed to try again, and succeeded. So his job was restored to him.

The then chairman of Everton, John Moores, remembers meeting Solti in Milan: he was, in fact, the only official from Inter with whom there was any contact. Moores said that Solti made 'a very good job' of providing accommodation and facilities for training. But that was just the tip of the iceberg. 'What does the manager do for a big professional club?' asks Solti, plaintively, in his odd memoir. 'It is a hard question to answer, because it is a road full of obstacles and twists and turns.' Indeed.

There was none more familiar with the 'twists and turns' than Italo Allodi, in the late 1960s and through much of the 1970s probably the most powerful man in Italian football. Like

Franchi, his origins were unexceptional. He was a professional footballer of modest accomplishments, who played for Mantova. Subsequently, he became the club secretary, and played a major part in the brief rise of the team into the First Division, Serie A.

Angelo Moratti of Inter, known as *il gran petrolifero*, the great oil man, plucked him out of the chorus and made him secretary of Inter. At Inter, Solti became Allodi's familiar, and his fixer. Wheeling, dealing and manipulating in the transfer market, Allodi became very rich. He acquired a splendid collection of paintings, which he often conferred in the shape of gifts. Gifts, indeed, were his stock-in-trade, from his early days in Mantua. He believed in liberally oiling the wheels, not least when it came to journalists and referees. From Inter, Allodi went, as general manager, to Juventus. Solti followed.

I met Allodi for the first time in May 1973, when we sat side by side at a roulette table in the Jugoslavia Hotel in Belgrade. He was playing; I wasn't. Juventus were about to meet Ajax in the final of the European Cup. At that time, I knew nothing of what had gone on over Lobo. Allodi was genial and friendly, an elegant, affable man, who would instantly forget me.

The next time I met him, strangely enough, was again in a hotel just before a European Cup final. It was at the Excelsior Hotel, in the Via Veneto, in Rome. Liverpool were to meet Borussia Monchengladbach that evening in the 1977 final. Seeing me standing in the foyer, Allodi marched across, shook me by the hand and said, 'We don't know each other, but I am Italo Allodi. I should like to talk to you.'

When, outside the Olympic Stadium before the match, I reported the meeting to Enzo Bearzot, team manager of Italy and Allodi's mortal foe, he burst out laughing. 'You don't know what riches are about to drop upon you from the clouds!' he said. But Allodi and I never met again.

All this is the preamble to a strange interview Allodi gave the Milanese daily paper *Il Giornale*, some time later. Was he upset, the interviewer asked him, by Glanville's continuing campaign against him? Yes, said Allodi, especially because, when Glanville was ill, 'I was one of those who sent money so he could stay in Italy.'

This was bizarre. I had indeed been ill in Italy, and had had to return from Florence to London for operations on my back, early in 1954, some 19 years before I met Allodi, and 23 years before he approached me in Rome and said that we had never met before. Far from staying in Italy, I had had to leave. I wrote a letter to *Il Giornale*, which they published, pointing this out.

Allodi's reply was more bizarre still. Perhaps, he said, I had forgotten my friend Mauro Franceschini, the youth soccer coach who worked in Florence. Well, it was through him 'that I and others sent money'.

This was, in its perverse way, shrewd of Allodi, for he knew he could not be contradicted.

For Mauro Franceschini, a few years earlier, had disappeared in mysterious, even sinister, circumstances. His car, its doors open with his passport still below the dashboard, was found one day beside the river Arno. Of Mauro, not a sign. There never has been. Did he kill himself? Was he murdered? Did he simply – the least likely explanation – contrive to disappear? To this day, no one knows.

But Allodi, by then appointed as head of the Coverciano coaching centre, would have met several old, mutual friends of Mauro and myself, would have known of our own friendship, would have picked up the fact that I'd been ill in Florence all those years ago, and made his own odd concoction out of the ingredients.

Shortly after our revelations in the *Sunday Times*, Allodi was off to West Germany for the World Cup. He had, for reasons obscure to most people, been made general manager of the Italian team – he and Juventus had already parted company – and the expedition was an utter disaster. The Italians took up their quarters at Ludwigsberg, in Bavaria, in a pleasant hotel. There, Gerry Harrison, of Anglia Television, and I repaired from Munich, a few days before the start of the tournament.

Nothing untoward happened. I glimpsed Allodi in the distance, but we did not speak. The following day, a short news item appeared on the sports page of the Milanese daily *Corriere Della Sera*, proving that not all Italian football journalists of that era, despite the hysterical response to the Solti revelations, lived comfortably in Allodi's pocket. Brian Glanville had come to Ludwigsberg, it said, and had been received by the players as though he were Father Christmas. 'But Allodi did a slalom to avoid him.'

Next day, when I was safely out of sight, Allodi roared and ranted. He had *not* done a slalom to avoid me, he informed a bewildered group of reporters, some not even Italian. If anything, it was I who had avoided him. But he'd bring me into court. *Magari* – even preferably – in England. Yes, in England! But it never happened.

Enzo Bearzot, the future World Cup-winning manager, was assistant manager of the Italian team then, and it took him nearly fifteen years to forgive Allodi for what happened in West Germany over the final group game against Poland. Defeat would mean Italy's elimination, after a stormy passage. In the opening game, in which it looked for a long time as if Haiti would beat them, Giorgio Chinaglia, once a Cardiff schoolboy and a Swansea centre-forward, was substituted. Infuriated, he made a lewd sign at the manager, Ferruccio Valcareggi, as he left the field, then went into the dressing room and smashed a number of mineral-water bottles. Full, said his critics. Empty, said Chinaglia.

In the event, Poland, whose fine team had already eliminated England in the qualifying rounds, beat Italy 2–1 in Stuttgart. Strange rumours were current at the time. Some months after the World Cup, Kazimierz Gorski, manager of the Polish team, gave an extraordinary interview to a Polish daily paper. In it, he said that 'wealthy Italian supporters' had come to the Polish training camp and offered money to the Poles to lose. They'd been refused. Later, clearly under pressure from his own Federation, perhaps because Poland were due to meet Italy again in the imminent European Championship qualifiers, he withdrew the allegation.

There were other rumours that bribes had been offered by Italian players to Polish players. These I myself followed up, obtaining statements from both Kazimierz Deyna, the Polish captain, when he played for Manchester City, and Jan Tomaszewski, the flamboyant goalkeeper, when he was playing for Beerschot in Antwerp. Both confirmed the story, but Bearzot, who was clearly anxious for the truth to come out, impatiently brushed this aside. Something had plainly happened, something grave enough to move Bearzot never to bring the Italian team to Coverciano, its former base, for training, so long as Allodi was in charge; but the case remains largely unproven.

With the World Cup over – very quickly – for Italy, violent criticisms descended on Allodi's head. He went, as did Valcareggi. A duo was installed, Bearzot and the former international centre-half Fulvio Bernardini.

What would become of Allodi? There were various speculations. Then, surprisingly, he was asked by the Italian FA to prepare a report on the future of Coverciano. I was among those who heaped scorn on the idea, on the sinecure.

Strange that so many crucial meetings in this saga took place in 'official' hotels, on the occasion of a European Cup final. So it was again in Paris in 1975, when Leeds United played Bayern Munich in what turned out to be another highly controversial game, strangely refereed. In the Hotel Crillon, Artemio Franchi took me aside and explained to me how Allodi had been neutralised.

Yes, he said, Allodi had been commissioned to draw up a plan for Coverciano. But who was to say that plan would ever be implemented? Who indeed? But it was. All Franchi's ingenuity turned out, not for the first or last time, to be so much camouflage. Allodi not only drew up a grandiose plan. He was appointed, on an excellent salary, to run Coverciano himself.

Artemio Franchi, alas, is now dead: in a wretched motor accident outside his native Siena. Such are the undercurrents and labyrinthine conspiracies of Italian public life that it has even been suggested there that his death was not an accident. Franchi, a captain of one of the *contrade* in the historic Palio horse race, where each *contrada* runs a horse, ran head on into a lorry, when driving back from a *contrada* meeting. He was, the conspiracy theorists point out, an excellent driver, well used to the road between Siena and Florence.

On the occasions I have been asked to categorise Franchi, I have replied, 'A man who prefers to be honest.' Given the ambience of Italian business and football, and given the nature of Franchi's own career, it was sometimes a difficult ambition.

A Sienese, Franchi was the son of a chef who worked in the

fashionable Sabatini's restaurant in Florence's Via Tornabuoni. Franchi was a bright, quick, subtle fellow, who got himself a university education, and eventually became secretary to Florence's chief football club, Fiorentina.

There he drew the attention of a Big Wheel, Dante Berretti, the top man in Tuscan football and a power broker. How well I still remember Berretti's massive, opulent presence in the Tribune of Honour – the directors' box – at Fiorentina's matches in the early 1950s. He was a huge, handsome man, with abundant, carefully brushed-back, grey hair. He it was who had Franchi made head of the so-called Semi-Professional League, which then had its headquarters in Florence. It was rather like being secretary of the English Third and Fourth Divisions.

Thereafter, it was upwards all the way. In due course the able Franchi became president of the FIGC – the Italian FA – and then of UEFA, with a seat on the FIFA Council. He was a beguiling man, humorous, lively, immensely intelligent. In Italy, he was known as 'a diplomat', with all the ambiguity attached to such a word. If there was any general criticism of him, it was for his tendency to '*insabbiare*', a word which means to cover something over with sand. At this, he was adept. Problems tended to be obfuscated, rather than confronted.

There was no better example of this than the appointment of Italo Allodi to run the Coverciano coaching centre in 1975; a decision which enraged decent men in Italian football. Fulvio Bernardini acidly remarked that the only thing Allodi was qualified to teach was how to give gold watches to referees. But Allodi stayed, spending huge sums of money on so-called Super Courses for would-be managers, sending them all over the world to study the game. He even, in 1982 during the course of the World Cup finals, held a convention of managers and coaches at Coverciano, in the course of which one of his minions, the Tuscan manager Eugenio Fascetti, made a vicious assault on Enzo Bearzot. He accused him of disgracing Italian football with the tactics he was using in Spain. Bearzot and Italy went on to win the World Cup. Fascetti was fined.

*

But I am getting ahead of our story. Publication of it in the *Sunday Times* in April 1974 led at once to an almost hysterical closing of ranks by the Italian media, a despicable *omertà*. In the sense, at least, that though the clamour was great, there was dead silence on the subject of our specific accusations. The newspaper for which I myself had written for many years, the *Corriere Dello Sport* of Rome, was bold enough to publish a translation of the whole long article on its back page. But in the editorials on its front page, it constantly attacked us.

'I had to do that,' Mario Gismondi, then its editor, explained to me. 'Otherwise, they would have said I was playing Lazio's game against Juventus.' Lazio, the Roman club, at that time being a powerful challenger to Turin's Juventus in the Italian championships.

A senior correspondent of *Corriere Dello Sport* came over to London in May for a match at Wembley between England and Argentina, and told Botsford and me, during a reception at the Argentine Embassy, 'I'd have given a year of my life for a scoop like that.'

There were, and still are, plenty of decent, honest, upright men in Italian football, but their voices then were scarcely heard above the screams of outrage and denial. Why traduce Italian football? newspaper demanded. Why not investigate the way England manipulated its way to the World Cup in 1966? Had there ever been an atom of evidence, rather than supposition, on the subject. I am sure we would have been the first to investigate. But this was no more than a question of *tu quoque*, an attempt to avoid at all costs looking facts in the face.

Peculiarly shocking and disappointing to me was the behaviour of the supposed doyen of Italian sporting journalists, Gianni Brera: though I suppose it was pretty naive of me to have expected any better.

Brera, a sturdy little man who prided himself on not being an Italian but a Lombard, from Milan, was a quirky, idiosyncratic writer, with curiously bigoted and inflexible attitudes over race and geography. Italians, he insisted – and a surprising number of people in the game took him seriously – hadn't the strength and stamina to play the running game Anglo-Saxons played. He resented the emergence, at that period, of footballers from

Italy's Deep South, though they were clearly enriching the sport. But I had expected him to be the first, rather than the last, to rise up in arms over the slimy stratagems which Botsford and I had exposed.

Instead, at first, not a word. Finally, I discovered that he had written something spiteful and malicious about me, a brief paragraph in *Guerin Sportivo*, then a weekly newspaper. Knowing nothing of it at the time, I greeted him cordially when I saw him during the 1974 World Cup.

Later, I took him up on his treachery, and there were violent exchanges in Italian magazines. The truth was, and he knew it, that he had not done his duty, that he had let down his readers, Italian football, and football at large. But goodness knows he was not alone.

Eight years later, immediately after Italy had won the World Cup in Spain, two young investigative journalists, Oliviero Beha and Roberto Chiodi, had the astonishing courage to allege that an early, drawn game against the Cameroons in Vigo had been bought. The Camorra, it seems, were involved. I am quite sure Enzo Bearzot, manager of that Italian team, could not have been. True or not, it heralded a new era in Italian sports journalism: a new, incorruptible, kind of writer.

One curious defence mechanism employed against our discoveries was to accuse the English of mounting a campaign to undermine Italy's chances in the ensuing World Cup: conspiracy theory indeed! Needless to say it was Italo Allodi who propounded it. By contrast, Gian Paolo Ormezzano, the exuberant, ebullient young editor of the Turin daily, *Tuttosport*, made an honest and open response. 'The fact remains,' he wrote, 'that it's a nasty affair for our football; but to confront it is the only way to come out of it. And it's not to be excluded that, in the end, the matter will reduce itself to the disappearance of a very dangerous personage, and to the umpteenth lesson in life-journalism given to us by the English.'

Giampiero Boniperti, Juventus' President, maintained his club were completely extraneous to the affair, and that its lawyers had been consulted with a view to taking legal action. They never did. Nobody did. How could they? There was nothing they could properly dispute.

Someone else did threaten to sue us. Not Boniperti, not Allodi, but an Englishman, Sir Harold Thompson.

Thompson might be described as a complex, perverse and gifted man. He was a celebrated scientist, specialising in Infrared Spectroscopy, a professor at St John's College, Oxford – a university where he had first arrived as an undergraduate from Yorkshire, winning a soccer Blue. He had been at once the creator and the destroyer of Pegasus football club, whose wonderfully romantic story began in Oxford in 1948. Composed of players from both universities, most of them initially war veterans, such as Ken Shearwood and Tony Pawson, it took wing with astonishing speed. In no time at all, the Pegasus club had delighted a packed Wembley stadium with a superlative win over Bishop Auckland, mightiest of Cup fighters, in the Amateur final at Wembley. They won the Cup again, thrashing Harwich and Parkeston 6–0.

But as the years went by the Cambridge men tended to go off to join the Corinthian Casuals, and mature students gave way to beardless boys. Thompson now became a menace rather than an advantage. Younger undergraduates disliked being cajoled, even bullied. Nor could they stand up to Thompson as easily as men who had fought in the Western Desert or commanded little ships. John Tanner, centre-forward for Pegasus in their great days and later a club official, was once so exasperated by Thompson in the dressing room before a game that he gave him a black eye. Thompson walked round the field saying, as he pointed to the eye, 'Look what Tanner did to me!'

Within the Football Association, he was a would-be *eminence grise*, a perpetual problem to the powerful secretary Sir Stanley Rous, who at times would swat him like a fly. But Thompson had his revenge. When, in 1962, the time came, after 28 largely remarkable years in office, for Rous to retire and become President of FIFA, he wanted his protégé, Walter Winterbottom, to succeed him.

Winterbottom seemed an ideal candidate. Since 1946, he had been both England team manager and director of coaching, and was a somewhat clerkly figure who had, in fact, once played for Manchester United. Thompson set about seeing that he did not get the job. In the event, an article in the *Observer* by

Clement Freud played into his hands. It trumpeted the praises of Winterbottom, taking it for granted that he would be elected. Thompson took it doggedly to each member of the electing committee, asking them whether they meant to be manipulated by a single newspaper. So they chose the compromise candidate, the obscure treasurer Denis Follows.

Rous disliked Follows, and the antipathy was reciprocated. Follows, a former secretary of the British Air Line Pilots Association (BALPA), was a small, somewhat pompous man, with no great presence; though in due course he would stand up to the Government, in his future capacity as chief executive of the Olympic Committee, and insist Britain send a team to the Moscow Olympic Games, in the face of the American-led boycott.

So Thompson had his way and Follows was elected. That evening, I was asked to interview him for BBC radio. As we waited outside the studio, he said, 'The secretary is the servant of the Association, and we all know what happened. The servant became the master.' Meaning Rous. And thank goodness Rous did become the master of an FA Council largely composed of pathetic, bumbling, insular old fossils.

Playing Mr Nice Guy to the FA did Follows little good. Thompson persecuted him. The genie was out of the bottle. He was a king-maker now, and a king-breaker, too. His constant bullying and pestering made Follows' life a misery. In the end, he succumbed to a heart attack. So Thompson, equally known to pester stewardesses on the England team's charter aircraft and the wives of fellow officials at banquets, set about making another king: Ted Croker. Again, he succeeded. Croker, once an heroic pilot, then a successful businessman and an ex-player for Charlton Athletic, became the new secretary in due course. But he was made of sterner stuff than Follows, and wouldn't be bullied. Thompson was frustrated.

In 1974, not long before our investigation and its results were published, Thompson had been largely instrumental in getting rid of Sir Alf Ramsey, the England team manager, winner in 1966 of the World Cup. In this, I do not think Thompson was wrong. The decision was jointly arrived at by the Senior International Committee, alias the old selection committee, now deprived of any such function. The usual bunch of fence-sitters, they would probably have allowed Ramsey to carry on, though for at least two years it had been perfectly clear that he had lost his way.

In the spring of 1972, his mistaken tactics had made a present of the home first leg of the European Nations Cup quarter-final to West Germany, who won the match 3–1. For the return leg, played in Berlin, he seemed to lose his nerve, and picked a ridiculously defensive side, full of harsh, physical players, which never had a chance of winning and eventually managed a useless 0–0 draw. 'The whole England team,' said the brilliant, blond German inside-left, Gunter Netzer, 'has autographed my leg.'

Technically, Thompson was quite justified in saying that he alone had not made the decision. But as the unquestioned moving spirit, it was Thompson who was seen as responsible, and his bitterness towards the press was great. It was said that he'd never forgiven Ramsey for telling him, years earlier, not to blow cigar smoke in his young players' faces. It may even have been true. Thompson was not a man easily to forget a slight, real or imagined. But there were moments when paranoia appeared to set in; and soon we should see one of them.

Thompson had just been made a vice-president of UEFA, and, as such, Botsford and I felt it our duty to give him a complete and regular briefing on the Solti–Lobo Affair, and its development. He seemed pleased enough at the time. But the following December in Budapest, of all places, where he attended his first meeting of the UEFA Executive Committee, he gave vent to an extraordinary outburst.

When Solti and his deeds were about to be discussed, Artemio Franchi, the UEFA President, volunteered to leave the room, since he was an Italian and an Italian club was involved. No, not a bit of it, said Thompson. There was no reason for him to go. He knew these journalists, and their fabrications. Why, they had recently and falsely accused him of getting rid of Alf Ramsey!

This bizarre explosion was faithfully reported to Botsford and myself by our Deep Throat in Budapest; and consequently reported by us in the *Sunday Times*. This produced, almost at once, a letter to me from Thompson, accusing us of 'printing quotations and statements about me which are false, and further, which reflect upon my integrity in football affairs. I am considering what further action should be taken.' I should not, he pursued, call upon his friendship or help in the future, 'for I cannot deal with people who write these cheap untruths'.

No action was taken, for our statements were not untrue. Indeed, we heard that Thompson's chief preoccupation, and that of certain members of UEFA, was to find out how we had received so accurate a report from the meeting. Apprised of what had happened, the Secretary of the Football League, Alan Hardaker, who detested Thompson and could show a nice, dry wit at times, remarked to me, 'They could take his braces off in those meetings, put them back on again, and he still wouldn't know what had happened.'

It was not much consolation, however, to know that the man who should have been our chief ally, the scourge of corruption in European football, defender of the English game, had effectively lined up with the opposition. For whatever perverse, tormented reasons.

One step, at least, was belatedly taken at the Budapest meeting. Solti was declared *persona non grata* in European football, a fairly empty gesture now that his cover had been 'blown', but an acknowledgement, at least, that dirty work had been afoot. Curiously enough, when Solti did go into a Hungarian gaol, it had nothing to do with football. He was stopped at the frontier and found to be in possession of a valuable Hebrew text, which he was trying to smuggle out of the country.

The Executive Committee also received the report of the two-man *ad hoc* committee which had been set up soon after the revelations by the *Sunday Times*, in an almost empty gesture. The members of this committee were a distinguished French lawyer, Jacques Georges – who would later become president of UEFA but hardly distinguish himself with his ill-timed, intemperate comments on the Hillsborough disaster – and a Swiss called Lucien Schmidlin. In the event, a mountain of seven months' labour produced a mere mouse of a report. Hardly astonishing, perhaps, given the fact that Georges and Schmidlin had no investigative arm, knew little or nothing other than what they had learnt from Botsford and myself, and could hardly put their witnesses, such as Italo Allodi, on oath.

The *ad hoc* committee reported on the ludicrous identity parade at the Hotel Atlantis, the previous year. Louis Wouters, the Belgian lawyer, furnished them with some interesting rationalisations. 'Solti,' he told them, 'is clearly guilty, and therefore why should the Disciplinary Committee bother with him?' Or, for that matter, interview officials of Juventus, since there was no evidence that any was implicated. None, after all, had visited Lisbon.

As for the extraordinary letter Hans Bangerter, the UEFA secretary, rushed off to Juventus, exculpating them, the Disciplinary Committee had discussed two options. We know, of course, that these were either to declare Solti *persona non grata* or to circularise clubs about him, and we also know neither was embraced.

As for Juventus, the *ad hoc* committee had scarcely bothered with them. They listened to the tape, discussed its implications with Wouters, and took another opinion, allegedly of no assistance, from the chairman of the Finnish FA, Poriola. That was that. The only evidence to appear in the committee's report consisted of internal UEFA documents, and even some of these were not given in full. The lack of will seriously to pursue so serious a case was evident. It was perfectly plain that, had it not been for the publication of our *Sunday Times* report, sleeping dogs would have been left to lie.

In March 1975, we published in the newspaper a chart which showed how mysteriously often the Big Three of Italian football, Milan, Inter and Juventus, had their European matches controlled by the same small group of referees. Dienst of Switzerland, who had refereed the World Cup final of 1966 at Wembley and the 1968 European Nations Cup final in Rome (refusing a manifest penalty to Yugoslavia, who thus failed to beat Italy), came top of the list, with the Italian clubs winning six and drawing three of the games he refereed. Tschenscher, the West German, took half a dozen games: three wins, two draws, one loss.

Ortiz de Mendibil, who refereed the notorious Inter–Liverpool semi-final of 1965, and a highly controversial Twente

Enschede–Juventus Fairs Cup quarter-final years later – Twente complained bitterly to me afterwards that they thought his refereeing in Turin had been shamefully biased – did not control a single game which was lost by an Italian team. Five wins out of five. Yet despite his controversial record, Ortiz de Mendibil, who allegedly had a gravely sick child, requiring expensive medical attention, was actually on UEFA's Referees' Committee. The Austrian Seipelt, despite his long acquaintance with Solti being well known, was the committee's chairman. Seipelt it was, of course, who had effectively disqualified Lobo.

As an exquisite envoi to the Budapest meeting, Lucien Schmidlin suggested that since Lobo had broken UEFA's rule of silence, he himself should be punished. A case of killing the messenger, indeed. Dr Franchi turned the idea down flat, but it showed clearly enough which way the wind was blowing. Lobo was regarded not as a hero, a very decent man, but an embarrassing nuisance.

As our investigation proceeded, other wretched cases came into the light. That, for example, of the Standard Liège–Inter European Cup quarter-final second leg in 1972, and the extraordinary behaviour of the referee, Gyula Emsberger, and a man called Istvan Zsolt.

Zsolt was a well-known former international referee, a known intimate of Solti, and in 'civilian' life once manager of the Hungarian State Theatre. Emsberger, on the line in 1966 at another notorious game, the Inter–Real Madrid European Cup semi-final when Vadas wouldn't be bought, refereed the Standard–Inter game, but there was a puzzle over his report, which had led to his suspension from two international games. He had not filled it in himself; he had inexplicably left it to Zsolt. Who, in completing the form, had equally inexplicably left out the fact that the Inter right-half, Bedin, had been cautioned; inexplicable too was Zsolt's very presence in Liège.

Once, when Zsolt came to London, the Hungarian actor and journalist, the late Leslie Vernon, brought him to my house, where I asked him about this curious event; and about a strange decision he once gave in a Switzerland–Italy game. It was hard to glean any cogent answer. He was a thoroughly evasive man.

In Tatabanya, when Botsford and I were doing our December sweep through Europe on the Solti trail, from Vienna to Budapest to Switzerland to Milan, we had interviewed Emsberger. But the man who would pin down both him and Gyorgy Vadas was the talented Hungarian investigative journalist Peter Borenich. He it was who would obtain from Vadas the full statement on the Inter–Real Madrid game which Botsford and I, subsequently, would try in vain to get him to make, in Budapest; at Budapest Radio, where all (football) roads meet. Borenich it was who would have Zsolt squirming, over the Liège affair.

Inter's Bedin had been booked once already in the European Cup that season. This meant that, if he was booked again, he would automatically be suspended from the next tie. But why had Emsberger allowed Zsolt to fill in his report at all? Under questioning from Borenich, he gave an explanation. Of a sort.

'Because he had completed many reports and had seen the game,' said Emsberger. (Let me say, in passing, that the translation is the work of the admirable Charlie Coutts, a Scot from Aberdeen, once a Japanese prisoner-of-war, who had for years been settled in Hungary, broadcasting in English for Radio Budapest, working for Reuter.) 'On the plane going home, I asked him to fill it up for me in German. He did. I posted it when we arrived in Budapest. The next time we met, I asked Zsolt why he had not written in the names of both suspended players. To which he replied, "Was it not just one yellow card?"'

'No, two,' said Emsberger. Zsolt asked him when he had given it. Two minutes from time, was the reply. Then, said Zsolt, he had not seen it. He had already been on his way down from the stand to ask the UEFA observers what they had thought of the refereeing. A curious mission.

But why, Borenich asked Emsberger, ask Zsolt to complete the report at all? 'Because I do not write well in German,' was the answer. 'My son usually helped me, once I was back home. After this incident, I was suspended for two international games. If one is as stupid as I was, the punishment is deserved.'

'Why was Zsolt at the game?' asked Borenich; the $64,000 question.

'I don't know. He never says much. A taciturn character.'

He did not say very much, at least of any relevance, when Borenich put him under pressure. A bold thing to do. Zsolt instantly called up senior people at Budapest Radio – senior figures in Hungarian football, too – to try to scare Borenich off the trail. But Borenich would not be scared.

Wriggling and squirming, as he did when he sat in my own house, Zsolt tried to evade hard questions behind a smokescreen of pompous verbiage. 'Your story is badly drafted. As a former referee, let me put you on the right lines. The story falls down, no matter how well it may sound, when it pictures the referee as not dictating the name of the player to whom he gave a yellow card. It falls down, because it was not drafted with expert knowledge. At the end of a game, if a referee, for any reason, asks someone to enter up the UEFA report sheet, then he tells that person what happens during the game, and details serious violations of the rules . . .'

Zsolt, clearly, was on the ropes; blocking, stonewalling and evading. The difference, however, between Borenich's investigation and my own was that he virtually had to take his career in his hands, and face the prospect of Zsolt calling up the peculiar mafia of Hungarian football big-wigs who had important positions in radio. This Zsolt did, but to Borenich's enormous credit – Hungary then was a very different place indeed, under Communism, than Hungary now – he still persisted. All roads, as Botsford and I found in our inquiries, seemed to lead to Budapest, and winding, circuitous roads they were. Hard, at times, not to remember the old definition of a Hungarian as the only man who can go into a revolving door behind you and come out in front of you.

Borenich would eventually put the results of his fearless investigations into a short book called *Only the Ball Has a Skin*. Hungarian football in the 1980s was an absolute sink of iniquity. Infinite games had been bought, sold and fixed. Many of the leaders of the game were disgraced, but there was always a sufficient quorum of honest men to ensure a better future for football there. Men like Borenich himself – and Gyorgy Vadas.

Keith Botsford and I had known about Gyorgy Vadas, about the Inter-Real Madrid game, for a long time. That Vadas had been approached by the ineffable Solti, had refused to 'bend' the game in favour of Inter, and had suffered as a referee in consequence. That was one thing. Proving it, getting any kind of confirmation, was emphatically another.

We had been to Budapsest, had tried and failed. What a vile visit that was! I was in one hotel; Keith, upon the hill above the splendid city, in another. Keith had been ill. I had waited endlessly in my hotel room for the call which would tell us that Vadas would see us. Cyril Connolly once wrote that the writer knows that he must always, in the end, return to the hotel room. But hotel rooms in those pre-war times were not the soulless, anonymous, debilitating rooms of an American hotel. I waited and waited. Keith continued to suffer. At long last, Vadas agreed that he would see us.

The meeting took place in the canteen of Radio Budapest; such a drab, dreary, sombre setting when one thought of the rogue millionaires, the great occasions, the grand conspiracies, which were implicated. Vadas was a large, good-natured, anxious man. He wouldn't talk. If we told him this and that, he might confirm it. He would go no further. Fear was in the air; he had suffered sufficiently. The walls could still close in on him. Perhaps he'd come to England; if we paid for the trip, he might talk to us there. We were willing to accommodate him but it never happened. It was Borenich, fellow employee at Radio Budapest, where all things led and all things seemed to happen, who eventually cracked it. After endless insistence.

And what creatures now crawled out from under stones! Solti, Allodi, Moratti. The ineffable secretary of the Hungarian Football Federation.

Back to 1966. The semi-final second leg, at San Siro, as it had been for the past two years, years in which Solti, and Inter, had suborned the referee. Now they needed to do so again. Needed to win, to go forward to the final. Under the steady pressure of Borenich's questioning, Vadas confirmed and elaborated on all the things we had already heard. It was a little late in the day, but yet another large, significant, repellent piece fitted into the arcane jigsaw. Let me quote the interview directly from Borenich's admirable book.

VADAS   I was approached in Milan by Solti. He was with us from morning to night. The only time he was not around was when we were sleeping. He was making sure we did not encounter anyone from Real Madrid. On the one occasion I was left alone with him in my room, he made a very serious proposition. Basically I was to referee the game so as to ensure that Real did not go forward ... I have never talked about this in public. The sum was enough to buy five, maybe six, Mercedes cars. [The going rate had certainly diminished by the time Solti approached Lobo.] To be paid in dollars. Not negligible. Starting from an initial payment in the event of a straightforward win by Inter, doubled for a win by a penalty award at the end of the game, quintupled for a win during extra time, multiplied ten times for a win by a penalty during extra time ...

     I told my two linesmen colleagues immediately. And we went out on to the pitch determined to control that game correctly and honestly. We may have made some wrong decisions, but of this I am certain: in our minds we were motivated by one aim, to control the game correctly.

BORENICH   I understand you met Angelo Moratti, the Inter president, in his house.

VADAS   It was a pleasant meeting. At 11 o'clock on the morning of the match, Inter's general secretary, Italo Allodi, accompanied by Dezso Solti, came to the hotel. They brought greetings from Signor Moratti, and an invitation to visit him at his villa. What a marvellous place it was! Name anything beautiful or wonderful, that place had it! ... We lunched in a pleasant environment and in an excellent mood ... To start the lunch, Signor Moratti presented the three of us with a gold watch. Then, as the meal progressed, he told Solti that he should buy us this or that. We just ducked our heads in wonder . . . Colour television sets – very rare in Hungary in those days – tape recorders, record players, electric razors, radios and other electrical devices. We three Hungarians looked at each other in amazement.

Solti showed great respect for Moratti. His behaviour was almost servile . . . At the same time, I knew that Solti was not employed by Inter, as such. Moratti and the Inter leadership commissioned him for successfully arranging this and that.

BORENICH   What was Solti's reaction at the end of the game, when Inter went out?

VADAS   His behaviour was not that of a sportsman. At half-time he had started bawling that I had refused three 'justified' penalties . . . I said to him, 'You must have been watching another game.'

BORENICH   And at the end, what did Solti say?

VADAS   Shouted and screamed that my refereeing had been a swindle. Threatened to spare no effort to have me struck off the FIFA list of referees. That was a threat he was able to make good. The screwing had been well done before I arrived home. At five o'clock in the morning after the game, Solti phoned the general secretary of the Hungarian Federation, Gyorgy Honti, to tell him that, in Solti's words, I had cheated them out of the game . . . Later, I was to learn that Solti told Honti, 'If you value my friendship, you must act to have him removed from both the FIFA and the Hungarian senior list of referees. I have never experienced such an example of unfair refereeing . . .' I am sure Solti held me responsible

for a loss of $30,000. That was what he said
he had lost through Inter failing to qualify.

Translation, again, by Charlie Coutts.

On his return to Budapest, Vadas was confronted by an
enraged Honti: 'Look at all the terrible things the Italian papers
have been saying about you!' Vadas was withdrawn from all
those UEFA games he had been chosen to referee, and removed
from the FIFA list. He reported the attempted bribery, but no
action was ever taken.

Nor was any taken when Botsford and I eventually dug up,
in Holland, the document Solti – that 'madman going around'
– had signed on behalf of Juventus in 1971. Damning evidence?
Not a bit of it. UEFA's response was that 1971 was 1971.
There was no indication that Solti was in any way connected
with them in 1973, when he went to see and try to suborn
Lobo in Lisbon.

A telephone call from a Dutch friend, then the general
manager of Twente Enschede, had put us on the track. He
remembered meeting Solti a few years earlier, he said, when he
came to Enschede and tried to persuade Twente to swop the
dates of their ties against Juventus in the Inter-Cities Fairs
Cup. Keith, on a typical inspiration, surmised that a letter might
have been signed, dropped in at Enschede on his way to
Germany, and found his guess was right. A photograph of
the letter was duly published in the *Sunday Times*, but there
was no sequel. Hans Bangerter's deplorable letter had set the
scene and the tone. There would always be reasons, good
or bad, for doing nothing about Juventus, perhaps, with its
FIAT backing, the most powerful club in Europe. Even in the
world.

Not that any great zeal was shown in other quarters, England
included. Harold Thompson, with his paranoiac outburst, had
not exactly set the tone, but if we did not meet outright hostility
we met massive indifference. A senior official of the Football
Association was heard to remark, 'I wish they hadn't started it,
because they'll never finish it.' Nor did we.

There was much more that we heard in our investigations in
Europe, above all in Budapest and Vienna, where the sweet,

cosy, outdoor-café life – of which Solti had been a part and Bela Guttmann still was – continued as it had for generations. How a certain official had protested violently because half the bribe he had been promised was pocketed by the go-between. How another was seen late at night in a Turkish hotel, having money counted into his hand.

And Allodi? He continued to flourish like the green bay tree, till illness overtook him in the late 1980s. It says much for the morality of Italian football that there was never any lack of major clubs panting for his services. Leaving Coverciano, he moved, so to speak, just down the road, to become general manager of Fiorentina. Thence, when things did not go as well as the club hoped, he moved down South to Naples.

There were occasional displeasures. Enzo Bearzot, in his deep seriousness and integrity the very antithesis of all Allodi seemed to stand for, was slow to forgive. Nor would he, indeed, till 1989, when meeting a clearly debilitated Allodi at Coverciano of all places, he made peace.

Relations were not as rosy in 1984, nearly ten years after whatever happened in West Germany during the World Cup. Once again, Allodi was threatening revenge; though once again, it was all huff and puff. He never succeeded; never sued.

Interviewed by the weekly magazine *L'Espresso*, Bearzot was asked whether he still had it in for Allodi. He replied somewhat opaquely, 'Not in that way.' But he considered Allodi 'an able but dangerous person'. He would say no more, for fear of 'poisoning the ambience'.

A furious Mr Fix-It protested. Bearzot's success in Spain, two years before, in the teeth of the opposition Allodi encouraged from Coverciano, had made Allodi's position there untenable. So he joined a complaisant Fiorentina; but he'd been planning, he said, to resign that job in 1985, in order to rejoin the Italian Federation. Now, he proclaimed, he was ready to resign straight away, so he could be free to sue Bearzot in the courts. Hopes that his case would be taken up by a Federation official, the grandly named Procurator of the Football Federation, had been disappointed. National team managers, it transpired, were too grand to be proceeded against in this way. Bearzot, who'd made

Allodi's removal from Coverciano a condition for renewing his contract, was inviolable.

Allodi, needless to say, did not resign, and he did not sue. His next little bit of bother came when he was in Naples. A strange anticlimax. The Italian Federation was carrying out an inquiry into the fixing of matches. Police investigating drug dealing had by chance stumbled on a network of corruption, run by gamblers. Allodi's name had been linked with a dubious character. Little more than that. It seemed the merest peccadillo by comparison with what had gone on, unpunished and largely undetected, in the Years of the Golden Fix.

But the prosecuting lawyer, acting on behalf of the Italian Federation, launched the most extraordinary attack on Allodi and his machinations. One agreed with almost every word, but wondered why this was happening now, in such a marginal context. The Freudian phenomenon of displacement seemed to be taking place. A great head of steam, a huge resentment, seemed to have been built up over the years, and here it was, finally being released.

Tearfully, Allodi protested that he was a pillar of rectitude, that he'd always kept himself respectable. When the tribunal gave its decision, it predictably exonerated him. How, after all, could it traduce a man who, when he did leave the Federation for Fiorentina, had the Italian sports press beating a path to his door, dedicating to him whole pages of sycophantic flattery? The man of whom Bearzot had said, 'How can I work when I've a Brutus at my back?' and who'd replied, 'If I'm Brutus, then he must think he's Caesar.' Who had bounced back with a vengeance; and a fortune. Nor would he ever lose that pitifully misplaced respect.

History repeats itself, wrote Karl Marx, the first time as tragedy, the second as farce. Rome, then, was in his mind, I recall, but not Roma. Not the famous, passionately supported, endlessly storm-tossed football club. But in the case of Roma, its president, Senator Dino Viola, and the case of the bribe that never was, the dictum will still serve.

In the semi-finals of the European Cup of 1984, Dundee United, managed by the explosive but effective Jim McLean, surpassed themselves by reaching the semi-finals. There they were drawn against Roma, whom they beat 2–0 in the first leg, at Tannadice. McLean, bouncing up and down on the bench, was heard to utter the words 'Italian bastards'; words which would not be forgiven or forgotten by the Roma players. Indeed, at the end of the second leg at the Olympic Stadium, Roma's footballers surrounded him and angrily abused him.

It was before the second leg, however, that there was dirty work at the crossroads. One day, Viola was approached by two people. One was Spartaco Landini, once a centre-half who played for Internazionale and even in the Italian World Cup team of 1966. The other was called Giampaolo Cominato, who had previously been general manager of two clubs, Bolzano and Avellino. The two made Viola an offer he couldn't refuse; or at least, he didn't. They could 'fix' Michel Vautrot, the eminent French referee, who was deputed to handle the second leg. All it needed was 100 million lire; about £50,000 at the time.

Viola agreed. Had he temporised, had he made even the most superficial inquiries, he must have learnt that Vautrot was the last referee to agree to be bought, that he was not only one of the best referees in Europe, but one of the most upright and honest. But conspiracy theory has been the name of the game – from chariot racing to football, through the Papal years – in Rome for a couple of thousand years now, and Viola clearly didn't need much convincing.

The two swindlers had made elaborate plans. The next stage in this *opera buffa* took place in a restaurant, the night before the game was due, where Viola's son and others took Vautrot out to dinner. It had been arranged, Landini and Cominato said, that a telephone call would be made to Vautrot during the meal. It duly was. Vautrot was called to the phone, and was baffled to be wished good luck by Cominato, calling himself Paolo. Be sure your sin will find you out! Had Cominato used one of the multiplicity of Italian first names that exist, he, Landini and Viola might have got away with it. But when the fond and foolish old Senator Viola heard that 'Paolo' had called, he jumped to the conclusion that it must be the well-known Italian referee Paolo Bergamo. It would cost him – and Bergamo – dear.

The game took place; I saw it myself and Roma won comfortably and deservedly, wiping out the deficit and going on to the final where they would lose on penalties against Liverpool. Viola was happy enough. Roma had come through; *ergo* it must have been money well spent. And Landini and Cominato went away to spend it. Vautrot, of course, was never even approached, let alone suborned.

That, doubtless, would have been that, had Viola, not long afterwards, run into Paolo Bergamo when they were both attending a refereeing course. The good old Senator blabbered on, ingenuously, about the 'fix', quite convinced that the astonished Bergamo had been a party to it. For thirteen months, Bergamo restled with his conscience, before it finally won. Should he or shouldn't he report what he knew, which was his statutory duty, to the Italian Federation? Finally he did. For delaying so long, he was suspended; but the delay was long enough to let Viola and Roma off the hook. For when an inquiry was held by the disciplinary body, the club and its president protested that it had come too late to be valid, that the bizarre statute of limitations in force at the time had been infringed.

What the statute laid down, an indulgent cheats' charter, was that any offence committed in a given season must be brought to trial before the end of the year which followed that season. To give the Italian Federation its due, it did its absolute utmost to circumvent the rule. Viola was brought to trial, but he slipped through the net. It was too late. Nor did he seem to lose any prestige or respect on this account. The rationalisation was that he was acting only to protect the interests of his club, convinced that if he did not bribe the referee then the opposition would.

What he had wanted to do, Viola insisted, was to give Landini and Cominato the money before the game, in order to disclose the identity of the 'Mr Big' whom he presumed to be behind them. Moreover, he pleaded that extortion had taken place; that the two tricksters had told him, in effect, give us the money, or your team will lose the match.

Landini, however, anxious to avoid being convicted for fraud by the State, insisted that the money had been paid to him *after* the game. He had, he claimed, the air tickets to prove as much; or at least to prove that he would not have been in a position to collect, the day before the game took place.

UEFA, however, had no such statute of limitation. They, in turn, 'tried' Viola, finding both him and Roma guilty of a serious offence. In consequence, Roma would be banned from the ensuing Cup Winners' Cup competition; a punishment which would cost them huge sums of money. Far more than 100 million lire.

Roma appealed, and to the general horror – shared, it must be said, in Italy itself, at least outside Rome – the sentence was commuted to a fine. Roma could play in the Cup Winners' Cup, after all. 'A scandalous decision!' thundered the *Gazzetta Dello Sport*, of Milan.

Fond and foolish old presidents, however, were a species to be found in Milan, as well as in Rome. When the devious Angelo Moratti departed Inter, and this world, his successor as president was Ivanoe Fraizzoli, a pompous manufacturer of clothing with a wife, nicknamed Lady Fraizzoli, who rejoiced in being in the public eye. By 1984, he was no longer president, and seemed to resent the fact. It is a little hard otherwise to explain, except in terms of his natural garrulity, why he did what he did at a banquet in Hamburg in 1984, held after Inter had played there in the UEFA Cup.

What he did, in brief, was to spill the beans about a notorious European Cup match played thirteen years earlier by Inter in Monchengladbach. At a moment when Inter were losing 2–1, and a hail of beer and soft-drink cans came on to the field of play, Roberto Boninsegna, Inter's Italian international centre-forward and a star of the 1970 World Cup final when he scored his country's goal, was hit on the back of the head, felled, and removed from the ground. Inter went on to lose 7–1. They appealed on the grounds of Boninsegna's injury; the appeal was upheld, the result annulled, and the game ordered to be replayed. Inter then comfortably won what became the first leg, at San Siro, and held Borussia to a 0–0 draw in Berlin, in the rearranged second leg.

Well before the appeal was heard, there was much controversy about the match, not least in Italy itself. By chance, I was in Florence at the time, and went to visit Fiorentina's famous manager, the former Swedish international Nils Liedholm, later to manager Milan and Roma, at Florence's Stadio Comunale. 'Very strange,' he said, dourly and drily. 'A team loses its centre-forward; and is beaten 7–1!'

But there was more serious speculation than that. Above all, had Boninsegna been struck by a full Coca-Cola can – not, as at first reported, a beer can – or by an empty one? The chairman of the UEFA Appeals Committee, a Swiss lawyer called Zorzi, whose name frequently crops up in the tormented annals of UEFA's disciplinary proceedings, accepted that the can was full. Hence the designated replay, hence Inter's passage to a European Cup final which they would eventually and very emphatically lose to the great Ajax side of that era.

To give the talkative old Fraizzoli his due, the game had actually been given away the previous season by Sandrino Mazzola, elegant centre-forward of that Inter team and himself another Italian hero of the 1970 World Cup final. The Coca-Cola can which had struck Boninsegna, he said, had been empty. The one he handed to the referee had been full. Devastating enough in itself.

But Fraizzoli, at that Hamburg banquet, went further. Before the appeals committee sat, he said, he had taken the precaution of sending a couple of representatives to Helsinki to put pressure on the Finnish member of the tribunal. Not only that: when the appeal was eventually heard in Zurich, the two hatchet men had gone into action again, this time to keep the Finn away from other members, who might influence him.

But then, Fraizzoli himself had had a very lucky escape over the Groningen Affair. Mere peanuts by comparison with the Years of the Golden Fix, when the prize was so much greater and Moratti, abetted by Allodi, was making referees offers they could so seldom refuse.

How had the mighty fallen! This time it was a mere UEFA Cup tie which was involved, and no Real Madrid, no Liverpool, but a little Dutch club, Groningen! In this shabby affair – needless to say quite unresolved by a UEFA Disciplinary Committee over which presided an old friend from the Solti era and its sub-committee, the Czech Vladimir Petra – the Fine Italian Hand of Moratti was missing, indeed.

Inter had lost the first leg of their second-round UEFA Cup tie against Groningen, 2–0. A week later, on 26 October, said the manager of the Dutch side, Hans Berger, he had been offered £55,000 to see that his team lost the return leg, by sufficient goals to let Inter go through. The intermediary, Berger would reveal after his team had in fact lost the second leg 5–1 in Bari – Inter were at the time suspended from playing at San Siro – was himself a Dutchman; an agent, the grandly named Apollonius Konijnenburg. Four days after Berger was approached, Renzo De Vries, the president of Groningen, passed the complaint on to the Dutch Federation. Two days before the return leg, the Federation conveyed it to UEFA.

It was only after his team's defeat in Bari that Berger spoke out to the press. 'Inter wanted to win at all costs,' he said. 'One of their representatives offered me £55,000 to throw the game.' To this, Fraizzoli rather clumsily responded, 'It's all a pack of lies. Anyway, how could you hope to buy an entire team for such a small amount?'

At the eventual UEFA enquiry, De Vries said that he himself had been illicitly approached in Bari, the day before the second-leg game. Berger, for his part, testified that he'd been told that, were Groningen to let Inter win through, Fraizzoli would pay for the club to have a new grandstand, and see that Berger himself was offered the managership of Pisa or Verona.

There was further testimony from Theo Huizinga, general manager of Groningen. He had, he said, heard at least one of Konijnenburg's damning conversations with Berger, in the course of which he had said that he was acting on behalf of Fraizzoli. But then, as we knew, Solti had said to Lobo that day in Lisbon that he was acting on behalf of Juventus, and Juventus escaped scot-free. So would Inter.

Curiously and ironically enough, UEFA's more permissive rules allowed, in such cases, the big Italian clubs to escape the consequences of their chicanery. In Italy itself, where realism, if not cynicism, ruled the day, the actions of such an intermediary implicitly involved the club for which he purported to be acting, which was thus held guilty until proved innocent. With UEFA, it was comfortably and comfortingly the other way round.

Who, meanwhile, was Apollonius? What was he? An increasingly significant Italo-Dutch agent, was the answer to that one. Fifty years old, he had opened an agency known grandly as International Football Management at Imperia, to sell players from the Low Countries to Italy. It had prospered sufficiently for him to transfer his base to Milan, where he enlisted the help of his son Ricky. So did Groningen themselves in Bari, where he was their interpreter.

The Disciplinary Committee was the usual fiasco. Apollonius didn't even turn up. At least you could say that Solti was present at the Atlantis Hotel, a decade earlier, even if he was never confronted with Lobo. A double room had been booked in the Dutchman's name at the Zurich Hilton, but he sent a message by special delivery claiming that he was ill. So the committee was adjourned to 15 December, which meant that FK Austria were obliged to play their Third Round matches with Inter knowing that they might have to play them again against Groningen. But being pretty sure, I'll wager, that they wouldn't.

And they didn't. When at last the committee did meet again, cosiness ruled once more. The impression of UEFA as an affable gentlemen's club, in which first-class hotels, splendid meals, limousines and jet travel were regularly enjoyed, in which the undeclared motto was Don't Make Waves, persisted. Groningen, the committee concluded, had produced no evidence to connect Apollonius with Inter, no evidence that Inter had been behind the approach. The committee could establish only that Apollonius 'had sought to have a talk with Berger with a view to manipulating the game'. In other words, 'If there are these madmen going about.'

All these years away from the Solti scandal, UEFA had still set up no investigating arm; and this time there was no *Sunday Times* investigation to embarrass them and force them to set up the sop of an *ad hoc* committee. One which would shuffle papers to and fro across a desk at irregular intervals, but do no more, largely because, even had it wanted to, it hadn't the means.

There is only so much a journalist can do, however popular or seemingly powerful the paper he works for. He can bring scandals to light, but however irrefutable his evidence, nothing will happen if the relevant body has no will to act. UEFA have never evinced that will. Their attitude is enshrined in the abject letter – a letter with no apparent authorisation – which the secretary Hans Bangerter sent so speedily to Juventus. Exonerating them.

When the journalists themselves, even the decent, honest ones, have no will to investigate, then there is less chance than ever of justice being done, the game made straight. It would be shockingly unfair to say that the majority of Italian football journalists during these years were corrupt, even if many did undoubtedly receive handsome gifts and privileges from the major clubs. But my thoughts go back to a train journey to Turin which I made with one of the best Italian football journalists of his time, Pier Cesare Baretti, pitifully killed in an aircraft accident early in 1988.

By that time, he was actually president of Fiorentina. Not the classical, moneyed president, but essentially an administrator, a nominee. Earlier, he worked for the Turin paper *Tuttosport*, of which he became the editor. When I spoke to him in that railway compartment about the Juventus–Lobo–Solti business, it was as though feet had walked over his grave. He became suddenly quiet, almost evasive, and said, '*Non mi interesso del costume*. I'm not interested in background.'

What an appalling, significant admission that was. For if the good guys, the Barettis of this journalistic world, were going to behave like the Three Wise Monkeys, what chance had Italian football got? And how could they square such a stance with their consciences? How could they go out seriously to report games when they sensed that they might be bought, fixed, manipulated? Only the season before the Groningen affair, Inter had been accused of throwing, or trying to throw, a match away to Genoa, to bring off a coup on fixed odds. But Bini and Bagni scored goals – for which not a single colleague congratulated them – and Inter won 3–2.

The Brazilian right-winger, Juary, who would later splendidly win a European Cup medal in Vienna with Porto, alleged that afterwards in the dressing room both players were beaten up, though he later withdrew his story. There was plainly no involvement, then, of the club itself. But the incidents, not to mention the massively greater fixed-odds betting scandal which led to the suspension of so many star players in 1980, was surely the consequence of the general atmosphere of chicanery and cynicism seeping through to the players themselves, so that when the two major tricksters, Trinca and Crociani, approached any *ritiro* – training-camp hotel – they were welcomed by the players where any other outsider would have been taboo.

What kind of an example, after all, were the club directors setting? Vittorio Pozzo, the grand old man of Italian football who had learnt his tactics in England before the Great War and won two World Cups, in 1934 and 1938, with his *azzurri*, had lamented the post-war decline many years before. A new kind of a director had emerged, he said, to replace the Old Guard. He had made a lot of money, very quickly. He had no background in the game, and not much real love for it. Above all, he wanted success quickly, and at almost any price.

He was unquestionably right, though whatever the affection of the Old Guard for football, they were seriously compromised by their acquiescence in Fascism. Pozzo's own militaristic approach to football was itself somewhat questionable. He was certainly an honest, decent man, but he shamelessly made use of the bombastic nationalism of the times to enforce discipline and invoke nationalism. Sometimes he could be comically hoist with his own petard, as he was over the case of the *oriundi*, the name given to players of South American birth and upbringing who held double passports as Italian citizens, and thus became eligible to play for Italy, not least in World Cups.

'If they can die for Italy,' said Pozzo dramatically, 'they can play for Italy.' Referring to the fact that *oriundi* were liable for military service. But playing was one thing, dying another. When the Abyssinian War broke out in 1936, Guaita, one of three Argentines in the Italian team which had won the World Cup two years earlier, was caught trying to sneak across the Swiss border.

Some of the old footballing dynasties remained, notably that of the powerful Agnelli family, the bosses of the FIAT motor company, and patrons of Juventus. They had held out as long as possible against the machinations of Fascism, but the end of it was that they and the newspaper they controlled, *La Stampa* of Turin, had fallen into line.

Gianni Agnelli would become one of the most powerful men in Europe, let alone Italy, after the Second World War. His love for Juventus was beyond dispute, and there was a certain feudalism in his assertion that football was a game which could 'be shared with everybody else'. Just as there was sound sense in his remark, when once I interviewed him in Turin, in 1962 for a BBC television documentary: 'If it's a business, it's a losing business.'

Sometimes president, always patron, sometimes mischievous, always committed, Agnelli was a figure of a very different stamp from the new era of *nouveaux riches* which Pozzo so deplored. All the more sad and deplorable then that his Juventus, however little he may have known about it, should allow themselves to become embroiled in the kind of chicanery practised by a relative upstart like Moratti.

But what strange presidential figures emerged from the shadows in the post-war years! There was one, the chairman of a major Northern club, who had made his fortune in the wartime blackmarket on the Ligurian coast, chiefly in cigarettes; so much so that cigarettes themselves were endowed with his own name, so that you were asked not whether you wanted cigarettes but, 'Will you have an X?' The name of the future president.

Milan had an extraordinary presidential succession, after the substantial publisher and film maker, Rizzoli, stood down. There was the fair-haired Riva, the son of a street sweeper who had married his rich boss's daughter. Riva's factories went bust in the 1960s, putting thousands out of work, and he fled to Lebanon, which was then a place of refuge. Then there was Felice Colombo, who was responsible for the bribery coup in a home match with Lazio which brought the whole house tumbling down about the ears of Italian football in 1980.

He it was who agreed to pay some of the Lazio players a bribe to lose a match which they would probably have lost, anyway. Unfortunately for him, when he got the cash out of a Lombard bank he did not bother to remove the wrappings, and it could not have been more easily traced. He was suspended from football, but continued blatantly to run the club for some time, just the same. After all, it was he who had the money.

'Giussy' Farina, a businessman who had transformed Lanerossi Vicenza into a major power for a short time, and then ruined them by vaingloriously outbidding mighty Juventus for their half-share in Paolo Rossi, also came to Milan. The consequences were severe. Years later, in late 1989, he and a string of Milan players were brought to trial for tax evasion. Almost all of them were heavily fined, and given suspended gaol sentences.

To pretend, however, that Italian clubs alone were involved in dubious incidents across the European years would be preposterous. The Greeks had a word for it – probably several – while in November 1984, perhaps the Viennese had one, too.

The case is interesting, in its depressing way, demonstrating once again the bizarre ineptitude of UEFA's disciplinary procedures and their extraordinary inconsistencies. The Swiss, Herr Zorzi, chairman of the Disciplinary Committee which upheld Inter's protest against Borussia Monchengladbach in 1971, was, these thirteen long seasons later, chairman of the Appeals Committee which would rule so bizarrely in favour of Rapid Vienna. *Plus ça change*. There has been a wonderful durability about UEFA's disciplinary figures. If only durability were all!

Celtic had lost the first leg of a UEFA Cup tie, 3–1 to Rapid in Vienna. In the second leg, Rapid emerged at Celtic Park with a thoroughly aggressive stance. Tommy Burns was the chief victim, hit in the back of the head by an opposing defender, brutally kicked by the goalkeeper as he ran through. Celtic eventually came out winners by 3–0, but there was a fourteen-minute stoppage, when two bottles were thrown on to the field from the crowd and the Rapid left-back collapsed to the ground.

There, the mystery began. What hit him? What had happened to him? The claim was initially that a bottle had struck him. Television showed that it hadn't. The appeals committee, bizarrely, would refuse to look at the televised recording. Rapid then quickly changed their story. Indeed, the aggrieved Celtic Chairman, Desmond White, pointed out that they were permitted to change their deposition no fewer than three times. Now they asserted that their man had been hit ... by something. Something: but what?

A coin? They can do nasty damage. A missile from a catapult, such as that which, by an irony, had apparently laid out poor Ronnie Simpson, Celtic's goalkeeper, before the start of the Intercontinental Cup game in Buenos Aires in 1967? Who could say? What *was* beyond doubt was that the injured man left Celtic Park in a bandage so huge that, in the words of Celtic's manager and former full-back, David Hay, 'It looked as if his head had been chopped off.'

Hay told me, himself, that ambulancemen who went to the left-back when he collapsed could detect no wound at all, though later Rapid would assert that he needed three stitches in his cut. This evidence was given solely by Rapid Vienna's own club doctor. True or false, it was uncorroborated evidence given by an interested party; such as would never have been accepted in any properly constituted court.

Piling Pelion upon Ossa, Herr Zorzi's appeals committee then ordered the second leg to be replayed – in Manchester. To decree a replay at all was a most dubious decision. To have it played at Old Trafford, Manchester United's ground, where police had none of the experience of their Glaswegian equivalents of dealing with the volatile Glasgow fans, was dicing with death. And so it proved.

I went to that game, and travelled on a bus full of aggressive Celtic fans rubbing finger and thumb together to indicate corruption, banging and stamping, threatening that there would be trouble if their team didn't win again.

It didn't. Alas, it played ineptly, succumbing to the only goal, scored resourcefully on the break by Peter Pacult, the centre-forward, after eighteen minutes. Three-quarters of an hour later, the police allowed a vicious Celtic fan to run on to the field and attack the Rapid goalkeeper, Herbert Feurer.

At the end of the game, another thug ran on and assaulted Pacult. Glasgow police, whose habit, as David Hay remarked, is to move round and round the ground throughout a game, rather than waiting for something to happen, wouldn't have allowed that. Manchester's finest, perfectly capable of dealing with their own kind of trouble, were taken unawares. Not only were Celtic thus eliminated from a competition in which they had previously and legitimately progressed, they were also now fined £17,000 and ordered to play their next home European game behind locked doors.

Nothing exonerates the brutal behaviour of those two fans, but if there was an accessory before the fact, it was surely UEFA.

But it wasn't the end of this horrid affair. Or unending sequence of affairs. The fact that UEFA had so often dealt so cravenly and ineffectively with suspected cases of corruption provided a kind of Cheats' Charter. Inter, after all, had got away with murder, or its metaphorical equivalent, right through the 60s. Juventus were never brought to book. The wells had been poisoned. The police often say that it isn't punishment but the possibility of detection which deters criminals. By that criterion, clubs which intended to bribe and cheat in the European competitions had little to dissuade them. And the clear corollary of that was the spread of cynicism. Matches became suspect to the knowing, or the cynical, when there may have been nothing the matter at all. As late as the 1989 European Cup final in Barcelona, when Milan thrashed Steaua, there were whispers about the Rumanians' supposed passivity, while 1975 had of course seen a deeply contentious final in Paris between Bayern Munich and Leeds United. Leeds had a Lorimer goal ruled out through a most debatable offside decision against Billy Bremner. They were refused a penalty when it was perfectly clear, as television and photographs would show, that Allan Clarke had been tripped by the usually immaculate Beckenbauer.

I remember Artemio Franchi – by now a man made rich by his involvement in the oil business, a bonus owed to his friends in football – telling me after the match that UEFA had awarded the French referee, Kitabdjian, only two marks out of a possible twenty. But that was where it ended. No attempt was made to dig deeper.

But then where was the spade, let alone the diggers? Botsford and I had done our best to dig, and that Football Association official had expressed the wish that we had never started. Don't make waves. Don't rock the boat. Have another drink, eat another meal, catch another jet, enjoy another good hotel. What could be done, after all, if there were these madmen going about?

Trainer

Town, August 1966

'CLAY WANTED TO use his left hand like Sugar Ray Robinson,' said Harry Wiley, 'and he said nobody could teach him that but me. He came to my hotel in London religiously every day and he'd take his shirt off and I showed him how to shorten that jab. He called me and said how disappointed he was I wasn't there in Miami Beach; he wanted me to raise his hand for the title. But he said he won't fight again unless I'm working his corner.'

Wiley is a short, plump, thickset black man, 56 years old, possibly the most accomplished boxing trainer of his day. He has trained Sugar Ray Robinson for almost a quarter of a century; now he also manages Bunny Grant, the British Empire lightweight champion from Jamaica, runs a gym on 136th and Broadway, a training camp on the Hudson, pops over to England whenever he has time, to instruct the British white hope, Billy Walker, and collects rents to make sure ends meet. His voice is lazy, thick and musical, its rhythms and undertones those of the South, rather than of New York, where he was born. He is endlessly courteous, enormously dignified and obscurely melancholy. Now and again, the mask lifts for a moment and one senses great reservoirs of disappointment and frustration, memories of slights, betrayals, ingratitude.

'Clay was up there in my room,' he says again, 'sweating, practising his jab, day after day, but *he* wouldn't tell you that. He's still seeking knowledge, but he don't want the public to know. "*I* won this fight." He becomes a Frankenstein. I don't mind. I've forgotten more about boxing than he'll ever know. I don't mind it.'

But it is plain that he does mind it; minds – more exactly – the perpetual role of Frankenstein to monsters who fight, succeed and take the credit.

We are in his gymnasium now. Above the dim doorway, a notice painted in straggly block letters reads: ONLY LICENSED MANAGER'S AND TRAINERS ALSO NEW'S PAPER REPORTER'S ARE ALLOWED TO COME INTO THE GYM FREE. Another notice says: YOU ARE CORDIALLY INVITED UP TO WATCH THE FIGHTERS TRAIN. CHAMPIONS OF TOMORROW TRAIN HERE TODAY. SINCERELY HARRY WILEY PROPRIETOR AND TRAINER OF SUGAR RAY ROBINSON.

The gym is a holocaust of sweat and exertion, of black bodies hitting, jumping, stretching, bending, lifting. The sharp beat of skipping rope is counterpointed by the drumming tattoo of a punch ball against the wall. One boxer has tied a scarf to the twin grips of the stretching machine and has put it round his neck, heaving and pulling like an ox at the plough. The ring is full of black boxers, jabbing, jogging, hooking, uppercutting at the empty air, each dancing around the others, each fiercely enclosed in his own hermetic world. To move about is dangerous: heavy punch bags are swinging; men are grunting and weightlifting and shadow boxing; trainers are calling to their protégés. 'Quit chewing that gum, Goddamn it!' shouts one of them, to a boxer in the ring. 'Take that gum outa your mouth!' Another, wearing a snappy sports coat, is instructing a tall, gentle, lanky boy who looks as if he'd be happier at home, playing the piano. 'Don't turn your head when you're doing it! Hold your head straight! Snap it, snap it, snap it!'

Wiley is wearing a good brown suit and showing plenty of white cuff; huge gold cufflinks display his initials, picked out in relief, and his tie is secured by a golden boxing glove.

'I used to have them cursing and swearing,' he says, 'but you'll notice it's run very decently now. I used to have four or five trainers; one time I came in and they were gambling; I don't allow that. *They* talk to their fighters, but nothing boisterous.'

'Snap it, snap it!' shouts the trainer in the sports coat.

'I said when I open a gym,' says Wiley, 'I'm not going to

have that violence, gambling, stealing one another's equipment, many things boys do. They will steal each other's equipment, they will say things and they'll have arguments. There've been one or two fights, but I've barred them. And it's good for the community; the police tell me I run a nice place. They usually gamble when they've finished training, they throw dice; here they sit down to watch; you go to any gym in America. You wouldn't know Doug Jones, the number two heavyweight, was training here. We've had Clay here. I don't allow *Clay* to run his mouth in this gym. If he does, I run him out of here; he's just here to train – let him train and get out. It's like in the army; I was sergeant, then they made me first sergeant. They knew I was tough, but I was fair.'

His army days were memorable days, although he got arthritis through sleeping on a ground sheet, and was blown up in an ammunition truck. At home, he has a photograph album, full of snapshots of himself, taken with English girls, jauntily inscribed. In one of them, a big, dark girl in a bathing costume has twined herself around him. BARBARA POSED FOR ME NICE, HUH? says the caption. BARBARA IGNORED EVERYTHING reads the next, and the one after that: BARBARA TOLD ME SHE LOVED ME TOO. Other girls appear: SHE OWNED A NIGHT CLUB: I WAS HER DAY CLUB.

A FINE CHICK IF I MUST SAY SO MYSELF. WHAT DO YOU THINK?

WHAT A MAN THAT WILEY.

'It goes without saying I was more than accepted over there,' he says, 'and I've never been treated any better and I can appreciate democratic viewpoints. They treated me so well, it's just one of those things you don't forget.'

A small, bald man in a white singlet has appeared, and is working frantically on a heavy bag, wearing light gloves, as though a fight is imminent and the fight will determine his future. 'Him?' says Wiley. 'He's a bug. B-U-G. My pet bug. He don't bother nobody. You know, they have stick-ups round here; there's some bad kids. We've had two cuttings-up in the street. Not round here; not here. We've had one fight here in eight years – one cut the other one. I put 'em both out. They've never been back since.

'You must be hard, firm but fair, you know what I mean? Like a fellow did something wrong, AWOL, or something, I would say, "Well, you know the rules. Take a shovel and dig that ditch." And when we went across on D-Day, you should have seen the fellows relying on me. "Gee, Sergeant Wiley, how do we get across to that beach, we can't swim?" I said, "What will be must be." "You not scared, Sergeant Wiley?" I said, "I'm as scared as you are. What's to be is to be." '

Doug Jones has his private dressing room in the northwest corner of the gym, and he sits there now after training, a tall, elegantly made man with a narrow moustache, who treats Wiley with odd formality. 'If Doug becomes champion, then my gym becomes popular,' says Wiley. 'They won't believe it. I'm very, very confident. I know he's got guts, which is what a fighter needs.'

'I think I should have got the last one with Clay,' Jones says. 'What you looking for, Wiley?'

'Handkerchief,' Wiley says.

'Toothpick?'

'Handkerchief. You want some coffee?'

'No thanks, Wiley – I usually get tea with my lemon.'

'Do you want me to send down for some?'

'That *would* be swell.'

A television director comes into the room, a pale, red-haired man with a worried, probing gaze. 'I tell you something as the son of a doctor,' he says, 'you've got to lose weight.'

'Well, I get fat very easily,' says Wiley, cutting the bandages off Jones's hands with careful expertise. 'I'm on a diet: bananas and skim milk.'

'They won't sharpen them scissors for nothing,' says Jones.

'What's given you the biggest satisfaction in all these years?' asked the director. 'Is it your life? What is it?'

'I would say it's my life,' says Wiley. 'The satisfaction is in the blood. You just go on and on and you see fighters come and go; eventually you're just part of them. I get the greatest satisfaction seeing these Golden Gloves fighters develop; I *like* kids.

'I want to ask you what you think as laymen about Billy Walker. I learn a lot from laymen. I'm not a guy who thinks he knows it all. This old man came up to me in training camp when Ray had retired and he'd come back and he'd been beaten by Tiger Jones. He said, "Can I speak to you, Mr Wiley? I seen a mistake in Ray. I've never been a fighter, never had a glove on, know nothing about fighting; I've only seen one fight in my life, but I've seen Ray on the screen, and I've seen a mistake in Ray. You know why he lost to Tiger? He tried to exchange punches with him. He always used to stand on his toes. Now he's standing cross-footed." The man was right. So you learn from the most unassuming people.'

Robinson still comes down to the gymnasium to work out; his name and achievements run like a motif through Wiley's conversation. 'I had the hardest fighter to discipline in the world, Sugar Ray Robinson, but he respected me. We had it out. I said, "If you can't respect me, get another trainer," and we stayed apart for a month, then he came back and said, "You were right." Everything goes together: man and wife, tea and sugar, cup and saucer. Respect goes with respect. Is that right?'

It was Wiley, indeed, who gave Robinson (alias Walker Smith) his *nom de guerre*, when he was running a church boxing club. 'Ray came into the gym there, a young kid fourteen or fifteen, and expressed that he wanted to be a fighter. He was a very spindly type of boy and I didn't believe he was ready to box; I thought he was too young. I let him come around with me and set up the ring. One night, through a break, he got his first fight. He didn't have any licence and I happened to have these licences in a drawer; one was Ray Robinson, who never fought; it was just lying around, and I put his name on it and he fought and he won. He said, "I told you I could fight. I always told you I could fight." I said, "You haven't turned pro yet." '

'So what's your satisfaction?' asks the director 'Sugar Ray's made millions; what have *you* got?'

'Just making him champion,' says Wiley. 'Making the champion of the world. I should be more interested in money. I don't know; the money comes secondary. Joe Louis made more than I did.'

'Has he kept any?' asked the director.

'No, not a penny. Joe is a philanthropist, he gives money

away. You come in a gym like this: "Joe, give me five dollars." He gives away all he gets. You say, "Joe, why do you give it away?" He says, "Oh, well, the guys need it." He did what he wanted, he's still living, he's got a beautiful home, he eats and sleeps, so what more do you want? I believe in putting money away for a rainy day, yet I would spend some of it, because what's the good of having it when you're old? I wouldn't even come in the gym; right now I'd be down in Florida. *I'm* happy; very poor, but happy. I walk through the streets: "Oh, Mr Wiley, how are you, Mr Wiley? He trained Sugar Ray." A little kid comes up to me "Will you teach me to box?" That's not my vocation, talking; I believe in producing.'

Going through Harlem with Wiley is indeed a small triumphal procession; everyone knows him, greets him and wants to talk to him. Huge cab drivers leap beaming out of their taxis to salute him; bar and club owners try to persuade him to lend his name to their places, offering as much as $150 a week. He had his own bar on Broadway once, but it was too much of a worry, and he closed it. Names drop like leaves: 'The great dancer Bill Robinson lived there . . . I started this church gym for Congressman Adam Powell; a very fine person, we were boys together . . . I carry a gun, I have a permit to carry a gun from the Mayor of New York. Mayor Impelliteri. Only three people in Harlem have permission to carry guns.' He carries it, he says, to protect himself when he's collecting rents in Sugar Ray Robinson's apartment block. He stops his blue Chrysler Imperial Crown outside a block of shops, and a man rushes towards it, addressing him in a bizarre parody of French. '*Comment allez-vous? Bien?* I was down there in Miami Beach with Cassius, it was great there, we was all living in the house.'

'Sugar Ray's barber,' says Wiley, driving on. 'You know what they make in that barber shop on a Friday or a Saturday? No Friday do they do under $800. And no Saturday under a thousand.'

Wiley and the barber were both members of the extraordinary circus with which Robinson travelled across Europe in 1951, when he was fighting almost every week, and ended by leaving his world middleweight title briefly in London. A dwarf went with them, too; Wiley found him in a bar in Paris, was surprised by his good English, and thought it might be good for publicity if they took him along for the ride. 'I said to Ray, "Take him around as a mascot or something, it would help *him*, too," because he was a midget, he didn't have many opportunities.

'We were like one big family. It was very inspiring for a fighter, because it made him feel like he *had* to be good. Ray was a fighter who was always like that, he always liked lots of people around him and he would pay for it, he spent thousands of dollars.'

Wiley lives in an apartment block, up a steep hill on 129th Street; a notice says NO SPITTING OR LOITERING IN THE LOBBY. 'We're going to get a home in the country,' he said, with faint unease, 'if I make enough money.'

His own door is protected by an arsenal of locks and bolts, which turn and click and rattle before at last it opens. His family greets him; his wife is a slender, elegant, dignified, pretty woman, with a mature, engaging smile. 'I didn't name her,' Wiley says, 'but she's got a name I disagree with – Bloundelia. I call her Bunny for short. Her mother named her before I got to her.' His eleven-year-old daughter, Pamela, is slim and pretty, too, though here the smile has a shy complicity. Harry Wiley III, a tiny, lively boy with wiry hair, is wearing a police badge, and displays a pair of boxing gloves given to him by Billy Walker. 'I'm a cop,' he says. 'I'm going to shut up the bad people. This is my muscle. That's why I'm strong; because I eat a lot of bread. I'm the boss in this house.'

'Sure break up all the furniture, these kids,' says Wiley, going into the small, hot sitting room. There is a cut-glass chandelier, a menagerie of china animals; a china bull and a china matador confront one another on the mantelpiece, and above them again hangs a photograph of a bull fight. Small, orange tropical fish swim insidiously amidst the fronds of a tank. 'I'm not going to get any more till he's bigger,' Wiley says. 'I'm not apologising; I'm just telling you what it is.'

'I can knock everybody out,' says the little boy. 'With that glove. A terrible glove puncher.'

'That little boy of mine,' says Wiley. 'He's really something.

I wouldn't take a million dollars for him; he's a very good kid. Sometimes he worries me, though.'

He has been married for nine years: 'I would have got married earlier, but my mother and father were very sick and my brother got married and they had no one at home but me.'

His father was a Post Office worker who never really wanted him to box, and took the first opportunity to put an end to it; but then, Wiley had no great love for fighting himself. Even today, there is a strange, unexplained paradox between the mild humanity of the man and the fact that he is involved in a brutal sport which has always demanded the sacrifice of the young. He talks about the technique, the various possible punches, without the least overtone of aggression, as though he were discussing the technique of the dance; blood, pain and violence have somehow been refined away.

'I was born two streets from here, a street called 131st and that was on the East Side. I never had no idea of going in for fighting. I didn't approve of gang fights. But there was a club called Boys' Welfare Club; Benny Leonard used to come there, Harry Wills, to encourage the boys. They brought a boy from Jersey called Jesse Collins who'd beaten everybody my weight, and I was approached by Harry Wills. He asked me would I box him and I told him, "Certainly." They put up the ring in the street, but anyway I knocked Jesse out in the second round. So they had me train and I went out to box and I didn't do too bad. I won the first fifteen. Then another boy in the block pulled my sister's hair. I said, "Don't do that." He said, "What do you mean?" I said, "If you do that again I'll do something about it," and he said, "What, you?" and he did it again, and I knocked him out, too. I turned professional and I got hurt by a car; then my father had a good excuse, he wouldn't let me box any more. I had had twenty-seven, twenty-eight fights.' Their souvenir is a slightly squashed nose, the sort of thing he tells fighters they will avoid, if they follow his methods.

After retiring, he went into the Post Office – 'like father, like son' – but 'they all liked the way I slipped punches and they wanted me to teach them, so eventually I got out and my first big job was when I was picked to train the Olympic team in 1932. That was when I met Henry Armstrong.' When

Armstrong, later to hold world titles at three different weights, came to New York, where Wiley was having 'a pretty uphill struggle', his managers sent for him as trainer.

'I took Ray Robinson to camp some time, and Ray was a cocky kid. He said, "Don't let him stumble into me, I'll knock him out," and I said, "Gee, you talk big for a kid." He said, "I don't mean to talk big, I believe I can defeat him," and sure enough, I lived to see the day that he did beat him.'

Wiley has his jacket off now, and the gun is revealed: a pearl-handled revolver sticking rakishly out of a leather holster, with an air of the Wild West. Again, there is something strange in the juxtaposition of the gentle man with the predication of violence. The pearl handle, perhaps, is a small gesture towards a milder ethos.

For though he is clearly a person who's been hurt, he will have nothing of racial extremism; Clay's adherence to the Black Muslims has displeased him. 'It's the persecuted being persecutor. Now we cannot solve our problem through these moves. To me, to get the things out of life we should get as a racial group, we should educate our children: we've got to work. I'll never forget this poem I learnt at school:

> A man who wants a garden fair
> Small or very big
> With flowers growing everywhere
> Must bend his back and dig.
> For things are very few on earth
> That our wishes can attain.
> Whate'er we want of any worth
> We've got to work to gain.

And that applies to us. We've got to work; we've got to sacrifice. We must educate our children: through that medium they'll get on top and they'll adjust themselves to society. Work to gain; not fight to gain.'

This attitude, in turn, goes with an almost mystic respect for authority as such. It's who you know that matters; or who they might *think* you know. Mayor Impelliteri gave him a gun, and he was all right. Jim Norris was head of the International

Boxing Club and always polite to him; *he* was all right. On the walls of the little room he calls 'Harry's junk room', where a rocking horse pokes its maned head above a sea of toys and empty Chianti flasks, there are signed pictures of both men on the crowded wall: 'To Harry Wiley with sincere good wishes, Vincent Impelliteri.' There are Frankie Laine, Jackie Cooper, Edward G Robinson – squaring up to a younger Wiley, in Hollywood.

But acceptance doesn't impinge on integrity: 'I've never had any dealings with gangsters or the underworld. I've never worked in a corner where I knew they were doing something wrong and I've never worked with a fighter that was controlled by gangsters. And I can name an example: Sonny Jones. Willis had won twenty-four straight fights and this Sonny Jones fought him at the Marciano arena and he beat Willis and I got numerous offers – I didn't even know who they were – to buy this fighter next day. And because I didn't take any of the calls up, he didn't get another fight.'

The telephone goes now. Wiley answers it and says, 'Listen!' pointing to the extension.

'I'm going to drop from 71½ to 66,' says a loud, harsh voice at the other end.

'I'll gladly give you a return match,' Wiley says.

'This is a match that means something,' says the voice. 'That I can talk about. The other, I can't talk about it.'

'OK,' says Wiley. 'We're still the best of friends.'

'I don't want it,' says the voice. 'I fought a guy in New York State I don't know. I don't want nobody I don't know.'

'I understand,' says Wiley.

'Look. Like I say, you gotta look after your fighter.'

'I'm capable of protecting him.'

'OK, Harry. Take it easy.'

'Likewise,' Wiley says.

Back in the living room, while his daughter watches, amused, from the small, adjacent bedroom, he moves about the carpet, demonstrating punches. 'Now, surprisingly, people think it's very complicated to learn boxing. I have figured it out to say this, that there are only six punches you can hit a man with, three with each hand. The left jab' – he gently advances his left hand – 'the only punch that's used without a muscle, so you must use your shoulder. Now the next punch is my left hook, thrown while pivoting on my left foot, and the punch must be made to fit against the jaw. Your next punch is your left uppercut, sometimes called the bolo. That's all you can do with the left hand. Now the right hand. The most effective punch any fighter can throw is a straight right hand. That's done with the right foot pushing the body forward. Now there we have the right cross over the top of the jab; it's called the counter-punch. Now you have here the right hand uppercut; there are no more punches.

'Now the thing that is best in boxing is feinting; feinting is best in boxing. Clay is beginning to use feinting more in his fights than any coming-up fighter today.' (But still, in Wiley's opinion, he cannot remotely be compared with Robinson, whose feints deliberately set a man up for the counter-punch, while Clay's are merely defensive evasions.) 'You can feint with the hands, stomp with your foot, anything to distract.

'Now the next thing a fighter should learn is how to train and what he should eat. There are certain hours in the morning he should run and no other times he should run. I would suggest he run between 6.30 a.m. and 7.0 a.m., because the air at that time is different from any other time in the day. A fighter should rest as much as he can, and he should rest before going in the gymnasium. The worst thing a fighter can be is over-trained and the next worst thing is undertrained.

'Bandaging of the hands is very important, very important. I think every trainer should teach his fighter to bandage his hands himself in the gymnasium and only the trainer himself should bandage his hands for a real fight.

'I suggest the first thing fighters should learn, which is seldom taught, is balance. Before they even get in the ring, they should spend two or three months learning balance. If you're properly balanced, the hands are co-ordinating with the body. You teach a fighter styles according to the contour of his body. Now, if a fighter is tall like Sugar Ray, you would not teach him as much bobbing and weaving as a smaller fighter, not as much as you would teach him to slip and you would teach him to use his hands in defence.'

He begins putting on his camel-hair coat, to go out, and suddenly the little boy is thrown into paroxysms of despair. 'Daddy, don't leave me!'

'Leave you?' says Wiley. 'Daddy's got to tend to business, then he's coming back.'

'No, Daddy, no!' pleads the little boy, following him down the corridor, to the door and its plethora of locks. 'I want to go with you! I want you to stay here!'

'You know your daddy's a poor man?' says Wiley. 'He must work.'

'Stay! Stay! Stay! Stay!' cries the little boy, till his mother carries him away, inconsolable.

'He doesn't want me to go,' says Wiley, standing by the elevator. 'He wants me always around. If his mother goes out, he don't say nothing. He'll holler like that for half an hour and I don't want him to holler, because he's not too well, he's got bron-icle asthma, number one, and then he's allergic.'

In the garage, he drives the blue Chrysler up to the petrol pumps. 'Hey, boss,' he says, 'give me some of your orangeade.'

'You don't mean orangeade,' says the garage man.

'Yea,' says Wiley, 'I ain't got no money either. When I duck you, I want to duck good.'

Along Broadway, the triumphal progress is resumed. We go into a Harlem bar. Pretty black girls are sitting at it, unescorted; the lights are very dim, and the bartender talks elegiacally and endlessly of how boxing has declined. A squat, tough, middle-aged man comes in with a pretty girl, dumps her at a table, and comes over to the bar: Wiley introduces him as the proprietor. 'You couldn't mention like you came here?' he asks, without much optimism. 'No? You came here, and you ate some real nice chicken?'

Farther down Broadway, where the lights are brighter, a girl is busily accosting men. 'Puerto Rican,' Wiley says, without censure. 'She's a sporty girl. There she goes, see; she's trying another one. What she don't know is there's detectives here; they'll pick her up eventually. She don't know them; *I* know them.'

He drives on slowly – it is after midnight now – talking about Sugar Ray again and Salem Crescent Church club, where the great black fighters come from. At last one asks him if he goes to church himself.

'No, I don't,' he said, contritely. 'True, I should do, I should go to church. I go when I can do; maybe time don't permit me to. My work don't.'

Gianfranco Zola

Times magazine, 12 April 1997

T HE MOMENT GIANFRANCO Zola looked up and saw Croatia's Mario Stanic sitting in the Parma stand was a propitious one for Chelsea. It was the moment that Zola knew his days with the Italian club were numbered.

Forced to play out of position on the right wing, Zola's frustration was obvious. 'If, at the beginning of the season,' he said, with untypical bitterness, 'they had told me that I would have to change roles, I would have discussed it and probably we would have come to some kind of an agreement. But these are things which should be worked out at the start. Before the game against Inter, Carlo Ancelotti [Parma's new manager] asked me to play on the right. He said to me, "Try it up to half-time," and I did try. I certainly gave it all I'd got, even if I thought that I could have given more in another position.'

So it was that on a November evening last year, Zola came to Stamford Bridge to address a press conference. Smiling beneath a blue cap, the tiny Italian announced in his fractured English that he was joining Chelsea for £4.5 million – £5.5 million less than the asking price when Chelsea had approached Parma the previous season. In the interim, Parma had made a mess of things. Dismissing their much respected manager of seven years, Nevio Scala – with whom Zola got on well – they appointed Ancelotti and paid a fortune for Enrico Chiesa, the Sampdoria striker. Another large sum went on the Argentinian attacker Hernan Crespo. This embarrassment of riches meant Zola wasn't given the room to shine.

Zola, whom Chelsea are paying the bagatelle of £25,000 a

week, can, in fact, do marvellous things from the right, as he has frequently shown at Stamford Bridge, where he is capable of cutting in, going first one side then the other of a defender, before beating the goalkeeper with a diagonal drive. But he likes to move out to the wing when he feels like it, not because he has been ordered to stay there. At Chelsea – and now for Italy – he can play where he likes best, just behind the front line. And in contrast with the Italian premier division, Serie A, where every game, he says, is like a European Champions' Cup match, the pressure in the English Premiership is only half as great, making it easier to play here.

London has clearly been good to Zola. He lives in a flat near Sloane Square with his wife Franca and two children, Andreas, six, and Martina, four, and can often be seen eating at Italian restaurants nearby. He gets to play the piano (Beethoven and Vivaldi, though he laughs at any suggestion that he does so well). He even has warm words for England's – and Chelsea's – much maligned fans. 'From the first day I've been touched by the atmosphere surrounding these matches. Here, the supporters go to the stadium as if they were going to church. They come to commune with the players. The match is a festival, the chance to live a day in good humour.

'And in London,' he says, 'you can walk about calmly in the streets; no one bothers you or follows you for hours. When supporters recognise you, they greet you, they politely encourage you, and that's all. The English are very reserved, like we Sardinians, and very respectful.' *Beato lui* – lucky old him – as the Italians say.

Yet he was happy, also, in two very different cities – Naples and Parma. So popular was he in the former than when he lost his husky dog and appealed, after a dazzling performance against Verona, for its return, he had it back in just a few hours.

Sedate Parma could scarcely have been more of a contrast with the anarchy of Naples, but Zola delighted in it too, at least until the ill-starred arrival of Ancelotti. 'The two cities, Naples and Parma, are ideal for footballers and important because they provide continuous stimulation. They also have in common their grand passion for football, and the fact that they have great teams.'

Now he enjoys the contrast of London and the challenge of getting the best out of Chelsea. 'I began this adventure with great enthusiasm. I was ready to move mountains. To be honest, I thought I might have a bit of trouble fitting into the team, to a football that was new to me. In the end, everything went ahead without any problems.'

Certainly it took no time for his British team-mates to accept him. Dennis Wise, Chelsea's captain, swears by him. Graham Rix, the club coach, no mean technician in his own time, says 'I think he's one of the most exciting players I've seen. He's got two great feet. He plays with a smile on his face. He's capable of producing something out of nothing.' And Ruud Gullit, Chelsea's player-manager, who was a long-time opponent of Zola on the field in Italian football, attests to the little man's physical strength. 'He's built himself up to be strong enough to cope with this fast football. After training, he always does stretches and other things, and that makes him the player he is now. He did it himself.'

For his part, Zola says the English 'are more difficult to conquer than the Italians. Day after day you have to show your worth. It's a question of mentality: they are more closed in than we are.' And yet, surprisingly, he believes it easier for the creative player with flair, like himself, to flourish and be appreciated in England. This despite the pace of the national game which most European players deplore. 'Delicate moves and technical exploits are much appreciated here. And yet it's customary to say that British football is wholly athletic and committed to extremes.'

But whatever Zola's successes at Chelsea, they were surely eclipsed by his decisive goal for Italy at Wembley in February. With a single strike he not only put in doubt England's qualification for the 1998 World Cup finals in France, but he achieved the one thing he wanted above all else: revenge.

Zola went into that match carrying a double burden. The first went back to the second round of the 1994 World Cup in America, where he came on as a sixth-minute substitute against

Nigeria. It was a bruising match and a difficult one to be thrown into, not least for a player who had long been waiting to return to the Italian side. Zola was on the field barely a quarter of an hour when, after a trivial foul, he was sent off by the Mexican referee, Arturo Brizio, who had long since lost control of the game. It was no way for a man like Zola to spend his 28th birthday.

His response to the red card, he told me, was one of total incredulity. 'I did not foul him. It meant I missed the rest of the World Cup. And I was still more upset when the Secretary of FIFA, Sepp Blatter, said I deserved to be sent off.' (He was wryly amused when I gave him a press cutting claiming that Brizio was in trouble in Mexico for wearing a tape recorder during a match and subsequently broadcasting his various exchanges with the players.)

Two years later, Zola was back in Italy's team for the Euro 96 finals in England. He began coruscatingly with an electric performance in Liverpool against a Russian team which could do little with him: all dancing feet, perfect balance and insidious free kicks. Zola put Gigi Casiraghi through for Italy's second goal.

He came on only as a late substitute in the second game, which was lost to the Czechs after Italy's controversial manager, Arrigo Sacchi, whimsically left five of his regular side, Zola included, out of the starting formation. So the third group match, against Germany at Old Trafford, would be decisive. After only eight minutes, Kopke, the German goalkeeper, tripped Casiraghi and Italy were given a penalty. Zola took it. Kopke flung himself to his left and turned the ball round the post. The game finished 0–0 and Italy were out.

Revenge at Wembley came from a long ball out of defence by 'Billy' Costacurta, the Italian sweeper. A static response from one England defender, Stuart Pearce, and belated cover by another, Sol Campbell, allowed Zola to streak through from the right. At first it looked as if he might have let the ball run too far ahead, but he caught it well enough and struck a right-footed shot between England's goalkeeper, Ian Walker, and the near post. Zola's debt was repaid.

Chelsea fans will more warmly remember the goal he scored

ten days later against Manchester United – a small miracle of technique and effrontery. Receiving a pass from the Romanian Dan Petrescu on the right, Zola advanced on United's goal, ridiculed the attempt by Dennis Irwin, the full-back, to intercept him, jinked easily past the challenge of the towering centre-back, Gary Pallister, before suddenly turning to put the ball cheekily between Peter Schmeichel and the near post with his left foot.

Zola exemplifies the sheer physical democracy of soccer. He stands just 5ft 6in high and weighs 10st 4lb. Yet the biggest and strongest of defenders find him a nightmare. In England, the only way opposing clubs have found to subdue him is to mark him man to man. Some, notably Leeds United, Sunderland and Nottingham Forest, have done this to effect. When Sheffield Wednesday eventually put Peter Atherton on to him at Stamford Bridge, Zola was asked how he had liked it. 'I prefer my wife,' he said.

Asked before the Wembley game whether he would close-mark Zola, England's manager, Glen Hoddle, replied that at the international level, thanks to changes in the laws of the game, such methods were extinct. As Zola left the hefty Pearce for dead, he may have regretted his decision.

Given his scintillating gifts – the ease with which he can beat a man, score from a delightfully flighted free kick, make a decisive pass – it's odd to reflect that Zola made such a slow and obscure start to his career. He didn't make his debut in Serie A, for Napoli, until he was 23. Before then he was deep in the boondocks of his native Sardinia, not even courted by the island's one major club, Cagliari.

Zola was born on 7 July 1966, in the tiny town of Oliena, where his father kept a bar. His first professional club was Nuorese, then playing in C2, the lower echelon of the Third Division. That season they did so badly they even slid out of C2 into the Interregional League. Zola scored ten goals for them from inside-forward in 27 games. The next season, 1986–87, he was back in C2 with another Sardinian club, Torres. Eight goals in 30 games and Torres were promoted to C1, where he spent the next two seasons.

At long last the sports director of the club, Nello Barbanera, persuaded Napoli's general manager, Luciano Moggi, to come to look at Zola. That in itself was quite an achievement, for Moggi, who now fills the same role with Juventus, is one of the most formidable wheelerdealers in Italian football. Moggi came, saw and, if he was not exactly conquered, he had at least seen enough to sign Zola to Napoli for £200,000. 'Moggi,' reflects an Italian soccer journalist, 'was taking a big chance. Zola was not just an unknown quantity, *un oggetto misterioso*, but *un oggetto misteriosissimo*.'

Yet it worked. Not least because in Naples Zola found his chief mentor, the player he will always admire, Diego Maradona. In character, the two could hardly be more different: Maradona flamboyant, recalcitrant, self-indulgent and self-destructive; Zola quiet and contained. But Zola learnt from him.

Not only was this Zola's first season in Serie A, it was a season in which Napoli defied the giants of the North to win the Championship for only the second time in their history. Zola played in eighteen of those games, though he scored only a couple of goals. Maradona was the fulcrum, the inspiration, the motivating force of this team, and Zola has never ceased, for all the Argentinian's vicissitudes, to admire him. Asked, years later, which players he most respected, Zola replied, 'The list is qualified, not long. Platini captured my imagination as a boy. Then I met Maradona. It was a flash of lightning. I don't think anyone like Diego will ever be born again. I've learnt so much just from watching him.'

It is interesting, by contrast, to note that when asked which manager had most helped him, he did not name any for whom he'd played in Serie A, but chose Giovanni Maria Mele, the manager of his first Sardinian club.

It was in Pisa on 17 February 1991 that Maradona made the ultimate, symbolic gesture: he gave Zola his number 10 jersey. From then on, it would be Zola who made the team move. He went on to score 32 goals in 105 league games for Napoli. His first international cap came with the first match that Arrigo Sacchi managed – against Norway in Genoa.

But they didn't get on. Sacchi, the self-made coach who never kicked a ball even in decent amateur football ('You don't have to have been a horse to be a jockey,' he'd say), never got on with what the Italians called the fantasists (unorthodox, imaginative, creative players), of whom Zola was ineluctably one, and that counted against him. Zola's appearance against Nigeria in July 1994 was only his seventh for Italy. A good performance against Turkey in Pescara the following December at last gained him a regular place in the national team, but even so, between him and Sacchi there was never much more than an armed neutrality.

When Sacchi walked out halfway through this season to resume his old job as manager of Milan, Zola shed no tears, least of all when he was succeeded by Cesare Maldini, the 65-year-old manager of Italy's Under-21 team. Just before Italy played Northern Ireland in Palermo in January, Zola said, 'Many things have changed since Sacchi left. We work with more serenity; we feel more loved. With Maldini, we can recover our harmony and mend our relationship with the fans.' As for joining Chelsea, he says, 'I believe I've made the right choice. In Italy, it's a difficult time for "fantasists", while in England that kind of player is loved and looked for.'

But he is also aware of how it can turn sour. He knows only too well the problems faced by his team-mate Gianluca Vialli: problems which emerged with the arrival at Chelsea of Zola himself; problems which have remained unresolved. At that first press conference, when Gullit was asked how Zola, Vialli and the Welsh international Mark Hughes could co-exist, he answered that it might be possible to use all three. In the event, it wasn't.

Vialli, for so many years one of the outstanding strikers in Italy, had surprisingly joined Chelsea in the summer from Juventus, soon after captaining them to success in the European Cup. It seemed a tremendous coup. As it turned out, however, Hughes and the proud and powerful Vialli duplicated rather than complemented one another. It was only when Vialli dropped out injured and Zola paired with Hughes that things began to hum. Behind them played another Italian international, the elegant midfielder Roberto Di Matteo, whom Chelsea had bought from Lazio of Rome.

It is strange to reflect that in December 1995, when Zola was asked which player he most envied, he replied, 'Without doubt Vialli, for the charisma that he gives out and the ability to galvanise others with his example.' That Vialli should be relegated to the substitutes' bench was, Zola had said, a situation which he was sure would change, given Vialli's great qualities. Hughes, meanwhile, has been grateful for Zola's inspiring presence: 'There would be something missing if I couldn't play with a player like Zola.'

Tomorrow, in the FA Cup semi-final at Highbury against Wimbledon, Zola could well be Chelsea's trump card. Wimbledon will be greatly tempted to man-mark him. But such a policy brings risks of its own.

Three or Four Cultures

Penguin Modern Stories, 1969

'D NEVER SEEN anything like what went on at the airport, when we landed. Talk about chaos. There were hundreds of them, hundreds of Mexicans, little dark people, clapping us and waving and wanting to touch us. All those strange, brown faces, smiling at you. You had to fight your way through to the buses; it was like running a gauntlet. When we did get on to our bus, they stood and rapped at the windows, all those teeth still flashing away. You'd have thought we'd come from outer space. I said to Bobby Wragg, our quarter-miler, who was sitting next to me, 'Phew! It's harder than running a race,' but he said, 'Nothing's harder than running a race,' which was the last thing I wanted to hear, because I always tend to work myself up. I need someone to soothe me down, not worry me; someone like Jack Drake, that's my coach at home; someone to say, 'Forget it, Marion,' or I'll brood. I'm a terrible brooder.

It was miles and miles out to the Olympic Village, a very dismal drive through ugly, tatty streets, terribly poor and run-down, till someone said, 'That's the Olympic Stadium,' and there it was, out on our right, this huge, white bowl. I imagined it full of thousands and thousands of people and thought, Oh, God, I've got to run there, and my stomach flipped, I grabbed hold of Bobby's hand. He said, 'What's wrong, Marion?' and I said, 'Just one of me turns, dear, nothing serious.'

Then someone else said, 'Popocatépetl,' and I looked out on the left. There were mountains, great, gaunt things, like nothing that I'd seen before, and I started wishing I was home, though I knew I'd be all right once I got there, to the Village, and I'd started training, because as soon as I'm on a track I'm OK; tracks are the same everywhere, if you see what I mean, even if one's cinders and another's Tartan.

And very soon we could see the Village, down on the right; huge, high, red, new blocks with coloured numbers painted on them. I didn't like the look of those much, either, to be honest, but at least we'd all be there together.

There were a lot of jokes among the boys about the Women's Village, how they'd have to use wire-cutters to get in, or pole-vault over the top. I told them, 'None of you can pole-vault high enough; the only ones that get over will be the Germans and the Americans,' and one of the other girls said, 'Very nice, too,' which of course brought a great, big roar from them all: 'Well, hi, there, baby!', 'Vy you don't like us?' and that kind of thing.

The Village looked so big when we got into it, much bigger than that at the Empire Games. When we got to our block in the women's part, I had to go up three flights of stairs to my room; I was sharing with Mary Gregg and Joan Paulton, 400 metres and javelin, and the first thing we did was try and make it cosy, sticking up all the photographs and pennants and things we could. Mary had a great big picture of the Beatles and I put my bears all over the place, Rufus the big, pink one, and Dylan, the green one, and the blue one, Ringo; Joan had a gramophone and put on a Stones record, till in the end it was quite like home, even if the cupboard space was terrible, just one measly little wardrobe and a chest of drawers between the lot of us, so we had to leave half our things in the cases.

Of course, what was driving everyone up the wall was the altitude business: would it affect us, would we acclimatise in time? My race, the 200 metres, didn't carry an oxygen debt, thank goodness, but you still had it on your mind, you couldn't help it, and when we came into our room Mary collapsed on the bed – she was always larking about – shouting, 'Oxygen, oxygen! Bring me an oxygen mask! I can't breathe, doctor, I can't breathe!'

Joan said, 'Here's your oxygen mask!' and shoved a pillow over her face, but it wasn't really any joke, and when we got outside, Joan said, 'Hey, we'd better hold on to one another, in case anybody folds up,' and we walked along very, very slowly, arm in arm – anyone looking at us must have thought we were drunk – till after about fifty yards Joan said, 'I think it's all right.' She was in the middle, and let go of us both very slowly.

But in fact you found that even if you just walked quickly there was this tightening in the chest, this heavy feeling after in the legs. It was ghastly.

In the city, the white dove on its black background flew everywhere: 'Todo es Posible en la Paz.' There was an air of vibrant hiatus, a lull between battles.

A week before, the tanks had been out in the Zocalo. In a sidestreet, eight single-decker buses stood, like wounded elephants, charred and gutted. The survivors, yellow, dirty, made their laboured way down the Paseo de la Reforma, ships in a beleaguered convoy, their front windows pocked and starred by bullets, their sides black with slogans: DIAZ ORDAZ ASESINO, GRANADEROS ANIMALES. *Young mestizos swarmed on their steps, clung to their rails, poised like statuary.*

The white buildings, the green expanses, of the university stood empty, but for the occupying soldiers: small, bored, enigmatic Indians. The students remained on strike.

Outside the schools which they'd invaded and desolated lounged the riot police, the Granaderos, squat, swarthy men, jowled under blue helmets, hung with guns and gas pistols and respirators, their plump faces set in a thin, derisive smile.

Though the sun shone, a low, grey haze pressed on the city. Fumes of exhaust smoke hung, insoluble, in the mountain air.

We didn't train for the first couple of days, just lounged around the Village, which was nice, really; there was a smashing swimming pool and the sun shone and we got brown. The breathing was all right so long as you didn't hurry and the food in our restaurant was quite good. Of course we couldn't drink the water, which was rather a drag, and we took our two little pills every day. We made a big joke of it in our room. Whenever Lucy Grainger came round, our team manager, Mary would yell, 'Lucy, Marion hasn't taken her pills today!' and Lucy would say, 'Well, we'll just have to administer them forcibly,' and I'd say, 'No, anything but that, I'll take them, I'll take them, I'll even swallow them without water!' Though we did hear about a couple of Americans who'd drunk the tap water and they were absolutely shattered.

Sometimes I went along to the track, which had a really gorgeous surface, Tartan. I'd sit there on the steep, green bank and watch the people training I'd be running against, sometimes clocking them, especially Martine Lechantre, the Belgian girl I'd beaten in the European Games. She had a very good action, with those long legs of hers, but I knew I started better, I was stronger. She'd run 23.1 in the Little Olympic Games, the year before, where my best this year, in fact my best ever, was the 23.2 I'd run at Crystal Palace, but I didn't take that too seriously, because everyone knows that in Mexico times are so much faster, sometimes in the sprints by as much as a couple of seconds.

When I did start training, I missed Jack dreadfully. The official coaches were all right – they tried to help – but it's never the same: you need your own coach, and Jack just couldn't afford to come. He was miserable, though he wrote to me every day, which was a tremendous help: how I should plan each day's training, when I should rest, what times I should be aiming for.

There was the Russian girl, Beskova, too. She was very strong, more like a man – I sometimes wondered how she'd passed the sex test – but I'd beaten her in the European Games, too, and I knew I could do it again. I knew I had a much faster finish.

It was nice, in a way, to be able to watch them without their being able to watch you. I'd lie back there in the sunshine on the bank and sometimes wave to them and wish it could go on like this; only, of course, it couldn't.

When I did begin to train at last, it was hard for the first few days, not so much when you were actually running as afterwards, when you had to recover, panting away for air that wouldn't come, frightened it would *never* come. I felt so sorry for Laura Bates, in the 800 metres; she had the room upstairs. After the first day's training she was practically flaked out; she lay on her bed and said, 'I'm dying, I know I'm going to die. I'd leave you my spikes, Marion, if you hadn't got such big feet.'

That first week, I did hardly any stamina work; Jack had told me not to. A few hundreds, well spaced out, a few two hundreds, but not the real interval thing, because it just took too long to recover.

There was quite a good atmosphere in the British team, everybody very friendly, but I think it was harder for those of us who were expected to win medals, because we were so few, only three or four; the others could relax more because they hadn't got the same pressure on them. If *we* did well, it was only expected of us; if they did badly, nobody would blame them.

I got photographed a lot and, once you went outside the Olympic Village, there were all the Mexicans, again surrounding you, trying to sell you things, asking for your autograph, touching you. We all bought masses of stuff, Mary and Joan and I: straw sombreros and bead handbags and paintings on bark and Indian jewellery, and strewed them all over our room till it looked like a junk shop.

Just nearby the Village we'd sometimes pass a terrible little shanty town, tiny little one-storey brick houses more like pig sties, some of them painted very jazzy colours, which in a way made them look worse. It seemed funny, somehow: us living there in these great, tall blocks, complaining about the cupboard space, and practically next door, these shacks. One or two of the boys said they thought it was a scandal, but I must confess I didn't think about it much. I'd come here for one thing, to win my event, and if I didn't do that I'd have let everybody down.

That was what was in the air at the Village, under all the jokes and the chatter, that was what gave it its atmosphere: everybody wanting to win, whether they were black or white or brown or yellow, runners or jumpers or rowers or swimmers. There were Indians in turbans and Africans in coloured robes and Japanese in spectacles and they were all there just for this one thing: to win. No wonder it was so difficult to sleep at night. Then I met Antonio.

It was one morning in the athletes' lounge, a big room they

had with chairs and newspapers and sofas, rather stuffy, and down below a basement where you could get coffee and Coca Cola and things for nothing – if you wanted them.

He was enormous but terribly handsome, like a gladiator; not huge like the shot-putters and people, who've been on the anabolic steroids and blow up like balloons, but just terribly muscular and strong, great big arms and an immense neck, and this very clear-cut, handsome face with blond curly hair, really fabulous. I think he must have felt me staring at him, because suddenly he turned towards me and stared back, and of course I looked away at once, shy little thing. That was one thing I'd promised myself before I came: there wasn't going to be anything like that. I'd come to win my races and, until I had, nothing was going to distract me or interfere with me, absolutely nothing and no one.

In a minute or two he strolled over to where I was sitting – there was a newspaper rack just by me – and I was wondering, Will he speak to me, will he turn and talk to me? My heart was thumping away even though I knew it was silly; I knew I mustn't get myself involved.

Then he did turn, he did talk to me. He turned and smiled; he said, 'Do you understand English?' I said, 'Yes, I do, I *am* English, actually.' It all came tripping out; I must have sounded quite gormless; I could hear the two girls beside me on the sofa, Mary and a long-jumper, Beryl, sniggering away.

He said, 'Then tell me please what this means,' and he held out the local rag they have there in English, the *Daily News*. There was a picture of some gigantic Russian girl lifting a barbell with a little Mexican watching her with his mouth open, and some funny caption underneath. I tried to explain it to him and he nodded; there was something very calm about him.

He said, 'You are a runner?' I said, 'Yes, I'm a runner and she's a runner and she's a long-jumper. What are you? Don't tell me; let me guess. You're a discus-thrower.'

'No,' he said, 'I am a wrestler.'

Mary said, 'Well, you're big enough.'

He said, 'I have to be big. I am heavyweight,' then he introduced himself, all terribly elegant. He bowed; he said he was Antonio something or other. I asked, 'Are you Italian?' He said, 'Uruguayan,' and I said, 'Where's that?' and Mary said, 'South America, you fool.'

His English wasn't all that good – he couldn't always understand us – but we got along; we went downstairs into the basement and we all had Coca Cola. He said, 'I hate it, but I drink it.'

When the other girls left to go swimming I said I'd join them later. They said, 'All right, *we* understand,' very sarcastic, then Antonio and I were left alone.

It was one of those click-click things that sometimes happen to me and I wish they didn't, especially at times like these. He didn't say much, just stood smiling down at me. I wanted to go but I couldn't; I seemed to be hypnotized. I think if he'd said, right there and then, 'Let's go to bed,' I would have gone. There was so much in his face, such strength and such a lot of understanding. In the end we just went out for a stroll across the Village and ended up sitting on the bank above the track, holding hands. I don't know who took whose, whether I took his or he took mine; it just happened. I could see two of the British men's team in their red tracksuits looking at us over the parapet, but I didn't care. I never do at times like this. Perhaps it would be better if I did.

On Wednesday evening in the Zocalo, a group of student leaders from the Consejo de Huelga, the Strike Council, addressed a meeting. With the serene bulk of its colonial palaces, the Zocalo was a haven from the city's cheap modernity: its boulevards of lethal traffic, its synthetic Americana of coffee shops, skyscrapers, twilit bars.

The crowd grew quickly, filling the square, boiling beneath the students and their microphones, its mood intransigent, its cheers directed not merely to the students in front but at the Presidential Palace behind. When the tanks rolled into the square, guns turning, probing, like the blind tentacles of octopi, the crowd gave way before them sullenly at first, till the police moved in behind the tanks and the square turned into a maelstrom of flailing sticks, fleeing men, falling bodies. Guns flamed now and then in the dusk; a student roared defiantly into his microphone till suddenly his voice stopped. Gradually the square was cleared, till at last there remained only the tanks, the police, the scattered bodies.

The place he took me to that afternoon was the Museum of Anthropology. Fabulous. I've never really gone for museums; I'd probably never have seen this one if it wasn't for Antonio wanting to go, but when we got there it was fascinating, very modern and not like a museum at all. They'd really tried to make everything interesting instead of just sticking it in glass cases so you could take it or leave it.

Outside they'd got this huge, carved stone Aztec pillar with water cascading all around it, marvellous, and inside the rooms were all lit up like an aquarium, full of these frightening Inca and Aztec masks, animal heads, and creepy descriptions of human sacrifices. I said, 'I'm glad they're not living here now.' Antonio said, 'In some ways it is worse,' but I didn't know what he meant, then.

There were quite a few other couples there from the Village, athletes and their girlfriends; it seemed quite a popular place. In fact some of them were so busy snogging they didn't seem to be paying much attention to the museum, especially one Italian couple who were walking through the rooms very slowly, arms round each other, looking into one another's eyes, till you wondered they didn't bump into something. Antonio looked at them and laughed; then, as we came into the next room and there was no one in it, he kissed me.

It wasn't the first time, but it was still all new and marvellous. I could feel him hard up against me. He was so strong I couldn't have pushed him away if I wanted to, and the trouble was I didn't want to. I was in a panic; part of me kept wanting to fight him off, the other part didn't, especially when I was with him like this, and, being me, I knew which part would win. The thing was, could I hold out long enough, could I keep him at bay till after the final? At this rate I knew I wouldn't. I wouldn't even get through the heats. Lying awake in the night, away from him, I'd think about it and I'd come out in a cold sweat. I'd told him, 'Look, Antonio, I think you're smashing, you're super, but I've come out here to *run*, can't you understand that?'

He'd said, 'Yes, but you cannot run all the time!' It was hopeless. I knew so many girls who'd messed up their chances in important races, Empire Games and European Games and so on, just through this sort of thing, and I jolly well wasn't going to be one of them. I owed too much to too many people, and I owed it to myself.

As we came into another room, there was a boy and a girl in Mexican Olympic blazers that Antonio said hallo to. He introduced me, then they talked in Spanish, all very serious, though of course I didn't understand a word, till Antonio put one arm round the boy's shoulder, the other one round mine, and the four of us went downstairs, to where they had a cafeteria. We sat down at a table with our coffee, and the three of them carried on their conversation, very low, looking round now and then as though they were afraid of being heard.

I got a bit restless, to be honest, not being able to follow any of it, though now and then Antonio would wink at me and pat my hand and say, 'Sorry, sorry.' We must have been there half an hour, with me getting more and more fidgety, which I do anyway when I'm building up to an important race. I can't keep still: I have to keep doing something, moving around, like a racehorse in the paddock. Then at long, long last the two Mexicans got up to go.

I asked Antonio, 'Whatever was all that about?' He said, 'His brother is in prison.' I said, 'In *prison*? What's he done?' He said, 'He is a student leader.' I said, 'I don't understand,' and I didn't. 'Why should they put him in jail just because he's a student leader?'

Of course I'd read about what happened in Paris, the demonstrations, fighting with the police and all the rest – there'd been a lot about it on the telly – but I'd no idea the same sort of thing was going on here. As far as I was concerned you came to these countries, you ran and you went away. You'd got enough on your mind with your own races; you just *had* to shut everything else out.

Antonio said, 'Many students have been killed here, many others are in prison. Have you no student movement in England?'

I thought a bit and remembered some strike or other at the

London School of Economics, students sitting down in the entrance. I said, 'I suppose we have. I don't really take much interest,' and he smiled and shook his head. I told him, 'I'm one of your ignorant athletes, I'm afraid.'

He tried to explain to me, then: what was happening in Uruguay, what was happening in Mexico, how the university students were on strike and the army had occupied the university, how it had blown down the door of a school with a bazooka, the sort of thing you see in the cinema. What with his English and me being so thick about that sort of thing, I didn't really follow a lot of it, and, besides, when he was talking I loved to look at him, his expressions, especially when he was so serious, very stern, and now and then this fabulous smile. It distracted me.

That night when we got back I went out on the track and I ran six hundreds, eight two hundreds and a couple of quarters. My recovery rate was miles quicker, now.

On Friday evening in the Plaza de las Tres Culturas, a 'mitin' was held by the Student Strike Council.

The square was colossal and amorphous, an immense, jarring co-existence of different epochs, irreconcilable moments in time; a paradigm of Mexico itself. First, the excavations, the Aztec remains, rising like stone whales out of a sea of grass. By them, the colonial church, built from the same stone, at once rugged and exotic, intransigent and bizarre, as if its builders, inexorable conquerors, had been touched despite themselves by what was in the air, by the arcane mysteries of the place. And all around the square, the shiny functionalism of the new, the yellow corrugated cliffs of workers' flats, born out of the anonymous present.

In one corner of the square, Granaderos lounged, with their saurian smiles, outside a school which had been closed. In its dusty centre, by a wall, stood Polytechnic students, small and poor, full of a throbbing intensity of grievance.

From behind the square there could be heard the thump, thump, thump of a relentless drum, where Indians were dancing in a little market place. They danced tirelessly, without joy, bidden by the drum, the drum itself beaten by a fat, middle-

aged woman, her face fixed in a showman's grin. A whole family danced; the man like a fine circus animal, marvellously muscled, his brown, thick legs descending with a stamp, as though on some hated face. He wore only a loincloth and a high feathered head-dress; the expression of his high-cheeked, narrow-eyed face was perfectly impenetrable. He danced as a slave might dance who had translated resignation into something positive and challenging, making the best of a bitter predicament.

His wife, by contrast, danced without the same defiance, a slight, worn woman in a black shawl, each step a small victory over weariness, while their children, a boy and a girl, danced rhythmically, though they, too, had their father's impassivity without his challenge. Thump, thump, thump went the drum as if worshippers were being called to attend a sacrifice, when they were being called only to buy.

Into the great square, an hour before the meeting was due, rivulets of people trickled. Imperceptibly, in small agglomerations, the crowd grew big, gathering in front of the yellow apartment block beside the school, from one of whose balconies the students would speak. The crowd, as it increased, was very quiet, expectant, but without the aura of fear. By the time the student leaders filed on to their balcony and set up their microphones, it must have numbered four or five thousand, dense but not congested, mild but determined, easy in applause. Amongst it, paler, alien faces, foreign journalists and cameramen moved, scribbling and focusing and clicking. Students moved among it, too, spreading blurred, mimeographed sheets of paper like confetti.

When the leaders began to speak, it was with raw inexpertise, hollering at the microphones as though they, too, had to be convinced, their words coming in distorted thunderclaps, the crowd responding fervently to each peroration: 'Justice . . . the corruption of the Government . . . the brutality of the police . . . we shall go out among the peasants.'

Suddenly it began to rain, not gradually but instantly, great gouts of water falling on the crowd like a punishment, the crowd accepting it and bearing it, shifting a little as in gentle protest, putting up coat collars here, newspapers there, but still unscattered.

Honestly, I'm going round the twist. What with everything that's happening, I'll be surprised if I even qualify for the semi-finals.

One thing I am *not* going to do is give way to Antonio; I've told him a dozen times but he still won't believe me. That's the trouble with your actual Latin male, he'll never take no for an answer, not even a qualified no, and it's very hard because I want to as much as he does, or rather I would do if it wasn't for these being the most important three weeks in my life. But it's no use telling him that, either; he just laughs. I said, 'How can you expect a wrestler to understand?'

When I've won, if I win, it would be lovely, but until I do, I need everything, every atom of strength, every ounce of concentration. Sometimes I watch those Russian girls and I really envy them: *they* don't have these awful distractions. I watch them thumping their way round the track and I know they're giving it everything, because it's all they've got to give it to, so unless I give it everything too, what chance have I got?

I've done a 23.4 and a 23.5, but I know Lechantre has done a 23.3, and the Polish girl, Juskowiaka, is meant to have done a 23.1. Lechantre's going really well – it scares me to watch her – but then she's always been better in training than in competition; I've always been better in competition than in training. I need all that, the crowd and the pressure. I flutter like a leaf, but it still brings something out of me.

Antonio came and watched me train now and then; he even timed me. But I asked him in the end not to come: it distracted me, not just because I have this thing about him but because of his attitude, his not taking my running seriously. I watched him wrestle once or twice, in the gym, heaving and hauling away; I told him one day it was like watching whales in labour. But he's incredibly strong.

On Monday morning, the mothers and sisters of imprisoned students began a silent march of protest through the city, from the Memorial of the Mother.

The memorial stood in a small square, north of the Reforma, abstract, squat and almost wilfully ugly. Beneath it was carved an inscription: TO HER WHO LOVED YOU BEFORE YOU WERE BORN.

The women gathered quietly, quite cheerfully. Though some, a little unsurely, carried placards and banners, they had an air of hope rather than despair, of cheerful unity in positive action. Most were middle-aged, a few were young; most poor, dressed in the self-negating black of the Latin woman who has resigned herself wholly to motherhood.

The procession took shape slowly, like molecules coming gradually together. While the women moved, unhurriedly and amiably, into a file, a motor-coach full of students drew up beside them in the square, and they broke into a smiling, spontaneous patter of clapping, the students smiling back at them through their windows, happy to be heroes.

As the students climbed down from the coach into the square, a dark man spoke sternly to them through a microphone. 'This is a silent demonstration of protest. A peaceful demonstration. You may walk beside it, but you may not take part in it. You must not interfere with it in any way.'

When at last the procession, and its vanguard of banners, were ready, the column began slowly to move out of the square, a sluggish stream, a snake uncoiling, gathering pace, momentum, as it did, filing down into the Reforma among the traffic, the yellow buses and the green collectivos, *the honking cacophony of cars. Of these, the women took no heed, as if, once started, there was nothing to stop their gently irresistible progress, or their cause itself. The students marched peacefully beside them, policemen looked on complaisantly. The women did not speak or sing.*

I'm afraid I've let it happen. Between me and Antonio. All I can say in excuse is that yesterday afternoon I ran a 23.5. In fact I think that had a lot to do with it, it was the mood I was in: not only feeling chuffed, but thinking, it hasn't done me any harm being distracted; if anything, it seems to have done me good.

I'd arranged to meet him that evening by the Post Office, after I'd trained, and when I did I was absolutely full of it. I said, '23.5, I did 23.5,' but he just gave me a glassy sort of smile. I said, '23.5, on my own, with nobody pacing me; the winning time in Tokyo was only 23!' He said, 'You are wonderful,' and he kissed me, right there, bang in the middle of the Olympic Village, and suddenly, pressed up against him, I wanted to make love, I didn't care any more, and he felt it, I could tell, because he didn't say anything, just put his arm round me and we walked across the Village to his block, the Uruguayan one, and upstairs to his room, without anybody stopping us. He locked the door, and we made love; it felt marvellous, having him inside me at last. I felt full of life, full of power, and I knew that I was going to win; the heats, the semi-final, the final, all of them.

When he asked me next day would I go to a meeting with him that Wednesday, a students' meeting, I said yes. I'd have said yes to anything. That afternoon, I went out again and ran a 23.4.

A march had been planned, to the occupied school at San Tomas; soldiers and their trucks, their tanks, girdled the Plaza de las Tres Culturas. When the first of the student leaders to speak announced that the march had been abandoned, the crowd gave up an instant, responding sigh; of surprise, relief, acceptance, disappointment. It was dense again, numbering perhaps 5,000; tranquil, as it had been five days before. The student leader assailed it through the microphone: democracy . . . equality . . . solidarity with the Olympic Games. As he spoke, the sun fled from the sky and night came very quickly, the square lit patchily now from the apartment windows, and a scattering of lamps. It was quite dark when the two helicopters came throbbing and droning above it, like giant insects in a mating ritual.

It sounded rather exciting when Antonio told me about it, going up on this balcony with all the student leaders, while they made their speeches. We were going with this Mexican friend of his, the one whose brother was in jail, Manuel.

We got a taxi out to the vast, great square, swarming with people, where they took us into a block of flats, up in the lift, through one of the apartments, then out on to a balcony, where we looked down at all these people. There was a church down on the left and what looked like some ruins, and farther away a big, glass building which Antonio said was some Government ministry.

Manuel introduced Antonio and me to the students on the balcony, all terribly intense, some of them wearing beards like Castro. One of them was already spouting away into a microphone, making a dreadful din. Naturally I hadn't a clue what he was on about, and when Antonio tried to whisper what it was I still wasn't any wiser. I'm a bit of a nit about politics – I can't even follow them in England, let alone in Mexico – but Antonio had his arm round me while we stood there, and that was smashing. I'd got to the point you sometimes do with a person, when you need to have them with you all the time, you need to be touching them; you don't care how many people are looking or what they might be saying, just as long as you've got them beside you.

Of course I'd been getting a lot of niggling from the British team, not so much from Marion and Joan now, except for the odd dig, like 'If they could only have her chasing an electric Antonio, like a greyhound, she'd win by streets!' but from some of the boys, especially in the restaurant, Latin lovers and all the rest of it, but funnily enough it meant even less since that evening we made love than it had before.

I think if Antonio hadn't been there beside me on the balcony I'd have felt completely strange, completely and utterly at sea, as far away from the people on the balcony as I did from the people below, looking up at them. They were like children, really, laughing and clapping; oceans and oceans of them, these brown faces, stretching right back across the square. I was glad when it got dark and it was harder to see them; I could almost pretend we were there alone, just me and Antonio.

When the helicopters came droning over, I didn't think anything of it; they were just part of the whole strangeness. Then all at once there was this great, green, dazzling light, blinding you, like sheet lightning, then again, and suddenly a bang, and then another bang, something going *whack* against the wall, beside me; then someone screaming, a woman, and

Antonio grabbing me and pulling me to the floor, coming down on top of me, bump, knocking all the breath out of me, then more bangs, more screaming, and in a flash it was all real, and I was terrified.

The flares hung briefly in the dark like green fire, then, in the moment that they vanished, came the shots, the first cries, prelude to a crescendo of alarm in the square, the bewildered shouting and scurrying of people stricken by some natural disaster, an earthquake or a hurricane. The shots seemed, to those running, panic-stricken, for shelter, to be coming now from the crowd itself, now from somewhere else. The roar and clatter of helicopters heightened the chaos, but these, now, rose higher in the air and droned away from the square.

Most of the shots seemed to be aimed at the students' balcony, which had become an obscene shooting gallery, the row of heads above its parapet diminished first by one then by another, tottering and toppling like wooden, one-dimensional effigies.

Then a new sound joined that of the bullets and the agonised yelling of the crowd: a sound of infinite, advancing feet, moving swiftly yet without haste, till soldiers burst into the square, invading it from every side, like implacable Indians, the explosion of their rifles turning the syncopation of firing into a sustained, relentless percussion.

The soldiers went about their work with the devoted ferocity of hounds tearing a hare. They shot whoever they found in front of them; their rifles scorched and crimsoned the white shirts of boys; their bayonets drove into the backs of women; they killed and killed, as if the square was a slaughterhouse.

Here and there, at the whim of officers, prisoners were roughly taken, thrown into the backs of trucks, then driven away. A bazooka roared; its shell hit the wall of the apartment block, beside the students' balcony, and burst in an aureole of flame, which seared its way up to the roof.

There were no heads to be seen, now, on the balcony.

They were *firing* at us. God knows who; God knows why. I daren't look up, but the bullets seemed to be howling in from everywhere; I could hear them bouncing off the wall behind, hitting the balcony in front; I just screamed and screamed, I couldn't stop myself, till Antonio put his hand over my mouth. I had my eyes tight shut; then at last the bullets stopped for a few moments, and I heard voices shouting just above us, footsteps all around.

Antonio took his hand away and I opened my eyes very slowly, then I squirmed round and looked up; there were legs standing over us; I saw a man's hand in a white glove, holding a big revolver; behind me it sounded as if somebody was being dragged across the stone floor. Antonio yelled, '*Atleta, atleta*!' then the bullets came in on us again, bang, one just above my head, and I ducked right down; my nose was flat against the stone.

I don't know how long I stayed there, but it seemed forever. Somebody just near me gave an awful scream – they must have been hit – and I started to cry, it came pouring out of me, I was shaking and trembling and crying. Antonio held me tighter, but I shoved him away with all my strength.

Then, thank God, it all stopped. Someone was pulling me to my feet; Antonio, I thought, and tried to break away, but it wasn't Antonio: it was a man I'd never set eyes on before, he seemed like a plain-clothes policeman. Two more of them had hold of Antonio; one had a pistol pointed at his head; both of them were wearing white gloves.

They pushed and dragged us off the balcony, down the stairs, out of a back door, then shoved us against a wall. Antonio was pointing to his blazer badge and mine and saying, '*Atletas, atletas.*' He looked white as a ghost, and then it all welled up in me, I started shouting at him, 'How could you bring me here? How *could* you, when you know I've got to run?'

World Cup 1958

The Carthusian, December 1958

G OTHENBURG WAS GROUCHO and Mr Fix-It. There were
other characters, of course, who may have appeared
more vivid: 'Manager Yakushin' of Russia, an immense,
weatherbeaten bear of a man, who looked as if he had been
through every campaign of the revolutionary war; when he
smiled, it was as though a sandstone cliff had disintegrated
before one's eyes; Feola, the plump Brazilian team coach; Didì,
the brooding, coal-black master spirit of the *carioca* football
team. Yet one's memories of these two are somehow more
immediate and personal.

Groucho and Mr Fix-It were press stewards; that is to say,
they were to be found at certain periods of the day among the
shining glass and metal accoutrements of the splendid new
Ullevi Stadium, where Mr Fix-It sold cheap cars and Groucho
pursued some activity which never became plain to me. Mr Fix-
It was a large, impervious man with the fixed and terrifying
smile of a toothpaste advertisement; it made two parallel lines
with his thin, invariable bow tie. His face was an inexpressive
moon; his hair, dark and abundant, was smothered with Bryl-
creem, or its Swedish equivalent, and parted down the middle
as if slashed by a Prussian sabre.

'Leave it to me,' he would say, 'I'll fix it for you': girls, cars,
parties, restaurants, tickets. He meant diabolically well, and
appeared alarmingly when least expected. One would wake
from an unhappy afternoon hotel siesta to see him standing,
unabashed, with grin and bow tie, at the end of the bed.
'Resting, eh?' The accent was peculiar; ostensibly it had more

to do with Golders Green than Stockholm. 'I came here to tell you about the party . . .'

Groucho fixed things, too, but with a sort of White Rabbit improvisation; his name derived from an embarrassing resemblance to Groucho Marx. The hair and the moustache, though grey instead of black, were strikingly similar. He wore glasses, and was forever imparting confidences with that peculiar, intimate wriggle from the hips with which his namesake snuggled up to wealthy women. 'Listen, I tell you something else. You won't believe this . . . That man over there, well, I *hate* him! Yes!' But the confidences were always very flat, the restaurants bad and expensive. One had the impression that while Mr Fix-It was lost and would never know it – insensitivity surrounded him like a magician's cloak – Groucho was lost, and vaguely did. On Independence Day, he appeared at the stadium in what seemed to be a Boy Scout's shirt, smothered in patriotic badges. Nobody dared to ask him what it was.

If Groucho dabbled in confidences, then Mr Fix-It's stock-in-trade was anecdotes, through which he tried to present a rounded picture of himself, a sort of official autobiography. In these stories, he appeared as a rock of commerce, calm and unaffected, while Swedes all round him were turning to schnapps and helping to maintain the remarkable suicide rate. 'So I called this chap into my office and I said to him, "Take it easy, what's the matter? What makes you think you'd be so good at this job, that the other fellow isn't doing it properly? You're nobody special, you know; you need all your time to do your own job."'

He was selling cars, it appeared, as a favour to the firm. The task was a difficult one; no one else had been anxious to take it on. Mr Fix-It had volunteered with absurd quixotry – and we were to understand, piercing the thin veil of diffidence, that he was doing well.

And yet, he had his weak spot. He liked the Gothenburg Exhibition Building.

In this, he was not alone, nor was it inappropriate. The building, a monstrous pseudo-Roman abortion in ochre brick, stands at the top of the Kungsportaveynen. Inside it are pictures and sculpture; on ceremonial days, its infinity of steps are used for interminable parades, as this most neutral of countries indulges a significant penchant for uniforms. Mr Fix-It himself took us to watch a parade there; his fiancée was among those holding the flags. There were soldiers and sailors and airmen, with their female equivalents; girl gymnasts with powerful legs, nurses, street sweepers and housewives. In a moment of aberration, I confided to Mr Fix-It that I thought the building a monstrosity. For a moment he did not reply. The smile altered in character; a certain *dolcezza*, even nostalgia, seemed to enter into it, as though one had suddenly told him that his favourite aunt had all the time been a homicidal maniac.

'Perhaps,' he said at last, still faint and far away, 'it's the difference in our ages. You see, I'm used to this building. I have *known* it so long.' I felt ashamed.

But he finally lost face with The Party. For my part, I had no recriminations. It had been made plain to me from the first that it was a Dutch treat; Mr Fix-It would play host only in a manner of speaking. But clearly the idea grew and grew within him. The evening was going to be a triumph, a triumph for himself. At a wave of the wand, he would conjure up a bevy of journalists from all over the world, eager to be acquainted with Swedish beauty. Another wave, and behold – as many Swedish beauties as there were journalists. 'Come,' he said to the journalists, 'I invite you.'

It seemed promising enough; after all, the streets and parks of Gothenburg swarmed with friendly, flaxen girls. But when Mr Fix-It's troupe filed coyly into the expensive restaurant, there was a terrible hiatus. Each member was more homely than the last.

'Thank you,' said each journalist, at the end of the long evening, 'thank you for the party,' and it was then that the real blow fell. 'That will be eighty kroner from you,' Mr Fix-It said, and he smiled.

He never retrieved his position. People were polite to him after that, but he was avoided; besides, it began to be noticed that the information he gave was often wrong. The last time I saw him was – absurdly – in the Vallhalabadet, broken but brave.

This, the municipal swimming baths, is, in fact, where the

inhabitants go to satisfy a collective obsessional washing neurosis. After being given a towel, one enters a locker room of transcendent, shining sterility. In the middle of it stands a large weighing machine. The next room, far longer, is lined on either side with dressing cubicles; the next is the true centre of the Vallhalabadet. Large, tiled and steaming, it contains an arsenal of showers, taps and baths of every description. Here, a myriad of Swedes are washing themselves scrubbing for dear life, soaping their hair, dipping their feet in foot baths, even shaving. Under a line of electric hairdryers fixed to the wall outside, more of them stand, luxuriously turning their fair, soaked heads from one side to the other, in the warm jet of air.

Two rooms later – one has passed sauna baths and massage rooms – one goes through a blast of cold air, and into the baths themselves. There are seldom more than three people there.

Indeed, it was not in the baths but in the locker room that I saw Mr Fix-It, a naked Mr Fix-It, appearing suddenly and disturbingly from nowhere, doubly naked without his bow tie, though the smile was present.

'Where were you?' he said, game to the last. 'What did you do at midsummer? We could have had a party; I would have fixed it.'

I believe he would.

Feet of Clay

Men Only, 1963

I was just sixteen then, and I said to myself, when I knew Leeds Town were coming up to play, I'll get his autograph. I'll get it when they stop at the halt. There was this train, see, that used to leave Newcastle at twenty minutes to six, and most of the visiting teams would be on it. It would stop at our halt for just three minutes, and I reckoned if I ran along the train, like, I could find which carriage he was in, and pass me book in, for him to sign. We were a tiny little mining village – that was all we were – but the trains would always use to stop there.

Mind, I'd more or less given up getting autographs then – it was more for kids, really – but with him it was different, I idolised him; there'd never be another like him, greatest centre-forward ever seen on a football field. But he was getting on then, and there'd been paper-talk about him retiring, so I thought it might be me last chance.

I was Newcastle daft, but whenever Leeds Town came up I always used to cheer for them as well, because of him, and he'd always get a goal. I remember one of them at Gallowgate, the first time I ever saw him play, greatest bloody goal you could imagine: he jumped up above the three of them, goalkeeper and all, and the ball went in off his head like a bullet. There isn't a centre-forward living or dead could have scored that one.

I'd have been there that day, too, only I was playing meself; I was in the colliery side, centre-half – I was a big lad for me age, eleven stone and nearly six foot, even then. On top of that, I was working for a butcher in the morning, and delivering evening papers after the game. So that I could be at the halt, I took on the morning round instead. I was up at six o'clock that day; it was one of those cold ones, with a northeast wind; I hadn't got but a thin coat on, and it was biting into me, and when I'd done with that, I'd got the meat to deliver. Usually when I played me mother would do me a poached egg for me lunch, but this time I didn't have time, and when I got to the colliery ground I felt frozen right through, honestly. But I'd got me autograph book in me pocket, and all the time I was playing I was thinking to meself about getting to the train there; only half me mind was on the match.

As soon as it was over, I rushed in and out of the dressing room and used a short cut I knew, over the fields – it was a mile and a half from the ground. I remember thinking the book was going to bob out of me pocket and I'd lose it, I was going so fast. I'd had it for years, it was all bound in leather, and it had players in it going back to Bill M'Cracken.

When I got to the halt it was dark, and the train was just coming in. I was right opposite the Pullman car, and I could see him there, Billy Green, already, from the bottom of the bank; that great fair head he'd got and the broken nose, like a boxer. He was sitting right by the window, and he was drinking a beer. Well, I rushed up that bank like me life depended on it, and I got on the platform below the window and I tapped on it, but he wouldn't open. So I knocked on it again, but he still wouldn't look round, and I was getting desperate. I went on tapping and holding up me book until at last he did turn round, not a smile or anything, and he opened the window and I handed in the book. He didn't even look at it; he didn't. He just took it and threw it straight out on the platform, right in the middle of a puddle. I picked it out but it was soaking, all the binding and everything ruined; when I got home the colours had run and there were pages all sticking together. While I was trying to wipe it off, the train pulled out, and that was the end of it. I walked back home across the fields and, I can tell you, I was near crying. I thought, What did he want to do that for, there was no necessity. Then I thought of the way I'd made him me idol and the trouble I'd took to get there, and I felt like I'd come to the end of the world.

My father said that night, 'If that's the kind of thing he does, he's a rat. I don't care how many times he's played for England, I don't care how many he's scored.' They'd lost at Gallowgate that day – I suppose that was part of the trouble – but anyway, from then on, I put him out of me mind, I was done with him. I thought, If I ever get to be any good and play professional, I'd never treat a boy like that, no matter what.

About a month later, Liverpool City came to me and offered me a trial. I'd rather have gone to Newcastle, but they'd never shown an interest; I'd wrote to them for a trial, and they didn't even answer. I was that keen to turn professional. I'd have gone as far as Aberdeen.

I did all right in the trial, so they took me on the groundstaff – I was too young to sign just yet – and I'd help on the pitch and clear up the terraces and that, then play the odd game in the A side. The summer I came back home, and soon after the new season started, they gave me a chance in the Reserves, and I stayed in.

About the fourth or fifth match, we were home to Leeds Town reserves, and I didn't think much about it; it was just another game to me. Then the Friday morning I got to the ground, and Danny Morris, our left-back, said to me, 'You're in for a caning, then; you know who you've got up against you?' and I said, 'Who?' and he said, 'Billy Green.'

Well, when I heard that, I must have surprised him, because I said, 'Grand.' I said, 'That's wonderful,' and he said, 'Wonderful? He'll run bloody rings round you,' and I said, 'We'll see about that, then.'

I was that excited I couldn't wait for the game; I didn't sleep that night, not a minute; I was just thinking of the time at home, and the way he'd thrown me book into a puddle, and how I was going to show him.

They'd just dropped him from the League team that week and, when he came on to the field, you could see he didn't ike it; he'd got those heavy brows and his face was all sullen; he stood and hardly bothered to play the ball, when they were shooting in. When we kicked off, I came up beside him, third-back style, and he gave me a look like as if to say, 'Who's this cheeky young bugger?'

The first time the ball came through to him, I really got dug in; he went down flat, and when he got up he said, 'None of that, son,' and I said, 'None of that yourself,' and the next time, when he went up for a ball in the air, I jammed me elbow in his ribs; I was getting stuck in, I can tell you. Ned Willis, our skipper, came up to me and he said, 'Here, steady, lad, what's the matter with you?' and I said, 'I'll show him, I'll show the bugger.'

The funny thing was, if it had been just a normal game, like, I'd probably have been scared, sixteen years old and him with a reputation like he had; but as far as I was concerned, he was a rat, like the old man said, and whenever the ball came near him I thought of that evening and I went right in.

He didn't score that day, and we drew one-all. When we came off the field, he said to me, 'How old are you, son?' and I said, 'Sixteen,' and he said, 'Dirty as you are at your age, eh?'

'Well,' I said, 'there's one thing I don't do: I don't throw youngsters' autograph books into a puddle when they ask me!' He stopped there looking at me like I was daft, and I went down the tunnel, and that was the last I ever saw him.

Feats of Clay

The Times, 20 May 1997

THE FILM DOCUMENTARY *When We Were Kings* tells, in its sometimes enthralling, sometimes anti-cinematic way, of Muhammad Ali's 'Rumble in the Jungle' in Kinshasa in 1974, his extraordinary victory over George Foreman. Enthralling for its filming of the event itself; engaging, in its portrait of Ali; anti-cinematic, in its plethora of talking heads.

The one that talks most is Norman Mailer's, by turns analyst and groupie. Mailer wrote a strange book about the contest, in which he described how, in an odd magical ritual, he walked around the balcony of his hotel room, propitiating fate on Ali's behalf.

At the end of the film, sheer embarrassment as Mailer tells a tale of how the ailing Ali complimented him on looking so young at 62, moving Mailer to go off like a dog – a fawning dog? – to urinate. At which Ali asks Mailer's far younger wife why she is still 'with that old man'.

The film shows Ali as an astonishing boxer, a supremely handsome human being, an infinitely charming and loquacious egotist, but claims by one of the talking heads that Ali might be a 'great political leader' are simply absurd.

As one who covered several of Ali's earlier fights, notably his sensational victory in Miami Beach over Sonny Liston in 1964, I found that the film omitted a complete dimension. Where it tries to show Ali as hero, it is surely more appropriate to see him as victim.

Another talking head tells us that, for all his present slurring and shambling, the cruel product of his Parkinson's Syndrome,

Ali is now a happy man. But who can be happy when, remembering him in his physical glory, he sees the Ali of today, a brutal parody of what he was? And, seeing him, reflects how it must have happened, the fights too far, the punches to the head sustained despite his marvellous evasive skills.

For me, the watershed, the ugly moment of truth, came in 1966 in the dressing room of the White City gym before Ali's second meeting with Henry Cooper. He was on the massage table, for once calm and serene. Indeed, he had been sending up his own, flamboyant style of earlier days.

'Let's go back to the past for just *five* minutes! If he give me jive, he'll fall in five! Let me go, Angelo; I want him *now*!'

Recumbent, Ali said, 'Presidents of the USA, they have their advisers. There's my brains right there.'

At which I expected him to indicate Angelo Dundee, who had trained and nurtured him so assiduously, but he did not. 'Herbert Muhammad!' Ali cried, and pointed to a short, plump, black man who stood smiling in a corner. Herbert Muhammad, the son of Elijah Muhammad, founder and baleful leader of the Black Muslims.

It was the Black Muslims, by then, who controlled Ali, who had persuaded him to change his name from Cassius Clay, to leave the group of rich businessmen from Louisville, Kentucky, who had skilfully guided his career up to the time that he took the title from Liston.

By an irony, however, it was supposed, at the time of Ali's conversion, that it had been engineered not by Elijah Muhammad but by Malcolm X, the rival whom the Black Muslims would eventually shoot down.

Had the Louisville consortium continued to look after Clay, as he then was, would he have kept much more of his money? Would he have been forced to keep on fighting for so long?

He had 22 fights after taking the title back from Foreman. A talking head assures us that Ali just loved fighting. Did he? The day after beating Liston, Clay told us that he did not like hurting people, he did not like fighting – neither had his hero, Sugar Ray Robinson.

As for his subsequent status, under the Black Muslims, an icon and a role model for young blacks, had he not been that already, by virtue of defeating Liston? A well-known liberal American journalist remarked to me the day after that Liston was 'the kind of coloured man who keeps other coloured men in line. I'm glad to see him get it.'

A few days later, I flew to New York to work on a boxing documentary for the BBC. Clay turned up at their Fifth Avenue headquarters to record an interview with Harry Carpenter, in London.

He arrived with an entourage – indeed, an entourage would surround him, flattering and exploiting, for the rest of his boxing career. Sam Cooke, the singer who would eventually be shot dead, was one of the noisy group. Clay was noisiest of all. He would not say a word until he had the cheque and halfway through the interview he stopped, to demand more money. Only his devoted camp follower, Bundini Brown, was missing – Brown, who pops up early in *When We Were Kings*, described as assistant trainer, solemnly predicting the fight; Brown, who claimed authorship of his and Clay's famous chant, 'Float like a butterfly, sting like a bee! Yeah! Rumble, young man, rumble!', Bundini Brown, who, in that dingy Miami Beach gym, where the Beatles turned up to be photographed with Clay, complained, 'I'm giving everything and getting nothing!'

'I'm so great,' Clay would cry, 'that the Beatles came to get *my* autograph!' Soon after the rumpus at the BBC, I went to Harlem to interview Malcolm X at the Hotel Teresa, where Joe Louis used to stay in his time as world champion. Clay was on the steps, haranguing a small crowd. Upstairs, in the hotel, was Malcolm X, lean, bespectacled, courteous and intense.

His analysis was persuasive. His solution was all cloud-cuckoo-land. Blacks constituted ten per cent of the American people. They should therefore be granted a separate state, with ten per cent of the territory.

When Ali talks, on this documentary, one hears the voice of the Black Muslims. Whatever the atrocious suffering of American blacks across the generations, Africa is surely no panacea. Ali insists that America's blacks have been brainwashed with white attitudes and must therefore be 'unbrainwashed'.

If anybody was brainwashed, it appears to have been Ali

himself. He showed courage, and was vindictively punished, for standing up against the Vietnam War, but at whose instigation was he standing? I much preferred the unreconstructed Clay, for all his exhibitionism.

In Miami Beach, Liston, before the fight, was the funnier man and, at the weigh-in, Clay appeared to go berserk, yelling and ranting at a passive Liston. 'You a chump! You a chump!' Jim Manning, of the *Daily Mail*, wrote that Clay was too sick to fight, but it was just one more manoeuvre.

In the event, Clay boxed beautifully, slipped punch after punch, until Liston, his shoulder strained, quit on his stool. In Kinshasa, Ali, who had been promising to 'dance', played 'rope-a-dope' instead, until Foreman had punched himself out and could be punched in his turn.

But in the last analysis, the exploited Ali just took too many punches.

The Dying of the Light

The Dying of the Light, 1976

MY FATHER HAS BEEN dead for twenty years, but looks quite well. A referee on a football field in some town drab and obscure, somewhere like Accrington or Barrow, somewhere full of cobbles and factory chimneys, put his whistle to his lips, blew a great, long, final blast, and my father fell, just like the walls of Jericho. Or rather, like some classical hero, Hercules or Achilles – he could always be sulky when he wanted – with an immediate apotheosis, deathless fame, a hallowed place in everybody's memory.

That should have surely been enough for him. If he'd had a proper sense of proportion, the merest grain of *comme il faut*, he would have disappeared, rather than linger on as an embarrassment to everybody, a nuisance to himself, as they say about the old. Except, of course, that he wasn't old, but old only for a footballer, so that by a strange paradox, as soon as he retired he became young again. Thirty-five. A whole life lived; half a life to go.

I wasn't there to see him die. It was an away game and we stayed in Southport, Mother, Tim and I. We lived in a club house and we'd have to get out, now. We'd never owned a house.

When Dad got home, he was very bright and breezy. I hadn't learnt then that these were the dangerous times, that he was chattering to keep his spirits up. 'Well, that's it, everybody, played my last game, made my last save. They didn't score!'

'That's the eighth time this season!' Tim said.

'That's right!' said Dad. 'Good lad!' and picked Tim up into the air and swung him round. 'Game's best goalkeeper. Now I'm going to be the game's best manager, aren't I?'

When he said that, I started to cry, a right little Cassandra I was, but something must have come through to me, some of his fear and misery. I cried and cried. They couldn't stop me. I couldn't tell them what it was. Dad put Tim down and swung *me* round. 'Here, nothing to cry about, young lass! Let's have a smile, then!' but it wasn't any good: I went on howling, till at last Mum told him, 'Put her down, Len!' and he did. He wasn't laughing any more, he dropped me brusquely and it made me cry still harder. I knew he was cross.

'What's to cry for?' he asked me. 'What's to cry?' And yet he must have known. What he meant was that Tim was the fan, the one to care, the one who went to matches, who helped Mother keep his cuttings, while I was the one who didn't want to go, who fretted when she got there. And now Tim began to cry too, as loud as me, on and on, long after I had stopped.

'Proper little miseries,' Father said, then walked off down the little hall in his sports jacket and his grey flannel trousers and his big, brown brogues; I still remember what he wore that day. He went into the living room and slammed the door. 'Now see what you've done,' said Mother.

I was twelve and Tim was ten. I'd gleaned enough to know Father was a hero; there were images that stayed with me and still do. My father soaring out of the mist, some winter's afternoon; the mighty jump, which was his Nijinsky Leap, soaring above a throng of striving bodies, sleek, bobbing heads; long arms, huge hands, outstretched to seize the ball, clutch it to his body, bear it to earth. The roar of relief and joy at the moment he grasped the ball, stretched in midair, superman and saviour, the voices all around me saying, 'There's nowt like him, never will be!'

My father in his green jersey, his ridiculous cloth cap, peak pulled down, rushing from his goal in a kind of dynamic crouch as attackers bore down upon him, a compound of marvellous courage, fearsome cunning, a Janus who looked beadily one way; plunging on the ball, beneath the thundering boots, grabbing it, smothering it, to the music of the roar, again.

My father standing in his goal, full of restless power, thick-thighed, broad-chested, jaws rotating as he chewed his gum, eyes forever on the play, suspicious as a policeman's, alert to danger as a deer.

My father sprawled bitter in the mud, the ball in the net behind him, his whole body exuding resentment, outrage and defeat, a man betrayed. And then, if his team were playing away, the roar would be one of mockery and triumph, a roar that frightened me, that seemed levelled directly at him, gloating on his defeat; a roar that would frighten me, so that I would clutch my mother's sleeve, bury my face in her coat, wanting to escape the sound, the sight of him, till she would say, 'Don't be a silly billy! It's only a game!'

Only a game! My father's whole, prone body, the wooden grimness of his face when he got back in goal, gave the lie to that, while there was a brutal quality about the roar itself, a note of retribution and revenge, over and above the mere insult of the goal, a hunter's passion to destroy. 'Got you!' it said. 'Got you at last!' As indeed they finally would.

He should have gone out gloriously at Wembley or at Hampden, rising, rising to the ball for the last time then, that last centre safely held, rising still, into the sky, to his apotheosis. Instead of which . . .

Instead of which, when the phone went beside my bed this morning at half-past six, waking me and waking Robert, it was Mother, crying, as I'd known it must be. And in me the same response as always, same reaction of pity, anger and despair, welling up inside. How extra vulnerable we are when we've been woken, when all the demons of the night are still to be allayed, all our defences are still down.

'The police were here. I don't know *what* to do. Can you come soon?'

Robert stirring beside me in the bed, stretching his long, pale arms, saying, 'Your father?' sleepily. Me nodding at him, trying not to cry myself, so grateful that he's there, with all his saving scepticism.

'Broken into a bank, has he?'

I shake my head, grimace and wave my hand at him, but still I'm glad.

'Mother, don't cry! What happened?'

'And they came. And they took a statement. And they said he'll be arrested.'

'*Why*, Mother, what's he *done*?'

More tears, then I could hear the word whispered, 'Fraud.'

'Fraud,' I told Robert, and he echoed, 'Fraud?' his hands behind his head. 'Suspended sentence. First conviction. No need to worry.'

'*Shut* up! Mother, *what* fraud?'

Oh, she couldn't really say. Raising money for some kind of club. Been borrowing it all over Croydon. What happens if he's sent to prison?

'He won't, Mother, Robert says he won't. Yes. Mother, I'll be down.' Again. And again.

'What's he been up to now?' Robert yawning, stretching.

'Some fraud about a club. He's taken people's money.'

Now he sits up. His hair's too long. Long and lank and brown. But at least there's still plenty of it, dangling back from above his long forehead. Beneath that, grey eyes, and below them, his nice long, bumpy nose.

'The Casino Club?'

'Why, did you know about it?'

'Yes, didn't you?'

'You should have told me, Robert.'

Because Father never would. He was wary of me: I was the Reality Principle. Mother would tolerate him, like a mother. But what he wanted was somebody who'd say, 'Fine, Len, fantastic, Len!' and they were always to be found. Failing that, Robert would do, because Robert would let him rattle on; Robert would do his fly-on-the-wall, grit-in-the-oyster act, and he'd never guess that he was being goaded. Noncommittal but encouraging. Oh, how well I knew the way he did it. We were all microbes under the microscope, butterflies wriggling on the end of the pin; yet *he* admired my father, too, or what my father *was*.

I remember how I found out. We'd known each other for a week; we were in bed together and I'd come so beautifully. I loved to make love with him. I loved him in bed and out of bed, which was so unusual; loved his detachment and how funny he could be. And his eye roved round the room, picked

out a book, my father's silly book. 'You're not *Len* Rawlings'
daughter?'

'*Yes!*' I said.

'Good God!' I'd never seen him quite so animated, propping
himself on the pillows, his face as open as an eager schoolboy's,
an expression that I knew so well, had seen so many times, the
expression conjured by my father's name.

'Not *you!*' I said. 'Not *you!*'

'*From Post to Post*! I thought I recognised it! Bought it when
it came out; used the money from my paper round. I'd go miles
to see him play. I queued up for his autograph, at Upton Park.'

'And got it?' I asked. Not everybody had.

'Oh, yes. Mind you, he could be stroppy at times. Formed us
up in a line, and sent me away because I queued up twice. I'll
never forget the goal he saved that day.'

Et tu, Robert. I closed my eyes. I wished he wouldn't tell me.

'Right in front of me; I'd stood behind the goal. Pressed up
against the railings. Anywhere else, I was too small to see. It
was the war. I was a West Ham fan; he was a guest for
Tottenham.'

'*I* know. In the Air Force.'

'Yes. The rain was pelting down; December. I'd got no coat
and I was soaked. The ball came over like a flying lump of
mud; footballs got heavy, then. Macaulay headed it, right for
the corner.'

'But Dad saved it!'

'That's right. I still don't know how; he should never have
had a chance, especially in all that mud. There was no take-off.
He was so big, too; you'd never think a man that size could be
so agile. Flew across the goal, parallel with the ground, and not
only got to it but caught it, held it. Fabulous!'

My God, I thought, you should know him now.

'I've still got that autograph. I think I have. There was never
anybody like him.'

Was, was, was. 'A fat lot of good that did him.'

'Why, what's he doing now? I thought he had a pub.'

'I wish he did.'

'He was a manager, though, wasn't he?'

'Oh, yes. Three times.'

'You'd think they'd listen to me, wouldn't you. Bloody directors. Thirty-eight England caps. Best keeper of my day. Blokes that never kicked a ball. But oh, no. So in the end I told them. You don't want a manager. I said. What you want's a bloody yes-man.'

'He's in Croydon,' I told Robert. 'He lives there in a little house. And he more or less does nothing.'

'Oh,' he said, and his head dropped. He looked very sad; I think he really was sad, which was nice; not like most of them, just a conditioned reflex, giving you ten seconds' sadness, as if you'd said your grandmother died. He *is* kind, he *is* warm, he *is* compassionate, yet all that co-exists with his killing curiosity. I don't know how he ever came to work for the BBC. He should have been a detective or an anthropologist or a psychiatrist.

'What does he *do* all day?' That was one of his characteristic questions; very simple, seemingly banal, yet full of hidden lacerations, the sort that pulls you up with a shiver; on the edge of a crevasse, looking down, down into absolute nothingness.

Though, thinking about it, it becomes less frightening, for my father's days in their way are surprisingly full, even when he isn't working. There are walks to take, striding across the hills with Ben, his Airedale. There's pubs to drink in, golf to play, though from time to time he has to change his club as the birds come home to roost. There's visitors, pilgrims; you'd be surprised how many. There's the television. God bless the television, which takes care of everything from six o'clock or so. And his occasional trips to London, when they send him the money for a train ticket, a hotel room and a hired dinner-jacket, put him on show for a few hours, drink his health, fill him up with wines and brandies, then pack him back in mothballs till the next time.

My father lives in the past and the future, never in the present, where children and savages are meant to live, though he's still so much a child and I suppose a bit of a primitive. My father lives through his memories and his fantasies and his memories feed his fantasies. He's *been* somebody, so of course he will be somebody again.

Attention must finally be paid to this man.

One more from the lumber room, and wrong. Attention *has* been paid to this man, immense attention, huge, disproportionate quantities of attention, so that now, the present, is merely a hiatus, a tiresome parenthesis in what ought to be and will be. When my father goes out walking with his dog, hurling the rubber ball, striding across the sparsely covered hills, he's full of joy, you can see it; there's a beam on his nice, silly, strong-featured face. He shouts to Ben; his thoughts are so obviously positive, which means they must be thoughts of the future, thoughts of the past.

Mind you, I'm guessing, for these thoughts are not revealed to me, if I go with him, nor to Tim so far as I can tell, while Mother never does go with him; she's very intuitive, Mother is, and she seems to know. My father doesn't want people in this past and future world of his, other than the people he peoples it with. There'd be lots of images, plenty of sensations; of old, far-off, forgotten games, and matches long ago. I'm too easily tempted. And images of the future, less dynamic: graciously greeting, presidentially presiding, translated from boots, shorts and jersey into black tie, hundred-guinea suits, though not the 'gear', the frilled shirts, pinched-in suits and kipper ties. Those are for the new football stars, and he isn't one of them.

'Does he read?' Robert once asked that, too, and the answer is oh, yes, he reads, and writes, too, in a very clear, copperplate, rounded Board School hand. He reads, as he always read, newspapers and sports magazines. The *Mirror*, the *Express* and now the *Sun*, the *News of the World, Shoot, Goal*. Sometimes his own scrapbooks, but not, so to speak, generically. Only to check a fact when people come, to pin down a specific memory. 'I can *remember*,' he'd say, with a wag of the head, a knowing smile. Man, the animal who can remember. Defeats and victories. Goals and near misses. Shots that beat him, shots that were saved, shots that hit the bar. Who said what in the heat of action. Who said what in the depths of the dressing room. No wonder even Robert could sit listening to him, hour after hour. Did Mother listen then? She sat and smiled, happy to see him happy. Why listen, when she'd heard it all before? Would Tim listen when he came down, from Rotherham, an executive in a plastics firm? He'd listen but he'd fret: he'd heard it, too, and besides, he'd had to define himself against Dad, decide himself not to be like Dad. Dad's past worried Tim, just as once upon a time it had smothered him, when he was doing what Dad wanted, trying to be a footballer, too. Tim, in his flared trousers and his lurid shirts, open at the neck when ties were out. Tim with his sideburns and his styled haircut, long at the back, full at the sides, still irredeemably curly. Tim with his bushy moustache. 'What's *that*?' Dad said. He'd been clear-shaven all his life, like every player in his time: short back and sides, bare upper lip. Tim keeping such a gimlet eye on London fashions, way up there in the North. And slipping envelopes to Mother, with a kind of surreptitious self-importance.

I don't like the expression on his face when he passes those envelopes; there's too much triumph there, too much self-vindication. Tables turned, boot – football boot? – on the other foot. You were so great, but now *I* keep *you*. And yet I can't blame him, quite apart from the fact that other sons, as put upon as he, might have said go to hell, stew in your own juice, and walked away. Yes, I can forgive Tim his petty generosity, his generous pettiness.

Remember those awful afternoons in our little back gardens, back gardens in Manchester, in Sunderland, in Southgate, Southport. 'Come on, now, son! Don't be afraid! Never be afraid! Dive in, that's it! No, no, no, you *must* keep your eye on the ball!'

Poor little curly-headed Tim in his short, grey trousers and his long, grey school socks, framing his fragile little knees; and Dad so big. 'Don't kick it! Head it!' Tim exhausted, crying.

'Let him come in, now, Len; you can see he's tired!'

'Not until he's got it right, Mary. He's got to learn. Now, stop that howling, Tim! You know what they did to me, when *I* joined Rovers? When they were teaching me to take a ball? They'd throw it in the air, and if I didn't climb high enough they'd boot me up the backside. How'd you have liked that, eh?'

If there's anyone I have to thank for turning a raw lad from a colliery village into what one scribe called Soccer's One-Man Wall, it was Rovers' assistant trainer, Jackie

Cochrane. Jackie had been a goalkeeper himself and the first day we met he told me, 'Son, I'm going to show you how to catch the crosses. A keeper that can't catch crosses is like a cow that can't give milk.' And teach me he did.

There were times, as a green fourteen-year-old, when I must admit that I half wished I'd gone down the mine, like my father, but looking back, I'm grateful to Jackie and what he showed me. He was right, too. A goalkeeper who stays on his line is only doing half his job, however many saves he makes.*

How Father wanted Tim to be good! Not as good as him, of course, but then I don't think that ever really worried him: he honestly felt that no one could be. Even now, when he talks about himself as a player, it's with a kind of detached reverence, the absolute faith of a believer.

'Here, did you see this, Dad?' Tim might ask. 'They're comparing you and Gordon Banks.' Then Dad would laugh and shake his head, almost pityingly. 'No comparison, lad, no comparison.' His past was sacrosanct.

Whatever Tim felt about Dad then, I know *I* hated him, those afternoons. I wouldn't look out of the windows – I just couldn't look – but the sounds came back to me: squelch of feet on the winter-wet grass, my father's hectoring voice, the ball bouncing off the wall of the house or landing on a rockery.

He'd even had Mother playing football at one time, back-garden football, it says in *From Post to Post*, but that was before I was born. What kind of football can it have been? I did ask her once. 'Oh, it was just fun!' she'd said. 'I was hopeless.' Mother's so quick to bury any kind of nastiness that you can never be quite sure. It was probably done out of love, albeit self-love; he'd wanted her to share his love for him.

But between that time and the time he was teaching little Tim, he never tried to teach me; I think he knew. Just as he'd hardly ever smack me, though he often clouted Tim. I frightened him, as I frighten him now. Intelligence always worried him, all the more when it combined with the feminine principle. 'She's

* *From Post to Post*, p. 24.

clever, Jenny is,' he'd say, as if it were something to beware of, like a wasp's sting. 'Very intelligent, our Jenny. Don't know where she gets it.'

From Mother, probably, though Mother was scared of her own perceptions; they could make life uncomfortable. It was easier to shelter inside a little cocoon of unawareness. When people make fun of Women's Lib, I think of Mother, look at Mother, and I know we're right. Right for men *and* women. What couldn't Mother have done for Father, if she'd only been allowed to? All the pain she could have spared him, all the pitfalls she might have led him round. She wasn't allowed to grow, so *he* never grew. There he still is, a child with a child's qualities. Greedy, but not greedy enough. Ruthless, but not ruthless enough. Ambitious, but not ambitious enough. Or rather, not for the correct things.

By the time I signed pro at seventeen, I had one ambition: to be the greatest goalkeeper in the world.*

Which he fulfilled; to find that it was not fulfilment, only a halfway house to something else that never quite materialised. If Mother needed Women's Lib, Father needed Footballers' Lib: a movement for saving professional players from themselves, to stop them living in a fool's paradise, an eternal present, in which they're encouraged to be mindless and dependent, to have everything done for them that doesn't take place on that green oblong, all the minor decisions made; until the day that they're no longer needed.

I suspect it's just as bad now, though they drive big cars, where Dad took buses; live in the stockbroker belt, where we had semis; go off to nightclubs, where Dad went to the pub. Victims, all victims; though Dad can't see it, and no wonder. That's what riles him more than anything: that they make money and he didn't. The obscene injustice of it. 'Honestly, Mary. Honestly, Jenny. People not fit to lace my boots. Two hundred pounds a week. If they're worth that, then what was I

---

* *From Post to Post*, p. 36.

worth? No one could ever have afforded me.' Overlooking the much greater injustices.

Before I even see or speak to him, I know that he's done whatever it is they've charged him with. And that whatever he's done is absolutely trivial and insignificant, by comparison with what's been done to him. I sense, too, that this time they mean to crush him, that their patience is exhausted, that there won't be any question of a fine or a suspended sentence or some footling little punishment they work out just for him. 'Look here,' they'll say, 'we've all been very tolerant with you, taken your past record into account, all those international caps, all the goals you've saved for England. We've overlooked your shoplifting, we've forgiven you your forgery, we've made allowances for your obtaining credit under false pretences, but that's the point: your credit has run out. We're scrupulously just. We weigh things very carefully. If only you'd won the World Cup, we might have let you get away with murder. As it is: three years, with possible remission for good football. You see, you've reached the point of no return.'

Which I feel, too. Hope's gone. Hope of change, I mean; if ever there was any. And going to prison will make surer still of that; it will destroy not just what's left of his public image – though not its past; oh, never, never its past – but his image of himself.

I've heard him bitter, though only for effect and self-indulgence; he didn't believe such things could ever happen to him. Such as the time when he was coming up for shoplifting.

'Well, look how Hughie Gallacher died; another bloody international.'

Quite different from him. I'd read about it. Tiny, self-destructive Scot, centre-forward, always in trouble, always getting drunk; one of the little, pathetic, doomed idols from the slums.

'Died on the bloody railway line. Just before coming up in court.'

For ill-treating his son.

'What was Hughie? Fifty-seven? I've still time!'

Somewhere up in the Northeast. The little, violent man, the great entertainer, the Mighty Atom, full of self-hate and helplessness, laid down his head on the line. His last, most violent deed.

My father mustn't die like that. If he's to die, then he must die majestically, as a reproach, a final, terrific gesture, like Samson, tearing down the pillar of the Temple.

'Gentlemen of the jury, the quality of mercy is not strained. Besides, you are all far guiltier than my father. How many of you saw him play? Be honest! How many of you saw him save a goal? How many of you screamed and cheered and were transformed, had colour brought into your squalid lives? How many had his picture in your room, pined for his autograph, collected his cigarette card? Come on! I see middle-aged men, grey heads, among you. Gentlemen, I submit there is no case to answer, or else that there's a collective case to answer, to be answered by you, not him. When Hughie's head rolled on the railway line did you know, did you care? Were you a little relieved?

'M'Lud, even you may be called into question. You're a Rugger man, M'Lud, I can see it from your fine, port-pink complexion and the healthy hang of your jowls; you're a Garrick Club and Athenaeum man, M'Lud; a Middle Temple man; but Gallacher *did* once play for Chelsea, where it was fashionable for Garrick men to go at times.'

I sentence this footballer to be run over by a train until he's dead, and may the Lord have mercy on his goal.

'M'Lud, gentlemen of the jury, our collective guilt is a cliché, I concede that to you, a sentimental cliché that makes justice impossible. And yet in this case I can produce specific evidence. My first witness is a newsreel, M'Lud. One hundred thousand people are applauding my father, who has just saved a penalty kick in a Cup-final. You might have been there yourself, M'Lud.'

No, no, it's hopeless, and I know it. Not even Manny Goldstone can save him now, as he did that other time, over the sports shop, paid the whole three thousand pounds out of his own pocket, looked at me with those spaniel eyes and said, 'Believe me, Jenny, for the pleasure he's given me, that isn't so much.' Mother crying. Me wanting to cry and wanting to hit him, terribly touched by what he'd done, infuriated by what he was, what he represented. He was better than almost all of them, yet still one of them, a myth-maker, a fan; still getting his kicks, in however benign a way.

'May be a bit of an old Jew-boy, Manny,' Father said, 'but he's stood by me when no one else would.' Father's a good, old-fashioned, instinctive, some-of-my-best-friends antisemite, with no malice in him; can't stand Jews in general, but takes any individual Jew on his merits, especially if he does him a favour. Which he wouldn't wholly see as a favour, because there's still a kingly condescension about Father: he tends to take tributes as his due. If it comes to that, perhaps they *are* his due.

Manny Goldstone with his kind, silly, over-fed face, his big status-symbol cars, his passionate addiction to comfort. Manny Goldstone, who'd come up the hard way but now lived the soft life. 'Give you a lift?' he'd said, once, as we left the house in Croydon together, the big Bentley parked in that shabby street like an orchid in a potato patch. And in the car, purring up to London, I couldn't keep myself from asking him. 'Why, Manny, why?'

'Why *what*?' Out of the corner of his spaniel eye he darted me a worried look. She's going to probe.

'The banquets, the charities, the testimonials,' I said.

'Is that so wrong?'

'It's very nice, but why?'

'It gives me pleasure. Other people gamble.'

'What *kind* of pleasure, Manny?'

Another hunted look. 'Do you think it's wrong to get pleasure out of doing things for people?'

Which prompted a thousand other questions. For *which* people? Very famous footballers, down on their luck. How famous do they have to be? How much pleasure must they have given *you*? And how much more do you get by being the Grand Panjandrum? Because I've seen you, Manny, I've been to your great occasions, you in the middle of them, with your blue velvet dinner-jacket, your exquisite pink ruffles, the cigar in your hand as big as the barrel of a pistol. Your nice little slim, strained wife dressed in a Dior gown that cost more than you'll raise from the whole evening. You circulating, shaking hands, pecking cheeks, East End boy made good. Oh, Manny, you don't have to tell *me* you're getting pleasure!

But he *had* been kind to Father; I didn't want to spoil that, so I just said, 'No, of course not, Manny,' and for a long time he drove without saying a word. Finally he asked, 'Are *you* happy, Jenny?'

'Now and then,' I said. 'I don't think about it much.'

'I'll tell you about your father,' he said. 'When I was a kid, down Clapton, and he was playing for Borough. We didn't have much of a life, my family. My old man was a tailor, but he got tuberculosis. At school they were all yiddified, the teachers as well as the boys. What kept me going was Borough, and your father. That was something they couldn't take away from you. Saturday afternoon, you put on your green and white scarf, you paid your way through the turnstiles, you stood behind the goal, and you were part of it. All the week, they made you feel like an outcast, home was always one long funeral, but there, you could lose yourself. Thousands of you, jammed in together, cheering together, going mad together, especially when your father made one of his fantastic saves.

'I can't tell you what he meant to me, to all of us there. He was like God, Jenny. Just to see him come out on the pitch. Always third in line, the captain first, carrying the ball, then someone else, then him. I tell you, I'd feel it in my stomach. The captain, the second bloke, that little flutter of anticipation: then him. Big legs, big shoulders, hair brushed down – red hair, like yours. Sort of loping along. This terrific feeling of *safety* that you got from him, the feeling he could never be beaten. We *were* him, really. He was us. He represented us; what we'd have liked to be. When *he* saved, *we* saved. When he got hurt, we got hurt. Just for the ninety minutes, everybody was your friend. You could even carry some of it away with you, in the buses or the tube, then you went back to being what you were.

'So if I try to do things for your father, Jenny, it's because he did something for me.'

How moving, I'd thought, and how pitiful. Life reduced to *that*. The endless adolescence of it all. Football Fans' Lib: liberation from perennial boyhood. And how pathetic that what Manny had now was still not enough.

'You might not understand that as a woman, Jenny.'

'I think I understand, Manny.' And just because I *am* a woman, watching the Peter Pans eternally at play. That's why I don't share your ecstasies and fantasies, Manny; not because I never played football, but because I think it's marginal; or it should be.

But there was another question that I wanted to ask Manny, and this was very hard to keep back. Finally, out it came. 'Why must you all be so *secondary*, Manny?'

Bristling again. 'What do you mean? *Who's* secondary?'

'Jewish people.'

'What about them?' Now he's really hostile.

'They *attach* themselves,' I said, 'instead of doing things.'

'What about all the boxers, then? Ted Kid Lewis, Jack Kid Berg, Al Phillips – all out of the East End. All Jewish.'

'But the footballers aren't,' I said, 'only the people who give parties for them.'

He'd been insulted now; he'd frozen stiff behind the wheel. What I'd said to him, I suppose, was that Jews were parasites, the old libel, and yet it wasn't what I'd meant. After all, they're primary in their own occupations, just like Manny in his jewellery business; but why shouldn't that be enough? Why should Manny still need my father?

And there was more that I'd have said to him, had I dared: that his charity was like all charity, a palliative rather than an answer. My father shouldn't have needed him; he shouldn't have needed anybody.

'Don't sulk, Manny!' I said, and I leant across and kissed him.

He softened then and smiled. 'It just didn't seem like you, Jenny,' he said.

'Oh, it's me all right,' I told him, 'always prodding and probing,' and I despised myself a little, for sliding out of it by flattering his male vanity. So we parted friends, because if you make a man feel that he attracts you, he'll forgive you almost anything else.

But there's no hope now, even from Manny; so what hope is there?

'A psychiatrist,' Robert said.

No; not another psychiatrist. Society's scavengers. Why should *he* change, instead of the world?

'You're a Laingian,' Robert says to me, 'lunatics are always right,' and I get furious with him. 'What should psychiatry be for?' I yell at him. 'To help people, or to make them toe the line? You might as well be in Russia!'

Society wants my father to disappear. Go away: you're an embarrassment! A psychiatrist would help him to 'adjust', to be content with what he's got, or what he's been left with, to stop pinching things and swindling people, which at best they'd see as cries for help, while I see them as cries of rage. They show he's still alive, at least to that extent; that he hasn't given in.

'Jenny,' Arthur Grace told me once, the smooth, pompous, bureaucratic bastard who's General Secretary of Borough, and was once the office boy, 'the trouble with your father is he seems to think the world owes him a living.'

'But it *does* owe him a living!' I snarled at him. 'Of course it does! It's lived off him; why shouldn't he live off *it*?'

When I told Robert, he was in his musing, hair-splitting mood. 'It won't stand up philosophically, will it?' he said.

'Then fuck philosophy!' I shouted.

'But you might say that of so many people. Soldiers, for a start. War heroes. Crippled for life, and all they get's a tiny pension. After all, they've saved their country. Football's only a game. Artists, too. Poets who dry up at thirty. Painters whose pictures sell for thousands, after they're dead.'

'I'm sorry for all of them,' I said, 'but it doesn't affect the issue. My father's a man who's lived his life backward. He's been sucked dry and slung aside to rot. And don't tell me there are plenty like him; don't tell me he was lucky to get out of the mines; don't tell me there are some who've made good! It's just irrelevant! They shouldn't have *had* to make good!'

Because this is a favourite line with his detractors: look what he *could* have been! Look at the opportunities he had! With *his* fame, *his* popularity! Threw it all away!

Irrelevant!

'He had his chance,' they say, 'the chance to be a manager. Look what Wally Grove has done!'

Look, indeed! My father's always looking. 'Think of him

now, and think of me. What was he? Just a good, average
player. A fair inside-forward, that was all. Never got more than
a couple of caps for England. To hear him, you'd think he'd
got ninety!'

I'd heard him and I'd seen him; seen him with my father.
How cool and sleek he was! How capably he dealt with Dad,
how plausibly! The double-hand clasp. The enormous smile.
The frank look, straight into your eyes. After all, it cost him
nothing. 'Wonderful to see you, Len!'

'Been in a few games together, haven't we, Wal?'

'We have that, Len, we have that!'

'Remember that Cup-tie down at Portsmouth? Two-nil
behind, two men off the park, five minutes left and we won it
three-two?'

'Ay, like yesterday!'

Lots of laughter. Another smile – for Mum. A smile for me.
'Your father was a great player, Jenny.'

My sweetest smile in return. 'Oh, yes, Mr Grove, I know.'

'And Wally's a great manager.'

'Never had a keeper like you, though, Len.'

'Never will, Wally, never will!'

More laughter. Dissolution of tableau. How well Wally slid
out of that one. Easy and painless when it might have been so
awkward. Comfortably clear of the hanging question, why are
you *there*, Wally, while I'm *here*?

Though it was really so easy to answer. Wally was shrewd;
Dad was naive. Wally was glib and adroit; Dad when he tried
to be cunning was transparent.

Dad watched him move on, squeezing arms and pumping
hands, shook his head and said, 'Wonderful, what he's done,'
meaning, considering what he was, compared with me.

But now Wally's sleek with the last twenty years' good living.
They've filled out the hollows in his rough old miner's face, a
boozer's face, eyes a little swimmy, although I bet you never see
him drunk. Man management is what they say he's good at,
which means manipulating people. 'Wally Grove, that master
of man management.' *He'd* never quarrel with his directors; not
like Dad. Or if he did, he'd wait and choose his time. I was sure
all the things the papers wrote about him were true; that he had

Authority and Vision – foresight, anyway – that young players stood in awe of him; that older players worshipped him. And yet, for all his success, I knew that Dad had brought more joy; and that they both knew it, too. That he was a politician; but Dad had been a prince. That here, too, Dad had been primary and Wally, for all that he'd accomplished, was still secondary. That people might revere him, but he'd never be talked about as Robert and Manny talked of Dad. That he was aware of this, so that, despite everything, whenever he met Dad there was this little worm gnawing away.

Dad wrote to him once for a job, and I remember the reply he got.

Very nice to hear from you. Unfortunately our coaching and training staff has no present vacancies. If any should arise, I shall bear you in mind.

Man management. The public face: cautious and inscrutable. I can see why Dad never made a manager.

World Cup 1966

Sunday Times, 24 July 1966

I T HAS BEEN a week of tottering dynasties and strange cataclysm; the week of Eusebio and Pak Doo Ik; a week in which Italy slunk home behind sunglasses to Genoa, and Brazil arrived at Euston as Napoleon's army must have arrived from Russia.

Amaral, the shaven-headed 'preparer', brushed condolences aside, and walked from train to coach as though from the condemned cell to the scaffold. Manga, Tuesday's goalkeeper, took refuge in the back seat, head tensely cocked, as though still looking for Eusebio; on the seat in front of him, alert and incongruous, perched a doll in a red dress.

'Look kind of disappointed, don't they?' asked a Scots boy, as the crowd gathered morbidly round, like people round a motor accident. 'Dejected.'

Indeed they did. Feola's brooding face might have been carved from Mount Rushmore; the dark heads were studies in mute melancholy. 'They're pretty bitter about European refereeing,' said an official.

Only Dr Gosling stayed wonderfully urbane: 'After the second World Cup, it was not the same; the first World Cup was a fiesta. The next future, they will start working very hard for the next World Cup.'

'Have you seen Pelé?' one cheerful porter asked another. 'He's a millionaire; he'll drop you all right.' But Pelé looked as if he'd been dropped himself.

Football, like the Toynbeean view of history, is a thing of cycles. Great teams are a thing of three or four great players.

Twelve years ago, we thought the Hungarians invincible, and Hungarian methods, axiomatically, *right*. Since 1958, it has been the turn of the Brazilians; what the rest of us lacked, it seemed, was a black element, and a beach like Copacabana.

Illusions, all of them. Brazil won the World Cup in 1958 – and 1962 – for neither of these reasons, nor even for the efficacy of their now exposed 4–2–4. They won because they had half a dozen great players, to whose talents 4–2–4 gave most free expression.

Take away Didì, Zito, Vavà, Zagalo, Nilton Santos and the real Garrincha, and what's left but to hope and pray that others of their stature will emerge? So far, they haven't. The mystery of how and why they do remains, for all the theorising, a mystery. Mysterious as North Korea . . .

They, indeed, have been the heroic surprise of this World Cup. Probably they would have done better still had they, immediately after thrashing Australia to qualify, abandoned their splendd isolation, playing as often as they could against European teams. Admirably quick learners, such experience would have been priceless.

Portugal, their quarter-final opponents, are a team of balance and incision. Simoes, their vigorous little outside-left, runs, wanders and passes with great intelligence. Graça, Coluña and Augusto work shrewdly in midfield, while there is always the menace of Torres' head.

But Tuesday night was Eusebio's: tall, infinitely graceful, moving with effortless, flowing speed, his right foot the weapon of a Titan. One couldn't, on the evening, compare him with Pelé, who didn't look fit from the first; but in general terms, the contrast is fascinating.

Broadly, though each has his special dynamism, Eusebio is fluent where Pelé is explosive. Pelé, all muscularity, goes off like a great time bomb; Eusebio's irresistibility is rather that of a cataract. Each, with his right foot, is a glorious striker of the ball. The cunning with which Eusebio, at free kicks, alternates the flying shell with the dipping, dropping, tantalising lob is formidable.

Yesterday, against the North Koreans, Eusebio perhaps surpassed even his achievement last Tuesday. He has been criticised in the past as a player who does not give his best when things are going against his team, and certainly he almost 'disappeared' from the 1965 European Cup final.

At Everton, yesterday, he gave his critics the lie. Four of Portugal's goals were his; so was the corner which made Augusto the fifth.

Eusebio has been a star since he was nineteen. In 1965, he was chosen European Footballer of the Year. In 1962 he had already demonstrated his remarkable power and skill with a superb performance in the final of the European Cup in Amsterdam. After the match, in which Benfica beat Real Madrid 5–3, Puskas insisted that he and Eusebio exchange shirts. It was a fitting tribute.

If Puskas had the greatest left foot in Europe, it became clear that night that Eusebio's was the greatest right foot. Born in Lourenço Marques, Mozambique, he's a portent of what African football may become in another ten or fifteen years.

Just as Albert, four days earlier, stood at the entrance to the tunnel, pulling at a bottle of water, waving, and at last, with an anticlimactic rinse-and-spit, disappeared, so Eusebio paused suddenly on Tuesday, before vanishing, to give the crowd a gay, triumphant wave. The crowd responded as he'd known they would.

Next day at England–France – a mediocre victory over a depleted foe – Argentina's Juan Carlos Lorenzo had lurked unnoticed in the rowdy chaos of the long bar; five yards away stood George Eastham, who might have given England's midfield some style and invention.

Lorenzo's dark, plump, gentle face looked quite unchanged from Chile, four years ago. In Europe, before the World Cup, he said, they'd put out a shadow team. 'We couldn't show our real team there, because everyone would be watching. Half Europe watched the match with Italy.

'Winning that first game with Spain gave us more morale, more spirit. Then the game with Germany was a game not to lose. We wanted a point.'

Though England's defence had two long, nasty spells on Wednesday, Moore, Jackie Charlton and Banks must have impressed Lorenzo. To make the two saves Banks made, after you've barely had a chance to touch the ball, is the mark of a really fine goalkeeper. Yet any victory, after Italy's fiasco, must be welcome.

The Italians, however, had one grain of consolation: they've provided, in Concetto Lo Bello, one of the tournament's leading referees.

A Sicilian, from the town of Syracuse – where he runs the fire force and plays a cardinal role in amateur sport – Lo Bello has the dark, wavy hair, the regular features, the thin moustache, of a hero of the silent screen. He is, above all, a referee with a philosophy: 'You've seen that I run miles on the field. I don't do it for exhibitionism, I do it because players must be aware of the referee, get wind of the referee, just as the fox gets wind of the dog: because a player who senses a referee at his shoulder won't commit a foul.

'I don't think a referee's on the field to punish; he's on the field to keep the play within the limits of correctness. It's the mere presence of a referee that puts players in a position to play the ball, rather than one another's legs.'

In common with many of the referees, Lo Bello believes the new drug tests have been a splendid innovation. 'Drugged players are not in control of their mental faculties. And besides the immediate consequences, which sometimes show during the game, drugs have a serious effect on the organism of an athlete. You know how doping works on it: like an accelerator on a car. The more the forced consumption of energy, the more he pays for it.'

The medical dispositions for the World Cup have, indeed, reflected the greatest credit on Dr Alan Bass and the medical officers in the various centres. Dr Gosling of Brazil, the very doyen of sports medicine, has said they're the best arrangements he has ever known.

But doping-control, though it helps the referee, still leaves him with a vast responsibility for the smooth running of a game. As Lo Bello says, 'The players sense at once if you're not in control. After all, it's their profession.'

At Everton last Tuesday, alas, the Portuguese sensed very quickly indeed that Mr McCabe was no mailed fist, and they exploited the knowledge shamefully. It was deplorable that, even after they'd plainly won the game with those two quick, softish goals, Morais should still cruelly foul and lame Pelé.

'By some chance,' said their selector, Alfonso, after the game, with sublime speciousness, 'Pelée injured himself today.' By some chance, Morais was allowed to stay on the field when he should certainly have gone straight off.

Later, Mr McCabe, radiating fussy good intentions, refused what looked a clear penalty for a foul on Jairzinho. More significant still was an incident in the second half when, little Simoes having been brutally hacked down, Mr McCabe – more ambulance man than arbitrator – quite ignored the culprit, but went anxiously to Simoes, on the ground.

When Simoes got up, Mr McCabe patted him indulgently on the head; perhaps he was trying subtly to shame the Brazilian.

What FIFA should have demanded from the first was that condign punishment be visited on intimidatory tactics. It is bad enough that star players be marked out for relentless shadowing. It's worse when they are hacked and cuffed as well. If, in the opening round of matches, Pelé's Bulgarian shadow and one of the two Argentinians who viciously chopped down Suarez had been sent off, the tournament would have been far more salubrious.

But to return to Italy's defeat by the Koreans: that second Caporetto.

Baffling explanation: this was a failure in spirit rather than ability. Only a group psychoanalyst could disentangle those strange inferiority feelings, that footballing equivalent of writer's block, which seem to afflict the Italian team abroad.

It is little use belabouring the players, as their press has done, calling them 'millionaires encouraged by megalomaniacs'. Their performances here had the quality of an anxiety dream; they needed a Freud, rather than a Fabbri.

As it is, one awaits news of the first Italian emissaries, modern Marco Polos, across the 34th Parallel. The motto of Italian football has traditionally been, if you can't beat them, join them. A 6–1 defeat by Yugoslavia in 1957 led immediately to an influx of Yugoslav managers for the leading clubs; when the present ban is lifted, it will possibly be the turn of Myung Rye

Hyung. As for the goalscorer, Pak Doo Ik, perhaps Juventus . . .?

The Italians might do well to recall the remark last week of the French coach Jasseron: 'Each match has its own story.' I shall miss Jasseron and the French. Down to ten fit men, they played boldly and cleverly against England, breaking swiftly out of a resourceful defence, cleverly served by Bonnel, Simon, Herbet.

Nor can one readily forget that moment at Welwyn when Jasseron, a Jacques Tati figure, moustached and hollow cheeked, appealed, hands outspread, to the French press: 'Bosquier played well. We're all agreed?' And they, anarchic to the last, replied in chorus, 'No, no! Not for me! Not for me!'

The Man Behind the Goal

London Magazine, 1963

H E HAD BROUGHT his own football. It lay on the ground beside the bench, where he himself sprawled in clumsy comfort, his head pillowed on his hands, his heavy, muddy boots propped against the wooden arm. The bench stood beside some railings, at the foot of a little slope of leafless trees. The park had gone from autumn into winter; puddles lay, blind and brown, in the declivities of the little football field; raindrops hung from the white crossbars of the goals.

I did not greet the man when I arrived; my first reaction was to resent him. He was filling up the bench where we always changed; his boots had fouled it with pats of mud and – supine and unembarrassed – he gave no sign of moving.

'It'll rain again,' he announced, in an accent I could not quite place. 'See those clouds up there? Black ones. It'll pour.'

I nodded, and began to take off my tracksuit. In a moment, I looked up and saw Don coming down the hill that led from the road, his fair, bushy head bowed; unseeing, or not wanting to see: I was never sure. His leather bag swung from his hand.

The man did not speak to me again; he seemed perfectly relaxed. From a haversack beside him, he took out an apple and, raising his head like a fish rising to a bait, began to eat it, in noisy bites.

Don was beside us now. We looked at the man, exchanged shrugs and glances, and hung our clothes over the spiked fence. Don took a football out of his case and rolled it on to the ground.

'Hard, is it?' asked the man, casting a sidelong glance. 'Yes, it looks hard. Mine's soft, soft as bloody putty. Useless. Can't get nobody to blow it up.'

Then, as though his attention could be switched on and off like an electric current, he went back to his apple as though he had never spoken, and finally, with a contemptuous flick of the hand, his eyes still fixed on the sky, he threw the core over the fence.

Don and I moved on to the football pitch, and he went into goal; the goal beneath the great, chimneyed monolith of the power station. I shot; the ball rose high over the crossbar, and Don turned to trot after it, a patient and unhurried sheep dog. Out of the corner of an eye, I saw that the little man had got off the bench, and was playing with his own football, a small, stooping, undernourished figure in a blue boiler suit, gambolling about the ball, half-gnome, half-puppy, head bent over it, in earnest concentration. In his fantasy, he was clearly a forward, tricking and bewildering a host of defenders, now skipping over the ball, now pulling it to him with the sole of his foot, now feinting to his left, and stroking it to the right. From a distance, the ball invisible, it must have seemed like a grotesque ritual dance, a leprechaun frolicking round his crock of gold.

There was a thump and a splash, as our football landed beside me in a puddle; as I turned to get it, the little man suddenly whirled, to kick his ball under the seat – obviously he'd scored a goal. I shot again, looked round again, and now the little man had recovered his ball and was dribbling it towards us over the bumpy ground, with the same dedication, the same ungainly diligence. I wondered for a moment if he meant to join us, but he made no effort to come on to the pitch, merely dribling the ball on and on, head bent, until he was behind our goal.

Again I shot. This time the ball sailed between the netless goalposts, high past Don's outstretched right arm; and at this the little man turned from his own soft ball and scampered after ours, catching it, turning on it with a short, self-conscious pirouette, as though he were demonstrating to a class, then, with the same, studied technique, he kicked it back to us.

I shouted thanks, feeling a stab of guilt, sorry I had dealt so brusquely with him. I half hoped that he would go away or, if he stayed, concentrate upon his own strange, intense gyrations. But each time the ball flew behind the goal, he was after it like a faithful bird dog, dribbling it back with his painful, stooping run, until at last, with a kick laboured but accurate, he would send it back on to the pitch. 'Thank you!' we called. 'Thank you! thank you!' But we were still uneasy; he had placed us in his debt.

We trained once a week, and we thought we had seen the last of him, but he was there again the following Thursday, boots up on the bench, his half-pumped pudding of a ball beside it. Again, he trotted behind the goal when we began to shoot, again he endlessly chased the ball and sent it back to us, but now he maintained a ceaseless and staccato commentary.

'On the ground . . . keep it on the *ground* . . . if you put it in the air, you've lost it, you're *wasting* it!' A breathless dash to retrieve the ball. 'The Scottish way's the best . . . I don't mean the new way, because that's rubbish; I mean the *old* way, the classical way.' Another dash. 'I told them at Tottenham, I was on the terrace . . . Spurs? I said . . . Great *team*, I said? They're not fit to lace the boots . . . up in the air, the whole time . . . that big Smith; the other big one, Norman . . . Up in the air, biff and bang . . . I *told* them, that's not football. Football is on the *ground*.'

I still could not locate his accent, which now, in its harsh fluency, seemed Welsh, now from the Northeast. When we left the field, he trotted beside us, still urging and admonishing, while we listened with half an ear, responding now and then in monosyllables. Close at hand, he cut an oddly contradictory figure, half-boy, half-man: boyish in his slim fragility, the clear, washed grey of his eyes, the straight hair dangling, like a boy's, over his forehead; unboyish in the greyness of that hair; the waxy yellow of his sunken cheeks. At moments, I would look at him and think of an old man; at others, almost of a child; but in his humped, compulsive movements, there was nothing childlike. I thought of him as some poor, harmless paranoid; a garrulous tramp with a strange obsession, who probably slept rough, out in the park; a cliché figure, made overfamiliar by playwrights of the *avant garde*; life imitating art.

He needed a disciple, this was obvious, and he must have

known that we – casual, mediocre Sunday footballers – were too old and frivolous for his purpose. But the next week, when we arrived in the rain, the pupil had been found: a sturdy, stupid boy who stood oxlike under the downpour, woodenly watching, as the little man pirouetted round his soggy football.

'He'll get pneumonia,' I said, and wondered at his toughness, his fanaticism. He was too frail to spurn the weather.

When Don and I reached the goal behind which he was standing – this time, the upper goal – we could hear him instructing the boy with the same, hortatory voice, as though he were addressing a youth rally. 'If you come *over* the ball like this' – a skip and a hop – 'it is useless. What you *want* to do is approach it like *this*, then you take it away like *that*, thus leaving your opponent in two minds.'

The boy nodded his heavy, pink-cheeked head; he was not invited to try it for himself.

'More *haste*, less *speed*; it's the same thing with your kicking. With the *in*-step. The toe of the boot *down* – like this, and *then*, the follow-through – like that!' The ball merely skidded across the muddy ground, but the boy did not laugh; nor did he fetch it. Instead, the little man set off after the ball, with his familiar, crablike run, caught it, dribbled back, and cried, 'I shall now demonstrate the pass with the inside of the foot!'

It was raining more heavily than ever. The boy's coarse, black hair was soaked; raindrops ran down his plump cheeks, but still he stood, impassive. It was twenty minutes before he left, plodding his stolid, unathletic way across the wet grass, to disappear at last over the hill. The little man resumed his old position behind the goal, and now it was us whom he exhorted.

'Too high, too high! I was telling that boy: *always* along the ground! Keep it down, and you'll go *up*! Keep it up, and you'll go *down*!' The slippery ball made his kicking more feeble and erratic than ever, and he began to complain. 'It's my boots are the trouble! If *I* could get these boots right! I can't kick with these. It's no use trying.'

Back and forth he ran, under the teeming rain, fetching and kicking, fetching and kicking. His hair, plastered damply to his forehead, gave him more than ever the appearance of a tonsured monk; I could see him in a brown cassock, hobbling after the ball just as he hobbled now.

'If *I* had my boots right! If *I* could only get some boots!'

The next time we trained, I brought him an old pair of shoes. I put them underneath the bench – clotted with mud, strewn with newspapers and ravaged brown parcels – while he pursued his ball, on the football pitch. I did not mention the shoes – somehow the gesture reeked of charity, a need for gratitude – nor did he himself ever allude to them; but he had them on his feet, the following Thursday.

I came upon him unawares that day, though at first I thought he knew I was there. He was talking in a loud, cheerful voice I had not heard before, smiling; stretched full length, again, on the seat. He was reading the *Daily Express* and I saw, with some surprise, that it was the latest.

'You read these things,' he was saying, 'and what do they expect you to believe? Three-quarters of it's lies; lies for gullible people. President Eisenhower accuses Khrushchev. If you bought the *Daily Worker*, it would say, President Khruschev accuses Eisenhower. Which of them is true? Probably neither! I don't bloody well believe one nor the other.'

I greeted him: 'Reading the paper?'

He tilted back his head, grinning at me. 'I was engaged in listening to the finest music in the world: the sound of my own voice.'

Suddenly I liked him better. For the first time, the harsh, hectoring tone had gone; the eyes, more palely luminous than ever, seen so close, were full of a humour at once subversive and self-deprecating.

'You're here every day?' I asked.

'Every day, rain or shine, wind or weather, hell or high water.'

'And . . . do you camp here?'

'No,' he said, contemptuously. 'I live down in Westminster, at the Salvation Army hostel – if you can call it living. What they give you to eat, you couldn't feed a sparrow on. One rotten little sausage for breakfast, a few mouldy baked beans at night. If I didn't go out and buy my own bread, I'd starve.' He gestured, and I saw beside him, half-hidden by his body, a brown loaf, crudely hacked by the penknife which lay beside it.

'Here every day,' he said. 'I never get bored. I never get bored, listening to myself. Out in the fresh air. Sometimes I have arguments; it's a way to pass the time. Other times I recite poetry.'

'What poetry do you prefer?'

'My own!' he said, and gave the same mischievous smile. 'They talk about great poetry. "In Xanadu did Kubla Khan a stately pleasure dome decree." Dee-dum, dee-dum, dee-dum, dee-dum. Dee-dum, dee-dum, dee-dum, dee-dee. Call that poetry? *I* don't call it poetry.'

It was a chance to ask him where he came from.

'Northumberland,' he said – as I had half suspected. 'A little village up there. Don't ask me what it's like now; I haven't been back there for thirty-five years; I never wanted to. I've been all over the world – India, France, Italy, Spain. Why should I go back to a village in Northumberland? I never liked it there. If I go anywhere, I'll go to France again.'

'What were you doing in France?'

'Learning the language. I was there a year ago. I was in Marseilles. When I think I'll go to a place, nobody stops me; I make up my mind, and then I go.'

'And India?'

'I was in the army. I was there till 1939, when the war came. Then I told them I was ill; my stomach, I said. Fifteen doctors looked at me; they had me in three different hospitals, but they couldn't get to the bottom of it, none of them could. They had to discharge me. Because I hadn't joined the army to fight a war: I'd joined the army in peacetime.'

'Is the boy coming today? Your pupil?'

'Oh, him,' he said, 'he'll be here later. I'll make a footballer out of him. I've told him, "I'll make you one, if it kills me. I'll make you one if it kills us both." I've got the perfect system, see. I have devised this system lying here and thinking; it is a triumph of mind over matter.' The hortatory voice was coming back. '*Whereby*, if the material is young enough, *any* player can be turned into a champion. I'm too old, now, or I'd use it on myself.'

I looked round; Don was making his steady, long-legged way down the hill. The little man glanced up suddenly at a tree above him and said, 'That's another thing I've been thinking about: photosynthesis. They say a tree keeps alive by what it draws into itself through its leaves. Well, how can *that* tree possibly be alive, then – ' and his voice rose as though it were a personal affront ' – how can it *possibly* be alive when it hasn't *got* a bloody leaf?'

Looking again at the little man and his pupil, I knew that, whatever scheme he had devised, the plump boy would never make a footballer. Indeed, it grew clearer and clearer as one watched that the scheme was an end in itself, the boy no more than a lay-figure, scarcely permitted a kick at the ball, while his master pranced and pirouetted like a lame little pit pony. Indeed, for the boy to be a pupil at all, it was essential that he *should* be inept; a more proficient boy would never have stood for it.

The following week, I brought the little man a parcel of food: a loaf of bread, a packet of butter, a few tins of soup and spaghetti. From his prone position on the bench, he thanked me seriously.

'I need that, it'll help me, that. The food they give you down there . . .' He was silent awhile, looking gravely into space. 'I have decided,' he said, at last, his tone implying lonely hours of contemplation, 'that soccer is the finest game of all: because there is nothing *evolutionary* about it. Cricket, croquet, hockey, billiards: they are all evolutionary. They are played with a club. A man with a club in his hand is only one stage further than an ape. Football is a game that Plato would have liked; it might have been invented by the Greeks; I can pay no higher compliment. That was the finest flowering of human civilisation.'

Looking at him closely, it seemed to me that his yellow cheeks were hollower than ever. Over his blue dungarees, which conferred on him a spurious dignity of labour, he wore an old khaki greatcoat, but it wasn't enough to sustain his Promethean defiance of the weather.

Again the boy arrived, again the demonstration and the exhortation, though, this time, he was allowed to do a little more for himself. He did it clumsily, without confidence or optimism; more, without visible enthusiasm. I wondered if he had simply been accosted while passing by, a wedding guest to the little man's Ancient Mariner, hypnotised first into staying, then into coming back, again and again.

The next week, he was for the first time wearing football shorts, showing his plump, white, heavy thighs, but his movements were as rigid as ever. A fortnight later, when I asked about him, the little man replied, 'I have decided he is ready. I have decided he is ready to take part in a game, using the principles that I have taught him. On Saturday, he's playing in a trial match for his school. I am going there, and I shall advise him from the touchline.'

'Have you seen him play before?'

'Never before; it wasn't necessary. It didn't interest me, because he had not imbibed my principles. But even in these few weeks, he has improved; I can see it for myself, and he's told me that he has: his teachers are amazed. Otherwise he wouldn't have been chosen for this trial.'

Suddenly I felt alarm for him. He was trying to impose his fantasy world upon the real, and the consequence could only be failure, disappointment. I could see him wandering up and down the touchline of the football ground, while loutish, spotted schoolboys giggled at him, and their teachers looked at him with outrage. He'd be disillusioned and humiliated; yet how could he be warned?

'Isn't it a bit early?' I asked. 'You haven't been teaching him long.'

'I have been teaching him three or four times a week, up to two hours, for the last five weeks. That is at least thirty hours. Thirty hours' tuition are all that is necessary to reach a good standard in boys' football. To reach the international standard, I have estimated it will take three hundred hours.'

For a little while, he kicked our football back for us, from behind the goal; then the boy came lumbering along, for his tuition.

The following week, the little man was not to be seen; indeed, his very bench had gone, and I surmised conspiracy, a persecution of park keepers. From time to time, as Don and I trained together, I looked up the hill, or behind me into the green distance of the park, half expcting him to appear; but he did not come. I missed him, wondering if we should ever see him again, whether he'd decamped from the park because the boy had failed, and he could no longer face us, the boy, the workshop of his failure.

A week later, the bench was still not there. We had been running up and down, passing the ball, for several minutes, and were just beginning to take shots at goal, when there was a scampering and a flurry of branches on the hillside beneath which the bench had stood, and the little man emerged, his eyes wide and staring – almost, I thought, like poor, mad Ben Gunn. He was wearing his army greatcoat, which hung nearly to the ground, and I wondered how he would negotiate the railings. But just before he got to them, he pulled himself up, with a quick, monkey-like movement, by the branch of a tree and, from the tree, he dropped over the fence.

He shuffled across the field towards us, and the goal, without taking off the coat. Even before I saw his face, I could tell his dejection by the way he moved. He could never be graceful, but now his old, obsessional vitality had left him, too. He seemed to be carrying out a duty, even – incongruously – a job. He took no notice of our greeting, but went on past us without a word. His face looked sick and ravaged, jaundiced, yellower than ever, crumbling away, like the face of a dying man; the eyes had nothing in them but a blank, possessed determination. He kicked the ball back to us as devotedly as ever, but in silence, without commentary or criticism. The change was such that it depressed us both, so that we finished training early. We thanked the little man, but he turned away without a word, hopelessly, making slowly towards the middle of the park.

I caught up with him. 'How did the game go?' I asked.

'Him?' he said, and stopped. 'Him? He was useless. I miscalculated. I hall have to go back to the beginning. I had decided that, using my system, *any* human material could be turned into a successful footballer. Now I can see that I was wrong; there *must* be basic talent, therefore the system is still not perfect. It may take years to perfect; I don't know if I have enough time left to me.'

'Of course you have,' I said, but the words sounded false, the consolation cheap. He made no answer, turning his back on me, as I felt I deserved, and trudged away again. For a few moments, I was half determined to go after him; then I, too, turned away. He was like a sick dog, wanting to be left alone.

He was not there the next week, nor the next, and I began to feel anxious for him; he looked in retrospect too much like a wounded animal, crawling off to die. In the third week, I met the boy; he came slowly across the football pitch, while Don and I were tugging off our boots. About him, too, there seemed to be a sadness, something over and above his usual stolidity.

I called to him and, without increasing pace, he came over.

'Do you know where he is?' I asked. 'The little man.'

'I dunno,' he said, in the incongruous, piping voice of plump adolescence. 'I don't think he's well. He may have gone to hospital.'

'Hospital? When did you see him last?

'About two weeks ago. I wanted him to teach me again, but he wouldn't. He wouldn't speak to me.' Aggrieved, the voice rose higher still. '*I* can't help it if I didn't play well. *I* couldn't help it if they told him to go away; it wasn't my fault.'

'Was he ill, then?'

'Yeah, he looked terrible. He said he hadn't eaten for three days. I came back the next day, I brought some apples for him, but he wasn't there. I never seen him again.'

That evening, I telephoned the Salvation Army hostel, who identified him without difficulty. Yes, they said, he had gone into hospital; they told me which it was. It was exposure, they thought; they were not quite sure. 'Well, I'm not surprised,' said the voice, as though I had somehow accused it. 'The *weather* he stayed out in.'

The following day, I went to the hospital with a paper carrier bag of fruit. I waited on a bench in the dim, bleak entrance hall, among a murmuring, worried crowd of visitors, dragooned and overawed; the poor at the mercy of the hospital. A bell rang and we filed along a twilit corridor. Here and there, we passed the entrance of a ward, where the patients sat up in their beds with taut expectancy. At each of these, a few of us would file away, and there would be small cries of joy, embraces.

At last I reached the ward where he was lying, and looked in through the door. It was very long; a row of beds ran down each side. At first I could not see him, but at last I made him out. He sat, motionless and upright, against the pillows, in a bed halfway down the left-hand wall, his face more wasted than ever. But it was not this which shocked me, so much as the expression of the eyes, void now of humour or defiance, merely staring out across the ward.

A nurse came up to me with her brisk, starched walk, and asked whom I wanted to see. I pushed the bag of fruit into her hands and pointed at him, then turned away, fearful he should recognise me.

Nemesis had caught up with him; society and the weather had beaten him at last. I hurried into the street, escaping with the memory of his courage.

Danny Blanchflower

Soccer: The Great Ones, 1968

I F ONE WERE to seek for the watershed between the old
school of professional footballer and the new, one might do
worse than look at Danny Blanchflower. Not that he was, in
any strict sense, representative of either; merely that, as a great
player of uncommon intelligence and versatility, he suffered
under the regimen which ended with the New Deal of 1961,
while suggesting to those who came after it what they might
become. By 1961, the erosion of social difference which followed our bloodless social revolution had already given pro
footballers a much less working-class orientation than they'd
had before the war. They no longer dressed in baggy suits,
mufflers and cloth caps, no longer felt content with an Andy
Capp life a few rungs higher than Andy Capp himself, their fan,
might have. But Blanchflower, fluent to a fault, articulate to a
paradox, fraternising with literary editors and philosophers,
writing for the intellectual weeklies and the posh Sundays,
pointed the way to wider horizons still. Thus, though he played
little or no active part in the crusade to abolish the iniquitous
maximum age, in 1960 and 1961, he had already given the pro
footballer a new concept of himself; or what he might, in some
remote future, become.

It is hard for me to write about Blanchflower, because I have
known him for many years, and moderately closely. I say
moderately closely, because Blanchflower is not an easy man to
know well. The charm, the eloquence, mask rather than illumi-
nate; there is a core of something secret, held back, concealed.
Thus, one can say of him that he is intelligent, humorous,

ambitious, competitive, even egocentric, but the inwardness of the man is elusive.

As a footballer, one could only admire him; it seems to me that he was indisputably a great player, with a vision of the game that was at once sophisticated yet simple; the qualities of the very best football. It was these characteristics which enabled him to be so fine a captain, at a time when football captaincy had grown to be little more than a question of tossing for ends before the kickoff. The freshness and originality of his approach to the game, combined with his remarkable poise, enabled him to give a team inspiration, confidence and a sense of tactical purpose. He did superbly with Tottenham Hotspur – and for a time, significantly, had the captaincy taken away from him. He did it just as well with a Northern Ireland team that, against all expectation, knocked Italy out of the eliminators for the 1958 World Cup, and reached the quarter-finals.

It has been said, possibly with truth, that the dominant force in his life has been his mother: once the pretty centre-forward of a women's football team, and Blanchflower's first coach. He was born and brought up in that hard, vigorous, bigoted city, Belfast, 'where they beat the big drum', as he once said; but there is nothing bigoted about him. He seems to have inherited the city's vigorous, robust humour, with none of its black undertones. He began there with Glentoran, joined Barnsley, in Yorkshire, as little more than a boy, from there went to Aston Villa, and finally, in 1954, joined Spurs, thus coming to London, where he must always have felt he belonged, where there was an opportunity to grow, to prosper and to spread himself.

If one were to describe him, as a player, in one word, I suppose that word would be 'scientific'. Certainly he owed nothing to force. Wiry and fit, he carried little weight, and though he did not flinch from tackles, it was his positional play, his highly developed sense of anticipation, which made him remarkable. Nor was he ever very quick – except in thought. And if there were some who criticised his defensive qualities, it might be answered that he was a little unfortunate to come slightly before what would have been 'his' time: that of 4–2–4, and the specialised midfield man. I remember, just after he had come back from the World Cup of 1958, his speaking enthusiastically to me in that great, grey clearing house of gossip and opinion, the Tottenham car park, of 4–2–4. What a good and simple idea it was, he said, simply to string a line of four defenders right across the pitch.

He was even, in season 1958–59, dropped from the Tottenham Hotspur team, and replaced by some young half-back whose name one can barely remember, on the grounds that he was not defensive enough. When, in March 1959, he came back, it was to inspire the team to a marvellous six-goal victory against Leicester City. You will deduce, from this, that he had to suffer a lot of pain for his uniqueness, his vigorous non-conformity. At Barnsley, at Aston Villa, then at Tottenham, he was never free from the reminder that he was, in the last analysis, a professional footballer, a paid servant.

It was at Barnsley, for example, that someone yelled at him for daring to be so unorthodox as to train with the ball. It would be many years before the Hungarians came to Wembley, thrashed England 6–3, and paved the way for a general acknowledgement that it really might be better to prepare for a ball game with a ball. Even as a youngster newly arrived in England, Blanchflower was shrewd enough to doubt the value of continued lapping, the mindless development of stamina. He has always believed – and it has come to be a heresy once more – that the great and dangerous forward may be dangerous precisely *because* he does so little, like a dormant volcano, always liable to erupt. This discussion, I recall, was provoked by a match against the Russian team Tbilissi Dynamo. Their international outside-left, Meshki, had stood inactive on the wing for much of the time, but looked wonderfully effective when he did come to life. Today, when all is 'work rate', a player like Meshki – or Greaves – might be considered a luxury. Blanchflower, always superbly economic himself, knew better.

One may see him today, perhaps, as a bruised idealist; not cynical, but hurt. Professional football is, to some degree, a paradigm of the larger world. Young players enter it full of hope and enthusiasm, only to encounter the proud stupidity of directors, the ineptitude of managers, the violence of opponents, the shallow ephemerality of the press. Thus Blanchflower, particularly aware and alert, was hurt more than most professionals.

There was, for example, the shock, as a very young international, of having the team's coach invaded by jolly, ultra-convivial men who turned out to be . . . officials. Where was the sense of high-minded purpose which he himself had brought to international football? And the awful anticlimax, the dazed disappointment, of the first international match in which he played.

It was in October 1949 against Scotland, in Belfast; and Ireland let in eight goals. Those were bad days indeed for Ulster football. The team, subject in any case to the whims of the Football League clubs, who need not release their players if they did not choose, met at the eleventh hour, and took the field with little hope, little in the way of history.

The Irish team stayed in Bangor, and Blanchflower spent a wretched night, trying unavailingly to sleep. 'The nervous anticipation of the big event had something to do with that,' he wrote. Then, in the small hours, when sleep seemed possible and imminent, a noisy band of Scottish fans arrived, and tore the peace of the night to tatters.

Blanchflower describes his recollections of that Saturday as 'mere shadows'. He was 'numb, dangling in a state of nervous suspension'. It is an interesting admission, given the absolute aplomb of his later career. Clearly he had none of the precocious *sang froid* of a Cliff Bastin or a Pelé, who, as teenagers, could stroll untroubled through a Cup final, or even a World Cup final.

'The game that day,' wrote Blanchflower, in the *International Football Book*, 'swirled past me, over me, around me like a fog. I chased fleeting figures through it; but all in vain. I felt weak and exhausted as if I had no control over my movements; and everything I did seemed strangely irrelevant to the game.'

In parenthesis, the most intriguing thing about this passage is that it should be written by Blanchflower himself, not, as in the case of almost every other footballer, by some assiduous 'ghost'. Blanchflower has a natural talent for writing as well as for football, but this is a subject to which I shall return later.

After the game, Blanchflower 'slumped into the dressing

room, a pathetic figure sadly humiliated by bitter experience'. He was ashamed and disappointed at what he considered his total failure, and wondered if he would ever be chosen for his country again. Though there were excuses to lean on, he acknowledged that the main responsibility was his own. But he was well aware of the sad inertia which grips a losing team, of the whimsical methods of selection, of the lack of any leader to give the team direction and morale. At the same time, especially coming from the Second Division, he had been made to realise what a gap there was between club and international football, where there were so many good players about.

It was, by his own admission, Peter Doherty who recovered him for international football; Doherty who was one of the few figures in the game he has ever admired (another, I think, was Arthur Rowe, in his days as manager of Tottenham).

Doherty had shared Blanchflower's resentment of the slap-dash, defeatist way in which Irish teams were put in the field. Like Blanchflower, he was an individualist, often a stormy one, and a wonderfully talented player. 'Always remembering Doherty,' he once said, 'I aim at precision soccer. Constructiveness, no matter what the circumstances, ball control, precise and accurate distribution, back in defence to blot out the inside-forward when necesary. I am described as an attacking wing-half, and I suppose that is correct. Sometimes I even score goals.'

Doherty's appointment as team manager gave Ireland, and Blanchflower, new life. 'Here was someone,' wrote Blanch-flower, 'it seemed right should be in charge; a great player, an idol to some of us, a man we all respected. There was hope; something to believe in, something to fight for.' Doherty told them they had nothing to lose: 'The biggest step forward,' Blanchflower has said, 'was a psychological one.' This in turn led him to a developing interest in the psychological aspects of the game at large. Though the individual skills and abilities of the Irish team had improved, he was aware that what Doherty had done, above all, was to remove an enormous mental block. Once the Irish team had convinced itself that it was as good as anybody else, it proceeded to prove as much, on the field. The climax of Doherty's partnership with Blanchflower, if one may so describe what it virtually came to be, was reached in the 1958 World Cup.

Blanchflower, though his background was largely similar, had had a better formal education than Doherty. He was born in Bloomfield, a suburb of East Belfast, one street away from Billy Bingham, who would become his outside-right in that notable Irish team. Bingham and Danny's younger brother, Jackie, in fact, played together in the boys' football team run by Mrs Blanchflower, after at first playing football in the street – a game in which Danny sometimes joined.

Blanchflower went to the local college of technology, to be trained as an electrician. In 1944, however, volunteering for the Royal Air Force, he was sent to St Andrew's University, for a short course in electrical enginering. It was a view into another, alien and beguiling world; the students, in their red gowns, represented a fortunate way of existence, a privilege of learning which had been denied to him. After this, he was subjected to another new experience, being sent to Canada for aircrew training. But the war was over, and he was still in Canada, before he could do any operational flying.

On his return to Belfast, Glentoran, with whom he had been an amateur, gave him £50 and £3 a match to sign professional, though until his demobilisation he played as a 'guest' for Swindon Town. In 1948, Barnsley signed him, and three years later they transferred him to Aston Villa, a great club fallen on barren times.

Blanchflower has related, often enough, the traumatising story of how he signed for Villa: travelling to Derby with Mr Joe Richards, the coal-owner who was chairman of Barnsley and later president of the Football League, in his chauffeur-driven car – then, when they reached Derby, being sent with the chauffeur to eat in the kitchen, while business was done in the hotel dining room. What was he, after all, but a professional footballer, and, as such, one consigned to the kitchen and the tradesmen's entrance? This, though Villa paid £15,000 for him.

Further disillusion lay in wait for him at Villa Park. Villa may have been a very great team indeed up to the Great War, and a goodish one in the early 20s, but ever since their relegation in the 30s they had been a stagnant, disappointing club. Playing for them, Blanchflower matured both physically and technically, but there was none of the stimulus a player of his capacities required; no manager there to inspire and lead him as Doherty had done; little chance, season by season, of anything better than staying in the middle reaches of the First Division.

In 1954, he agitated long enough for a transfer to get it. He wanted London; and London wanted him. Both the great North London clubs, Spurs and Arsenal, were eager to sign him. Tom Whittaker, the manager of Arsenal, came up to Villa Park, met Blanchflower, and told him that of course he would be coming to Highbury, that Arsenal could match or top any offer that was made. But in the event, they couldn't. The bidding rose to £30,000, a larger sum than had ever before been paid for a half-back, and Arsenal's board of directors refused to allow Whittaker to go so high. The same kind of penny-pinching would lose Arsenal Denis Law, when he was a £55,000 rather than £100,000 player. Blanchflower never forgot it. He was convinced from that moment that there was something rotten in the state of Arsenal – like Villa, a great club fallen on mediocre times – and his scepticism would flare into a silly row, twelve years later. After a somewhat intemperate article in the *Sunday Express* criticising Arsenal's treatment of an injured player, the club suspended him indefinitely from their press box.

Blanchflower has written amusingly of the cameo at Villa Park when he was due to be transferred: how the directors sat in the boardroom while he waited next door with a local journalist called Tommy Lyons; how it was Tommy Lyons, not Blanchflower, who was eventually and mistakenly called into the boardroom. Still, the transfer to Tottenham Hotspur went through, conducted by Arthur Rowe, who justified the price by saying, 'In nine matches out of ten, Blanchflower has the ball more than any other two players on the field – it's an expression of his tremendous ego, which is just what a great captain needs.'

From this you will divine not only that Rowe had a deep appreciation of Blanchflower's qualities, but that he was prepared to allow him to exercise them. In other words, he was a big enough man and manager himself to give Blanchflower free rein on the field; as a real captain. Yet Rowe, a sensitive, vigorous, idealistic, enormously stimulating man, had not much time to go at Tottenham. He had been bitterly wounded by the opposition and hostility of certain directors, which was manifested even during the most successful days of his push-and-run strategy.

The fact was, however, that Blanchflower was the last player to adapt himself to push and run. This game of wall passes, of immediate parting with the ball over short distances, was quite alien to his own, which was more deliberative. The beauty of push and run, in a way, was that it did not require any specific midfield general. Certainly, Eddie Baily, the little English international inside-left, was a fine constructive player, but in fact every player carried a field marshal's baton in his knapsack. Blanchflower liked to give the ball room and space; was always adept at chipping it, floating it, lobbing it. Endless, hurried movement was not for him; any more than it was for the brilliant little waif of an inside-forward, Tommy Harmer, a footballer's footballer who had been in and out of the Spurs first team for years, because he did not fit into the push-and-run formula.

Blanchflower and Harmer were to establish a marvellous, telepathic partnership. There could scarcely have been two more sharply contrasted figures. Though both had enormous technical talent, and what the Italians call 'a vision of the game', Harmer did it all by instinct, while Blanchflower, besides the natural good instincts of a fine player, had his ratiocinating intelligence as well. He was from Belfast; Harmer was a Cockney of the Cockneys, uneasy anywhere too far from Hackney. Yet they combined marvellously, each perfectly understanding the needs and intentions of the other, and they set up some famous victories; not least one which brought ten goals against Everton.

There were moments, not least when Spurs were awarded a free kick, when they appeared to be arguing. 'They really *were* arguing,' said a London journalist who, like Harmer, came from Hackney. 'Tommy's quite serious about it; he says, "Got to keep Danny down, you know!"'

Later, the partnership with Harmer would give way to one with the marvellously elusive John White, 'The Ghost', who floated unobserved, by all but Blanchflower, into open spaces, unmarked positions, especially out on the left – where Blanch-flower would reach him with impeccably accurate balls.

When Arthur Rowe, who had already been driven into one breakdown, had another and left the Spurs, he was succeeded by a very different manager, Jimmy Anderson. Anderson had, like Rowe – once a Tottenham captain – been with Spurs for many years, graduating from the position of third-team trainer slowly and steadily up to manager. He was regarded essentially as an interim appointment; a figure without glamour or allure who, whatever hidden qualities he might have possessed, was unlikely to hit it off with a Blanchflower.

A crisis point was reached when Spurs lost to Manchester City, in the semi-final of the 1956 FA Cup, at Villa Park. Spurs, in the concluding stages, were behind, their attack making little impression on the City defence. In desperation, Blanchflower, in his capacity as captain, called the gigantic Maurice Norman, centre-half, up to inside-right. Norman was very tall, very heavy, rather clumsy, but undoubtedly a fearsome figure, par-ticularly efficient in the air. The gamble might have worked, given a grain of luck; but it didn't. The other possibility, that of City exploiting a weakened defence, was the one that came about, and Tottenham lost. City went on to win the Cup.

Blanchflower was deprived of the captaincy, and for a long time steadfastly refused to resume it. He was not going to be captain, he said, in name alone: either he exercised the rights of a captain, or someone else could have the job, or the sinecure. At the end of that season, he was even, briefly, dropped. The announcement was that he was unfit. Blanchflower said this was nonsense: he was perfectly fit. 'I turned up at White Hart Lane all ready to go. I thought the lads were kidding when they told me.'

In due course the dim interregnum of Jimmy Anderson came to an end, but the manager who succeeded him was – if much more forceful – little nearer Blanchflower in temperament. Billy Nicholson had been a dour, conscientious right-half in the splendid push-and-run team, a Yorkshireman without frills or exaggerated ambitions, content to chase and tackle and cover till the cows came home. Some, cruelly, had said that he did Alf

Ramsey's tackling for him. He was anything but a stupid man; his exceedingly shrewd tactical thinking had provided England with a plan to hold Brazil to a goalless draw in the Swedish World Cup of 1958; no other side had prevented Brazil scoring. But Nicholson, though subject to refreshing bursts of good humour, was in the main close, wary and cautious. Besides, a player of Blanchflower's stature and loquacity was not the easiest kind for a young manager to inherit. They had, inevitably, their ups and downs, but in the end they worked together in sufficient harmony for Spurs brilliantly to achieve the League and Cup double which had eluded every other club in this century.

I don't think I myself saw Blanchflower play at all till the middle 50s – I had been living in Italy – and was not, initially, too impressed. He was, at the time, being used at inside-right, a position that manifestly did not suit him. He hadn't the acceleration, nor the ability to turn quickly, while his many qualities of foresight and construction largely went begging. He regained his rightful position, of course, and Spurs, buying Dave Mackay from Hearts, transferred their ultra-attacking left-half, Jim Iley.

Blanchflower and Mackay were to form a magnificent partnership. By utter contrast with Blanchflower, Mackay was all muscle and flamboyance, capable of what might loosely be termed 'tackles' (he was to sober down in time) which made one's hair stand on end. He clapped his hands; he stuck out his barrel chest; he took, *ad infinitum*, what Peter Cook once called 'his long, boring throw-ins'; he flung himself among flailing boots. He was essentially a hectic player, certainly not without skills, but with none of Blanchflower's cool, rational artistry. They complemented one another splendidly, though if I were asked which had the greater importance to the team I should reply, unhesitatingly, Blanchflower. This became very obvious when he retired, and Spurs all at once lost the direction and detachment which he had given them. Mackay, John White, Jimmy Greaves were all, in their way, remarkable footballers, but it was Blanchflower, finally, who gave the team its stamp and character.

I remember in particular a European Cupwinners' Cup game, at White Hart Lane, against Slovan, Bratislava. Spurs had lost the first leg, in Czechoslovakia, and they made a bad, nervous beginning. Maurice Norman, the centre-half, was clearly on edge, plunging and lunging at balls, committing himself and being drawn out of position. But there beside him was Blanchflower, like a groom calming a highly-strung racehorse, slowing the game, covering mistakes, till at last Norman and the rest of the team settled down for an easy win.

Similarly, the triumphs of the 1957–58 Ireland side would have been unthinkable without Blanchflower; as they would have been equally impossible without Doherty. The team had in it a handful of very talented players, a few who were naturally gifted but unreflective, others who were frankly moderate. Among the most talented was Blanchflower's own brother, Jackie, at centre-half. A player of immense versatility, Jackie had begun with Manchester United as an inside-right, been turned into a right-half, and finally, with immense success, into a centre-half.

Danny admired him, as a footballer, a great deal, though they were temperamentally quite different: Jackie hadn't the same, consuming ambition as his older brother, and seemed prepared to make less stringent demands on life. In the 1957 Cup final, when Manchester United's goalkeeper, Ray Wood, was injured, Jackie went in goal, and won Danny's admiration for the clever way he distributed the ball. Goalkeeper's distribution, indeed, has always been one of Danny's hobby horses. Given this, and his love of paradox, perhaps it was explicable that one day, in the Burnley team coach, he should reach a point where he seemed to be advocating distribution as the chief quality any goalkeeper needed, where others might feel that the first duty was to keep the ball out of the net!

One of the chief reasons Danny enjoyed playing for Ireland with Jackie was that his younger brother's great all-round skill and confidence allowed him to be left chiefly to his own devices. Danny himself could go upfield and occupy himself with the build-up in midfield. But in February 1958, Jackie was involved in the appalling disaster of Munich Airport, when the Elizabethan airliner carrying Manchester United back from Belgrade crashed. Mercifully, Jackie himself escaped, but he was painfully injured, and never again graced a game for which he had been so well endowed.

This meant that Ireland had to find a new centre-half for the finals of the World Cup, in Sweden, and they manufactured one out of the tall, blond full-back, Willie Cunningham. Cunningham was a solid enough footballer, but he could aspire to none of Jackie Blanchflower's class, with the result that Danny had to play a much more cautious and defensive game. It is interesting – and rather sad – to speculate how much better Ireland might have done in Sweden had Jackie Blanchflower played.

But the footballer who had the greatest affinity, both temperamentally and in his approach to the game, in that Irish team was Jimmy McIlroy. Dark haired, pink complexioned, modest and dry, McIlroy, at inside-forward, brought to football the same cool perfectionism, the emphasis on skill and science, as Blanchflower. They both thought about the game a great deal; they liked each other, perhaps a little warily – they were wonderfully humorous together – and they had the Irish team playing football their way, and Doherty's way. They delighted in working out new moves and strategies, such as the penalty kick which involved both of them, running into the area, the first pushing the ball forward for the other, following up, to shoot home. Blanchflower, as might be expected, was particularly good at taking penalties, with success usually guaranteed by his cool composure.

On the right wing, the ebullient little Billy Bingham, later to become the Irish team manager, was a player of another mould, more of a force of nature. It was no use McIlroy and Blanchflower expecting Bingham to share their quizzical, rational approach to the game. If he had, no doubt they could have worked out some remarkable triangular schemes. But football is a house of many mansions, and there is always room, and need, for the gifted, instinctive player; as Garrincha, in that very World Cup, was to show with Brazil.

To qualify for Sweden, Ireland had to accomplish the 'impossible' feat of eliminating Italy, not to mention Portugal. The Portuguese had yet to reach their heights of the early 60s, when Benfica would produce a team to delight and dominate Europe, but they were no easy victims. As for the Italians, invertebrate though they may have shown themselves in away matches, they had the tradition of two World Cup victories behind them, and a crop of native talent laced and reinforced by *oriundi*, South American stars of Italian descent. In Rome, Ireland were obliged to put the tiny Billy Cush, a wing-half, at centre-half, but played so well and with such spirit that they lost only by a goal.

The following autumn, they came to Wembley and, wonder of wonders, defeated England. Harry Gregg, the Manchester United goalkeeper by the time Munich came, and a great admirer of Blanchflower, worked wonders in goal. Clearly, if the Irish were capable of that, they must have felt themselves capable of anything.

As they were. Early in the New Year, they were due to play Italy in mid-week in Belfast. M. Zsolt, the Hungarian referee, was held up in the fog and didn't get there, so that the teams had to play a futile friendly instead. This didn't please an already violently partisan crowd, which became increasingly more violent as the referee lost control, and foul succeeded foul. The limit was reached when Beppe Chiappella, the Italian right-half, jumped with both knees into the back of Billy McAdams, Ireland's centre-forward.

At the final whistle, with the score 2–2, the crowd brutally invaded the pitch and attacked the Italian players. Police and the Irish players helped them to escape; it was the kind of scene to which Blanchflower himself was totally alien.

For another of his qualities was his absolute sportsmanship on the field. No doubt he committed fouls now and again, but it is hard to remember any of them. Nor can one dismiss this by saying that the really gifted player has no need to indulge in roughness. A long, long line of Scottish international wing-halves bears depressing witness to the contrary. Violence was simply remote from Blanchflower's nature, and when it was visited on him he became understandably bitter. One of the few occasions I can recall him being really angry was when, on a train journey, he was talking of a recent match at Everton, in which he had been brutally charged down from behind, the referee looking on with indulgence. Competitive almost to a fault, his career – at a time when so many vital matches turn into brawls – reassures one that competitiveness need not always turn into cynicism and viciousness.

A few weeks later, Ireland played Italy again and this time beat them, deservedly, 2–1. It was a triumph for Blanchflower and for McIlroy, who scored one of the goals. This time, both crowd and Italians alike seemed purged of anger, so that the Irish, by and large, were able to play the pure football of which they were capable. Their victory was an appalling blow for Italy, who thus failed for the first time to reach the finals, but it was an uplifting achievement for Doherty and little Ireland.

It is notable that Blanchflower, for his behaviour after the first, savage affair, was praised by Ottorino Barassi, the Italian vice president of FIFA. It was Blanchflower who had seen to it that each Italian player had an Irish escort from the pitch, moving Barassi to remark, 'Blanchflower is a man of many parts, and a gentleman.'

At the end of the season, he was deservedly voted Footballer of the Year, an honour which would be conferred on him a second time, when captaining Spurs to their successes.

There was another absentee from the Irish team which travelled to Sweden. Or rather, Billy Simpson, the big Rangers centre-forward, though he made the trip, was too badly injured to play. So Ireland had to manufacture, from their bare resources, another centre-forward as well as a new centre-half, and, though they did amazingly well in the circumstances, they did not really manage it.

They stayed at a little seaside town called Tylosand, in a hotel above the beach, with a pitch situated picturesquely in a nearby wood, to play on. The atmosphere had none of the cold formality of the England party, where every man seemed to be looking over his shoulder. Doherty, though he never lost control of his team and its players, knew how to weld them into a cheerful family – and in Blanchflower and McIlroy he had mature lieutenants.

Their opposition was alarming: Argentina, re-entering the World Cup after long sulks and silence; Czechoslovakia; and the World Cup holders, West Germany. Clearly it would be a splendid achievement if they finished in the first two of their group, to qualify for the quarter-finals.

And they did. They beat the Czechs, they lost to the Argentinians, they drew with the West Germans, then, in a play-off, they beat the Czechs again. Finally, an exhausted and depleted team, they went down to the French, in the quarter-finals. Obliged, as we have seen, to mask his batteries, Blanchflower only came fully into his own, perhaps, in the play-off against the Czechs, in Malmo. These, a few days earlier, had thrashed Argentina 6–1, and were locally the favourites against what was by now a scratch Irish side. But the wonderful morale of the Irish players carried them through. In extra time, with the score 1–1, Blanchflower floated one of his long, immaculate free kicks across the Czech goal, and McParland scored with a right-footed volley, to put the Irish, incredibly, into the final eight.

With seven injured players and the imbecility of a 210-mile coach ride to Norkopping, they had little real hope from the first. The French, thanks to the anomalies of the competition, had benefited from four days' rest, and it was clear that Ireland needed some kind of miracle. They did not get it but, if one of the ideas that Blanchflower, Bingham and McIlroy had devised had only been fully worked out, things might have been different.

For almost half the game, Jack was as good as, and better than, his master. Then the idea was put into practice, took the French by surprise – but it was not exploited. It involved a throw-in on the Irish right flank. The intention was for Blanch-flower to throw the ball to Bingham; Bingham, with his head, to flick it to McIlroy; and McIlroy to run through for a shot at goal.

It worked; up to a point. Blanchflower threw in, Bingham duly headed on, and McIlroy ran into the penalty area. But instead of shooting he squared the ball across the goal, and the chance was gone. France went on to score four times, and Ireland's brave attempt had ended in anticlimax. Still, it was a superb achievement to get to Sweden at all, and an even finer one to reach the quarter-finals against such strenuous opposition.

For the future, Blanchflower's greatest triumphs were reserved for club football with the Spurs. This, now, had a more fascinating aspect than it ever had in the past, for victory in the English Cup and League meant entry into European competition, the sort of thing that was meat and drink to

Blanchflower, always looking for new challenges, new approaches, fresh aspects of the game.

He had settled in a pleasant house in a North London suburb with Betty, his second wife, and their three agreeable children. His first marriage, which came to an end while he lived in Birmingham, had been to an Ulster girl – and he was to marry a third time, to a South African. On arrival in London, he had begun an amusing column for the *Evening News* which, while it did not extend him, was often humorously inventive.

In 1960–61, Spurs began the League season with a remarkable unbeaten run, and cantered on to win the Championship. They were essentially an attacking team, highly talented, if not a great club side in the manner of Real Madrid. Blanchflower, John White and Dave Mackay were perhaps their three outstanding players, but there were also the lean, professional Bill Brown, of Scotland, in goal, and the tremendously brave Cliff Jones, on the right or left wing. Blanchflower's clever crosses into the penalty area were as well tailored for his flying headers as Alf Ramsey's had been, a decade earlier, for the headers of Leslie Medley.

Looking back, Blanchflower has said that he enjoyed playing with them all; that there was no player whom he enjoyed playing with more than any other. There were times, he added, when Jimmy McIlroy would tell him he thought he played badly for Ireland, to which Blanchflower would reply, 'You don't play badly; you just play differently.'

The Ireland team had reached its apotheosis with the 1958 World Cup. The following October, it lost at home, 5–2, to England. 'How England won 5–2 nobody knew,' Blanchflower said. 'We should have won 5–2. They were meant to have been playing 4–2–4; all they'd done was play two centre-halves to stop our two centre-forwards, and afterwards they went on like that for thirteen games.'

His account of the scene outside the England dressing rooms, after the match, shows him at his best as a raconteur and a close observer. 'X of the *Daily* —— is very excited, this is England's greatest victory for years, and he says to Walter Winterbottom, "Walter, would you say England was playing 4–2–4?" And Walter looks up, and he doesn't find the answer up there, and he looks down again, then he looks up, and he says . . . "Yes." And X says, "What I thought was so-and-so and so-and-so. And so-and-so and so-and-so and so-and-so and so-and-so." And then Bob Pennington of the *Daily Express* comes forward with a big smile, his rival, and he says, "Thank you very much, Walter. And now do you think we can have X's views?" And all the little local journalists standing round, amazed at this quarrel between the big boys!'

Spurs won the 1960–61 Championship with a forward-line led by the powerful Bobby Smith, with Les Allen an excellent, incisive inside-left. The following December, however, they paid some £99,000 to buy Jimmy Greaves from Milan, so that Blanchflower was captaining a still more richly gifted side. At that time, he feels, Spurs and Benfica, the holders of the European Cup, were the two best club teams in Europe, Real Madrid having passed their zenith. The two clubs met in the quarter-finals, and Benfica got home by a goal. Blanchflower thinks that Spurs had two and possibly three good goals disallowed for offside, the first two in Lisbon – particularly one by Bobby Smith – the other by Jimmy Greaves, early in an exciting match at White Hart Lane. Spurs won it, hectically, by the odd goal, but it wasn't enough to keep them in.

Intriguingly, Blanchflower endorses the fast and physical nature of Tottenham's football in the second leg, although it was very much in the image of Mackay, rather than in his own. Many of us criticised Tottenham for their methods; it is significant that Blanchflower, though they were so foreign to his own approach, should still feel they were right. 'It wasn't football,' he has said, 'but that was what was needed. If a team came out to play defensive football, the very thing it wanted was for the other side to play a rational, cool, elaborate game.' Others might think that pressure defeats itself, that the modern game has, for the last forty years, been built on the sudden break-away, but Blanchflower's view is an interesting one.

He scored from a penalty kick in that game: cool enough, as usual, to make a very good job of it, selling the excellent Costa Pereira, in goal, a dummy, then sliding the ball into the left-hand corner, after Pereira himself had moved right. Afterwards, Pereira told him that it was the first time anybody had sent him the wrong way. This penalty kick had an interesting sequel, for, a few months later, at Wembley, during the Cup Final, Blanchflower was called upon to take another one, against Burnley.

He was so convinced that Adam Blacklaw, Burnley's Scottish goalkeeper, would have seen his penalty against Benfica on television that he decided to try to send him the other way from Pereira. As he walked up to take the kick, Jimmy McIlroy, who 'used to take them for Ireland, and miss them, said to me, "You're going to miss it." I said, "I'm glad *you're* not taking it." ' And Blanchflower did not miss it. He duly sent Blacklaw to the left, and put the ball in, to the right.

The following season, he and Spurs had consolation, when they thrashed Atletico Madrid 5–1 in Rotterdam, to win the final of the European Cupwinners' Cup. By this time, Blanchflower was 'assistant to the manager, whatever that meant', and on the morning of the game Billy Nicholson decreed that there should be training. The team, already demoralised by its poor form over the past six weeks, resented this; all the talk was of bonuses, of who would and who would not be playing.

'I'd been playing terrible,' Blanchflower said, 'because unconsciously I was carrying my knee. I told them, "You're all afraid of this match. I deserve to play more than anybody and I don't know if I'm playing, and I'm not worrying. I'm going out to train. If you're not training, please yourselves; you can sit and play cards, if you like." ' The players trained – and they won.

From this, it can be deduced that Blanchflower might have become an exceptional manager, yet, while playing, he always denied any ambition to do so. He had, he said, been disappointed too often and one cannot imagine him suffering directors gladly. Even at Tottenham, where things had certainly improved since the 50s, 'I said that the team at Tottenham was bigger than the club, when I left. I felt that Tottenham never made the best of those years.' It may also be that Blanchflower was too much the individualist, even the egoist, to have submitted to the grinding compromises of management. Shrewd about the psychology of footballers – I remember his once saying of a successful manager, 'X hasn't done anything. He's just sat there and sucked his pipe and given them confidence' – one nevertheless sees him as a lone wolf, impatient of stupidity.

He had by now become a 'fashionable' figure, taken up by such as Professor Ayer, the logical positivist philosopher, author of *Language, Truth and Logic*, whom Blanchflower once reproached on a television programme for being superstitious, and Karl Miller, the young literary editor, then, of the *New Statesman*. Blanchflower wrote frequently for the *New Statesman*, sometimes very well, and later had a fruitful period on the *Observer*. One has always felt it a pity he left them to spread himself over the wider but less exacting spaces of the *Sunday Express*, for he seemed to have there the direction and discipline his writing demands. It is hard for a footballer who has, as Blanchflower admits, been 'adulated', and has reached such peaks, to buckle down to the needs of another *métier*; yet just as the tension between his own talent and the demands of organisation probably brought the best out of him as a footballer, so a similar tension might bring the best out of him as a writer. A tendency to sentimentality, mild vendetta and a sacrifice of individuality to the fashions of American sports journalism might thus have been avoided.

Not surprisingly, perhaps, his admirations in literature have tended towards the romantic, in particular to Scott Fitzgerald, that doomed, gilded, perennial adolescent of the protracted 1920s. Though he writes, now, for the popular press, his relations with it have long been uneasy; one remembers a ferocious *New Statesman* column, after the World Cup finals of 1962, in Chile, which presumed that one writer must have come home to be sick into his well-advertised bowler hat. Misquotation, malice and the cynical kite flying which he so often met during his playing career were not likely to be received by him with tolerance.

Despite the breadth of his interest, he testifies to the shock of leaving football; which he did, at last, in 1964. 'There's a strange awakening when you come out of the game, because we're all very spoilt in the game. You've had so much adulation. You've spent ten years having things done for you, army style.'

Retiring, he embarked, with bright success, on television as well as journalism, and in 1967 became one of the commentators on the CBS network of the first professional soccer league to be played in the United States. Beyond question one of the great footballers of his day, a great captain in an age when captaincy was moribund if not dead, his major contribution, perhaps, was to give the professional footballer a rational, articulate voice.

Still Looking for an Idiom

Prospect, October 1995

'BRITISH SPORTS JOURNALISM is still looking for an idiom; still waiting for its Red Smith, its Damon Runyon, its AJ Liebling, let alone its Ring Lardner; still waiting for the columnist who can be read by intellectuals without shame and by working men without labour. Meanwhile, it is afflicted by dichotomy: a split between mandarin indulgence and stylised stridency, this in itself a valid reflection of the class structure.'

I wrote those words almost thirty years ago in an article called 'Looking for an Idiom' for *Encounter* magazine. The piece was an attempt to analyse the dichotomy in British sports journalism between the quality and the tabloid press. It described the obstacles faced by writers on both types of newspaper. The tabloid journalist was forced into stylised self-betrayal. He was condemned to cliché and jargon, and could not express himself freely. Still, at least covering mass sports ensured that he reached the masses who followed them. By contrast, the quality journalist was free to write largely as he pleased, though unable to reach a wide audience.

I compared this unhappy situation with that in the United States, where a language had long since been found which embraced all levels of the sporting public: 'What is wholly lacking is an idiom which will throw a bridge across the two cultures, avoiding, on the one hand, bathos, which is the nemesis of "good" sports writing, and on the other stylised vulgarity, the nemesis of the popular school. The American sports writer, though now in a barren period, a period of pygmies, has never had this problem, precisely because, in a more fluid society, the idiom lay close at hand.'

In retrospect, I am not quite sure why I limited the comparison to the US and didn't include countries like Italy and France. Good sports journalism had long been flourishing there and I had been closely acquainted with it for many years. Indeed, in 1949, when I was seventeen years old, I began writing for the Roman daily sports paper, the *Corriere Dello Sport*; and still do. In France, the sports paper *L'Equipe* and its companion, *France Football*, were and continue to be a rich source of comparison for the sports journalist.

Thirty years on, have we found a sports idiom for everyone, like the United States and the Europeans, or are we still stuck with the two cultures? Notwithstanding the new wave of football writing, Nick Hornby *et al.*, not much has changed – primarily because our class polarities have themselves largely remained in place.

We are forever being told that the working class is disappearing, the middle class steadily expanding, and that an underclass is being left at the bottom. But the success of a paper such as the *Sun* and the change in the profile of its rival, the *Daily Mirror*, are evidence of a group identifiably working class and identifiably none too literate. Forecasts that print would become a marginal, obsolescent, medium have not been borne out, but there is no doubt that television has come to dominate the media, and that it has elevated the visual over the written and the read, especially among the poorer, less literate, sections of British society.

Perhaps the box's dominance in the US is linked with the falling-off of American sports journalism, too. Its giants have gone and they have not been replaced. American newspapers carry sports columns in superabundance, but they are seldom as idiosyncratic as those written by Ring and John Lardner, Red Smith, or AJ Liebling in his *New Yorker* days.

Nevertheless, unlike Britain, American and most European newspapers regard sports writing as an honourable profession. Runyon and Lardner became well-regarded writers of fiction. Liebling could and did write on anything imaginable. James

'Scoop' Reston was a sports writer long before he became a famous commentator on international affairs.

But there was another side. In his 'Farewell to Sport', Paul Gallico gave his reasons for abandoning sports writing. He was reporting on an important boxing match in New York when another sports writer entered the press box and made a great display of taking off his hat and coat and laying them on his desk, before almost ritually opening up his typewriter. Then a voice rang out from the bleachers: 'Siddown! You're only a sports writer!'

Such a reproach could scarcely be imagined in Italy, where, for many years now, sports writers have been the heroes and sometimes the Saint Sebastians of their profession, avidly followed and royally rewarded. There, and in most Latin countries, most sports journalists have university degrees. It would be unthinkable for a senior Italian newspaper executive to suggest, as one of his counterparts in England suggested, that 'Sport is the arsehole of Fleet Street.'

Thus to compare the sports pages of an English tabloid newspaper with those of, say, the *Corriere Dello Sport* or its Milanese rival the *Gazzetta Dello Sport*, is to undergo some culture shock. Here is the *Daily Mirror*: 'Ruud Gullit spent two years as a dreadlock star in the making lying back and thinking of England. Every night he'd picture himself whooping it up on our pitches and after in the reggae bars of London. But . . . it was wearing the red of Arsenal that became the biggest ambition for the Rolls-Royce of Rastafarians.'

Now look at this, from the *Corriere Dello Sport*: 'But to the great teams, the imprint of genius has always been indispensable. Look at Milan, so perfect and calibrated in all its mechanisms, but unexpectedly vulnerable without the sublime whims of Savjicevic. Baggio can't be measured just by his goals . . . he is the lethal weapon against desperate situations, days that go wrong, games which are bewitched.'

In other words, Italian readers were and are treated as literate, while the English tabloids have seldom ceased to treat their readers as morons.

This attitude has been reinforced by the sad fact that when a really gifted sports writer has emerged from the working classes, he has not been willing to waste his talents on the popular press. Neville Cardus, the supreme cricket writer, was (as he admitted in his autobiography) chance born in a Manchester slum. Hugh McIlvanney is the son of a Kilmarnock coal miner. John Arlott was a country boy from Hampshire, formerly a policeman. It was as though such talented figures, having acquired a patrician style through their own endeavours, were not going to waste it on the popular prints, however well rewarded they might be thereby. Consider Arlott's beguiling account of his love for Reading Football Club: 'Bacon was a tall man from Derby County, with a shaving-brush tuft of hair growing out from a shallow forehead above a mighty jaw. His chest was like a drum, his thighs hugely tapering, and he had two shooting feet which he threw at footballs as if with intent to burst them.'

The reluctance of gifted writers such as McIlvanney, Arlott and Cardus to work for the tabloids has inevitably meant that such papers have been starved of talent. Whatever its increasing rewards, the English equivalents of the university men who so eagerly take to journalism in Italy and France have been reluctant to commit themselves to the demands of the tabloid press.

On the other hand, some journalists have left the tabloids to write impressively for the quality press. In the 1960s, Brian James went from the *Daily Mail* to become a football commentator on the *Sunday Times*. The same path from tabloid to quality was followed by Rob Hughes (*Times*), Joe Lovejoy (*Sunday Times*) and Colin Malam (*Sunday Telegraph*).

In 1992, after 33 years as football correspondent and sometimes sports columnist on the *Sunday Times*, I moved the other way to become a sports columnist on the Sunday tabloid the *People*. The move gave me the chance to try to prove what I had always preached: that sports writing should be an indivisible whole and that popular papers need not patronise readers. It is hard to believe that the fans at Highbury, Villa Park or Old Trafford are less intelligent than those who watch on the south bank of the Olympic Stadium at Rome. Roman fans can be as rough and aggressive as English ones; yet they read the flights of fancy of the *Corriere Dello Sport* with as much satisfaction as any Roman businessman or film director.

To write for a paper like the *People* means that concessions have to be made. For one thing, literary allusions aren't encouraged. But with a competent desk of subeditors and an encouraging sports editor, there is no reason or pressure to 'write down'. Saturday reports present the problem of 'editorialising', and an addiction to printing quotes from managers and players (which feature far less in the qualities). In the sports dailies of Italy, France, Spain, Portugal and South America, more space allows the ideal situation of having a match report alongside a quotes piece on a page.

So has popular British sports journalism deteriorated or improved these past thirty years? It's hard to say. Part of the sportswriter's problem has been the growing eagerness of the tabloids for scandalous stories about footballers. Since the iniquitous maximum wage was abolished in 1961, soccer players' exponentially increasing earnings have turned them into showbiz figures.

However, as often as not such lurid revelations are made not by the sports writers themselves but by those working on the news pages. Sports writers traditionally keep infinitely more secrets than they disclose about sports stars' private lives. But the tendency to tar all journalists with the same brush is sometimes irresistible. It was never so plain as during the Italian World Cup of 1990, when Bobby Robson and his England players would scarcely give the football press the time of day – although the 'revelations' which had upset them had been made by news journalists, known by the football writers as the 'rotters'.

Making up stories is nothing new, of course. Indeed, in the days before wall-to-wall television it was rather easier. Consider the career of Desmond Hackett of the *Daily Express*, whose name was made at the so-called Battle of Berne during the Swiss World Cup of 1954. At the end of a torrid match between Hungary and Brazil, bravely refereed by the Yorkshireman Arthur Ellis, Hackett peered hawkishly out from the edge of the press box, picked up his telephone and dictated: 'The World Cup quarter-final was a riot. My jacket is ripped, my shirt torn, and I am minus a tie. But I do mean a riot . . . I tried to cross the field and ended up being thrown over a fence by two policemen. Considering the riot going on about me I was glad to be out of it. But I was able to help Mrs Ellis, the wife of the Halifax referee, and her two frightened young sons through a side entrance into her husband's dressing room.' When FIFA, the international football association, investigated the incident, it established nothing concrete. But the *Daily Express* rewarded Hackett with a new suit and a £50 bonus. And so – frivolous, jocular, happily amoral – he continued to flourish for many years to come.

Continental journalists were far from being moral paragons either. They may not have made up stories, but they notoriously failed to distance themselves from the soccer authorities. It is ironic that a footnote to my original piece paid tribute to the Italian journalist Gianni Brera for writing as a 'whole man, whose subject happens to be sport'. Nearly a decade later, he surprised and disappointed me with his craven behavior over the Lobo-Solti scandal.

This involved a failed attempt by the notorious Hungarian fixer Dezso Solti to bribe Francisco Marques Lobo – the referee of the 1973 European Cup semi-final between Derby County and Juventus of Turin. Lobo not only refused a bribe to aid Juventus, but reported the attempt to his Portuguese refereeing association. But the European ruling body, UEFA, swept the dirt under the carpet by means of a farcical sub-committee meeting in Zurich.

It was only in the following year that I found out about the scandal – from sources of mine in Budapest. Keith Botsford and I began a long investigation for the *Sunday Times*, in which it was authoritatively established that a handful of rich Italian clubs had been bribing (or trying to bribe) European tournament referees for years.

Since Brera was regarded as the very prince of Italian sports journalism – a stocky, outspoken and polemical little Lombard – I expected him to be incensed, and to back me to the hilt. Instead he made an insulting reference to me in a weekly magazine he thought I wouldn't see. But I did see it, and bitter words flew between us.

As far as I was concerned, Brera had shamefully betrayed his trust and connived at corruption he must have long known existed. We were never reconciled. When he died, in a motor accident, he was still a much revered figure in Italian sports journalism. I should point out that its practitioners have improved in the past twenty years – they are now far more ready than before to denounce chicanery on the part of the great clubs.

Coming back to the present, what of Britain's new football literati? Actually, they are not new at all. As early as 1956 the *Observer* frequently employed intellectual heavyweights who were delighted to write football reports; alas, they usually did so very badly. They included Professor AJ Ayer, famed then not only as a logical positivist but as a Spurs fan and a friend of the team captain, Danny Blanchflower; John Sparrow, the Warden of All Souls and an expert on buggery in the writings of DH Lawrence; John Jones, author of a study of Wordsworth: all these writers were used by the *Observer*'s then sports editor, Michael Davie. All emerged as dilettantes. Nor were things any better at the *Sunday Times*, where an academic called John Sellars was appointed football correspondent after he chanced to meet the paper's editor, Henry Hodson, on a train from Oxford to London.

But David Sylvester, the art critic, who reported for the *Observer* (and recently won the Venice Biennale Prize) was in a rather different category. His passion for football and cricket was long standing, and he knew what he was writing about.

The invasion of the literati in the 1950s was of comparatively short duration. Quite soon the broadsheet 'heavies' saw that soccer should be treated as seriously as cricket or rugby. I was a beneficiary of that, no longer to be told that I would not be wanted that week because a friend of the sports editor would be reporting. (An Oxford friend, of course.)

In the 1990s, a group of writers has emerged which has 'discovered' football and written about it with varying success. Among them is Nick Hornby, whose lavishly praised bestselling memoir of an Arsenal fan, *Fever Pitch*, has caught the zeitgeist to perfection. I think it's as valid to write about soccer from the outside as from the inside, and Hornby's love of the game is manifestly genuine. However, the idea that Hornby and a core of rather less well-informed intellectuals take the game away from its natural constituency is ludicrous to anyone familiar with football commentary abroad.

Twenty years ago, *La Stampa*, the celebrated Turin paper, appointed as its chief football correspondent Giovanni Arpino, who covered the World Cup of 1974 in West Germany. Arpino was not a sports journalist; indeed, he was not a journalist at all: he was a novelist. Instances could be multiplied. French, Italian and South American intellectuals who write about the game, among them the Peruvian novelist Mario Vargas Llosa, are usually well informed and have something to contribute.

Such work stands in sharp contrast to the interventions of the poet and critic Ian Hamilton, who wrote two books about Paul Gascoigne's experiences in Rome. His largely second-hand accounts were thrown into relief by the scabrous memoir, by Jane Nottage, Gascoigne's former amanuensis, published about the same time.

Elsewhere, fanzines are a sporadically interesting sub-genre, giving a welcome voice to supporters. The best of them, such as Scotland's the *Absolute Game* and Arsenal's *One-Nil Down, Two-Nil Up*, are refreshingly abrasive. At their worst the fanzines seem to be written by 'wannabe' football journalists who have not yet cut the mustard and most probably never will.

So will an idiom ever be found? As a sports journalist who is trying and hoping to find it, I must be optimistic. The public, I am sure, would be much more receptive to good writing than tabloid sports editors believe. But the battle will be a long one – where it is fought at all.